FIGHT OR DIE...

LOST Boy

WALL STREET JOURNAL & USA TODAY BESTSELLING AUTHOR

M. ROBINSON

LOST BOY

WALL STREET JOURNAL AND USA TODAY BESTSELLING AUTHOR

M. ROBINSON

This book is a work of fiction. References to real people, events, establishments, organizations, or locations are intended only to provide a sense of authenticity, and are used fictitiously. All other characters, dead or alive are a figment of my imagination and all incidents and dialogue, are drawn from the author's mind's eye and are not to be interpreted as real.

To Yoda.
I. Love. You.
Thank you for EVERYTHING you do.
"Did we just become best friends?"

One

I jumped on my dirt bike in a hurry, wasting no time to pull back the clutch and kick-start the engine. My hand jerked the throttle as the motor revved to life, rumbling beneath me. The smell of exhaust immediately filled the humid summer air while the bike idled in neutral.

I'd been riding since I could walk. It was part of being a Jameson, and my old man wouldn't have it any other way. He'd shit a brick if he ever saw any of his three sons on anything other than two wheels with wicked horsepower. Reminding us all too often that we were Jameson men and real men only ride Harleys and women, rough and hard. So until the day my older brother Luke and I were old enough to have our own Harleys, like our oldest brother Creed, dirt bikes would have to do.

I leaned forward, gunning the engine a few more times before holding down the accelerator and front brake to do one hell of a burnout. Finally releasing it and hauling ass off of school grounds. Making sure to leave a nice little trail of dirt and rubber in my wake as I saw Principal Salisbury running out of the building in my mirror.

"Noah, you get back here right now! You hear me?!" he shouted in the distance.

I lifted my middle finger in the air, giving him a friendly gesture in response. There was nothing I loved more than to stir up trouble at school. I hated being there, especially now because it was summer school. It was just another place I was being told what I could and couldn't do, and I already had no say in my life to begin with. I learned early on that if I raised hell at school, I'd get suspended or expelled, and I wouldn't be allowed to step foot on school grounds, period. Which was exactly what I wanted.

You see, I was born into a world where no matter what, violence solved everything. It was the answer to every question, the solution to every problem, the consequence to every action delivered by none other than my father. I sure as hell blame him for the man I would eventually become.

I was born into this so-called *family*.

I was born to the *devil's* son.

The President of the mother chapter of Devil's Rejects Motorcycle Club in Southport, North Carolina. I'd be twelve-years-old in a few weeks, and I was already such a little shit with a sharp tongue and wise-ass attitude. Feeling and looking much older than I actually was. I may have only been a kid, but you sure as shit couldn't tell me that. Bred to not take shit from anyone, it was beaten into us and the only way of life in my father's eyes. The only way to survive. There were no other options. Surrounded by a family, a brotherhood of ruthless men whose only enemy was the law. Wearing their 1% patches proudly like I would have to wear one day.

Whether I wanted to or not.

My last name, *Jameson,* made sure of it.

Raising hell while we ride or die was our only code growing up and living in the MC life.

I sped through the grass, busting a sharp right onto one of my favorite trails. Ducking and dodging trees, listening to the motor accelerate up and down, faster and faster, around and around. Tracking from one side to another in nothing but mud and debris from the recent storm we had. I could see the sun up ahead through the tree clearing, showing me I was almost to the old, broken-down bridge that crossed over the Cape Fear River near my school. It was known for its heavy and strong ass current, and if you swam out far enough, it could haul even the biggest man under, which was how the river got its name in the first place. It was deceiving, but that didn't stop people from swimming and hanging out in the murky water without a care in the world.

I rode up to the edge of the bridge to judge the distance across the vast space and to look around for any cops that may have been hiding on the ridge. I shut off the engine when all of a sudden I overheard a voice singing, *"The sun'll come out tomorrow, bet all those dollars that tomorrow. There'll be sun shining bright and happiness. Just thinkin' about tomorrow,"* coming from the river surrounding the bridge.

My eyes instantly shifted to the girl floating on her back in the water, wearing one of those two-piece bathing suits all the girls wore on the beach. Hers was hot pink. I don't know how long I stared at her, but it was the calm look on her face as she belted out the lyrics, *"Just thinkin' about tomorrow. Clears away the sadness, the rain, and the emptiness. Till it's not there,"* that had me narrowing my eyes. Getting lost in her peacefulness and her raspy, distinctive voice, it was an expression and sound I'd never experienced before.

The low pitch in her tone soared its way through my core, the same way the motor of my bike rumbled beneath me. It wasn't until she started singing, *"So just hang on 'til tomorrow and work through the pain. Tomorrow! Tomorrow! I love ya all of the days and nights of tomorrow! You're almost there! And only a day away!"* that her soothing, crystal blue eyes suddenly found mine, as though she felt me too. The intensity of her stare made me quickly jerk back, and I roared up my bike again. Instantly proceeding with why I was at the bridge in the first place.

I pulled back the clutch, shifting into first gear, revving up the engine for a few seconds before slowly letting the clutch out. Once it caught up with the RPMs, my front wheel purposely rose when I shifted my weight back on the seat. Hanging on while controlling the wheel so I wouldn't get tossed off, keeping the balance of my wheelie as I drove over the bridge. I didn't usually take this way home, but I wanted to see how long I could ride out a wheelie over this bridge.

Being an adrenaline junkie, I lived for the moments when nothing else mattered but the thrill of the rush surging through my veins. It didn't matter what it was, if I could get hurt doing it, then I pushed every boundary just to prove that I could conquer it. Coming home bloody, bruised, cut up—you name it, I'd probably broken it. My momma had my ass every time, ruining more clothes than I cared to count.

After thirty-five seconds of riding out my wheelie, I smiled. It was my new record I'd been trying for weeks to beat. Right when I was about to revel in my latest stunt and let off the gas to set my bike back down, I glanced over at her again and she was still staring right at me.

"Shit!" I shouted, accidentally accelerating the throttle, causing my bike to come out from under me. Losing control of my wheelie. Immediately tossing me to the ground as if I weighed nothing at all. My body skidded and rolled across the wooden planks, along with my bike tumbling beside me. With one last hard thud, we finally came to a complete stop, crashing together. "Ugh," I groaned, instantly feeling the sting everywhere, and it wasn't from eating shit on the bridge.

I don't think I could've been any more embarrassed than I was from getting caught staring at the girl, and then making a fool out of myself right in front of her. Before I could even try to save face, I heard loud laughing from behind and above me, and I knew things were about to get much worse than just my pride taking a hit.

"Well, lookie here, boys! If it isn't big, bad Noah Jameson! Last time I checked your ass should be on the seat, not the pavement, dumbass!" Billy hollered over at me.

"Aww, poor baby, did you hit your head?" Chad added, standing beside him. "Doesn't matter... he's already dumb as shit."

"Get up, you pussy!" Mark added in front of them.

My hands balled into fists, and my nostrils flared. All three of these dipshits went to my school and were notorious for being assholes. The times I actually went to class and didn't ditch, I mostly kept to myself. I guess you could say I was somewhat of a loner, avoiding dickwads like these guys. Not because I couldn't defend myself, but I wanted to avoid more problems than the ones I already had. Trust me… I'd seen my fair share of Pops slapping Ma around, Pops slapping my brothers, Creed and Luke, around. Shit, even Pops slapping me around.

Although, I wasn't at the receiving end of his fists quite as much as they were, in their eyes I was the baby boy in the Jameson household. Not that it mattered to my father, he was a ripe ol' bastard through and through. But that didn't stop my momma and brothers from trying to shield and protect me as best as they could. Especially from the violence surrounding us on a day to day basis in our shithole we called home and, more importantly, at the MC clubhouse where I spent most of my time. Witnessing men being put to ground was a thing of the norm. We learned how to fight, or we got our asses kicked by our old man until we fought back or was spitting blood.

Usually both.

"He can't even ride his dirt bike! Your daddy must be so proud. Head of an MC and his boy can't even ride. Jameson, you're such a waste of space! Boys"—he nodded to me—"don't breathe, you'll catch his stupidity. I heard it's contagious, which is true judging by his stupid ass brothers. Especially the one covered in ink. Have you heard that bitch talk? He can't even form a proper sentence!" Billy continued baiting me, and I clenched my jaw and gritted my teeth, trying to move my bike off of me to get up.

"Come on, you pussy! Can't even defend your family?" Chad taunted, kicking my hands out from underneath me. Making me fall back down again.

"The only good thing in your family is your mama!" Billy taunted, snapping my searing glare to his sly grin as he hovered above me. "Yeah, lost boy, you heard me… your mama has the best pair of tits I've ever seen."

Before he got the last word out, I pushed off the ground, throwing the bike to the side, and his eyes widened. Using all my strength, I gripped onto Billy's head and started kneeing him repeatedly in the face. Forcefully pushing and pulling his skull toward my knee, crudely connecting them at the same time, and smiling as I did. It didn't take long until his boys were on me, frantically trying to pull us apart, but I wouldn't let go. If anything, I nailed him harder, proving to them once and for all I wasn't one of their victims they could bully around.

The loud, familiar rumble of a dirt bike, followed by "Noah!" broke my focus for just a second, and it was enough to get myself punched in the face by one of the guys. Abruptly tearing me apart from Billy's skull.

I stumbled back, trying to regain my footing, but yet another fist landed right into my stomach, and I heaved forward from the wind being knocked out of me.

"That's right, you bitch!" I heard one of them say as I gasped for air. My vision instantly clouded, making it hard to see.

For some reason, in that moment, when I should've been thinking about getting my shit together and beating some ass, I wasn't. I thought about the girl in the hot pink bathing suit who was swimming in the river, hoping like hell she wasn't watching me get my ass handed to me. All because my brother Luke wouldn't mind his own business and involved himself by showing up and hollering out my name.

I couldn't tell you why it bothered me, it just did.

Impressing her mattered more than it should have, and I didn't even know her name.

More shouting.

Kick.

Punch.

Ground.

I spit up blood, still wheezing for my next breath.

"You're gonna pay for that, you motherfuckers!" Luke roared. "No one fucks with my brother and gets away with it!" The next thing I heard was him cocking back his BB gun and sounding off, lacing them with pellets. One right after another with no end in sight. He'd been carrying that BB gun in the back of his jeans since our old man gave it to him almost four years ago for his eleventh birthday. Finding any reason to use it. "That's right, you pussy ass bitches! Run! Run your coward asses home! Right to your mama! Try my brotha' again and next time it'll be real bullets goin' through your bodies, you pieces of shit!"

I sat up groaning with my hand over my stomach, wiping away the blood on my busted lip with the back of my hand. Without even thinking, my eyes darted toward the river, looking for the girl, but she was nowhere to be found. Pissing me off even more. Luke's hand suddenly dangling in front of my eyes brought my attention back to him. I scoffed, roughly shoving it out of the way, and stood up by my damn self.

"What the hell?" he coaxed with a sincere expression on his face I wanted to knock off.

"Yeah, what the hell is right!" I snarled, stepping up into his face. "Luke, who the hell do you think you are? I had them!"

"Had them what? About to kick your ass?" He reached over, trying to point out my bloody lip, but I slapped his hand away again. "You can fight, Noah, I'll give ya that, but three against one ain't ever good odds! For anyone! You should be thankin' me, you ungrateful little shit!"

"Thankin' you for what? For makin' me look like a pansy ass bitch?" I shoved him hard.

He cocked his head to the side, eyeing me up and down. "Don't try me, baby brother," he gritted through a clenched jaw. "I'll lay your ass out."

"Is that right? Well, step in line, big brother, 'cuz those guys," I nodded in the direction they took off, "are gonna be chompin' at the bit to do it first." I sized him up. "Thanks to you."

"They won't fuck with you again if they know what's good for 'em."

"You won't fuck with me again—" I stepped away from him, walking toward my bike. Putting some much-needed distance between us, never taking my eyes off his—"if you know what's good for *you*."

He jerked back, grimacing.

"We ain't brothers right now. You're just another bully who made me get my ass kicked, just like Pops."

I picked up my bike and hightailed it out of there before we started using our fists to speak for ourselves. Jolting the accelerator faster with every jagged turn I sped around, hearing her looming voice again and again. Louder and louder each time. Fuming the entire way home when all I wanted to do was go find her and explain something, anything, just to find out her name. I never cared to be around girls, to have friends, to get to know anyone, always preferring to be alone instead. And there I was obsessing over a girl I'd only seen briefly.

Why?

I tried to shake off her calm, pretty face, her crystal blue eyes, though it was her haunting voice that caged in my mind the most.

"Tomorrow! Tomorrow! I love ya all the days and nights of tomorrow!"

There was so much feeling, so much emotion, so much depth in just a few simple words. A song I never cared about until I overheard her belting it out of her small frame.

How could she sing like that?

I hit the brakes on my dirt bike, letting it fall on the grass in our front yard, and rushed inside. Stopping dead in my tracks when I saw my momma dancing around the living room with music blaring from the speakers.

"Noah, baby!" she exclaimed with a smile on her face that was quickly replaced with nothing but concern. "Noah, not again," she griped, hurrying over to me after she lowered the volume on the stereo. She grabbed onto my chin to get a good look at my busted lip and swollen eye.

I jerked my face away. "I'm fine."

She sighed in defeat, knowing I hated when she tried to baby me. "Honey, that nasty gash on your lip and those broken blood vessels in your eye tells me otherwise. Not to mention, the blood on yet another shirt. Baby, what happened? How many times do I have to tell you to use your words, Noah. There is no need to provoke any more violence."

"Tell that to the Prez, you married him," I spewed, instantly wanting to take it back. Momma didn't deserve my smartass remark, she was as much of a victim of his bullshit as we were.

She winced, her face frowning. Tearing into my heart a little more.

"I didn't mean that."

"Yes, you did." She grinned, wanting to make light of the reality of our world, like she always did. If it wasn't for her, my brothers and I would be completely shit out of luck. She was the only saving grace in our lives, the only good mixed in with all the bad, and I for one wouldn't know what to do without her.

I hissed when I tried to smile, causing her more distress. "Momma, I'm fine. You should see the other boys."

"Boys?"

I spun, not answering, and made my way over to the stereo.

"Noah, there was more than one? Baby, what—"

Turning the song up, I looked over at her with my hands out in front of me. "Do ya wanna dance?"

She reluctantly sighed again, shaking her head. She'd been making me dance with her since before I could walk. Teaching me all the moves she claimed my old lady would be forever grateful for one day. Mostly, I just did it to shut her up and make her smile. She didn't do enough of that either.

None of us did.

I spun her around in a slow circle, tugging her back to me, and we swayed to the soft beat of the music.

"Noah baby, you know I'm always here for you. No matter what. Your momma is always here."

I nodded. "I know."

And the worst part was…

I truly believed her.

Two

An hour later, I was riding shotgun while Momma drove to the clubhouse, lost in the singing voice that wouldn't leave my mind as if she was right in front of me.

"Whatcha thinkin' about over there?"

"Nothin' important," I lied. "Pops know we headin' to the clubhouse?"

I wasn't surprised in the least when she silently shook her head no. Women's place in the MC was always in the background. They didn't have an opinion or a voice to be heard. The club brothers came first, no matter what. The ol' ladies like her weren't even allowed on the property unless invited. Usually during big parties when they were needed in the kitchen, where Pops said they belonged, cooking for the club members.

On those days, it was a free for all. The golden rule allowed the brothers freedom, not having to worry about catfights breaking out from sticking their dicks into whores, instead of their wives. Club whores ran rampant in the MC, itching to spread their legs, screwing any brother at any given time. They'd bounce around from one guy to the next, hoping one of the brothers would be stupid enough to make them their ol' lady one day. They were all the same—slutty, fake tits, wearing barely any clothes and too much makeup.

Even my father regularly bit into the forbidden fruit. I couldn't remember a time when he didn't have a side piece, and Ma always knew about it. Everyone did. He didn't even try to hide it, throwing it in her face often with one slut or several. Not giving a shit how it made her feel, he already owned her. He knew she had too much to lose if she ever left him. Having three mouths to feed with no education will do that to a woman. She stuck right by his side, proving her loyalty to him and the club, which was the only thing he ever truly loved. It was all that mattered to the bastard.

I think she would purposely come to the clubhouse unannounced because she wanted his attention in one way or another. Deep down she still loved him, making me realize early in life that love could kill you.

"Tomorrow! Tomorrow! I love ya all the days and nights of tomorrow!"

"Stay in the car, baby, I'll be right back," I overheard her say, closing the door behind her. Not paying her any mind, thinking about the girl who made me feel things I couldn't even begin to explain or understand.

Why?

The sound of bikes rumbling from behind the car tore me away from my thoughts. My eyes followed the group of bikers who were officers of the MC, all holding titles from Vice Prez to Secretary and Treasurer, just to name a few. They were part of the executive committee and the only members who were permitted to attend when spur-of-the-moment meetings were called. Where they discussed anything and everything that needed to be addressed immediately.

However, the scheduled monthly meetings were less formal, and the patched-in brothers were able to attend those. I knew all of these men too well. They weren't just family, but more like corrupt uncles who taught me entirely too much shit I shouldn't know at my age. Playing a huge part in me feeling, thinking, and acting older than I was. I'd been to titty clubs, drank beer, and even tried pot a few times. By the time I was five, I knew how to shoot a gun. Glocks, rifles, pistols—you name it, I shot it.

Diesel, who was the Sergeant of Arms and the closet friend to Creed, would often go out back to the woods with me and fire off rounds, seeing if I could hit the target at various distances, and he was impressed every time I did. Pops already had my very own Glock waiting for me, and if it were up to him, he'd have given it to me by now, but he knew the risk was far greater than the reward of seeing yet another one of his sons strapped with the lethal metal. Ready to take bitches out, or anyone else who crossed me or the MC. Exactly like the brothers.

Though Ma did almost shit a brick when the Treasurer, Phoenix, tatted "Zion" and "Road" on my knuckles for my eleventh birthday, which meant finding my path in life. I had always been intrigued by different cultures and their ways of living in the world. Knowing I'd never get to see it, I started tatting their scriptures in hopes that they would spiritually become part of me.

The tattoo was my present from Phoenix and Pops, saying I was already a year behind since Creed and Luke got their first tattoos from Phoenix when they were ten. You'd think Ma would be used to it by now, but she still gave me shit every time I came home with a new one, and I only had four so far. Creed was covered in them by the time he was fifteen, Luke was halfway there, and I was sure I would be too.

Although we were brothers, we all looked different. The only features we had in common were our light eyes and our tall, bulky frames that we inherited from our old man. My deep-set eyes changed from blue to green and vice versa, depending on what mood I was in. My skin was darker than either of my brothers from hanging outside so much, being a dare devil and getting myself into trouble. It only emphasized my chiseled, square jawline, masculine chin, and long face. I was also almost six-feet-tall, making me look much older, at least that's what Momma said. She loved that I got her brown wavy hair and slender nose, expressing that it was one of her favorite things about me. I was her baby boy.

I watched as the brothers walked inside the clubhouse, an old machine factory that was transformed into this hangout decades ago. The run-down building was in the middle of nowhere, just outside of town with nothing but acres of open fields surrounding it. A privately-owned organization governed by its own laws. The exterior was painted black with a massive mural of the club's logo out front. The club's colors, black and red, with a badass-looking tattooed pin-up girl with huge tits sporting devil ears and a tail. Straddling a custom chopper, holding a skull with flames beating out of its eyes in one hand and an AK-47 rifle in the other.

Over the large steel door was the club's plaque that read Devil's Rejects MC, Southport, NC. The building also housed several small loft apartments where club members would stay when they got too fucked up or to screw whores, who, like I said, were always hanging around. Some members even used them as their homes.

Once they were inside, my eyes landed on Creed and Luke. They were sitting on top of the old, wooden picnic table toward the back of the compound. Creed was resting his elbows on his knees, flicking the ashes off his cigarette into the grass as Luke fumbled with something in his hands. They looked like they were having some sort of private conversation, enjoying each other's company. Luke had always looked up to Creed, who was almost eighteen, probably because he was more of a father figure than our own dad.

I guess in my own way, I did too. He was a good older brother, they both were, which suddenly had me feeling like shit for giving Luke hell for defending me earlier. He was only doing what I would have done for him if the roles were reversed. It was just the way things were between us. Brothers first, regardless of all the other bullshit surrounding our lives. Out of all of us, Creed was definitely the son who got the shit end of the stick. Destined to be President of this hellhole one day, whether he wanted to or not, and he sure as shit didn't want it.

None of us wanted to be part of this lifestyle, and if our father was aware of that fact, he'd probably put us to ground himself. I reached for the handle to get out of the car and walk over to them, but the sound of our old man's voice bellowed from afar, holding me back.

"There you are, you piece of shit!" he hollered, loud and proud. Standing at the back screen door, staring straight at them. Completely interrupting their conversation. I couldn't tell who he was yelling at.

At first, I thought he was shouting at me, and I was still not entirely convinced he wasn't. Each of us were "pieces of shit" at any given point of the day, it was hard to keep track of who his anger was geared toward. It changed as much as his whores did.

"You fuckin' deaf? You not hear the bikes pullin' up? Get your ass inside right now, before I think twice 'bout lettin' you attend," he added, only looking at Creed.

"Pops, it was my fault," Luke interfered.

"Don't," Creed voiced to Luke, putting his hand up to silence him.

"Did I tell ya to speak? You're just like your fuckin' Ma, always speaking when not spoken to. You're weak and worthless like her too." He came through the door like a bat out of Hell, storming down the three steps, grabbing Luke by his shirt, and yanking him off the table, knocking whatever was in his hand to the ground. "Do I need to teach you another lesson, boy?"

My hands worked into fists the second I saw Luke's do the same. His face flushed and his jaw clenched like he was about to say something he'd surely regret. I reached for the handle again, but this time it was Momma opening the driver's side door that stopped me from going to help him out.

"Noah, don't," she ordered in a stern tone. "You stay right here, ya hear me? Creed can handle it, he won't hurt Luke in front of him."

She was right, he wouldn't. I think part of Pops knew not to cross that line with Creed. Not that it mattered. Sometimes it felt like his verbal abuse was far worse than anything his fists ever inflicted. The bruises eventually faded away, his mental and emotional abuse stayed with us forever, and I constantly found myself thinking I was exactly like him. It was always worse when Ma tried to defend us too, his anger would just turn to her. Furious she was trying to raise us into a bunch of pussies, claiming all he was trying to do was make us into men.

I snapped back the rubber band on my wrist as far as it would go, feeling the sharp sting on my skin. I did it three more times, *snap, snap, snap,* needing to feel the bite from the elastic so I would stay put and listen to Ma. I never took it off, it was the only thing that calmed the rage running deep in my blood. Fighting the internal battle to hurt the son of a bitch. I hated him. There wasn't one ounce of love in my body for my father, and as I sat there helpless, an emotion I recognized all too well, I visualized it was his face I was kneeing repeatedly this afternoon, not Billy's.

What I would do to my father given the chance was something I had never shared with anyone. Stirring an endless stream of feelings I knew were wrong but felt so right. When Creed got up, he stubbed out his cigarette on the wood, instantly grabbing ahold of Luke's arm, and firmly tugged him out of Pops' grasp. I finally let out a breath I didn't realize I was holding. He placed Luke securely behind him, shielding him from Pops' wrath, and my rapidly beating heart slowed down. The craze in my mind subsided, and I could feel my core unlocking, already gearing up for the next time my hatred would want to take control.

Take over.

Me.

They exchanged more heated words that ended with Pops mockingly jeering, "Now run along, the real men have important business to take care of. When you grow a pair of fuckin' balls, you'll be able to play too," he provoked Luke, wanting to have the last word.

I somberly gazed at Luke as he walked toward our car and over to where Ma was standing with so much pain and regret in her eyes, and it hurt me to once again just sit there, unable to do a damn thing about it.

"Get your ass inside," Pops demanded to Creed before he turned and went inside the clubhouse. More concerned about starting church on time than his own family.

"Thanks, baby," Ma called out to Creed, bringing his attention to her and then to me.

Our eyes locked for what felt like the millionth time in my short life. Both of us searching for the answers to the questions that hounded us since the day we were born.

Were we just like him?

Did people see him when they looked at us?

Was this all there was to life?

I was the first to break eye contact, shaking my head and looking out the window instead. I casually blinked and there she was, a figment of my imagination belting out, *"The sun'll come out tomorrow, bet all those dollars that tomorrow. There'll be sun shining bright and happiness. Just thinkin' about tomorrow,"* instantly making me feel her presence through the lyrics of the song, as though she was singing them only to me.

As her voice replayed over and over in my mind, it brought me to another place in time, causing shivers to run down my spine and back up to my neck. *"Just thinkin' about tomorrow. Clears away the sadness, the rain, and the emptiness. 'Til it's not there,"* triggering my scalp to tingle and my face to flush. Goose bumps rose on my arms, and more chills coursed through my entire body. My nerves felt like they were on fire, engulfed in flames.

The physical ache in my chest connected with me on a much deeper level, in a way I'd never experienced before. *"So just hang on 'til tomorrow and work through the pain. Tomorrow! Tomorrow! I love ya all of the days and nights of tomorrow! You're almost there! And only a day away!"* The stabbing pain in my heart only intensified with each lyric that left her lips. Each word that escaped her mouth echoed somewhere deep within me.

She wasn't just singing that song in the river this afternoon, she was living it. She sang with all her heart, with her entire soul. Her whole world was shared and expressed in a few seconds, a few moments…

It gave her peace like my rubber band provided for me. It calmed the chaos in her mind, the storm in her eyes, the feeling of needing to purge the hurt and the pain. It was then I realized why I couldn't stop thinking about her.

The depth.

The longing.

The sadness and sorrow.

She was *me*.

Three

I tried to shake her off, but it was no use. I thought about her for most of the evening, and I knew I was headed to the bridge at the same time tomorrow, silently praying and hoping she'd be there. Counting down the hours until I could talk to her, find out her name, and who she was. I wanted to know everything there was to know about her, but more than anything, I wanted to hear her sing again.

Hear her sing *for* me.

And only me.

I finally shook off the reminiscent thoughts, focusing on yet another attempt to apologize to Luke. After the third time of being blown off, I gave up and went into Pops' room in the back of the clubhouse. It was the only room I was really allowed to hang out in. Ma tried to set up the private living area as a game room for Luke and me, claiming she wanted us to feel at home and comfortable. Buying us video games and whatever else we were into at the time. We knew she was full of shit, she was just trying to keep us away from the bullshit. Probably praying if we were there, she could be too, keeping a closer eye on the prez and everything he stood for.

"What's up with you and Luke?" Creed asked, following me into Pops' room.

"Don't worry about it," I replied, sitting on the couch. Turning on the TV to play Mortal Kombat.

He snatched the controller out of my grasp. "Don't gimme that shit. I saw ya tryin' to play ball wit' him out back. Luke don't turn down basketball. So what's up? What happened? I'm guessin' it got somethin' to do wit' that shiner and busted lip on your face? Luke knows better than to put his hands on you, yeah?"

"It wasn't him."

"Good. Now, tell me who it was so I can return the favor."

I scoffed in disappointment, shaking my head. If I thought anyone would understand, it would be Creed. He hated being babied and talked down to as much as I did. "The fuck?"

"Noah, watch your mouth."

"Why? So Pops can knock me out for spittin' like a pussy." I learned cusswords before I could even talk. Swearing was a normal way of speaking around these parts. Our father made sure of it, slapping us around if we weren't cussing.

Creed narrowed his eyes at me, fully aware it was the truth. "He do that to you?"

"Not this time."

"Noah—"

"What?! You don't think I can handle myself either? I don't need you or Luke to protect me!"

"Hey…" He put his hands up in a surrendering gesture. "I'm on your side, no need to come for me. Ya feel me?"

"Yeah." I nodded.

"This about a girl?'

Our eyes locked.

"Ah."

"It ain't like that."

"It never is, baby brother." He grinned, leaning forward to place his elbows on his knees. "This the same girl Luke was tellin' me about earlier?"

"No." Luke was into some Barbie doll at his school. Big tits with a pair of long legs was all I saw in her.

"Damn. That woulda been some shit. Two brothers fightin' over the same tail."

I breathed out a chuckle.

"Your balls dropped earlier than Luke's. You've always been an old soul, though. Don't surprise me you already wanna get your dick wet. Like I told him earlier, I was your age when I first did, thanks to our old man. Only good thing he ever did for me too," he chuckled, remembering God knows what. "I know you can fight, but that ain't gonna stop us from tryin' to protect you, and that's just the way it's gonna be."

I didn't say anything, because what could I say to that.

"You know Luke had good intentions."

"It's why I've been tryin' to talk to him all night."

"Give him some time. He'll be over it by tomorrow." He stood, making his way toward the door. "Ice that eye, yeah?"

I laughed, "Just can't help yourself, can ya? You're worse than Ma."

"Where do ya think we get it from?" he joked, looking back at me one last time before closing the door behind him.

I went back to playing PlayStation for the rest of the night, avoiding the clubhouse and its usual festivities of booze, drugs, and women. As the night progressed, more and more people started showing up. I could hear them scattering around the hallway like cattle, knocking into walls and laughing at shit that wasn't even funny. I'm sure the clubhouse was busting at the seams beyond capacity with people, most of which were corrupt. Everyone shooting the shit, dancing, playing pool and darts, and getting messed up on their drug of choice.

I started getting tired just after one in the morning when the party was in full swing. My eyes weighed heavy with each passing second I was awake, my face burned, and my body ached. I felt like shit inside and out. I began dozing off with the controller still in my hands when the door flew open and in walked Luke, looking just as tired as I felt.

"Hey." I nodded to him, but he ignored me. "Come on, Luke, aren't ya a little old to be givin' me the silent treatment?"

"Ain't got shit to say to you."

I stood, blocking his way to the bathroom. "Well, I got plenty to say to you."

"Get out of my face, Noah."

I cocked my head to the side. "Or what? What are you gonna do, huh? My face is already jacked up thanks to you."

"Just gonna keep rollin' wit' that?"

"It's the truth, but I shouldn't have—"

"You're still givin' me shit when you woulda gotten your ass kicked if it wasn't for me. Instead, you just got a black eye and a cut lip. Boo fuckin' hoo, I saved your ass today. As much as you think you had 'em, all you were doin' was diggin' yourself into a deeper hole. If I hadn't shown up when I did, they were probably gonna land your ass in the hospital, and kickin' that fool in the face only proves my point more. You crossed the line today comparin' me to that son of a bitch, but you wanna know what really fuckin' hurts… you tellin' me we weren't brothers no more. Those are fightin' words! Now get the hell out of my face before you get your ass kicked for the second time today."

I jerked back, caught off guard. He'd never been this pissed at me before. It was a whole different side of him, and I hated it was directed at me. I was wrong for taking my anger out on him, I knew that. Especially when it had nothing to do with him. I was mostly peeved about the girl, getting caught staring at her like I was some jerk off and then biffing it right in front of her. Followed by her probably watching my ass getting handed to me. It was one thing after another, and I hated not having control.

He stepped back, never taking his eyes off mine as he walked toward the door. "I wanted to crash, but I don't wanna be around you right now. So thanks for not only ruin'n my day, but for ruin'n my night too."

"Luke, I'm sor—"

"Save it for someone who gives a damn." He turned, taking one last menacing look at me. "You know, you're right, we ain't brothers because *my* brother woulda never said that to me." With that, he turned around and left, slamming the door behind him.

I breathed out a heavy sigh, frustrated as all hell that he wouldn't even let me explain myself. I resisted the urge to follow him and make his stubborn ass hear me out, regardless of the consequences. If he needed to hit me to feel better, then so be it. We could beat the shit out of each other in front of everyone and go back to being brothers after. It wouldn't be the first or last time these walls had seen blood. Pops would probably get a kick out of it too, seeing his sons throw down like we'd been raised to do.

Ma and Creed, on the other hand, would be shooting daggers at us, involving themselves by breaking us up, and it would cause more problems than it was worth. So I stayed put, laying down on the couch and staring up at the ceiling. Throwing on some headphones to tune out my thoughts and feelings of being a piece of shit brother.

I hated that Luke was beyond pissed at me, I hated that the girl caught me staring at her, and everything that followed. I just hated how everything went down today, but mostly, I hated that I had no control over it. All I could do was lay there and wait for I don't know what. Nothing would change, at least not what mattered. My life was jaded and ugly, and all sorts of fucked up. I turned the music higher, drowning myself in the lyrics she was singing today, not in what I was listening to. I closed my eyes, seeing her face.

Thinking about tomorrow.

Everything would be better tomorrow. Luke would get over our fight and what I said to him, I'd see her again, and for the first time in my life, I looked forward to the next day. It was all I had to hold onto.

A few lyrics to a song.

Her voice.

And the thoughts of tomorrow.

I must have dozed off again because the next thing I knew, I jolted awake, shooting straight up on the couch to look around the room. Through the music that was still playing loudly in my ears, I could hear commotion outside the room. Throwing off my headphones, I tried to figure out where it was coming from, dazed and confused. Not fully awake. My hazy eyes quickly darted to the door as fast as my body jumped off the couch, rushing my way toward the screaming coming from the halls.

"What the hell?" I said to myself, swinging the door open. Only to be met with crowds of people running in all directions. "What's goin' on?"

No one answered, no one even looked at me as if I wasn't even standing there.

Was I dreaming?

I didn't recognize anyone, just their panic-ridden stares. I shook my head, more confused, then started to move, walking in the direction most of them were running from. Pushing my way through the swarms of people. I was still so out of it, exhausted from the day that had me moving on autopilot. My feet stepping left to right and vice versa, my eyes shifting in the same momentum while my mind tried to keep up with what was going on around me.

One step.

Two steps.

Three steps.

Four.

Slower and faster I went, almost being knocked over several times like I was a ghost. Failing miserably at maintaining a steady pace as I tried to find the source of the ruckus. Feeling more disoriented with every passing second, navigating the dark space with only multi-colored lights bouncing off the black walls. Loud music still blaring from the speakers but not loud enough to drown out the screams. It was almost like I was walking through a dream within a dream, knowing that didn't make any sense. I felt like I was swimming against a current, pushing, shoving, forcing my way through the waves of people.

Till suddenly I heard, "What the fuck did you do, boy?" Pops roared, and I followed the direction of his voice.

"It was an accident! I swear to fuckin' God it was an accident!" Creed shouted in a desperate tone, barely able to get the words out.

I walked into the room next to the makeshift bar where Pops was standing with Creed right in front of him. Ma was on the floor with her back to me, and I couldn't see her very well because a few brothers were crowding around her.

"Momma, what's going on?" I asked, making everyone turn to look at me with wide eyes and terrified expressions marring their faces. My heart sank as I realized there was someone in her arms, and for some reason I instantly let out, "Where did Luke go?" Like my conscience already knew the answer.

Diesel acted fast, scooping me in his arms and rushing me backward into the hallway I had just come from. He held me against the wall to block my view, but I could still see Ma looking over her shoulder as she solely concentrated on me being escorted out. She turned around when she thought I couldn't see her anymore, but I could.

I saw everything.

Diesel firmly grabbed ahold of my face. "Noah, look at me!" he ordered, trying to get my eyes to focus on him instead of the scene unfolding in front of me. "Noah! Look. At. Me!"

"Let him call 9-1-1, Jameson! It was an accident! Where the fuck were you?!" Ma yelled, turning her frantic attention to Pops.

"Accident or not, we can't call the cops! You want your son to go to prison?" he replied, ignoring her question.

Prison? Why would Creed go to prison?

She shook her head violently, finally understanding something. "No! Not Creed! I can't—"

"Noah! Goddamn it, look at me!" Diesel rumbled, but I was too far gone.

Watching.

Waiting.

"It was an accident!" Creed shouted at Pops, reaching for the phone in his hands.

He jerked it away and shoved him, causing Creed to stumble. "We will all go to prison over this!" he added, looking at everyone with his dark, cold, calculated stare.

"Where's Luke?" I found myself asking out loud again.

"Noah!" Diesel held my face harder, but I couldn't feel anything other than my rapidly beating heart.

"Where's Luke?" I repeated, my vision zeroing in on Ma.

"Look at me, pay attention to me," Diesel countered, trying to jerk my intense stare to him and not to the room that held the answer to my question.

Ma shook her head. "You fuckin' bastard," she wailed, her usually strong frame breaking into pieces.

"I'm tryin' to save all our asses! Do you want to lose another son?" Pops argued, his eyes meeting hers.

The floor suddenly felt like it came apart beneath my feet, and I started to fall. Deeper and deeper into the ground, faster and faster into the hole where I couldn't breathe. I felt like I couldn't breathe.

Why couldn't I breathe?

"Noah! Stay with me! Stay here with me!" Diesel stressed, but his voice sounded so far away, even though he was right in front of me.

There was a loud, overbearing ringing in my ears taking over every last part of me. "Where's Luke, where's Luke, where's Luke?" I called out, over and over again. Lost in an alternate universe where I was suffocating.

Where I felt like I was dying, slowly and rapidly and all at once.

I watched as Creed stepped away and his back hit the adjacent wall. The truth of our father's words was too much for him to bear. Too much for all of us to bear.

"Where's Luke, where's Luke, where's Luke?" *Was I still talking? Was that my voice?*

Around and around my mind spun. Up and down, and in and out, it whirled and tumbled, taking me on the ride of my life. Slowly sinking further and further into the corner of my soul, seeking refuge from this hell. From the truth, from the brutal reality of our world.

"Noah, please, man… don't do this to me… look at me… please just fuckin' look at me," Diesel demanded in a tone I'd never heard before.

I couldn't move.

I couldn't breathe.

I couldn't take my eyes off the lifeless body Ma was cradling in her arms.

"Where's Luke, where's Luke, where's Luke?" Tears fell from my eyes, and my knees couldn't hold me up any longer. I slid and fell down the wall, losing every ounce of control that I had left in me.

All my will was gone.

All my fight had vanished.

I was there, but I wasn't.

"No one fucks with my brother and gets away with it!" I heard Luke repeat from this afternoon.

I couldn't tell what was real or what was an illusion. It all blended together, forming more truths, more lies, more demons.

"Noah, I got you. I got you, boy," Diesel coaxed, gliding down to the floor with me.

"Try my brotha again and next time it'll be real bullets goin' through your bodies."

Blood.

There was so much blood.

All I could see was blood.

On Creed's hands and body, on Ma's hands and body. Blood everywhere. Puddled on the floor beneath them, splattered on the walls behind them, in my eyes, right in front of me. Caging me in with memories from this afternoon.

It was my words I heard this time. *"We ain't brothers right now. You're just another bully who made me get my ass kicked, just like Pops,"* I heard viciously spewed, regretting it immediately. "Where's Luke, where's Luke, where's Luke?"

More chaos.

More shouting.

More pain.

"NO! You can't do this! You can't take my baby!" Ma screamed with everything inside her as they pried the lifeless body out of her arms. "Please! Please, God! Just bring him back! Bring my baby back!"

She prayed.

She sobbed.

She fell apart.

And I died a little more inside.

"Look what you did, boy! You did this, Creed! You shot and killed your brother!" Pops yelled, getting right in his face.

I jerked back, desperately repeating, "Where's Luke, where's Luke, where's Luke?" Pops' words not making any sense to me.

Not when I could hear Luke restating, *"You crossed the line today comparin' me to that son of a bitch, but you wanna know what really fuckin' hurts... you tellin' me we weren't brothers no more."*

With wide, dilated eyes, I continued to watch as Phoenix picked Momma up from the floor. "Give me my baby! You let me hold my baby!"

She kicked.

She screamed.

She fought.

For me.

For Creed.

For Luke.

"I wanted to crash, but I don't wanna be around you right now. So thanks for not only ruin'n my day, but for ruin'n my night too."

Luke left the room because of me…

"Noah! Talk to me, Noah! Please just talk to me," Diesel urged in what sounded like an echo, far, far away.

"Where's Luke, where's Luke, where's Luke?" I weakly whimpered, shuddering, shattering, stumbling.

It was when I saw a black body bag being laid on the floor that I finally found Luke.

His dark eyes stared back at me with no life, no warmth, no love.

No soul.

"You know, you're right, we ain't brothers because my brother woulda never said that to me."

I realized right then and there that Luke was right, we weren't brothers anymore.

Because my brother…

Was dead.

And I was to blame.

Four

My left foot shifted from first to second to third then fourth gear, blazing through the woods at high speeds. All I could hear were the voices in my head and the faint sound of a train's horn in the distance. I revved the throttle of my dirt bike harder, finally shifting into fifth gear and maxing out at a hundred miles-per-hour. I pulled back the accelerator as far as it would go and raced onto old McMullen train tracks near the clubhouse, with an endless stream of torturous memories clouding my mind and attacking my body. Driving me to go faster and faster and faster.

My vision zeroed in on the task at hand, desperately trying to escape what had become my life. It had been over a year since Luke died. Over a year since Creed accidentally shot him. Over a year since my whole world came crashing down, burying me like my brother's rotting body under the dirt. If I thought things were bad before, I was dead wrong. Everything changed for the worse, in a way I never imagined it could. I started racing my memories of what followed the night Luke died, speeding quicker on the train tracks to outrun them. Knowing it was no use, my guilt wouldn't let me, and a huge part of me…

Would never allow it to.

"Momma, Momma, Momma, can you hear me?" I asked, kneeling right in front of her. She was still covered in Luke's blood, but I didn't care, I grabbed her hands anyway. Needing to feel her warmth.

Her safety.

Her love.

"Momma, please..."

She blankly stared out in front of her with her eyes wide open, but she was nowhere to be found. She couldn't see me.

Feel me.

Love me.

Nothing.

"Momma, I'm sorry. I'm so sorry about Luke. You have to believe me," I pleaded, looking up at her with tears in my eyes and my heart in my throat.

I had to tell someone.

I needed someone to understand.

I wanted her to understand, to tell me everything was going to be alright. To lie to me.

I just needed her to lie to me.

"I'm so sorry. Please believe me. I didn't mean it. I didn't mean what I said to him. Please... please tell me you believe me. You believe me, right, Momma? I didn't want him to die. He shoulda never left the room. I'm sorry, I'm so sorry, Momma..."

Not one look.

Not one word.

Not one lie.

Nothing.

She was as gone as Luke was. His blood now on both our hands.

I gripped the handle bars on my dirt bike as hard as I could, feeling as though I was still holding onto her hands. Knowing I would forever be holding her bloody hands, begging her to forgive me.

Pleading with her to lie to me.

To make it all go away.

To please just make it all go away.

I not only lost Luke that night, I lost my momma too, and I had no one to blame but myself. It was no one's fault but my own.

I. Did. This.

I frantically shook away my thoughts, trying to outrun them too.

Wanting…

Needing…

Anything…

Something…

The front tire on my dirt bike steered side to side, navigating the rough and narrow tracks. My bike flew through the air on more than one occasion as I drove up and down each bump on the terrain. I could feel the motor vibrating deep within my bones as I continued to push the engine beyond the max. Never letting up, persistent and adamant on riding at dangerous speeds.

Every time I closed my eyes, every time I blinked, every time a second passed by, all I could see was Luke's lifeless eyes staring back at me. Never once forgetting that haunting night when my brother was put to ground.

Not on my twelfth birthday that followed a few weeks after.

Not when I was awake or asleep.

Not even on my thirteenth birthday that just came and went a few days ago.

Not then… not now… not ever…

Every morning, noon, and night the images would play out like an old broken record for as long as I was breathing. Always overpowering my mind.

Controlling my actions.

Directing my thoughts.

I remembered every step I took into those woods, following far enough behind my father, Creed, and some of the brothers, unseen. Witnessing Diesel, Stone, and Phoenix carry Luke's black body bag deep into the forest, behind the clubhouse, before dawn. I remember the thick, suffocating fog in the night's air, the way the wind blew a cold breeze through the trees exactly how it was doing at the moment. I remember the sounds the wildlife made all around me as if they were the horn on the train in front of me right now.

Blaring.

Blasting.

Sounding off.

Most of all, I remember what followed once they stopped walking…

And started digging.

"You did this. He's dead because of you, boy. Now, I'm not going to make my brothers pay for your sins. You dig that grave and lay your brother to rest in it. I want you to remember he's six feet under because of you," Pops ordered, tearing the shovel out of Stone's grasp. Throwing it in Creed's face, daring him to defy him.

Woooooooooo! Wooooooooooo! The train whistled.

The horn booming again, pulling me away from my never-ending memories. The flickering headlight in the distance, warning me to get off the tracks, but I didn't heed the warning.

Instead, I decided to play fight or die, really push my boundaries like I had been doing since Luke died.

Waiting.

Always waiting for that moment I'd die too.

I instantly down-shifted into second gear, purposely slowing down. My body surged forward, using my knees to squeeze the gas tank as my right hand applied light pressure on the front brake. The back wheel lifted off the ground, my knees pulling the bike upward into a nose dive. I gradually eased off the brake, gaining some speed, wanting to see how long I could ride out the reverse wheelie without falling on my face.

Never once breaking away from the memories.

They never went away, I couldn't get them to leave my soul even if I tried. So after thirty seconds, I set the wheel back down, fucking pissed, and gunned the throttle once again, causing my tires to skid across the rocks as I reached top speed. Swerving from one side to the next, practically dumping my bike to the ground, almost dragging my knees with it. I didn't let up, jumping the tracks a few times to catch air, causing the suspension to protest when I landed.

The bike telling me no.

My mind telling me yes.

Go, go, go…

Quicker, faster, firmer.

Go, go, go…

The motor revved up and down with every jump and bump I hit, and all it did was toss me right back to that night.

Creed forcefully drove the shovel into the dirt, digging our brother's grave while our old man watched. Acting like it was just another person they were putting to ground in these woods that already housed more bodies than I cared to count. He didn't even show any signs of remorse, like it wasn't his own flesh and blood. His son. The life he put into this Hell that he called our home.

I never hated him more than I did at that moment.

I never hated Creed until that moment.

I never hated myself as much as I did in that moment.

"That's enough," Pops ordered. "Get your ass out of that hole and come get your brother. You're goin' to carry him into the ground by your damn self, and then you're goin' to bury him by your fuckin' self too."

"Prez, we can—"

"You can shut your fuckin' mouth! That's what you can do!" Pops interrupted Phoenix, looking from Creed to him and back to Creed. "I'm not going to tell you again, Creed! Get your brother and lay his fuckin' ass to rest!" He roughly grabbed Creed by the front of his shirt and lifted him out of the grave, shoving him over by Luke's body.

The train whistled louder, two long, one short, followed by one long bellow, bringing me back to the present.

Woooooooooo! Wooooooooooo!

Warning me, letting me know it was getting closer and closer. The RPM's on my bike were going crazy, higher and higher, making the bike shake from the daring game I was playing. Another horn sounded even closer this time, blaring through the morning sky.

Woooooooooo! Wooooooooooo!

Red lights flashed, and smoke suddenly filled the air as the train came barreling down the tracks. Getting louder and louder every second it approached. The polluted air made it hard to breathe, hard to see, and it felt like I was suffocating again in the exact same way I was that night.

Dragging me unwillingly right back to Hell.

Creed cradled the black bag that held Luke's body to his chest and whispered something I couldn't make out.

I didn't get a chance to apologize.

I didn't get a chance to make things right between us.

I didn't get a chance to say goodbye.

"Let go of him, Creed! And get your ass out of that hole!" Pops demanded.

"Please... let me say goodbye. Just fuckin' allow me that..." Creed bellowed, and I wished for the same thing.

Begging.

Praying.

Hoping.

"I don't give a fuck what you're pleadin' for! The only thing you deserve is to be lyin' in the ground instead of him. Now get your ass up here so you can bury him!" Pops replied with disgust in his voice.

"Jesus Christ! Just let me—"

"Fuckin' Hell!" Pops jumped into the hole and pried Luke out of his arms, and just threw him to the dirt.

The sound of his body thumped to the ground, echoing through the woods and right in my heart where I would forever hear that sound. I saw Creed lean forward to do something, but the second he took a step, Pops punched him. Instantly gripping onto the front of his shirt, getting right in his face.

"Prez, come on, that's enough," Stone coaxed.

"Yeah, Prez, leave him alone. He's been through enough," Diesel added.

"You listen and you listen good, boy," Pops roared, ignoring the other brothers pleas. "I don't give two shits about you, or what you're feeling. You're lucky I'm savin' your sorry ass from servin' a life sentence in prison for murder, you ungrateful dick. When I tell you to do somethin', you fuckin' do it. Do you understand me? I won't hesitate to remind you of your fuckin' place in my clubhouse."

Woooooooooo! Wooooooooooo!

The train sounded more and more, closer and closer, warning me repeatedly to get off the tracks. I didn't pay it any mind, I wasn't done.

I was far from done.

I down-shifted again and leaned back to pop a small wheelie, and as soon as the front tire hit the gravel I took off faster toward the oncoming train. Exhaust smoke bellowed out of the tail pipe as I pushed the limit, red lining the engine.

But nothing was going to stop me.

Not the tires smoking as I hit fifty, sixty, seventy, eighty miles per hour.

Not the brakes on the train squealing, protesting against the tracks. The conductor trying like hell to stop the massive steel from taking an innocent life.

Not the flashing red lights blinking all around.

Nothing.

Not one damn thing.

All I did was stare straight into the train's headlight right in front of me. The train that was coming right for me and still…

All I could see was Creed burying our brother.

It didn't matter that the blare of the train's horn roared through the trees, all I could hear was the sound of the shovel burying our brother over and over again.

Woooooooooo! Wooooooooooo!

The train's brakes pumped harder, clinking against the tracks as it barreled toward me. I desperately tried to tune out the chaos of that night, replaying in my mind with no end in sight.

Woooooooooo! Wooooooooooo!

Woooo!

Woooooooooooooooooo!

I shut my eyes just for a second and all I could see was blood, so much fucking blood, with Luke's lifeless eyes staring back at me.

Repeating, *"You know, you're right, we ain't brothers because my brother woulda never said that to me."*

All I could think about was this couldn't be happening, this couldn't be happening again. Silently praying it was all a nightmare playing out, and I would soon wake up from it. For over a year, I'd been existing in a living nightmare.

When a horn began blaring through the air again and again, I finally opened my eyes and saw that it was right fucking there, just a few feet in front of me.

And that was the moment…

I finally smiled.

Finally feeling what I craved.

What I strived for.

What I always desired, more so now than ever before.

A new high.

I felt the thrill of the rush running through my veins. Replacing all the hurt and the pain, all the memories of what I could never change.

The life and the future I couldn't control.

Suddenly, I felt my heart jump to life, making me feel for just a second, I hadn't died with Luke.

That I was…

Truly alive.

And it was all it took for me to abruptly jerk the wheel to the side, right as the train was about to hit me head on. Propelling my bike off the tracks, hurling my body through the air.

I flew through the wind, savoring that moment. Feeling free from everything that weighed heavy on my mind, my body, my soul.

"*Tomorrow! Tomorrow! I love ya all the days and nights of tomorrow!"*

I felt her.

I finally felt her.

But it didn't last, it never did.

It wasn't until I roughly landed on the ground that everything…

went…

Black.

NOAH

Five

"The sun'll come out tomorrow, bet all those dollars that tomorrow. There'll be sun shining bright and happiness. Just thinkin' about tomorrow," I heard her singing as if she was right above me. I'd never forget that voice for as long as I lived.

I'd never forget her.

For over a year I searched for her, going back to the river like I planned that next day. I never once saw her again. The only place I heard her sing and saw her face was in my mind, in my memories. She was the only good thought in my life, the only good memory that constantly battled the bad.

"Just thinkin' about tomorrow. Clears away the sadness, the rain, and the emptiness. 'Till it's not there."

"Hmm…" I weakly groaned, trying to wake up. Needing to wake up.

Wanting to see her again even if it was only a dream, it would still be the best damn dream I'd ever had.

"So just hang on 'til tomorrow and work through the pain," she sang, and it was just as memorable, just as powerful. Feeling her through the words was everything I remembered it to be. Her voice vibrated deep in my chest, deep in my body, deep in my bones. There wasn't a chance in

hell she wasn't there with me. She couldn't be a figment of my imagination or an illusion of my lonely mind like I was used to.

She had to be there with me.

It was too real.

She was too real.

"Hmm…" I faintly groaned again, slowly shaking my head. Willing my eyes to open, cursing them for not complying.

"Shhh… I'm almost done. You'll be good as new, I promise," she spoke to me for the first time, and it was the sweetest sound I ever heard.

I think the sensation returned to my body because I felt something cold on my forehead, before I felt her hands dabbing what seemed like water on my face.

"Hmm… sing…" I softly muttered what I had been wanting to say for so long. Instantly hearing her lightly gasp as if she was just as surprised to hear my voice as I was hers.

Talking to her.

Asking for what I'd been dreaming about for over a year.

Her body tensed beneath me, suddenly making me realize my head was in her lap. Her hands froze, not moving an inch, and I swear I could hear her heart beating as fast as mine.

She smelled like blueberries and bubble gum, and I knew it would become my new favorite scent.

"Please… sing…" I breathed out again. My mouth felt so dry, but I didn't care.

All I wanted was to hear her sing for me.

Even if it was just this once.

To sing only for me.

She took a deep, steady breath and did exactly that. Belting out, *"Tomorrow! Tomorrow! I love ya all of the days and nights of tomorrow! You're almost there! And only a day, away!"*

I also knew right then and there she was sunshine and happiness. She was a blessing, *my* blessing. One that I finally found again, except this time…

She'd found me.

Sluggishly, I shook my head a few more times and my eyelids started to flutter open. Only to be met with a pair of crystal blue eyes staring right back into mine. She was the most beautiful thing I had ever seen. Her dark, thick eyelashes flickered every time she blinked, emphasizing the black ring lining her cat shaped eyes. Her long, wavy, sandy brown hair framed her expression, caging in her round face with high, accentuated

But it was her big, pouty lips, that were almost too big for her face, that had me wanting to kiss her.

I never wanted to kiss anyone as much as I did in that moment.

These feelings were all so new to me, and yet I never wanted to let them go.

They would now be part of me, exactly how I needed her to be.

She swallowed hard, taking me in as well. Call it wishful thinking, but for some reason I just knew she felt the same way about me.

She was meant to come into my life.

I was meant to come into hers.

We were destined to meet each other. For what, I still didn't know.

Though it didn't matter, I immediately learned nothing did when I was with her. When we were together, I didn't think about Luke, about my family, about my mother. Especially not about that night. All I could see, all I could hear, all I could think about…

Was her.

Although she was right in front of me, she still consumed my mind, my heart, my soul. I fell for her when I was eleven-years-old and I didn't even know her name. We stared at each other for I don't know how long, lost in our thoughts that I just knew mirrored one another.

I was the first to break the silence, finally needing to hear it from her lips. "What's your name?"

"Skyler."

"Skyler," I repeated, wanting to hear it come from mine. "My name's Noah. Noah Jameson."

She smiled, her teeth were straight and white, and perfect. She was perfect.

"I'm Skyler Bell, but everyone calls me Sky."

"Well then, I'll just havta' call you Skyler, 'cuz I don't wanna be like no one else."

She chuckled, making me laugh too. My hand instantly went to my ribs, hissing from the pain.

"I don't think you broke anything," she informed, checking me over. "You had a nasty landing, though. What exactly were you trying to accomplish, aside from knocking yourself out?"

"You watched?" I asked, taken back.

"I didn't have much of a choice. I was down at the river and the train's horn kept blaring, so I rode my bike over to see what all the commotion was about. Thank God I did, or your dirt bike may have crushed you." She nodded over to the mangled metal and I knew just by looking at it, it was damaged beyond repair.

"Fuck," I murmured under my breath.

Her eyes widened, caught off guard.

"Sorry, I gotta bit of a foul mouth."

She smirked. "I see that."

"So you been cleanin' me up, yeah?" I questioned, wanting to change the subject.

She nodded. "Yes. After I threw your bike off you, I rode mine back to the river and grabbed the water bottle off my bike. Filled it up and came back to you. You've been unconscious for probably twenty, maybe thirty minutes. So are you going to tell me what happened here?"

I shrugged, not wanting to answer, mostly because I didn't want to ruin this moment between us.

"You have something to hide, Noah Jameson?" she asked with a smile. However, her eyes expressed something I couldn't quite place.

"Doesn't everybody?" I simply replied, making her eyes narrow in on me. Like what I said really hit home for her. "Besides, ya need to stop swimmin' at that river by yourself. Won't take much for that current to take you for a ride."

She sighed, smirking, and grabbed my head. "Alright, Evel Knievel, you're good to go." She helped sit me up, waiting until I caught my bearings before letting go of my arms once I was standing.

My hazy eyes immediately took in her body, noticing her frame was petite too. They landed right on her bare stomach where her shirt was torn under her perky tits.

On my twelfth birthday, a few weeks after Luke died, my piece of shit old man decided it was time I became a man. I crashed at the clubhouse, which I found myself doing more and more, wanting to get away from home. From Ma, especially when Creed wasn't around. It was easier that way. Pops had him traveling a lot, taking care of club business more so now than ever before.

I woke up in the middle of the night with my dick in some young blonde chick's mouth, sucking my cock like a damn pro. She blew me until I came all over her lips, my whole body shuddering beneath her. I barely had time to figure out what was going on before she got me hard again. She pulled out a condom and ripped it open with her teeth, rolling it down my shaft. Her luscious frame crawled its way up my body, slid down my dick, and just started riding me. I think I came again in less than fifteen seconds.

There was no kissing.

There was no hello or goodbye.

She got up and left like she was never there to begin with.

The next morning Pops informed me her pussy was my birthday present. Saying some shit about it being a family tradition, and it was what he did for his sons to make sure they weren't homos. I never saw her again, I couldn't even tell you what she fully looked like, it was too dark. Since then, my dick had a mind of its own, but never like it was with Skyler.

It was always different with her.

She followed my stare, looking down to where I still hadn't stopped gawking. With only her eyes, she peered up at me through her lashes. Smirking again. "You like what you see, Noah? Because you ruined my shirt too. I had to rip the bottom off to tend to your wounds."

I loved that she called me out on my bullshit. No one ever did.

Even though I wanted to say I fucking loved what I was looking at, I ignored her question and simply replied to her comment about my wounds. "I'm fine," I smugly stated, standing up straighter although it killed my ribs.

"Oh yeah? Tell that to all the blood still pouring from your legs, arms, and face. I'd like to see you get home without my help."

"You gonna help me home?"

"No." She shook her head, smiling. "You just said you were fine."

"You gonna believe a person who just knocked himself out? I'm clearly outta my mind. Thinkin' wit' the wrong head."

Her eyes widened with a great big smile on her face, shocked as shit by my response. Her eyes quickly wondered to my dick and back up. So I decided to keep going.

I was a Jameson after all.

We didn't have a filter.

"Wanna help me out with that too? I mean… help me home that is. Sorry, it must be the huge bulge... on my head doin' the talkin'."

"Noah Jameson!" She blushed, her jaw dropping to the dirt. "I… what… I… mean…"

"It's alright, Cutie, didn't take long to have ya blushin' and tongue-tied for me. I have that effect on girls."

I wasn't bullshitting her, I had girls throwing themselves at me since they found out I was fair game. My pops made it known to everyone, besides Creed, I was a man now and needed to get my dick wet. Over the last year, I started hanging around girls because of it. Talking dirty was what I was used to, it was all I ever grew up around. The chicks I was chilling with didn't think anything of it either, they were used to it too. But with Skyler it was different.

It was more like playful banter than anything else, just to see her smile for one more minute. To make her laugh, blush, think about me when I wasn't around. Something told me she had never met anyone like me before, and I'd be lying if I said I didn't love that. She was the breath of fresh air I'd been waiting for, pulling me from the quicksand I had been rapidly sinking in since I was born. My world suddenly seemed brighter. She chased away my darkness without even knowing it, and a huge part of me knew she would. It was probably why I couldn't stop thinking about her.

Skyler Bell was mine.

And I knew that at thirteen-years-old too.

She shook her head, smiling even bigger. "You—" she pointed at me— "are trouble! I knew I should've stayed away, especially after catching you gawking at me in my bikini the last time I saw you!"

I grinned, purposely eyeing her up and down. Not holding back this time, I spoke the truth, "What can I say? I like beautiful things."

She narrowed her eyes at me still smirking. "Just so you know, your flirting isn't going to work on me. I'm surrounded by actors all day, and I know when someone is full of it. And you, Noah, are so full of it, I'm surprised you can even stand."

"Actors?" I asked, jerking back.

"Yeah." Her smile eased, looking everywhere but in my eyes. "I'm uh… I'm an actress. Actually, I'm a performer. I can sing and act. I've been doing it all my life. I'm actually on a show filmed here in Southport, it's why I live here for a few months out of the year. But um… anyway…" She shrugged, playing it off like it wasn't a big deal, when it was such a huge one. She turned and started walking away from me, stopping a few feet ahead, calling out to me over her shoulder, "I can help you *walk* home where you can take care of your *bulge* by yourself, Mister. Or I can just watch you pitifully trying to once again save face and walk home by yourself, while laughing my ass off, of course," she added all proud of herself, and I think I fell for her a little more.

Her brightness overshadowing my dark demons once again.

"Choice is yours, Noah Jameson, but if it was my choice, I'd go with the first one. It might make your hand tired, but I'm sure you're used to it by now." She winked and I busted out laughing, instantly hissing and grabbing my ribs again.

Not only from my injuries but from the foreign feeling laughter brought upon me. The sensation was so unexpected as the noise left my lips.

When was the last time I laughed? Really laughed?

"Ugh, you boys… come on, I'm making the choice for you." With that she walked back over to me, carefully placing my arm on her shoulder and wrapping hers around my waist. Gently tugging me to her side before we started walking, and I milked it for everything it was worth.

"How old are you?" she asked, looking up at me.

"Thirteen. You?"

"Same. When's your birthday?"

"A few days ago."

"What?" she asked, pulling back. "When?"

"August eleventh."

"Huh," she breathed out, peering out in front of her again.

"Why?"

"That's my birthday too."

"No shit?"

She giggled, "No shit, Noah."

"Don't cuss, Cutie, you're far too innocent for filthy shit to come out of that sweet mouth."

"You don't even know me," she stated, trying to hide another smile.

"It don't feel like that, yeah?" She met my stare as my tall frame loomed over her. I couldn't take my eyes off her face.

"You sure you're only thirteen? You look and act a lot older, besides you already have all those tattoos." She pointed to a few of them on my arm.

"I get that a lot. Happens when ya havta' grow up fast I guess." I looked away for the first time, not wanting her to see the sadness build in my eyes. The dark trying to overtake this new light.

Her.

"Yeah." She nodded. "It does, doesn't it?"

It was my turn to narrow my eyes at her, silently asking her to keep going. Feeling like she had more to say but was hesitating.

"You are trouble," she coaxed, making me grin. Changing the subject by nodding to something beside her, she ordered, "Now get on my bike, *Rebel*."

I looked in the direction she nodded and cocked my head to the side, blurting, "Fuck no."

"What? Why?"

Our eyes locked again.

"Skyler, your bike is pink. I'm a guy, we don't do pink."

"Oh my God! Are you serious? You can't be serious."

"Does it look like I'm fuckin' jokin'?"

"Noah, I'm five-foot-four and you're every bit of six feet or more, not to mention you probably weigh twice what I do. You can't expect me to help you all the way to your house, wherever that is. You tower over me, I won't be able to help you walk that long. Just get on my bike and I can wheel you home. No one will have to know, it'll be our little secret, okay?"

"Fuck. No," I repeated, slower that time so she could understand because she obviously hadn't the first time I said it. "Besides, I like your arms around me." And to prove my point, I pulled her closer.

She rolled her eyes before sternly glaring up at me. "Cute."

"No, you're cute, Cutie. Thinkin' I'm gonna get on that. I'll walk home by my damn self before I get on your pink bike."

"You're being ridiculous. It's just a color, and you're with me so if anyone does see us, it's going to be a dead giveaway you're on my bike because you're the dumbass who decided to play chicken with an oncoming train."

My patience was wearing thin. "Look, Cutie, I'm gonna spit it out for ya. I only ride things with horsepower or two long legs. So unless I'm ridin' you, looks like I'll be staggerin' home with my pride still intact."

"Ugh!" She shoved me off her, not giving a shit about my ribs. I groaned out in pain, my hand instantly applying pressure.

"You"—she pointed at me, stepping backward towards her bike—"can walk your stubborn, chauvinist ass home *by your damn self*." She turned, getting on her bike.

"Cutie! I was jokin'! How you gonna be so cruel, bustin' my balls like this!"

"It wasn't funny!"

"I'd want you to ride me anyway!"

She looked back at me with a hint of mischief in her eyes, trying to pretend like she didn't like my foul mouth.

"Come on… ya can't leave me here. I'm wounded, remember?"

"Watch me. Have fun staggering home, Rebel." With that, she started peddling, and I couldn't help but chuckle, loving that she didn't let me get away with shit.

"If I hurt myself, you're gonna feel really bad!" I hollered out.

"No, I won't! I don't feel bad for stupid!"

I laughed, shaking my head. "At least tell me what show you're on!"

She hit the brakes and stopped, pausing for a minute before peering back at me. Contemplating if she was going to answer. I wasn't surprised in the least when she responded with, "I'm sure you could figure it out." Not giving me a chance to reply, she took off again.

It took me three hours to get home when usually it was a half an hour walk. I had to keep stopping from the crippling pain in my ribs, laughing every time I did. Thinking about her just leaving me there to fend for myself.

I'll tell you one thing though, she was right.

As soon as I got home, I jumped on my computer and found what show she was on. I barely used the Internet, let alone watched TV. I had no fucking clue who she was. So I spent the rest of the day and well into the morning, catching up on every episode I could. Knowing damn well, I couldn't wait to see her again. My sunshine and happiness.

More so now…

Than ever before.

NOAH

Six

My fourteenth birthday was almost a month ago. I celebrated by waiting for Skyler down by the river for most of the day, thinking maybe she'd finally show up after all this time. Another year had flown by since I last saw her at the train tracks. The day I knocked myself out and unexpectedly woke up to her beautiful face taking care of me. Singing that song that would forever be engrained into my mind, relentlessly playing. Constantly thinking about tomorrow. The next morning, following our first real encounter, I'd woken up with a smile on my face for the first time since Luke died, thinking I would see her again and again, and again.

I hadn't.

It was like she dropped off the face of the earth, and I was starting to think I'd imagined it all. A hallucination my mind created just to fuck with me. If it wasn't for seeing the episodes of her show on television, I'd think she was an illusion too. But she wasn't, she was very much real. I could still feel her touch on my scars, smell her intoxicating scent all around me, and see her pouty fucking lips sassing me. I missed her, which was so fucking absurd.

How did I miss a person I didn't even know?

I tried to find out everything I could about her online, wanting to feel close to her in any way I could. She'd been a performer all her life, from commercials to print ads, from productions to big and small roles on television and in movies. She wasn't a huge celebrity by any means, at least not yet, but I knew it was only a matter of time before she hit it big. Skyler had a gift, a talent like no one I had ever seen before. The girl could sing and act as if she was born only to do that, like her sole purpose in life was to entertain others. To stand out in a crowded room, to leave people speechless with her voice, to captivate an audience with her natural beauty. The list was endless.

Above all else, Skyler Bell was meant to shine.

I read all her interviews in magazines, watched all the shit she ever appeared in, and even looked at every photo I could possibly find of her from the tabloids and red-carpet appearances. I was borderline fucking creepy and obsessed with the girl whose voice and face I thought about every day and dreamt about every night. It was the only time I felt at peace. I'd smile to myself and think about a future with her on a daily basis. She gave me hope that there was more to life than what I had been living for all this time. I wanted to see her, I needed to see her as much as I needed to take my next breath. But she was gone like dust in the wind, taking a piece of my heart I didn't know I had left to give.

Leaving me alone with only my memories of her.

After the first few months of searching for Skyler at the river and coming up empty, I'd started to go there less and less, losing hope that I'd ever see her again. It was just as depressing as it fucking sounded. Believe me, I was living it.

When our birthdays rolled around, I couldn't help but go search for her yet again. I hadn't been back to the river in months, give or take a few. I sat there all afternoon by myself, skipping rocks across the shallow water. Watching the ripples descend as the pebble sank, taking a little piece of my patience with it each time. Waiting for a girl who never showed. Once I realized the river was a lost cause, I decided to make my way back home. Taking the train route just to feel her presence for a few more minutes before I had to let her go. I hadn't been back since.

Each step I walked toward my house felt like a step in the wrong direction, like I was being pulled out of the happy and back into the reality that was my life. And even though I should've known better, I still held onto the hope that I wouldn't be walking into a vacant house, filled with nothing but empty liquor bottles.

My momma used to make a big fuss over our birthdays every year. She was always there with a cake and some gifts, waiting to serenade us. It didn't matter how many times we begged her not to sing, she never listened. Singing "Happy Birthday" at the top of her lungs and loving every second of it. But that was another time, another life. One where I still had two brothers and a mother. Where I still had somewhat of a family.

Creed was barely around anymore, going on more runs for the club, leaving me behind to take care of what was left of our momma. He was a fucking mess, worse now that his girl was gone. Pops was no help either, he practically moved out, spending most of his time balls-deep in his whore. Not giving a flying fuck about Ma and her mental state. He probably wished she'd just kick the fucking bucket so he'd be free of that burden.

When I walked into my house, it was just as I expected. She was nowhere to be found, and in her place were empty liquor bottles piled on top of each other and scattered around everywhere. The scent of booze and stale cigarettes assaulted my senses the further in I stepped. Stopping in the middle of the living room, I looked around at the messy space that used to always be clean. The stacks of laundry that hadn't moved in weeks from the couch, the trash sprawled about. I could still hear my momma's voice, yelling at me to use a coaster under my drink on the coffee table that was now coated in cigarette ashes and who the fuck knows what else.

I shook my head, thinking about how my life had come to this.

Happy birthday to me.

I spent the next few hours cleaning up, praying maybe it would help her not drink. Out of sight, out of mind. To have her back, even if it was just for a few minutes, would have made my time and effort worth it. I missed the times she was so full of life, dancing around the house, making the best of the shitty hand she was dealt. Most of all, I missed talking to her. I hadn't had a coherent conversation with her since Luke died over two years ago. She was always drunk, it didn't matter what time or day it was. My momma was always plastered, shitfaced on the regular.

There was nothing left of the woman who raised me because I'd killed her too.

After I was done cleaning up her mess, I went to the clubhouse, desperate to just forget about how shitty our lives really had become. Which was exactly what I did. I rolled a blunt and smoked it to the face with some blonde chick with big tits and no IQ. We smoked and drank and fucked and that was how I celebrated my fourteenth birthday. High and drunk as hell, inside some chick I didn't give a shit about.

Wishing for a different life.

Hoping for another tomorrow.

It was better than the alternative. I started picking fights, purposely brawling with guys I didn't know and some that I did. Craving to feel in control with any aspect of my life. Nothing described the feeling of taking my anger out on someone's face. It made me recognize that maybe my old man and I were more alike than I had ever imagined.

Terrifying me in ways I never thought possible.

"Where you headed, boy?" Pops called out from behind me as I was walking out of the clubhouse.

Pulling me away from my thoughts about my birthday almost a month ago, I stopped and turned to face him. "Home," I stated.

He snidely scoffed, "For what? They ain't nothin' for you there but a fuckin' drunk."

"No shit. Gonna go check on her."

"Why? She don't give a fuck 'bout you. The only thing she gives a shit 'bout are her liquor bottles. Let her fuckin' be. I hope she drowns in her fuckin' puke, save me the money to havta bury her when her liver finally fuckin' kicks it."

"Jesus Christ," I muttered under my breath.

"What the fuck you say?"

I shook my head. "Nothin'." It wasn't worth arguing with him, and I wasn't in the mood for a bloody lip or a black eye.

"That's what I thought. Now get the fuck outta here, and take your bullshit of checkin' on that waste of fuckin' air with you. Shoulda' known better than to make her my old lady, she can't even suck my dick let alone take care of her family. Go make yourself fuckin' useful and scratch off the serial numbers on the new gun shipment in the back, you pussy ass momma's boy. I ain't raisin' no lil' bitch."

My eyes caught Diesel's from across the room, giving me a curt nod. Silently, letting me know it was alright to go check on her, he'd take care of the serial numbers for me.

"What dafuq you lookin' at, boy?"

"Nothin'." I shrugged, meeting his eyes again. "Just listenin' to ya."

"Good. Now go before I change my mind and make you clean the fuckin' toilets instead."

I didn't have to be told twice, I got the hell outta there. Not that where I was headed to was any better. Ma's car was in the driveway, so at least she wasn't out drinking and driving again.

"Ma!" I shouted, closing the front door behind me.

There were piles of empty liquor bottles everywhere, it didn't even look like the same house I had cleaned a few weeks ago. The place was a wreck again, smelling of booze and cigarettes.

"Ma, you here?" I asked, walking around the house. Checking every room until I finally found her. "Fuck," I breathed out, taking in the sight of her on the dining room floor. I couldn't tell if she fell off the chair and knocked herself out, or if she just passed out from a liquor-induced coma.

It was hard to decipher, given the half empty bottle she still clutched in her bony hand, while Luke's baby blanket was firmly grasped in the other. He still used it up until the day he died, it laid on his bed and he'd bitch every time Creed or I hid it from him. Which only made us hide it more. I shook off the memory, glancing at all the open photo albums that were on the table, and then to the Polaroids on the floor surrounding her. They were all photos of Luke, happy, smiling, alive.

And I swear it killed me a little more.

"Ma," I urged, crouching down beside her. "Come on, Momma, please get up." I shook her, trying to wake her up but she wasn't responding. I called out her name a few more times, shook her harder, and when I was just about to reach for the phone to call 911, she finally stirred awake. Babbling some bullshit that made no sense.

I breathed a heavy, deep sigh and closed my eyes. My head suddenly pounding, the walls feeling like they were caving in on me as I fell back to lean against the wall.

"Luke…" she groaned, making me immediately open my eyes. She was sluggishly shaking her head back and forth.

"Ma, can you hear me?"

"Baby…" She lazily opened her bloodshot eyes, and it was the first time, in I don't know how long, I really took a good look at her.

Staring deep into her drunken, vacant gaze that once showed so much love for me. Desperately searching to find her, needing to see the real woman staring back at me. The mother I still had and wanted in my mind. The same one I prayed still lived inside of her, buried under all the hurt and pain. Hidden behind all the happy memories that had become her worst nightmares.

I cleared my throat and looked away. I had to. Hiding behind the pain in my tears, I blinked those away too. There was nothing left of the woman I remembered and silently hoped I would eventually forget. Knowing I wouldn't, she'd always be my mother, and at the end of the day I'd take her any way I could.

"Come on, Momma," I coaxed, picking her up and cradling her frail body in my arms. She was nothing but skin and bones, she weighed nothing. It was like carrying a child. A hollow shell of a human being too far gone.

The second I stood, she threw up all over me and herself. "Ugh…" she groaned. "Sorrrry, baby… I'm just soooo tirrrred."

I swallowed hard, battling the stench of liquor, puke, and her. "I know,

Momma. I know," I reassured her, walking toward the bathroom. Fighting the urge to vomit, the bile raising in my throat every second it took to get her to her bathroom.

"Baby, haaave you seeeen Luke?" she asked, her head wobbling all over.

"No, Ma, I haven't seen Luke."

She did this sometimes, asked me about Luke as if he was still alive. I shouldn't have encouraged it, but I couldn't help myself. The guilt was eating me alive. If it made her feel better to think he was still with us, then who was I to take yet another thing away from her.

"Baby, you thinnnk he commmin' home today?"

"I don't know. Maybe. I'll tell him to come see you, okay?"

She lethargically smiled. "Okay, baby… where we goinnn'?" she slurred even worse as I softly set her against the cold tile next to the bathtub, making sure to lean her upright so she wouldn't fall over and hurt herself. Not that it mattered, but I wasn't going to let it happen when she was with me.

"We ain't goin' nowhere. Gonna draw you a bath, Ma. Get ya nice and cleaned up, alright?"

"Mmm kay, baby."

I sat up to turn on the tub's faucet, leaning over her to adjust the temperature. Once it was warm enough, I plugged the drain and grabbed some fruity bubble shit I found under her sink. She used to love taking baths, it must have been left over from before. Grabbing a towel, I threw it beside me and crouched down in front of her again.

"Alright, Momma," I exclaimed. "Gonna take you out of these dirty clothes, and I'm gonna give ya a bath, yeah?"

"Isss Luke home now?" she asked with great big hopeful eyes. Looking at me like she was the child and I was the parent.

"No." I shook my head. "But the faster you let me clean you up, the quicker we can go wait for him."

She drunkenly nodded. "Okkkay, baby."

I grabbed the bottom of her dress and slid it off her, throwing the ruined fabric in the trash behind me. In normal circumstances this would have been awkward as all hell, me seeing my mother in only her bra and panties, but the only thing I fucking noticed was how skinny she was sitting there in her drunken stupor. She was nothing but skin and bones and liquor.

"God, Momma, I'm so fuckin' sorry. I'm so sorry I did this to you," I murmured to myself, feeling like the piece of shit I was.

She was beyond out of it, not paying me any mind as I pried Luke's blanket out of her hands and carried her willowing body into the bathtub. Turning off the faucet, I grabbed a cup that was sitting on the edge of the tub and slowly began pouring water over her head. Pulling out chunks of god knows what from the puke in her hair. I washed it a few times because who the hell knows when she was going to shower again.

"Hmm," she groaned when I was massaging her scalp.

"Feel good, yeah?"

"Thannk you, baby."

She was in and out of consciousness the entire time, babbling incoherent shit or asking about Luke. It was one or the other. It didn't take me long to get her washed up though, and I dressed her into some fresh, clean clothes. When I was done, I brushed her hair and laid her in bed, trying to get her to drink some water but she refused, clinging on to Luke's blanket instead.

I waited in the bedside chair until she passed out, lost in my own plaguing thoughts, and just when I thought I was going to lose my shit and start bawling. Falling apart like my mind and body yearned to do, I heard Skyler's voice.

Singing for me.

"Just thinkin' about tomorrow. Clears away the sadness, the rain, and the emptiness. 'Till it's not there."

Giving me the push I needed to keep going.

I kissed my momma's forehead, whispering, "I love you."

Only to hear her murmur back, "I love you too, Luke."

I jerked back, hurt and winded. She hadn't said she loved me since he died, and when she finally does it wasn't even me she was saying it to. I don't know what hurt worse, never hearing her say the words or hearing her say it to the son I took away from her.

Taking one last look at her sleeping body, I turned and left. Moving on autopilot, needing to run away.

I couldn't breathe.

I couldn't fucking breathe.

I needed some air, some clarity, something.

Anything.

Other than what I was feeling.

Before I knew it, I was riding on the bridge over the river, to the one place that gave me peace. Never in a million years expecting what was happening in front of my eyes. Making me feel like I couldn't fucking breathe all over again, because another life was being taken away…

From me.

Seven

"Fuck!" I shouted at the top of my lungs, all the blood suddenly draining from my face and body.

My heart lodging itself in my throat as I flew off my bike toward the bridge railing. Watching her body float face down, being dragged by the rampant current. My eyes frantically searched for a passage, whatever I could find to help her. They landed right on a boulder that was slightly sticking out of the river, a few yards in front of her lifeless body.

"Skyler! Help! Someone help me! Skyler!"

And I didn't think.

I didn't hesitate.

I didn't allow the fear to take over.

It was instinctual.

She was instinctual.

I jumped, feet first and fully clothed.

Soaring through the air off the bridge, plummeting into the dark depths of the freezing water beneath me. As soon as my body went under, I fought with everything inside of me to resurface, not knowing which way was up or down. Already feeling the current sweeping my body away.

It was stronger than anything I could have ever imagined.

Pushing…

Pulling…

My way to the top.

My lungs felt like they were going to burst the longer I battled my way to the surface. The longer the water denied me air. Thinking only about Skyler and how I needed to get to her. She was a ticking time bomb in my core, in my mind, in every inch of my body.

Twenty seconds with no air.

Thirty seconds.

Forty-five.

Fifty.

Each second that ticked by was another moment of hell. My adrenaline kicked into overdrive, replacing everything but the need to get to her. Until finally…

I gasped.

Long and deep and hard.

My head above water, fresh air in my lungs, coughing, wheezing, greedy for my next breath. I didn't have time to catch my breath before I was battling again, this time with the full-fledged current. Being hauled in the same direction her body was being dragged by the treacherous stream. Despite the distance between us and the water propelling my body with so much force as I swam, paddling and kicking as hard as I could along with it, I saw her.

I finally fucking saw her again.

She was a few feet in front of me, being towed just as fast as I was, and she wasn't even swimming. There was nothing that could compare to the strength of Mother Nature when she was fucking pissed. Nothing compared to that current as I struggled to keep my head above water and my body from giving out on me from the force of her fury and rage. Not to mention the frigid temperature that had my body fighting from going into shock. But the bitch didn't deter me from what I needed to do, even though I knew I might get fucked. I paddled faster and harder, mirroring her anger and wrath. Trying to shake off the looming feeling in the back of my mind that Skyler might be dead. That I was risking my life to save hers.

It didn't matter.

Nothing ever did when it came to her.

The boulder came into sight and I only had seconds to reach her, grab her, and ultimately pull this off to hopefully save both our lives. I took a deep, sturdy breath and for the first time in all my life, I peered to the heavens above and prayed.

"Please, please, let me save her. Please…" I internally pleaded, praying to whoever was up there looking down upon me.

And just as I returned my gaze to the water, I realized she was finally within reach and I acted fast. I knew I was out of time, so I forcefully gripped onto the first thing I could. Grabbing her hair by the nape of her neck, yanking her as hard as I could toward me. Instantly spinning my torso around so my chest was to the current, strategically hugging her motionless body against me with all the strength I could muster.

"Skyler! Come on, baby, wake up! I'm here, I'm going to get you out of here," I reassured with no response from her at all. I held onto her for dear life, there was no way in hell I was letting her go.

Not now, not ever.

If we weren't to survive this, at least we'd be together when we took our last breaths. Like Romeo and fucking Juliet or some shit. I shut my eyes and waited, trying to mentally prepare myself for what was yet to come. Bracing myself as best I could for the impact that could possibly take me under.

With or without my consent.

Moments later, my back and head hit the boulder with so much intensity it almost knocked me out cold. My ears began to ring, my head rolled to the side, and I hissed and grunted loudly, my whole body seizing with sudden pain surging through every inch of my frame.

Burning.

Aching.

Throbbing.

Crippling my senses and vision. I repeatedly blinked, seeing only white spots as the current continued to ram my body deeper and firmer into the solid rock with Skyler still held tightly in my arms, against my chest. Feeling her dead weight along with the rapid flow jamming into me made it almost impossible to move. I felt agony in places I didn't even know possible, burning like hell. I had no time to contemplate how bad I fucked myself up because I needed to get us out of danger before my core completely shut down.

The force of the raging water against the boulder becoming too much, crushing bone by bone in my body. The undertow digging into my ankles, trying to pull me under. More water filling my lungs. I fought, I fought with everything I had left in me to save us. Keep our heads above the surface.

"HELP! Please someone help us!" I let out a gurgled yell, but it was no use.

My ribs ached from the ruthless beating, and my throat felt raw from all the water intake I couldn't control. With my vision still hazy, I wrestled getting my hand up to Skyler's chin so I could angle her head against my shoulder. Wanting to get her face out of the water. When I finally did, I breathed out a sigh of relief and satisfaction, feeling like I conquered at least one more task. When all odds were against me.

My defeat didn't last long because my body rapidly started feeling numb and the staggering pain slowly began subsiding. I knew I didn't have much time left until my body turned against me, until the current knocked me off this boulder and then there'd truly be no hope for us. I was panting, exhaustion trying to take over.

Mind over matter.

Kill or be killed.

Fight or die.

I shut my eyes one last time and prayed again, this time out loud. Hoping it would make a difference. That my prayers would be heard once again.

"Please… please… let me save her… I'm almost there."

It was now or never.

I let the current drift my body to the side of the boulder, and with shaky legs, I pushed with the strength of a thousand men off that rock toward the fallen tree branch in front of me.

Tugging.

Jerking.

Heaving our bodies out of the merciless stream and into the rapid flow of the river. I didn't waver, I couldn't rest, not even for a second. I flipped over onto my back so Skyler's body laid on top of mine and her face was completely out of the water, and then I firmly wrapped my arm around her waist and started to swim us backward to the shore. Struggling repeatedly to keep my own face above the surface from her weight and my exhaustion. Once again paddling and kicking my way onto the shore, already thinking about what I had to do next.

This wasn't over.

It was far from over.

I ignored my pounding head and the piercing pain in my back, and sprang into action as soon as we hit a patch of grass. Laying her securely on her back, I frantically knelt beside her.

Hacking.

Winded.

Trying to find my own breath within my shattering body.

"Think, Noah, think," I huffed and puffed, breathing heavily. My chest felt as if it wanted to cave in on me, undecided if it was grateful for the fresh air I was breathing or rejecting the massive amount of water I choked down while trying to save her. "You know what to do. You learned this shit in health class," I added, still feeling every forced breath my lungs heaved out.

Flashes of the CPR video started running through my mind, and my body moved in sync with the images. Getting a second wind from somewhere inside of me, I opened her mouth to check her airway and angled her chin toward the sky, lifting her head slightly back.

"You're going to be okay. Do you hear me, Skyler? Come on, baby." Leaning forward, I checked for any signs of breathing from her nose and mouth. Listening carefully for a few seconds like my life depended on it.

Nothing.

"Fuck," I breathed out, sitting up. Looking at her from head to toe and back up to her head again, taking in the blue hue to her normally tan skin. "I can do this. I know I can fuckin' do this." Placing one trembling hand on top of the other, in the middle of her chest, I sat up and used the weight of my body to push down, hard and fast.

"One, two, three…" I counted until I got to ten not remembering how many compressions I needed to do, just hoping it would be enough. Trying to get a response from her, needing to get a response from her.

Nothing.

"Fucking A!" I shouted, leaning forward to her open mouth. I pinched her nose shut and placed my lips over hers, blowing two deep, long breaths into her airway.

Watching out of the corner of my eyes as her chest lifted, remembering it was a good sign. It meant there was nothing she was choking on. I sat up again, placed my hands in the same position in the middle of chest, and repeated the same steps from before.

"One, two, three…"

Two deep, long breaths into her mouth.

"One, two, three…"

Two deep, long breaths into her mouth.

"One, two, three…"

Two deep, long breaths into her mouth.

Nothing.

"Goddamn it! Come on, Skyler! Don't do this to me! Don't you fuckin' do this to me!" I seethed, with nothing but fury and determination filling my drained lungs.

"One, two, three…"

Two deep, long breaths into her mouth.

"One, two, three…"

Two deep, long breaths into her mouth.

"One, two, three…"

Two deep, long breaths into her mouth.

Again and again and again.

Nothing.

"Please, baby, please don't do this to me! I can't lose you too! Please, for me… please breathe for me!" I roared, seeing Luke's lifeless eyes staring back at me.

"One, two, three…"

Two deep, long breaths into her mouth.

"One, two, three…"

Two deep, long breaths into her mouth.

"One, two, three..."

Two deep, long breaths into her mouth.

And then…

Time finally stood still.

Eight

Skyler gasped, throwing up. Instantly choking on the water purging from her lungs and out of her mouth.

"Fuck yes," I exhaled, immediately flipping her to her side so she wouldn't keep choking. Brushing her wet hair away from her face, I rubbed her back as she continued to hurl water from her lungs until there was nothing left for her to spew. Her tiny frame shuddering, accentuating all the bones in her body. Making her look so much smaller and innocent.

I shook my head, grateful that she was still there with me.

Alive.

Breathing.

That I was able to at least save her.

My sunshine and happiness.

"Cutie," I coaxed, slowly laying her down on her back. Immediately noticing the color was already returning to her face, and I breathed another sigh of relief. "For fuck's sake, don't ever do that to me again."

Her eyes fluttered to my face, her expression disoriented as all hell. "Noah?" she whispered in a raspy voice, meeting my eyes.

"Yeah. Where the fuck you been, baby? Been waitin' for you for over a year," I chuckled, trying to lighten the severity of the situation.

The fact that we could have died.

But mostly, the fact that *she* could have died.

"Am I in Heaven?" she asked, blinking away the haze.

"No. 'Cuz trust me, I sure as shit ain't goin' there."

She scoffed out a chuckle, her hand instantly going to her chest, wincing in pain.

"Looks like it was my turn to take care of you. I owed you one."

She blinked a few more times, looking deep into my eyes as though she couldn't believe I was sitting there, hovering above her. I don't know how long we stared at each other, lost in our own thoughts before her eyes shifted. "You're bleeding," she stated out of nowhere, reaching for the side of my head, but I caught her wrist midway.

"I'm fine."

She weakly smiled, shivering. "Yeah, me too, Rebel, me too."

"You're so full of shit and you don't listen very well, do you? I told ya to stop swimmin' by yourself. That current is all sorts of fucked up. If I hadn't shown up when I did, you woulda died."

She narrowed her eyes at me, looking me over. Realizing for the first time my clothes were soaking wet. "You saved me? What were you thinking? Oh my God, Noah, you could've died."

"No shit."

Her eyes widened, shocked by my response. "I don't know what to say. I didn't think… I mean I just… it all happened so fast," she stuttered, stumbling over her words, translating her thoughts. Confusing the two. But there was something from the look in her eyes that told me she was referring to something that had nothing to do with today. Shaking her head, she added, "I'm so sorry, are you okay?"

I nodded, the concern in her tone tearing up my heart. And for some reason, I found myself blurting, "I'd do anythin' for you."

She grimaced. It was quick, but I saw it. "You don't even know me."

"What are you talkin' about?" I grinned. "I'm your number one fan, borderline stalker."

She chuckled, pressing her hand against her chest again. Her mind shifted, focusing on the present. Her expression settled, reminding me of the girl who would always haunt my dreams.

"Stay off the Internet and don't believe everything you read. Most of it is bullshit lies."

"What I tell you 'bout cussin'? And why you tryin' to break my heart, Cutie? I was about to start a fan club and shit. Now you tellin' me you aren't who they say you are?"

She smiled. "No one ever is, *yeah*?" she mocked, trying to sit up by herself.

"I gotcha," I intervened, scooping her up and carrying her instead.

Once I started walking, she argued, "I can probably walk."

"No shit, but I'd rather feel you in my arms," I honestly replied. Holding back was never one of my fucking virtues. I disregarded the shooting pain running down my spine the longer I walked, carrying her, knowing I was really hurt. She couldn't have weighed more than Ma did.

"Noah, you're not carrying me all the way to my place."

"No shit, I'm carryin' you to the hospital."

"What? Put me down! I do not need to go to the hospital. I'm fine. You saved me, remember? Like my very own Prince Charming."

I looked down at her, smiling. "I'd rather be your knight in shinin' armor. Prince Charmin' is a pussy."

She laughed, full force. Holding her chest the entire time, but not caring. And it felt as though it was the first time she'd really laughed in a while too. Maybe even since the last time we were together.

"If I call you my knight in shining armor, will you put me down and let me walk home with your help."

"No."

"Noah!"

"Shut up, Cutie."

"Noah!"

I laughed, I couldn't help it. Nodding to my dirt bike a few feet in front of us. She followed my stare.

"You jerk! Making me think you were going to carry me."

"You're even cuter when you're angry, can't help myself."

She peered up at me through her lashes, puckering her pouty lips.

"Don't be lookin' at me like that."

"Looking at you like what?"

"Like you want me to kiss you."

She gasped, her mouth dropping open. "I don't want you to kiss me!"

"Then don't be lookin' at me like that."

She instantly turned her face away, still slightly glancing at me from the corner of her eyes. Trying to hide back a smile. "So you got a new dirt bike, I see. You're not going to crash this one too, right?"

"Not with you on it."

She smiled big and wide, not trying to hide it that time. I gently sat her down on the back of the seat and put my helmet on her, when she asked, "What are you going to wear?"

As soon as I was finished adjusting the strap to fit her face and making sure it wasn't going anywhere, I leaned back, getting a good look at my handy work. I never wore the thing, but I wasn't going to tell her that.

We locked eyes.

"You look cute as shit," I responded, smiling. Ignoring her question, I stated my own, "I'm gonna take you home on two conditions."

"Is that so?" she countered, cocking her head to the side.

"Damn straight," I affirmed, cocking my head to the side too. "You gotta promise me you'll get checked out by your doctor, your parents, I don't give a fuck, but by someone who can make sure you're really okay."

"I'll tell my dad. What's the next condition?"

"Ya not gonna disappear on me again. 'Cuz now I'll know where ya live, so don't try me. 'Cuz I'll take my stalkin' skills to the next level if ya do."

She giggled, and it was still the sweetest sound I'd ever heard. "I didn't disappear. I told you I only live here when we're filming for my show."

"Well fuck, I didn't know that meant you were hightailin' it out of here the next day."

"You didn't ask," she sassed, shaking her head.

"That how you gonna play it?"

She shrugged, smirking.

"Alright, Cutie. I'm game. When you leave again?"

"I just got here yesterday. We start filming next week, and I'm here for the next six months."

My grin mirrored hers. "Then that's six months you'll be on the back of my bike, yeah?"

Her eyes glazed over, unable to resist my charm. "Noah Jameson, what am I going to do with you?"

I didn't think twice about it, I leaned forward, getting close to her mouth. Causing her eyes to widen and her lips to part.

Waiting.

I licked my lips, almost touching hers before muttering, "Whatever the fuck you want."

She smiled once more, nearly taking my breath away. I swear I heard her sigh in disappointment when I pulled back, turning to grab her things on the grass nearby. I slipped her sandals on her feet, and when she threw on her yellow dress over her bathing suit, I resisted the urge to take one last look at her body, knowing it wasn't the right time. Considering what had just happened.

She nodded when she was ready and I jumped on my bike and kick started the engine, jerking back the throttle. Without me having to tell her to do so, she wrapped her arms around my waist as if she wanted to feel me too.

"Where am I headed?"

"Larson Ave," she answered, holding me tighter against her.

I took my sweet ass time driving her home, wanting to feel her arms around me for as long as I could. Taking trails I knew were soft, not wanting to cause either of us anymore pain. Though it didn't stop the empty feeling already filling my heart when I turned down her street.

"It's the fourth townhouse on the left!" she shouted over the motor.

I killed the engine on the side of her driveway and when I was about to lay down the kickstand, so I could help her off my bike and into her place, she jumped off herself. Not giving me a chance.

"Thanks for the ride, my knight in shining armor," she sassed, handing me my helmet while her other hand was firmly pressed against her chest.

I knew it must have hurt like a son of a bitch, jumping off by herself like that.

"Tryin' to get rid of me?" I questioned, arching an eyebrow.

"No. I just… I mean… my dad… he uh… he doesn't let me have guys in the house without him being home. That's all."

I narrowed my eyes at her, sensing she was lying to me. About what? I had not a fucking clue.

"But, anyway, umm… Noah, I really, really enjoy your company, it's just that I don't have any extra time to myself. Especially when I'm here. They have me on a tight schedule, working almost every day. I just don't—"

"What day you have off?"

"What?"

"You heard me."

Before she could think of an excuse, she blurted, "Sundays." Jerking her head back, surprised by her own response.

"Alright, then Sundays are our day, yeah?"

She bit the corner of her lip, thinking. Before she finally gave in, whispering, "Yeah."

"But I gotta tell ya, Cutie. I'm good at spittin' lines, so if ya ever need any help rehearsin' yours, I'm here."

She scoffed out a soft chuckle, aware that I meant it as a double innuendo. "I have no doubt." With that, she turned around, slowly walking toward her front door.

"Cutie!" I called out behind her, making her turn to face me. "Noon on Sunday at the river."

She nodded, biting her lip again with an expression I couldn't quite read. And it wasn't until I watched her walk inside her house that I realized...

Skyler never thanked me for saving her life.

Skyler

NINE

I woke up to my cell phone ringing beside me on my nightstand. The light from the screen illuminating the dark room with the morning sun trying to peek through the curtains.

"Mmm," I grumbled, not wanting to wake up. Pulling the pillow over my head to drown out the noise. It was the only day I could sleep in.

I was beyond exhausted, at least my body was. I knew it had everything to do with almost drowning in the river at the beginning of the week. My body was still punishing me for my poor decisions while my mind was trying to play catch up. To make matters worse, my call time had been before sunrise all week. You'd think after all these years of working in the industry, since I was in diapers, I'd have gotten used to waking up early.

Nope.

I still hated it.

"Mmm," I griped, throwing the pillow off my head and chucking it across the room. Reaching for my cell phone that wouldn't stop ringing until I finally answered it. "What is so important that you're calling me this early, Keith?"

"Good morning to you too, Sky," my agent/manager replied in a sarcastic tone, that was way too early for him to be using.

Flipping over onto my back, I rolled my eyes. "Good morning, Keith."

"See, Skyler Bell, was that so hard?"

I rolled my eyes again. "You do know Sunday is my only day I get to sleep in. Can you cut me some slack? I'm tired."

"Fine. I'll just wait to give you the good news then."

"Wait, what? What good news?" I asked, shooting straight up in my bed. Wiping the sleep from my eyes.

"Oh, now you want to talk to me."

"I always want to talk to you, Keith. I love you, you know that."

"Ah, now you're just buttering me up."

"Please…" I begged in the sweetest voice. "Can you tell me?"

He chucked, "You got the part, Sky."

"No! You're lying! Please tell me you're not lying!"

"I wouldn't lie to you."

"Oh. My. God! How? When? Are you sure?" I couldn't get my questions out fast enough. This was the break in my career I'd been waiting for.

A hot new Hollywood director was remaking the movie *Chicago*, putting his own spin on it. Getting together a cast of young up and coming actors and actresses, and marketing it toward a younger audience. I auditioned for one of the main female leads, Roxie Hart. She was the hero of the story, but she was also the villain. I'd taken roles where I had sung and acted before, small parts though. They didn't come close to a role like this. But it never mattered to me, I just wanted to sing and act, it was all I ever wanted to do.

"I got off the phone with the director before I called you. Whatever you did, you did it right, girl. He said you were made for the part." Before I could contemplate what he just shared, he added, "Proud of you, Sky."

Although he couldn't see me, I smiled and shrugged. "I'm happy my audition went so well. All I did was what you always tell me to do. Gave it my all."

"You were born to do this. I knew it the first time your mom brought you into my agency, demanding I meet you."

"You always say that."

"It's the truth. You were barely walking when I first met you, and as soon as you smiled, I knew you'd be a star. Signed you that very day. I still remember the first time you heard *Annie* years later, and you just started singing at that audition. Belting out the lyrics with a voice that didn't match your body. A powerhouse vocal ability coming from this small, little girl. You couldn't have been more than what? Four, five-years-old?"

"Six. I was six-years-old."

I know they say it's impossible to recall something when you're that young, but I did. I remembered everything about that day. I'd been singing little things here and there up until that point, but when I heard Annie sing

"Tomorrow! Tomorrow! I love ya all of the days and nights of tomorrow!" Something inside me awoke, and when I walked out of that audition, I knew my life would never be the same.

And it wasn't.

"Production on the movie starts the day after your show's season ends, and will wrap right before the new season begins. You'll be flown out to Colorado for the next six months and then back to Southport in time to start filming for the next season."

"Wow, so I don't get a break?"

"Not this time. You're on a tight schedule as it is, and the director is already working around it because he wants you for the role. The first two months you'll be learning all the choreography and songs. There'll be a vocal coach training with you day and night. I'll send you the script later today, so you can start learning your lines."

I listened intently, not saying a word.

"You can do it, I have full faith in you," he stated, knowing I needed to hear it.

No one knew me like Keith did. He'd been such a huge part of my life since before I could walk. Not only was he my agent and manager, he was part of my family, and I don't know what I would do without him.

"The world will finally hear Skyler Bell's voice and see her acting ability full force. You'll be surrounded by an all-star cast, and the role alone can get you nominated for an award, Sky. Or, at least, finally get you some recognition from more A-list directors."

I nodded. "Right."

"Jesus, I called in a lot of favors to get you this audition, little girl. How about some more enthusiasm and a thank you?"

"Right, no… I mean… of course… yes!" I anxiously exclaimed. "I'm excited and thrilled for this opportunity, I'm just… overwhelmed," I paused, trying to govern my thoughts and emotions. "I just… I… I… didn't expect to get the role, and it's a lot to take in. I don't want to let anyone down, especially *you*, Keith. I know how hard you work for me. How hard you've always worked for me, and I'm forever grateful and thankful for you. I'm sorry if I didn't sound like I was."

"Get your shit together, Sky. You're about to become a star."

"I—" He ended the call. "Great… now he's mad at me," I said to myself, placing my phone on the nightstand. I sat there for a few minutes, staring off into space. Going over the audition in my mind, trying to figure out what I did different to earn me the role.

My body jolted the second I heard the phone ringing again, except this time it was the landline. Breaking me away from the memory of that day.

Not looking at the caller ID, I answered, "I'm sorry, Keith, please tell me you're not upset. You know I hate it when you're mad at me."

"Who the fuck is Keith?" a familiar voice growled from the other end.

I pulled the phone away from my ear, looking at the unknown number on the screen. "Noah?" I questioned, recognizing the Southern accent.

"You makin' someone mad with that sassy mouth of yours, I don't believe it," he mocked in a sarcastic tone. "You gonna tell me who Keith is?"

"How did you get my number?"

"It's called the Internet. You be amazed how much you can find when ya know where someone lives."

I laughed, I couldn't help it. Noah had this ability to pull me away from *anything,* which was why I needed to stay away from him.

"So who's Keith? I got competition? 'Cuz I'll tell ya, I fight fuckin' dirty."

My cheeks flushed and my belly fluttered. If there was one thing I learned about Noah right from the start, it was he spoke his mind anytime he opened his mouth. He never held back, and it was one of the things I liked the most about him. He was as genuine as they came, and I hadn't met a lot of honest people in my life. Especially not in this business.

It was refreshing.

He was my breath of fresh air.

Which was yet another reason I needed to stay away from him.

"He's my agent and manager," I replied, putting him out of his misery. Though I was enjoying thinking about him fighting over me.

Stop it, Sky.

The bright sunlight blinded me through the shades, reminding me of how early it was and my eyes wandered to the clock on the nightstand, it read 7:10.

"What are you doing up this early, anyway? I thought all guys slept the morning away."

"Don't think 'bout other guys when you talkin' to me, Skyler."

I rolled my eyes, but I still found myself smirking.

"Imma ray of fuckin' sunshine. Don't need that much sleep. Can't stay asleep for very long as it is."

I could hear the humor in his voice, but I also heard pain in his tone, and I'd be lying if I said I didn't want to know why.

"Somethin' tells me you can't sleep for very long either. So since neither of us are sleepin', how 'bout we start our date now."

"Date?" I jerked back.

"Yeah, ya know… when two people go out, guy pays for everythin', they get to know each other. Maybe there's a reach-around?"

I giggled with a great big smile on my face.

"There's my girl," he rasped, making me bite the corner of my lip.

"I've never been on a date," I blurted, instantly smacking my hand on my forehead. Noah also had this ability to get the truth out of me, without even trying. "I mean—"

"I ain't ever been on a date either. We can be each other's first. Would ya like that? Me bein' your first?"

My eyes widened, and my belly did this somersault thing that only happened when he spoke to me in that suggestive way. I never had anyone talk to me like he did, and I'd be lying again if I said I didn't like that too.

"I… ummm… I—"

"It's alright, Cutie. I'd love for you to be my first."

I breathed out, "Noah Jameson, what am I going to do with you?" I pondered, shaking my head.

"I already told ya. Whatever the fuck you want. See ya at the river in an hour."

"An hou—" He hung up.

What is it with guys hanging up on me this morning?

I threw the covers off my body and made my way into the bathroom. After brushing my teeth, I took a quick shower and threw on a light pink summer dress with Chucks. I never wore makeup unless I was on set or going to an audition, but I decided that today was as good a time as any to put some on. I coated my already long, thick lashes with black mascara which always made my blue eyes pop more than they already did on their own. Sweeping a peach blush across the apples of my cheeks, I finished off my look with a blueberry-flavored lip gloss, and left my hair cascading down my back and framing my face.

"Dad!" I shouted, walking across the hall toward his room. "Dad, you up?" I asked, knocking on his partially open door. When he didn't answer, I announced, "I'm coming in."

There he was, exactly how I knew he would be. Still dressed in his dirty clothes and filthy work boots, passed out on top of his made bed.

He worked highway construction and worked crazy hours, mostly at night.

"Dad." I shook him, trying to wake him up.

"Mmm… not now, baby…" he grumbled in his sleep.

"What time did you get home last night?"

"Working, baby… I'm tired. Talk… later."

I sighed. "Fine."

"Love you, baby."

"I love you, too. I'll be gone for most of the day, but I'll have my phone on me."

"Going to set?"

"It's Sunday, Dad."

"That's right… I knew that…" He slightly opened his sleepy bloodshot eyes, looking me over. "You going to an audition with Keith?"

I shook my head. "No. Keith's in LA."

"Why do you look like that then?"

I scoffed, "Thanks, Dad. You saying I look like crap?"

"No, baby. You look just like your mom. Beautiful."

I smiled. "Thanks, Dad. Oh! Guess what?"

"Hmmm…" he groaned, closing his eyes again.

"I got the role!"

"What role?"

"Dad… you know what role. The one I haven't stopped talking about. The *Chicago* remake?"

"Oh yeah, that's right… I knew that too." He opened his eyes, once again taking me in. "Congratulations, Sky."

"This is huge, Dad! It could be my big break. I'm Roxie Hart, she's one of the lead roles."

"You're already a big star to me, Skyler. Always have been, always will be."

I smirked.

"Now let me get some sleep. We'll celebrate later tonight."

"Really?" My eyes widened. "You promise?"

"Of course, baby."

"Okay. I'll be back by dinner. I can make your favorite—"

"Nonsense, I'm going to take my baby girl out to dinner. Anywhere you want to eat."

"Really?!" I beamed.

"Anything for you, now go. Let me get some sleep."

I leaned forward and kissed him on the cheek, his familiar smell lingering all around him. "I'll see you later." Taking one last look at him, I turned and left, closing the door behind me.

Rushing down the stairs, I threw a bagel in the toaster, spread some cream cheese on it, and ran toward the door. Grabbing my purse and throwing it over my shoulder, I took the porch steps two at a time and grabbed my bike leaning against the house.

It didn't take long until I was peddling up to the river, ditching my bike near an old willow tree and walking over to him. I hadn't been back there since Noah saved me a few short days ago. I was more nervous to hang out with him than I was from what happened the last time we were together. He looked better than I remembered, and it had only been a few days since I'd seen him.

I could pick Noah out from a crowd in a room full of people. He stood out in his own way, with his tattoos, his bright blue-green eyes, his stocky build, and he had this stare that almost appeared murderous. He was the first guy to ever catch my attention, and I'd probably been around more males than any other girl my age.

When his eyes bared into mine, they rendered me speechless. Usually locking me in place like they were right now. I couldn't move even if I wanted to, and the truth was, I never wanted to. He walked over to me with that same swagger and confidence he exuded every time we were together. It was another thing I liked about him, he was consistent, never a phony act to impress the actress. Even though I picked on him for it, I just knew in my heart he wasn't showing me anything but the real him. It was still entertaining to call him out on it, letting him think he wasn't getting to me.

When in reality, he was.

Adding to the endless pile of reasons I needed to stay away from him.

TEN

Once his tall, muscular stature towered over my petite frame, he gazed at me with the same longing in his solemn expression that he always wore when he peered down at me. There was something about him, since day one, I couldn't tear my gaze away from. A magnetic pull I was instantly drawn to.

It came from something deeper.

More meaningful.

A connection I couldn't explain happened every time we were together, and it only seemed to grow stronger each time we saw one another. The familiarity in his intense gaze made me weak in the knees. I hoped he didn't notice, although I knew he was the type of guy who would notice everything.

Especially when it came to me.

Neither one of us said a word, but it didn't matter. Our eyes spoke volumes, exactly the way they always did, causing the nervous feeling in my core to subside as if it was never there to begin with.

"Hey, Cutie," he rasped, licking his lips. Eyeing me up and down with an infatuated regard. Almost like he wanted to eat me alive. "You look really fuckin' pretty. You do that for me, yeah?"

"No," I simply stated with a glimmer in my eye. "I'm just pretty."

He smiled. "That you are, pretty girl."

"I thought I was a Cutie."

"Cutie, pretty, beautiful, fuckin' gorgeous. Takin' my breath away all the damn time. That sassy, pouty mouth doin' things to me that I won't say, 'cuz imma gentleman. Need me to keep goin'?"

And like clockwork, there were the somersaults. A back flip, triple twist with a perfect landing in my stomach.

"Gentleman? Now you're just reaching."

He busted out laughing, and so did I. Extending his hand out for mine, he led me down to the river and we sat there on a blanket for most of the morning. Just talking and getting to know one another some more.

"What's your favorite place you ever been?" he asked, setting his arms on his knees.

"Like a state or a place?"

"Both."

"Well, that's a hard question to answer."

"Why's that?"

"Because most of the places I've travelled to have been for work."

"Don't ya get any time to yourself when you workin'?"

"Not really. I mean, maybe when I'm a little older and I can do stuff on my own, like drive, but usually I'm on set, or I'm with Keith."

"Keith, huh?"

I smiled, picking up on the jealousy in his tone.

"Tell me 'bout him."

"I thought you said I wasn't allowed to think about other guys when I'm talking to you."

He grinned. "I'll let ya this one time."

I laughed, shaking my head. "There's not much to say, he's like a father figure to me. I guess… I don't know. I've known him all my life."

"He know that?"

I lowered my eyebrows at him. "Know what?"

"That you see him only like a father figure?"

"I mean, I haven't said that to him, but I'm sure he knows. I live with him when I'm not filming here."

He jerked back. "You live wit' him?"

"Yeah, I mean… only when I'm not here. I'm from Southport, Noah. I was born here, but there's not much opportunity in good ol' North Carolina. I got lucky my show is filmed here, that doesn't usually happen. So when I'm not filming, I live in LA with him. I have a teacher on set and another one who comes to his house when I'm there."

"What 'bout your parents?"

"What about them?"

"They're okay wit' this?"

"Yeah, definitely. It was actually my mom's idea to advance my career when I was younger. It's been like this since I was maybe four or five. She actually used to stay at Keith's with me when she could."

He narrowed his eyes at me.

"I know it sounds really weird, but it's not. A lot of young actors and actresses live on and off with their agents and managers. They usually become more of a parent or family member than your actual parents and family members. It's easier this way, he takes me to auditions, coaches me, gets me ready. Rehearses my lines, and everything else in between. I'm lucky, he's one of the best."

He cocked his head to the side. "Used to?"

"What?" I responded, confused.

"You said your mom used to stay wit' you."

"Oh… right," I nervously laughed, shaking my head again. "What's this, Noah, twenty questions? It's my turn now. Where's your favorite place to be?"

He was silent for what felt like forever, gazing at me in that *Noah Jameson* sort of way. It made my stomach flutter for entirely different reasons, knowing he could see right through me. And as much as it terrified me, it also thrilled me. Finding someone who could see past the girl I was supposed to be.

Not just someone.

Him.

"Wit' you, Cutie," he merely replied.

"Me? What?"

"Bein' wit' you is my favorite place to be."

I smiled. Despite the awareness in his eyes, I looked away. I had to. Sometimes Noah was just too much to take, the truth in his eyes were too much to take…

Reaching into my purse, I turned my attention to a piece of bubblegum I was pulling out, avoiding the look in his eyes that I wasn't ready to feel. I put it in my mouth, needing some sort of distraction from the sudden realness between us.

"Care to share?" he asked, nodding toward the packet of gum in my hands.

"Oh, yeah." I looked down, realizing it was empty. "Shit, I don't have anymore."

"What I tell you 'bout cussin', Cutie?"

I peered up at him through my lashes, smirking, shrugging and chewing my gum.

"Share the piece in your mouth then."

"What?"

"You heard me."

As if on cue, my stomach did that somersault thing again. Except, this time it felt like it was never going to end, twisting and turning and flipping.

"Ummm…" I arched an eyebrow. "Okay." Before I gave it too much thought, I tore the piece from my mouth in half, handing it over to him. "Here."

Never taking his eyes off mine, he leaned over with a mischievous grin and bit it right off my fingers. The second his lips touched my skin, I felt this jolt of what could only be described as electricity. This immediate spark that made my mouth dry and my face flush, a burning sensation all over my body. I had never experienced anything like it before, and yet I couldn't wait to feel it again.

He cunningly smiled as if he knew exactly what I was feeling, thinking, wanting.

"Come on," he chimed in, nodding toward his dirt bike. "Takin' you for a ride, yeah?"

"Yeah." I mindlessly nodded, swallowing hard.

He chuckled, enjoying the fact that I was dumbfounded by what just happened between us. Reaching up, I grabbed his hand and he pulled me toward him. Whispering, "You look good in that shade of red, Cutie," into my ear. Causing sparks to ignite over every inch of my skin.

I thought he was going to kiss me and when he didn't, I couldn't tell if I was disappointed or relieved.

Disappointed, I was definitely disappointed.

He didn't let go of my hand until he was helping me onto his bike. "You should just keep this," he muttered while strapping me into his helmet.

"Then what are you going to wear?" I asked, already knowing the answer.

He winked and jumped on his bike, and we spent the rest of the afternoon riding around. He showed me all his favorite spots to do jumps and tricks, saying he and his brothers built a few of the obstacles for stunts themselves. But he quickly changed the subject when I asked how many brothers he had by simply telling me to hold on tight. Right when I did, he gunned the throttle and we went full speed into a course of jumps.

I laughed and screamed the entire time, begging for the next trail when we were done. I couldn't remember the last time I'd had that much fun, doing something completely out of the ordinary for me and loving every second of it. Being part of his world meant more to me than it should, and I was already counting down the days till we could see each other again. Shutting off the voice in the back of my head that kept trying to remind me I needed to stay away from him.

I just wanted a day to be free.

To act my age, to enjoy being outdoors, and be by Noah's side. To not have to worry about tomorrow. Where nothing else mattered but living in the moment with him. I knew right then and there that Noah Jameson was my escape away from the life I always wanted, to another world I didn't know I could have.

"You did not just bring me here," I teased, grabbing onto his hand as he helped me off his bike. "You read that interview, didn't you?"

"What interview?" he played it off as we walked side-by-side, still holding hands.

"The one where they asked me what my dream date would be, and I said a park so he could push me on the swing set."

"Not a clue whatcha talkin' 'bout."

"Sure… you just want to try to see up my dress."

"I'd prefer to see it on the floor next to my bed, but I'll settle on the swing set." He glanced over at me. "For now."

"Ugh!" Letting go of his hand, I teasingly pushed him. "Tag, you're it!" And I hauled ass away from him. Thankful that I was at least wearing Chucks for easy running. He wore combat boots.

He chuckled, "You better run, Skyler Bell. 'Cuz once I catch you, you're mine!"

I ran as fast as I could, but it didn't take long until I started getting tired. The sand only added to my exhaustion, ducking, dodging, moving out of his reach as quickly as I could. Noah's reflexes were insane, and it took a lot of effort to avoid his advances. However, once we were on opposite sides of the horizontal bars, I placed my hands up in the air in a surrendering gesture.

"Truce, yeah?"

"Fuck no." Like a lion attacking its prey, he threw himself under the bars and tackled me to the sand. "Mine!" he roared, landing right on top of me, but catching himself before he crushed my body beneath him.

I fell into a fit of giggles, laughing so hard it hurt my sides. It wasn't until I caught Noah's predatory glare that I stopped laughing. We were both panting profusely, suddenly looking deep into each other's eyes in a much different way than we ever had before.

It was new.

It was exciting.

It was all *him*.

He caged my face in with his arms, devouring me with his eyes, consuming every last part of me. His fingers started brushing the hair away from my face until there was nothing left between us.

But wants and needs.

I *wanted* him to kiss me.

I *needed* him to kiss me.

"Imma kiss you, Skyler," he stated as if he could hear my thoughts.

I think I nodded or moaned, or maybe I didn't do anything but lay there like an idiot. Waiting, anticipating, licking my lips for my first kiss. Whatever I did made Noah groan, and when he leaned forward, I closed my eyes. My heart beating rapidly.

Feeling him almost there…

So close…

Just one more breath.

Just one more second.

Until I felt his lips on mine.

Skyler

ELEVEN

"Well, lookie what we have here, you redneck motherfucker!"

My eyes shot open as Noah's body jolted off mine, weightlessly lifting me onto my feet before I could even blink. I mindlessly tried to search for who had just said that and what was going on, when he protectively secured me behind him with one hand on my hip as I looked out in front of us. Coming face to face with the guy who must have interrupted us.

"Walk away, Billy. Not now," Noah gritted through a clenched jaw, squeezing my hip. I glanced up toward the side of his face and saw his murderous stare aimed right at the six-foot-one brick house walking through the trees.

From the way they were both staring each other down, I knew there had to be something brewing between them. Something that went back months, maybe years. There was definitely history there, that much was crystal clear. The guy he called Billy cocked his head to the side, looking over at only me. I instantly recognized his heated stare, and if I noticed it, I knew Noah did too.

For some reason Noah's words from earlier registered in my mind as if he was saying them to me right then and there.

"So who's Keith? I got competition? 'Cuz I'll tell ya, I fight fuckin' dirty."

"Walk away?" Billy mocked in a condescending tone. "Now where would the fucking fun be in that?"

Noah's grip tightened further at my side.

"Does she know about your white-fucking-trash family? Probably not. I mean, it's not something I'd go bragging about, but I'm sure she can already tell by how fucking stupid you sound when you talk."

My stomach was in knots, knowing this wasn't going to end well.

For any of us.

"Ever heard of the Devil's Rejects, sweetheart? I'm sure you have, they're on the fucking news enough. His piece-of-shit family is a bunch of motorcycle riding, fucking killers! *Ain't that right, Noah?* And his daddy leads the pack. He's the President, or how do you say it? *Prez*, right?"

My eyes shifted to the side of Noah's face, who's concentrated glare hadn't moved from Billy's. I'd heard about them, everyone had. They were the talk of Southport, outlaws you were either with or against. And if you went against them, you'd mysteriously disappear into the night like you never existed to begin with. Sometimes I'd even hear people on set gossiping about them, but I never paid it any mind.

"How many men has your daddy buried, Noah? I mean, besides your brother."

Noah's grip tightened to the point of pain, and I held back a yelp. I must have still made an expression because Billy didn't let up.

Adding, "Ah, you don't know," he snidely chuckled. "Well, actually no one really knows what the fuck happened to his brother, Luke. I can without a fucking doubt tell you no one believes the bullshit story that he shot himself. *Ain't that right, Noah?* I think the Prez killed him, or maybe it was his dumb as fuck older brother… That would explain why their momma is suddenly a fucking drunk. Damn shame too, she had the nicest pair of tits in town. Now she's just skin and fucking bones."

With each word that left Billy's mouth, I could feel Noah's pulse quicken, and my heart broke a bit more for him. It would have been one thing if *he* had shared this with me, but hearing it come out of Billy's mouth made it so much harder to stomach. Noah hadn't moved, hadn't made a sound. He just kept staring at Billy with those lethal eyes, and if it wasn't for the fact that he kept tightening his hold at my side, I'd think Billy's malicious words weren't getting to him at all.

"By the way, how is your drunk ass mom these days? Word around town is she's been seen coming out of bars with a different man every night. Fucking them in their pickup trucks for everyone to see. I guess it serves your daddy right, he's been fucking anything that walks for as long as anyone can remember. Be careful, Skyler Bell, the Jameson men don't have a faithful bone in their fucking bodies. You don't want to look fucking pitiful on those tabloids, now do you?"

I narrowed my eyes at him, glaring.

"Oh yeah, baby. I recognize you. I know who you are, you see…" He stepped forward, and Noah stepped us back. Billy took one last look at me and then turned his full attention to the furious man beside me, sadistically spewing, "I watch her show, Noah, and jack off to her face like I used to with your momma's tits."

The last word didn't even leave Billy's mouth before I screamed, "Noah, no!" jolting out of my skin the second he charged Billy, ramming his shoulder into his torso. Instantly slamming him to the ground. "Noah, stop! Please stop!" I yelled, hovering above them. Frozen to the sand beneath me.

I couldn't tear my eyes off the brutal scene happening in front of my eyes. As if I was watching a train wreck unfold and unable to look away. I'd never seen a fight in real life before, and it was as scary as I thought it would be. Noah didn't hesitate, as soon as Billy's back hit the sand, he was on him. Straddling his waist, repeatedly punching him in the face.

Right hook.

Left hook.

Upper cut.

"Noah, please! He's not worth it! This isn't worth it!"

He ignored me, growling, "You piece of shit!" Hitting him in the stomach and again in the face, continuing his assault on Billy's body. One fist after the other connected with the guy's mangled face, showing him no mercy. His knuckles dripping with blood, so much blood.

I couldn't take it anymore, so I did the only thing I could think of. I grabbed onto Noah's shirt and started tugging it as hard as I could. Desperately trying to pry him off Billy. Praying it would work. His rage was the most violent thing I'd ever seen.

"You don't know shit 'bout Luke! If I ever hear you talk 'bout my brother again, I'll fuckin' kill you! Ya hear me, you motherfucker?!"

"Noah, enough! He's passed out! That's enough!"

Right punch to his face.

Left hook to his stomach.

It was like Noah was possessed, he wasn't even there with us.

With *me*.

I didn't recognize this guy beating on Billy, and that scared me more than anything.

"Don't ever, ever, fuckin' talk 'bout my girl, 'cuz I'll put ya to fuckin' ground, you fuckin' pussy! Where are ya now, huh? Not so fuckin' tough when I'm fuckin' ya up!"

Jab to the side of his head.

Fist to his nose.

"Noah! Come on! Stop! Please! Stop!"

"If you believe anythin' you just fuckin' said about me and family."

Blow to his throat.

Hit to his chest.

"Then you know what I'll do if you ever fuckin' try me again, motherfucker!"

I yanked as hard as I could on his shirt, stumbling backward and hearing the cotton fabric rip at the collar. With tears in my eyes, my fingers brushed the back of his neck, bellowing, "Noah! Stop! Please just stop!"

I don't know if it was the despair in my voice or the touch of my hand that finally made him stop, but I didn't care because he did. He stopped, sitting up, hovering above Billy's knocked out body. He was panting, I was panting, it was a mess. Filled with questions and not enough time for answers.

"What the fuck, Noah?" I breathlessly cautioned. My chest heaving with tears flowing down my face.

It was only then that his murderous glare flew to my panic-ridden eyes. Almost like he snapped back to reality, finding his way back to me. The fatal expression on his face vanished just as quickly, replaced by nothing but remorse and shame. There were so many sides to Noah, so many truths to see hidden behind those captivating eyes.

"Fuck," he rasped, peering from me to Billy, then back to me again. As though he just realized what he did.

Who he allowed to take over, controlling him.

"Cutie, I'm so fuckin' sorr—"

The sound of police sirens echoing in the distance cut him off, and he sprang into action. Rushing to his feet, he grabbed my hand and ordered, "Whatever you do, don't stop runnin', yeah?"

"Noah, we can't just leave him here to die!" I roughly ripped my hand out of his grasp. "We can just explain to the cops it was an accident. I saw it, I witnessed him provoke you!"

"Skyler, they'll take one look at me and cuff me. Now unless you want me to go to juvie, we gotta go!"

"But he's just going to rat us out to the police anyway, he knows who I am, Noah. Fuck!" I shouted, running my hands through my hair. "This is bad, this is really bad. I should have never… I mean… Fuck!" I paced back and forth trying to govern my breathing and my racing heart. On the verge of having a panic attack. Hearing Keith's voice in my head about being irresponsible and risking my career for a foul-mouthed hothead from the wrong side of the tracks. "What was I doing? Why did I come here?" I questioned to myself, searching the woods for answers like they'd miraculously appear. That's when my eyes connected with Noah's, and a sense of something I couldn't place fell over me.

Noah was over to me in two strides, sensing my panic. "The fuckin' dick will be fine, he's just knocked out. Now, look at me." He lifted my chin with his calloused fingers to look up at him again. I did, this time with tears streaming down my face. "It'll be alright, Cutie. He won't be openin' his mouth, and if he knows what's good for him, he will forget about ever layin' eyes on you. Yeah?"

I frantically nodded. "Yeah." Knowing he was right, something told me this was far from over between them. With one last glance at Billy, I grabbed ahold of Noah's swollen, bloody hand as we heard the sirens getting closer.

Noah didn't have to be told twice, he started hauling ass, and I ran with him. Trying to keep up with his pace the entire time as we sprinted through the park toward his dirt bike. I swear I blinked and he was carrying me onto the back seat, throwing his helmet on my head, jumping on right after me, and we were off. He hit the throttle, kicking up debris behind us as the back tire skidded across the dirt. And before I knew it, we were riding through the woods at full speed in ten seconds flat.

I glanced behind us seeing red, white, and blue lights flashing through the trees in the distance, sirens becoming louder and louder. My arms snuggly wrapped around his torso, leaning into his back trying to shake off the horrific images of Billy's bloodied face, while easing Noah's pain that I felt radiating in my heart.

He was so broken.

"Noah!" I yelled over the motor, loosening my hold.

He dropped the speed, glancing over at me.

"Go to my house. Just go to my house."

He hesitantly nodded, thrusting the throttle again. Taking unfamiliar trails until he was driving up to the back of my house, instead of the front.

I jumped off his bike just as fast as I did the last time he dropped me off, stopping him from getting off too. "Wait here, please. I'll be right back. I just need to tell my dad something."

He simply nodded, still unsure of how to proceed with me. I think he was more shocked I still wanted to be with him after what I'd just witnessed.

I darted inside through the sliding glass doors by the pool, calling out, "Dad! Dad, I won't be able to do dinner! Can we do it tom—" I stopped dead in my tracks when I saw his truck was gone from the garage. He left.

I checked my phone, it was after six o'clock.

Not one text.

Not one phone call.

Nothing.

I shook my head, disappointed in myself for believing in him when I knew better. I grabbed a piece of paper and pen and scribbled a little note but crumbled it up. If he didn't have the decency to message me, neither did I. Ignoring the stabbing pain in my heart, I made my way back to Noah, knowing he needed me.

Probably just as much as I needed him.

"Skyler, I'm so fuckin' sorr—" I placed my finger over his lips.

Lightly smiling, I assured, "I know."

That was all that needed to be said between us. I jumped on the back of his bike again, and we rode around the woods for I don't know how long. Both of us lost in our own thoughts, taking refuge within each other. My arms securely wrapped around his waist, his warmth, his skin, his scent comforting me in ways I didn't know were possible. It was well past nine o'clock at night when he pulled up to what I assumed was his house. After what Billy shared about Noah that afternoon, I thought I knew what he must have been going through, but nothing compared to actually seeing it with my own two eyes.

Nothing.

Only making me fall harder for the guy…

I needed to stay away from.

Twelve

I cut the engine and hopped off my bike, nervous as fuck for bringing Skyler here. I grabbed her hand and helped her down, feeling leery of her presence standing in front of the shithole I called home. It was mind-blowing that she was still there with me. Choosing me after what she heard and saw at the park earlier. I couldn't believe she didn't run for the hills, and I'd be lying if I said I didn't think she was going to when she told me to go to her house. I swear my heart paused for a beat when she stopped me from getting off my bike. The whole ride to her house, I was already contemplating what to say to her. How to explain myself. Do anything to get her to understand my life and how fucked up it was.

I still didn't have a fucking clue how to do any of it. What to say and how to say it. So when she told me to wait for her, I swear she brought life back into me. Not just in that moment either. Since Luke died, a part of me died with him, and all it took was Skyler to come into my life to show me it was worth living.

That she was worth living for.

"Skyler, I'm so fuckin' sorry," I expressed with as much sincerity in my voice that I could muster up. Looking deep into her eyes, needing her to see the guy I thought was long gone.

"What happened back there, Noah? I know you said you fight dirty, but that was… that was like you weren't even there. How do you know how to fight like that?"

I shrugged. "My old man, I guess. Been teachin' me to fight like that all my life."

"Do you fight a lot?"

"If I have to."

She frowned.

"Please, Skyler. Don't need ya pity, don't want it either."

"How do you want me to feel then, Noah? Because I can't help it. I care about you."

"Yeah?" I coaxed, longing to hear her say it.

"Of course. I wouldn't be here if I didn't. This" —she pointed to me and back to her— "between us. I have never felt anything like it before. I don't really have any friends because work takes up all my time. I have acquaintances in the industry, but none I'd consider as friends. My career has always come first, and it's the only way I know how to live. All I ever wanted to do was sing and act, but when I'm with you… when we're together… it makes me realize all the things I've been missing out on, and you make me question everything I've worked so hard for. Everything I've sacrificed and given up to get where I am now. It's messing with me. *You're* messing with me."

"I don't wanna fuck up wit' you, 'cuz I like you. I like you a lot, and I want ya to like me too."

She shyly smiled. "I do, Rebel. A lot too."

"Don't really wanna bring you here." I nodded to my house. "But don't know where else we can go. It's here or the clubhouse, and I sure as shit don't wanna bring ya there."

"Come on," she coaxed, eyeing my house.

I took a deep breath, already feeling like this was going to be a huge mistake, but what other choice did I have? This was my life. I led her through the back door, closest to my bedroom, thinking I could dodge the shit-show that was my mother.

As soon as she shut the door behind her, Creed's voice echoed through the hall from the bathroom. "I keep makin' excuses for you, enablin' you, and I can't fuckin' do it anymore, Ma. It ain't right. You're nothin' but a drunk and a sorry-ass excuse for a mother. Noah deserves better."

I shut my eyes, fucking hating myself for not listening to my gut. When I opened them again, Creed was walking out of the bathroom, so I hid Skyler and myself behind the wall as he made his way out to the porch. Putting a finger up to my lips to tell her to be quiet. When the coast was clear, I led Skyler to my bedroom and softly closed the door behind us. Grateful as all hell that my room was toward the secluded part of the house, but we could still see out my bedroom window toward the porch.

Creed sat on the steps, smoking a cigarette. The only light coming from the full moon in the pitch-black sky. He looked so run-down and exhausted, like he had aged so much in the last few years from the bullshit hand he was dealt. I looked away, knowing this was all my fault to begin with. My momma's sobs wreaking havoc on her body could still be heard throughout the house, and it took everything inside me not to go to her.

Instead, I sat on the edge of my bed, setting my elbows on my knees. Placing my head in between my hands, trying to drown out the noise of her wailing. I had almost forgotten Skyler was there, too consumed by my guilt to notice.

She rubbed my back, and I resisted the urge to fucking cry because all this shit was becoming too much to bear.

"Noah—"

"Creed, I…" Ma's voice interrupted Skyler, and we both looked toward the window where she was standing, crying behind Creed. "I just… I don't know how to stop…" she bellowed, sucking in air, trying to find her breath. "I was his momma for God's sake. My only job was to protect him. I failed. You may have pulled the trigger, baby… but he was only there because of me. He should have been home, in bed. What kind of momma am I? I don't deserve you or Noah… I don't deserve anything."

I closed my eyes, leaning my head back down against my hands. Needing a minute. It was the first time I'd ever heard her say anything like that. Heavy footsteps filled the silence, coming up the driveway, echoing through my thoughts. I didn't have to wonder who it was, knowing this was about to get so much fucking worse.

The second I heard Creed announce, "Gonna enlist in the Army." My eyes snapped toward my brother, but he was now blocked by our old man.

"The fuck you are, Creed!" Pops instantly drawled out.

Creed immediately stood, flicking out his cigarette, not backing down. Coming face-to-face with him.

"Jameson…" Ma coaxed, slowly stepping up beside Creed. Fixing her wet dress and wiping away her tears.

"Don't wanna hear your shit tonight, woman! Do you hear your son? Where the fuck did this come from? What bullshit are you tellin' him?"

"Nothing. I haven't told him anything. Leave him alone! He wants to do some good in his life. He's your son! Start treating him like one!"

"I give my boys everything. The fuck you talkin' about?"

"And Luke—"

"Jesus Christ… back to this shit again," Pops viciously spewed, eyeing her up and down. "It's been one less mouth to fuckin' feed. I ain't even sure that little shit was mine."

Ma never reacted to his abuse, but even with the distance between us, I could still see the look in her eyes. Reaffirming that this wasn't going to fucking end well.

"You son of a bitch! You piece of shit!" Ma screamed, lunging at him off the porch.

I didn't falter, instantly rushing toward the door. Only to be stopped when Skyler blocked my way. I jerked back.

"Noah, don't," she intervened, her eyes laced with worry and panic.

"It's your fault! It's your fault he's fucking dead! Your godforsaken club is just violence and death! You did this, and I hope you burn in Hell for it!" Ma seethed, instantly turning our attention back to them.

Creed was holding her back, and just by looking at Pops' face and body, I could tell she laid into him and a sense of pride came over me. Finally, she hit him, after all these years. I only wished she could have wiped that smug ass look off his face.

"Ma, enough! Enough!" Creed yelled, trying to calm her down. Locking his arms tighter around her.

"You stupid bitch! Look around. I have given you everythin' because of that godforsaken club! This is how you treat me? After everythin' I've done for you! After taking you back, after you—"

"I wish I would have stayed! I wish I had never come back to you! That was the worst decision of my life!" Ma wrestled her way out of Creed's grasp, getting right up in Pops' face. "You aren't half the man you think you are. You're nothing like he—"

I saw it before it actually happened, Pops reached for his gun and the barrel was right under her chin, rendering her speechless.

Skyler loudly gasped, bringing her hands up to her mouth, and this time I didn't let her interfere. I moved her out of the way, exiting my room as fast as I could. Hearing Skyler's pleas echoing behind me. "Noah, no! Please, no!" she cried out from the doorway in the hall.

"Stay in my room! Don't move!" I didn't wait for a reply. By the time I got to the porch door, Ma was on the ground and Creed was now standing in line of fire, right at the end of that barrel. Stopping me dead in my tracks.

I couldn't move.

I couldn't fucking move.

"Creed, no!" Ma tried to get back up. "Let—" And Creed shoved her back down.

"Do it!" Creed roared at our old man. "Wanna kill someone? Then fuckin' do it, Prez," he mocked, gritting through his teeth. "Pull the trigger. It don't matter to me anymore." Grabbing the barrel of the gun, he held it firmly in place over his heart.

I shook my head, shocked and disappointed. *Selfish fucking bastard.* Creed didn't think about me, about Ma, about anything but himself. Knowing we'd already lost one family member, what the hell would happen to us if he was gone too? Creed's attention shifted to me, noticing I was there. Watching everything go down, and it made me sick to my stomach. Pops followed his stare, taking a long, deep breath, and stepped back. Lowering his gun.

I didn't catch the next words that came out of their mouths, my mind was held captive by the thought of what would have happened had I not run out of my room. Had they not seen me standing there.

Would Pops have killed Creed?

Or would Creed have made him?

"Turnin' your back on your brothers? On your fuckin' family?!" Pops shouted, tearing me away from my thoughts. He pushed Creed, but he didn't waver. "Don't deserve to wear that fuckin' cut." His fist collided with Creed's face before he got the last word out.

His head whooshed back, taking half of his body with him. Ma screamed and rushed over to me, ushering me inside, and I let her. I couldn't believe Creed was going to leave me behind to deal with this bullshit. When he knew he was all I had left. I never wished for our old man to kick his ass more than I did in that moment. Resisting the urge to do it myself.

"Noah, baby… how long you been standing there?" Ma questioned, her bloodshot eyes narrowing in on me.

"Long enough," I simply stated, meeting her hazy stare.

"Baby, go to your room. You don't need to see this, you know Creed can handle him. He can take care of himself."

I scoffed, "No shit, Momma. What the hell you think we been doin' our whole lives?"

She instantly jolted back like I was now the one aiming the loaded gun at her.

"Where the hell you been? We lost Luke, we lost *you,* and now we're losin' Creed too."

Her eyes watered with fresh tears, and her lips trembled. "I… baby, I'm… I'm…"

"You what? Nothin' but a drunk?" I angrily retorted, needing to call her out on it for so long. “I don’t know you no more, ’cuz my momma wouldn’t have abandoned us when we needed her the most.”

Tears fell from her eyes and slid down the sides of her face.

“Don’t wanna fuckin’ fight you!” Creed roared, breaking our conversation. “You old fuck! Calm down and let me explain!”

I took one last look at her and backed off, needing to get away from her before I said anything else I knew I would regret. I walked into the kitchen, wanting to hit something so damn bad. Still hearing Creed and Pops going at it outside, fist-fighting on the back porch. Knowing Skyler had heard and was seeing everything go down. There was no way in hell she wasn’t going to run away from me now. I wouldn’t be surprised if she already hauled ass out of my bedroom and this fucking house. Not that I could blame her, this was all fucking bullshit. Drama any sane person would steer clear from.

“Goddamn it!” Creed hollered. “Not takin’ off my cut! Don’t want outta the club. I earned these fuckin’ colors! You dick! I just need this! Not just for her, for me! I’m fuckin’ losin’ myself, old man!”

And then…

There was silence, they stopped fighting.

“All my life, all I’ve done is follow your fuckin’ orders, never asked you for a damn thing in return. Need you to be my father this one fuckin’ time. Need to make this right and take those motherfuckers out. You can understand that more than anyone, Prez. Just need a leave of absence, ain’t no different if I was locked up, my loyalty is still to the club when I get discharged. I just need this,” Creed shared with seriousness in his tone.

What about me?

What about what I need?

A brother…

A mother…

A fucking family.

“Don’t make me beg…” Creed added, fueling my anger.

I heard his footsteps walking toward the house, when Pops’ voice filled the air. “Callin’ church. Your ass better be there at noon tomorrow.”

I shook my head again, feeling like I was shattering inside as Creed staggered into the kitchen. Not realizing I was there, he grabbed a dish towel for his bloody nose and lip before heading into the living room. Ma came running up to him as soon as she saw he was still standing.

“I’m fine,” he groaned, wrapping his arm around his ribs. He hissed through the pain as he took a seat on the couch.

“Let me get the first aid kit,” she coaxed, hurrying out of the room before he could refuse.

I didn't move from the place I stood because I could still see him. "You really leavin' us?" I murmured in the darkness from behind him, just loud enough for him to hear.

Silently hoping he'd change his mind and stay here. For *me*.

"Noah, I—"

"You gonna leave me with them? You're all I got, Creed," I honestly told him, my voice breaking like my heart. Tearing at my insides. "What if you die? Like Luke? What if someone accidentally pulls the trigger on you, Creed? What happens then?"

He opened his mouth to say something but quickly shut it. My feet moved on their own accord as if I was being pulled by a string. Standing in front of him, I added, "Joe's dad never came back from war," I reminded, talking about one of the MC members. "I don't wanna lose another brother," I spoke from the heart, it was all I had left.

As soon as the words, "I gotta do this, Noah," came out of his mouth, I tuned him out. Feeling so much fucking hatred for him, blinding all my senses. When I caught him saying, "Don't expect you to understand, but I do need you to respect my decision and know this is for you too."

"I call bullshit," I argued, pissed he was feeding me scraps like I was a fucking dog. Looking for a handout.

He shrugged. "Don't know what you want me to say, Noah."

I stepped back, eyeing him up and down. "Just go, Creed! Don't worry about me. I'll figure shit out on my own."

"I love you, Noah. You're my brother. You're in my blood. Nothin' gonna change that."

I slowly backed away, I had to. Standing there pouring my heart out and him not giving a shit, hurt too damn much. "Whatever you have to tell yourself. Go die for your fuckin' country," I scoffed, took one last look at him, I shook my head and left.

I walked back to my room where I knew I'd be alone, knowing in my heart my girl was gone. Tears swelled my eyes, and I snapped the rubber band on my wrist as far back as it would go, but even that didn't take away the sting in my mind. I opened the door to my bedroom, about to lose my shit for the first time since Luke died when all of a sudden…

There she was.

Skyler.

My sunshine and happiness.

Sitting on the edge of my bed, crying.

"Fuck," I breathed out, shutting the door behind me with my foot. I leaned against it, realizing she was probably fucking terrified.

Of my father.

My mother.

My brother.

And especially, of *me*.

"I'm so fuckin' sorry, Skyler. I'll take ya home or call ya a cab if you don't wanna be around me. I get it. I'm no good for you. Shoulda never brought you here, I fucked up." I closed my eyes, the expression on her face added to all the hurt and the pain in my heart. Eating me alive. "God-damn it," I whispered, feeling like a bigger piece of shit, knowing I really blew it with her. "I'll let ya be. Leave ya alone after tonight."

I held back the tears.

This was all too much.

It was just too fucking much.

I locked it up though, holding it together. Not needing her to think I was a pussy too, but what happened next nearly dropped me on my ass.

With my eyes still closed, I scoffed, "Come on, I'll take ya hom—"

Her lips touched mine, cutting me off. Opening her mouth against mine, baiting me to move my lips in sync with hers. Pressing her perfect tits firmly against my chest as her arms snaked around my neck. She smelled so fucking good and tasted like everything I ever wanted. When she tenderly pecked my lips once again, this time running her tongue along my mouth, she moaned, a soft, sultry hum, luring me in. The shock wore off and I reached up, holding her pretty, little, round face between my hands. Gently kissing her back, my walls crumbling down around us. All thoughts and emotions breaking apart with it.

I groaned from deep within my chest, kissing her as if my life depended on it. Knowing she was giving me her first kiss, and it felt like I was giving her mine.

I lost myself in that kiss.

In that moment.

In *her*.

Where nothing else mattered, but her. Right then and there, I knew there was no going back for me because Skyler Bell…

Was. Mine.

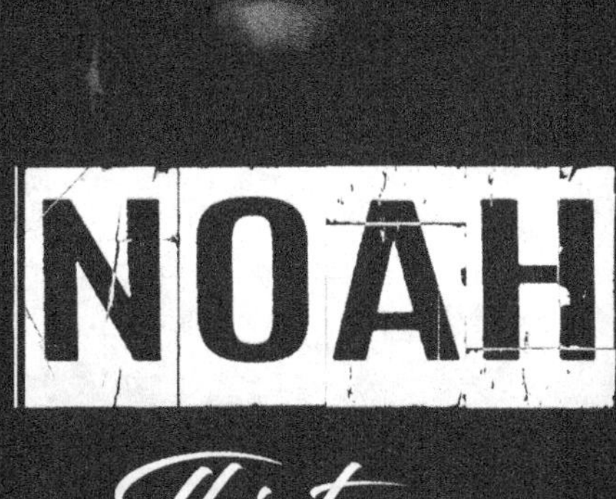

NOAH

Thirteen

Six months came and went in a blink of an eye, flying by and taking all our new firsts with it. I spent every second I could with Skyler, never missing a Sunday and stealing extra moments whenever possible. She wasn't exaggerating, she worked around the clock. Spending most of her time on set or rehearsing the lines for her upcoming role as Roxie Hart.

I still laughed, thinking about the one Sunday she took me up on my offer to help rehearse her lines. We sat down by the river's edge with our feet in the water, and I made sure I put on a straight face, trying to take this as serious as possible but failing miserably.

"Wake up, kiddo, you aren't never gonna have an act," I repeated the lines off her script from Chicago, *scowling when I was done. "I already hate this fuckin' dickwad, tellin' you this bullshit," I added my own commentary.*

Skyler giggled, smacking my arm with her script. "Noah! He's not talking about me. He's talking about Roxie, the character I'm playing. Remember?"

"What-the-fuck-ever, he's still a dickwad."

She shook her head, smiling. "Can we get back to the task at hand,

Romeo? Or do I need to find another leading man?"

"What did I tell ya 'bout thinkin' of other men while you're with me?" I gave her a stern look, trying not to crack a smile.

She rolled her eyes and cleared her throat before getting back into character. Reciting, "Says who?" With a sincere expression on her face.

I looked down at my lines, reading, "Face it, Roxie. You're two big towers with skinny legs. And I'm just a furniture salesman." Peering back up at her, I stated, "This dickwad sells furniture, and he's tellin' her she's got two big towers with skinny legs? What the fuck does that even mean? He talks worse than I do."

She busted out laughing, "Oh my God! Stop! You're making me forget my lines."

"I got my own lines." I threw the script on the grass beside me. "Shoot or action, or however the fuck you say it. Take two." I nodded to her.

She rolled her eyes again, taking a deep breath and clearing her throat. Going right back into character. "But you got connections. You know, that guy down at the club…"

"I am the connection. I'm all ya need. Fuck everyone else, so you can just fuck me."

Her mouth dropped open, scolding, "Noah Jameson!"

I grinned. "I love when you scream my name."

"Noah! Stop!" She beamed, her face turning that cherry red color I loved. "You're supposed to be helping me rehearse. This is not helping."

"Sure it is. It got you turnin' red and smilin' for me, more than dickwad was gettin'."

She smirked. "What am I going to do with you, Noah Jameson?"

Sweeping the hair away from her face, my thumb caressed her rosy cheek. I didn't hesitate in repeating the same lines since the first time she asked that question. "I already told ya, whatever the fuck you want."

Needless to say, that was the first and last time she took me up on my offer to help her with her lines. I didn't blame her, I couldn't act if my life fucking depended on it. She was the busiest person I knew, especially for being so young. I drove her to set and even picked her up a couple of times, just so I could spend some more time with her, though those were few and far between. Hoping one day I would be able to watch her on set, see her in her element, but she said it wasn't allowed. Which only made me more curious as to what goes on behind the scenes. I hated that her whole world revolved around her career, and I couldn't even be part of it. It almost felt as if I was missing out on a huge part of who she was. Getting only half of her when we were together.

A few weeks after my Oscar-winning performance, we watched the movie *Chicago* because I wanted to see what it was all about. Needing to feel like I was at least a little involved in that piece of her life. As we laid there on my bed watching, I could see how thrilled she was about this role. Her eyes sparkled when she mouthed her lines during her scenes, and as excited as I wanted to be for her, it was hard to watch it unfold. The scene where Roxie gets thrown around by the man I was playing at the river, the kissing and sex scenes, the overly sexy costumes and performances. Even some of the dialogue was hard to swallow.

It was difficult for me to understand that it was just acting, it wasn't real. She wasn't Roxie Hart, she was Skyler Bell.

Mine.

I played it off as best as I could, but the lingering feeling in the pit of my stomach and mind never wavered. It was always there. I knew she was only going to get bigger and more famous as time went on. I guess it wouldn't have been such a big deal had I felt like I was… I don't know…

Included.

I hated that another guy was going to be kissing, touching, putting his hands on what belonged to me. And that the world was going to watch. Looking at her in costumes that left little to nothing to the imagination tore me up inside. I probably should have told her how I felt, what I thought, what I wanted to hear from her in return, but I didn't.

I couldn't.

We spent every Sunday together, though we never talked about what we were to one another. Laughing, joking around, flirting, living in the moment became our thing. She was the distraction from life I needed so desperately, and I think I was the distraction she needed just as bad, just didn't entirely want. I could see it in her eyes when our conversations turned personal about her life. She'd change the subject or revert the question back to me. I didn't know a damn thing about Skyler, other than what I found online or read in magazines. She didn't talk about it, she barely even talked about acting and performing.

As much as I wanted to be part of every aspect of her life, it was obvious she wanted to keep us separate. I tried not to think about it, focusing on the fact that when we were together, the whole world faded around us. Nothing else mattered but each other. I hung onto that feeling of want, until I'd see her again. The good versus the bad, battling to make sense in my mind. It was the days we were in two completely different worlds, her with her career and me with the bullshit Creed left behind for me to deal with on my own. Those were the hardest times to get through, since we were usually only together one day a week. My life became my worst fucking nightmare.

With Creed off fighting a war he couldn't win, it gave our old man full leeway to me and what he wanted for my future. I wasn't officially a prospect yet, but my time was coming. Pops was waiting until I turned fifteen, however he still began paying me for jobs only a prospect would do. Making me fuck people up who crossed him, telling me I'd carry a Glock soon. He showed me more ins and outs of the clubhouse, concentrating all his attention on the only son he had left. My momma was worse than ever. I lost count of how many times I'd taken her to the emergency room to get her stomach pumped. It became a thing of the norm for us. I was almost positive she was trying to drink herself to death.

I barely went to school anymore, ditching more often than not. It was pointless, I was so far behind anyway. Pops wanted me to drop out, and without Creed or Ma on my ass, I was considering it. Creed was off playing GI fucking Joe, sending letters and money every chance he got. Even though I didn't want to, I still read them, but I never wrote him back. I said everything I needed to say the night before he decided to fuck me over. Leaving me to endure this hell by myself. I used the money he'd send for groceries and shit around the house. Not that it mattered, the food went untouched, the house was always a mess, and no amount of dollar bills would change that.

To make matters worse, Skyler was leaving in a few days for her movie. And for the next six months, I'd have no escape, no distraction, no sunshine and happiness…

She'd be taking it all with her.

Along with my heart.

We hadn't kissed since that first time in my bedroom, and I'd be lying if I said I didn't fuck my hand to the memory of that kiss. Of course, I wanted to kiss her again, touch her, be with her in an intimate way. Her beneath me, me on top of her, taking yet another first from her. The most intense part of it all was that none of that mattered. Being with her was enough for me, and if she wanted to initiate another thing between us, I'd give her whatever she wanted.

It'd be on her terms, not mine.

My cell phone pinged beside me on my bed, waking me up from a light sleep. It was too early, even for me. I grabbed it, turning my face over to read the message that just came through.

This isn't a goodbye. It's an I'll see you later. Talk soon, I'll call you once I'm settled.

I barely read the last word of Skyler's text before I bolted off the bed, throwing on the first pair of jeans and shirt I could find on my floor. I stumbled into my combat boots and sprinted out the door of my bedroom, hauling ass toward my dirt bike. I jumped on the seat and floored the throttle, almost eating shit as I drove like a bat out of hell, rushing to get to her house. Praying she wasn't already gone. I swear my heart was pounding the entire drive through the woods while my mind raced with more questions I needed answers to, and something told me she'd never answer.

Once I turned down the street, I shouted, "Skyler!" as soon as I saw her getting into a black Escalade. Adding to the pain in my heart that she really was going to just take off like that. Simply sending me a text as if the last six months didn't matter.

I didn't matter.

We didn't matter.

By the expression on her face, she knew I was fucking pissed. My hurt always reflected itself as anger. Another Jameson trait I couldn't change, it was just who I was.

"Noah—"

"What kind of bullshit text was that?" I interrupted, springing off my bike. In three strides, I was in her face. "What the fuck, Cutie?"

"Whoa," she breathed out, placing her hands out in front of her. "I'm… it's just… I'm…"

I cocked my head to the side. "You scared of me?"

"What?" She shook her head. "No. I'm just… you're really mad. I've never seen you this mad… I mean, not at me."

"No shit. Wakin' up to a text like yours will do that to a guy. You fuckin' lied to me, sayin' you were leavin' in a few days. Not today."

"I… I… I know… I'm just," she staggered on her words, making me feel as if she didn't know me or something.

"It's me, Skyler. *Me*," I affirmed, hoping she'd remember who I was and what she meant to me.

She frowned, murmuring, "I know that."

"Then what the fuck? You just gonna leave like that? Like I mean nothin'?"

"Noah… that's not fair. I'm sorry, okay? I'm just not very good at goodbyes. I suck at them, obviously," she noted, finally meeting my eyes. "I didn't want to say goodbye, alright? Not to you." She peered over at the driver. "Give me a few minutes."

The driver nodded, and she shut the door, walking toward the back of the Escalade so we could have some privacy.

"I'm already having a really hard time leaving, and that never happens. Ever. I'm always excited to start a new project, and I am… but it doesn't take away from the fact I'm going to miss you."

"So leavin' without tellin' me was what? Your cop out?"

"I don't know." She shrugged. "I guess. I figured it was easier for the both of us. I'll see you again, Noah. I'm coming back. And we can talk on the phone, email, text, but I have to go," she reassured, mostly to herself because I already knew that. "I need you to promise me something, okay?" She narrowed her eyes at me, and I never expected what she was about to say. Her intense stare connected with mine as the words, "Please, please don't fall in love with me."

I instantly jolted back, caught off guard.

"This is what I was trying to avoid. That look in your eyes."

"How do ya want me to feel? You were gonna leave, just like that. And now you're spittin' this shit? What the fuck happened since Sunday when we were together? Or every time before that?"

"We're friends, Noah. You're my friend, I'm yours. It needs to stay that way, so please don't wait for me. You need to go about your normal life while I'm gone. I don't want to be worrying about you."

"Worryin' about me what? Cheatin' on you? Jesus Christ, Skyler, do you not trust me?"

"What? No! That's not it at all. You're pretty much my best friend, but we're from two different worlds. I don't want to be worrying about you waiting here for me. That's all."

I nodded, stepping back. Looking her up and down. "I see. You're ashamed of me, yeah?"

"What?" She stepped toward me with tears forming in her eyes. "Of course not! That's the furthest thing from the truth, and you know that, Noah. I've tried so hard to keep you at distance, but I can't. And it's not fair to string you along for the next six months. Please understand… I'm just trying to do what's right."

"What 'bout what I think is right? Huh? That don't matter? You makin' my choices for me now, Skyler?"

"Noah, come on… you're not making this any easier."

"Miss Bell," the driver stuck his head out the window and intervened, looking back at us. "We need to go, or you're going to miss your flight."

Skyler nodded at her before peering back at me. "I have to go." She threw her arms around my neck, holding me as tight as she could against her body. "I'll call you when I'm settled, okay?"

I didn't say a word.

I didn't even hug her back.

Because at the end of the day, I wanted to beg her to stay. I wanted to swallow my fucking pride, drop to my knees, and beg. The truth was…

I was already in love with her.

And I knew she was in love with me too.

I wish I would've known then that this was only the beginning of our fucked up love story. Maybe then I would've been able to change the course of our lives. But they say everything happens for a reason.

And Skyler…

Was *my* reason.

Fourteen

"Ma! Come on, Ma! Wake up!" I roared, loudly clapping my hands in her face, hovering over her passed out body on the living room floor. "For fucks sake, Ma! Wake up!"

Nothing.

I'd been trying to get her to open her eyes for me for the last five minutes.

"Ma! Wake up!" I slapped her face, hard.

Nothing.

"Fucking A, Ma!" I stood above her body, panting profusely with my heart beating out of my chest. "Fuck, what do I do?" She'd never been this unresponsive before. I checked her breathing, it was slow and shallow, but that was normal when she passed out like this.

Reaching for my phone, I frantically scrolled through my contacts. Trying to find someone who could help me. I was on the verge of losing my shit, not knowing what the fuck I should do. My vision began tunneling, the sound from the TV echoed in the distance, and my hands suddenly started to sweat. My mind swirling back to the night Luke died, lying in Ma's arms. His lifeless eyes still fucking staring at me even after all these years.

I froze on Diesel's name as his face came into view holding me against the wall that same night.

"Noah! Goddamn it, look at me!"

Anxiously shaking away the images, I hit call on his name, still trying to wake Ma the fuck up like Diesel had tried to get me to look at him.

His phone went straight to voicemail. "Yeah, this is Diesel. I can't come to the motherfucking phone, so fuck off."

Beep.

Just as I was about to leave a message, Ma began foaming at the mouth and her body started convulsing uncontrollably out of nowhere.

"Fuck!" I panicked, ending the call. Falling to my knees at her side. "Ma! What's goin' on?" I stressed in a tone I didn't recognize, pulling her into my arms as her body violently thrashed around. Her eyes flickering, rolling to the back of her head. It was the most terrifying thing I'd ever seen, and I'd seen some fucked up shit. Nothing compared to watching her shake as if she was possessed.

"Oh, fuck," I muttered with tears pooling in my eyes. I grabbed my phone again and dialed the only number left.

"9-1-1 what is your emergency?"

"My mother! She won't stop shakin', foamin' at the mouth, and her eyes keep rollin' to the back of head. I… I… I can't get her to stop shakin'! Fuck! She won't stop shakin'!"

"Sir, you need to calm down. Help is on the way, but I need you to listen to me and do as I say so we can help your mom until the EMS gets there, okay?"

"I'll do whatever you say! Please help her! I don't want her to die! Please, don't let her die!" I begged. Tears flowed loosely from my eyes, falling onto the woman who gave me life. The woman's life I was trying to save. Feeling as though my body was convulsing just as badly as hers.

"Is she in a safe place? Anything around her that she could hurt herself with?"

"No, she's in my arms."

"Alright, I need you to lay her on the floor and roll her onto her side.

"But her legs and arms are whippin' around, she won't stay still."

"I know, sir, but you need to try. We need to make sure she doesn't choke."

I frantically nodded. "Okay." Slowly, I laid her back down on her side, holding her in place. "She's still thrashin'! How do I get her to stop? How do I make her stop?!"

"Sir, there's nothing you can do to stop it. The EMS is en route and will be there in one minute. I just need you to make sure nothing is near her mouth and she's still breathing."

"Ma! Come on, don't do this to me! Fuckin' stop! Please stop!"

"Sir, you need to calm down. You can't help her like this. She needs you to be strong. Can you do that for me? Can you do that for her?"

"Yeah… she just ca... can't die. I can't lose her too," I wholeheartedly stated. My eyes snapped to the front door when I heard knocking, seeing the red and white lights flashing through the front window. "Come in!" I shouted, ending the call with the operator on the phone. "Hurry! She won't stop shakin'! You need to help her! You need to make her stop shakin'!"

Two men and one woman dressed in uniforms rushed into the room, ushering me out of the way.

"Please! Help her!" I yelled, backing up to the adjacent wall. Using it to support my weight.

"Noah! Goddamn it look at me!" Diesel rumbled, but I was too far gone.

Watching.

Waiting.

"Noah! Look. At. Me!" This time it was Skyler's voice ringing through my ears instead of Diesel's. My mind playing tricks on me.

"Please! Help her!" I repeated, my vision zeroing in on Ma. I dragged my hands through my unruly hair, trying like hell to shake the feeling that this was my fate. To walk through life with no one but the Devil guiding me.

"Sir, calm down," the woman coaxed with her hands out in front of her while the two men hovered around my mother, holding her down much harder and firmer than I was.

"You're hurtin' her! You're fuckin' hurtin' her! Can't ya see she needs help!"

"They're not hurting her. I promise they're just doing what they're trained to do," she advised with her hands still in front of her. "Please calm down."

"Calm down? You want me to calm down when my mother won't stop fuckin' shakin'! She ain't your mother, so don't tell me to fuckin' calm down!"

"I understand, but I need you to stay calm, alright? You could go into shock, and we don't need that right now."

"Then get her to stop fuckin' shakin'!"

"She drinks?" one of the men called out, shifting my attention to him as he looked around the room filled with empty liquor bottles.

I nodded, unable to form words.

"She allergic to anything?" the same man asked.

"I don't know… I don't think so, but I don't know."

"What's her name?" the other uniformed man questioned.

"Diane," I replied, watching as her body gradually returned back to normal.

"Diane, we're the EMTs. We're here to help you." He placed something on her finger, saying it was checking her O2 stats or some shit. The other man knelt beside her and stuck a needle in her arm, injecting something, I assumed to stop her fucking shaking before they carried her onto a stretcher. Wheeling her now still body toward the ambulance parked out in front of our house.

I followed close behind, hurrying into the ambulance with them, refusing to let her go without me by her side. They hooked her up to all these machines, one right after the other. Trying to explain to me what they were doing as they poked and prodded to start an IV Drip. I just held her hand, hoping she could feel my presence, so she wouldn't think she was alone. That she still had a son who loved her more than anything in this world. I bit back the tears, hiding behind the pain I'd been used to all my life.

With glossy eyes, I watched them wheel her into the ER, paging the doctor on call. One of the nurses told me to have a seat in the waiting area to my left and they'd update me as soon as they could. I sat in one of the cold chairs at Docher Memorial hospital in Southport doing exactly that, waiting. A place I had come to know, remembering all the times in the last year and a half, since Creed left for the military, that I drove Ma to the ER to get her stomach pumped.

I pulled out my phone from my back pocket, calling the first person who came to mind. Needing to hear her voice, I hadn't spoken to her in weeks or seen her since she left over ten months ago. My stomach was in knots the whole time her phone rang until it went to voicemail. I hung up and called again. It rang five times and went to the same voicemail.

"Fuck! Come on, please answer." I hung up and tried two more times with the same result.

"Hey, you reached Skyler. I'm away from my phone, but leave me a message, and I'll get back to you as soon as I can."

Beep.

I gave up, pissed that I was always there for everyone, but no one was ever there for me. So there I sat yet again, not having one fucking person to call that'd give a damn, and the only girl that would was living another life. Which wasn't surprising, she was always working. Our schedules were completely opposite of one another, and the three-hour time difference didn't help. When we finally did talk I tried to keep most of our conversations light and short, mostly because I was still so fucking confused with where we stood.

I growled with frustration, abruptly standing to my feet. Practically crushing my phone in my hand. I started pacing the small waiting room, trying to govern my plaguing thoughts and reel in my self-pity that was fucking consuming me. I really needed her for the first time since she left. Six months turned into ten with no end in sight, and I don't think Skyler even knew when the fuck she was coming home. At this point, I was just as exhausted as she was when we talked. I didn't want to burden her with my bullshit of a life, feeling as though she was dealing with her own shit.

As if on cue, I heard her name on the TV above me, stopping me dead in my tracks. The ENews reporter spouting some shit about paparazzi catching her out the night before. A picture came up on the screen of her holding hands with an older man wearing a black hoity-toity suit and some shades. I assumed it was her agent/manager, Keith, but who the fuck knows. I sat back down, watching the coverage, letting my mind wander to the breathtaking girl on the television. Over the last couple months, I watched a few interviews here and there with her and the cast. She looked so fucking beautiful every time. Always taking my breath away. Still smiling, laughing, going on about her world like I had never been in it at all. Somewhere along the line, I slowly started resenting her for choosing that life over me.

But who the fuck was I?

Nobody.

To her or to anyone else.

I spent our fifteenth birthday a few months ago at the river, getting high and drunk by myself. Impulsively getting yet another tattoo on my leg. A music note, for her. I was covered in ink now, the needle had become a vice for me. A way to deal with my emotions by permanently engraving them onto my skin, hoping one day they'd just be a memory and not a life I was still living. I didn't stop there, picking up another unhealthy habit. Cigarettes. Needing the nicotine to calm the never-ending chaos running wild through my mind. It didn't help that I dropped out of school, losing myself in liquor, drugs, and chicks, but seeing Skyler's face every time I did.

"Noah, right?" a man dressed in scrubs and a white coat announced, pulling me away from my thoughts.

I went outside to smoke and must have lost track of time. Taking another long, hard drag, I blew out, "Yeah."

He nodded toward the cancer stick between my fingers. "Those things will kill you."

I cocked my head to the side, breathing out, "Not fast enough."

He scoffed out a chuckle. "How old are you?"

Narrowing my eyes at him, I drawled, "Old enough. So unless you got somethin' to say about my mother, you can turn your ass back around. Don't need your bullshit of what's wrong or right."

For a few seconds, he mirrored my stare. Before replying, "How about you let me buy you a cup of coffee? I can update you on your mom's condition on our way to the cafeteria."

If it wasn't for him having news about my mother, I'd tell him to eat shit, but I gave him the benefit of the doubt. Inhaling one last drag, I flicked out my cigarette. Nodding to him to start walking.

He held out his hand, stopping me. "I'm Dr. Pierce, but you can call me Aiden."

I warily glanced down at his gesture and shook his hand, not remembering the last time someone wanted to shake mine. Making me realize, no one ever did.

Once we walked back into the hospital, he was Chatty-fucking-Cathy all the way to the cafeteria.

"I've been the doctor on call when you've brought your mom in before. Seen her the last few times in fact."

"She gonna be alright?"

"To be completely honest with you, she got lucky this time. Overdosing on alcohol caused her seizure. I pumped her stomach again, like I have every time she's been in my ER. You know the drill by now, I'm sure. I want to keep her overnight for observation and get some fluids in her. She's severely dehydrated right now. How long has she been an alcoholic? From the looks of her liver, it's been a few years."

"Somethin' like that."

We stepped into the elevator and he eyed me carefully, as if he was contemplating what he was going to say. "It's only a matter of time before her liver starts giving out on her, Noah. Is there anyone who can help you get her into a rehab?"

"She won't go," I stated, hitting the fourth floor button to the cafeteria.

"You've tried to talk to her about it then?"

"Listen, Aiden, yeah?"

He slowly nodded.

"No need for this heart-to-heart, cut the bullshit. She gonna be alright or not?"

"For now, yes. For the future, no."

I took a deep breath, running my hands through my hair. Wanting to tear it the fuck out.

"She needs help, Noah. You can't keep enabling her."

"Enablin' her?" I growled in a throaty roar. "Don't talk like you know shit 'bout me. You don't know what I do for her. She's my mother, and half the time I want to ring her fuckin' neck for drinkin' herself into a coma. But what the fuck am I supposed to do? Huh? I can't make her stop drinkin', and if you think I'm just gonna let her drink herself into the ground then"—I nodded at him—"fuck you. I'll take her to another damn hospital. Didn't ask, and don't need your shit on top of all the other bullshit I deal wit' on the daily, *Dr. Pierce*."

The elevators dinged open, and it was the first time he took a good look at me. From my tattoos to the cut I was wearing on my back. It was Pops' present for my birthday, my own Devil's Rejects Prospect vest.

"You're right, I don't know *shit* about you. What I do know is that you keep bringing your mother into my ER to get her stomach pumped, and one day her liver is going to stop working and you won't have a mother to bring into my ER anymore."

I grimaced. It was quick, but he saw it.

"I'm trying to help you, it's my job," he stated in a sincere tone. "I know what it's like to grow up too fast. I've been in your combat boots, but I chose another life." He didn't hesitate, eyeing the 1% patch on my cut before bringing his stare to meet mine again. "And you can too, Noah."

It was my turn to get a good look at him, instantly shifting my eyes to the three crosses tattooed on his neck that he was trying to cover with his white doctor coat and stethoscope. I recognized it from one of the brothers who had the same tattoo, it signified Father, Son, and the Holy spirit. Someone doesn't just get a religious tattoo for shits and giggles, it meant something to him. Something deeper on a personal level. They reformed him like mine did to me.

I took one last look at him and backed out of the elevator, leaving him in there. Shaking my head, I scoffed out, "Not when your old man is the one holdin' the gun to your head, ready to pull the fuckin' trigger."

He jerked back, instantly understanding who my father was. Putting two and two together seeing Jameson on my cut and my momma's chart. You'd think I would be used to this reaction and for the most part I was, but for some reason…

It still fucking stung getting it from him.

FIFTEEN

It nearly killed me to walk away from Noah that morning ten months ago. Till this day, I still don't know what I would have done if he had begged me to stay. Certain scenarios ran wild in my mind, picturing a life where I could act my age and just be a normal teenager with regular problems, but that wasn't my reality.

Nor was it my destiny.

Production on *Chicago* was running over, and costing thousands and thousands of dollars a day to stay up and running. The staff, on its own, must have cost the studio a small fortune, but that was showbiz. Our days consisted of the same thing morning, noon, and night. The re-shoots alone were making the cast feel like the director was never going to say, "That's a wrap."

We were all tired, drained from pulling all-nighters several days a week for months. I couldn't even remember my last day off. I spent most of my time on set or in my trailer, waiting to go back to shooting my scenes. Sleeping in between my call times so I didn't go completely insane. Thank God for hair and makeup, they were magicians at this point with the exhaustion written clear across our faces.

"Sky, what the hell was that?" Keith scowled, following me into my trailer.

"I'm over it, Keith! I need a day off," I argued, fully aware he was about to give me shit for messing up some steps in my last routine.

We'd been repeating the same dance routine for "Cell Block Tango" the last four hours, filming it again and again because the director kept yelling, "Cut!" I wanted to cut his tongue off. He wasn't the one holding these precise positions while he fixed whatever issue he had at that moment. Mostly, it was his ego needing to fix something that didn't need fixing in the first place.

Hence, why we were running four months over production.

Keith stood there all agent-like with his expensive signature black-fitted suit that always made him appear taller and broader. His arms crossed over his muscular chest, wearing one of his big, bulky silver watches that I swear weighed a couple pounds by itself. His black hair was tousled which meant his hands were running through it while he watched me on set. That was his tell-tale sign he wasn't happy.

Yeah, well, neither was I.

The stern expression on his face only accentuated his hazel eyes, strong jawline, and slight widows peak as he continued glaring directly at me. I hated that stare, but most of America couldn't get enough of it. Not only was he one of the best agent/managers, he was also one of the most attractive ones. Making him hot shit for tabloid gossip and aspiring actresses, wanting a chance to make it in this industry. But to me, he was just Keith. A very pissed-off version of Keith at this moment.

"So slacking off is your way of trying—"

"Slacking off?" I interrupted, wanting to cut his tongue off now. On the verge of raging.

He turned, shutting the door to my trailer. Knowing he was about to get an earful from me.

"You can't be serious! That director is his own worst enemy!" Before he could reply and tell me I was overreacting or being overly dramatic, I turned and made my way back to my room instead. Hearing the steps of his stupid crocodile leather shoes, or whatever other animal he decided to wear that day, behind me. Those luxurious shoes were all the craze in Hollywood, all the men were wearing them.

I abruptly halted and started pacing the space between us, heated with irritation. "This movie should've wrapped months ago and you know it!" I stressed my frustration, still pacing. I was too wound up to stop. "Everyone is over it! Including *me*! And we still have to do press tours, promo photoshoots, red carpet events and that alone is going to take several more months!" I stopped, peering up at him. Needing to look at his face when I asked, "When do I get to go home? I see the emails that are coming through from the production crew on my show. Their threatening to terminate my contract, Keith!"

"You let me worry about that. Haven't I always taken care of you?"

I sighed, "Yes."

"That's right, I have. No one is going to fire you. Not on my watch."

"Fine… then what's the new wrap-up date? It changes every week."

"Sky, you're whining—"

"Whining?" I chimed in, looking at him like he'd grown three heads. All of them still staring down at me. "Have you heard queen of the set, Lola?" I ranted, stomping my foot to get my point across. "She's part of the reason we're running over, with her stupid diva demands. Just because she thinks she's God's gift to the world since her daddy scored her the lead in Anderson's new movie. She's an entitled, spoiled fucking brat! And if she asks for one more break to check her phone again, I'm going to throw it at her, Keith."

"Skyler," he warned in that fatherly tone I also hated.

I pretended like I was throwing something. "Right in her face, knocking out those fake ass veneers that are way too white to be real teeth. But she probably wouldn't even feel it with the amount of Botox and filler she's injected into her face."

"Skyler," he cautioned again in the same voice.

"Ugh!" I scoffed, turning back around to sit at my vanity and take off the pound of makeup on my face. "This is bullshit!" I sat down, roughly wiping at my eyes, showing him my anger. "For someone who is supposed to take care of me, Keith, I'm not feeling very taken care of! I'm tired and I'm hungry and I'm really freaking tired."

"You said that already," he pointed out, walking up behind me. Setting his hands on my shoulders in a comforting gesture. "Look at me, Sky," he ordered through the mirror.

I threw the makeup wipes on the counter and peered up at him through my lashes, gathering my best upset face I could.

"Breathe. Come on, in and out. You can do it."

I adamantly did.

"Again."

I yieldingly did.

"One more time."

I sincerely did.

"Good girl. Feel better?"

I shrugged, grumbling, "Maybe a little."

"Alright, now you need to take a second and appreciate this opportunity. Not to mention the doors it's going to open for you once this movie hits theaters. I know you're tired, I get it, but you know this industry,

Skyler. You've been in it your entire life, and everything we've worked so hard for is about to pay off."

"I know. I just want a day off. I need to sleep, I'm starting to feel like a zombie, Keith." I pointed to my face. "Do you see these bags under my eyes? This is not a good look for my age."

"You look beautiful as always, Sky."

I rolled my eyes. "You don't get it."

"Then explain it to me? Is this a hormonal thing?"

"No!" I snapped. "I spent my fifteenth birthday on set four months ago, when I was supposed to be at home with my dad. I haven't seen him since he visited a few weeks after I got here. I just want to make sure he's okay."

With a solemn expression, he spun me around and sat on the edge of my bed, holding my hands in his lap. "I will talk to production tomorrow and get you a day off, alright?"

I nodded, feeling better already.

"But, Sky, you know your dad. He's a workaholic, you would have spent your big day alone regardless."

"Yeah," I whispered, knowing it was the truth. "I still want to make sure he's eating, you know how he gets. Especially when I'm not there. He drowns himself in work."

"Skyler Bell, this is your moment to shine. He's a grown-ass man, and if he wanted to see you, he knows it only takes one phone call to me, and I'd have him on the next flight out here. I used to do it for your mom all the time, it was never an issue. Besides"—he smiled—"there was a birthday cake for you on set, and you even got some gifts. It wasn't that terrible of a day."

I narrowed my eyes at him, glaring. "Lola gave me the same gift bag that's in all of our trailers."

He laughed, "Well, now you have two expensive bags full of shit."

I chuckled, I couldn't help it. He always knew how to talk me down. So I simply replied with the truth, "I just miss home."

He leisurely nodded, taking me in for a second. "This is new, Sky. You never miss home this much. Something you're not telling me?"

"No," I lied. He wouldn't understand. I barely understood my relationship with Noah.

We still talked, texted, and emailed, but with my demanding schedule and his challenging life, our conversations were becoming less and less. Noah wasn't a huge phone talker to begin with. He was better at email and texting, though for some reason, those felt less personal to me. I could never judge his tone via writing, and never truly knew what he was really feeling. Plus, I had to find the time to write him back which was always a few days later. Neither one of us brought up our last encounter, when I was going to skip town without saying goodbye. I think he was saving it for when we saw each other again.

"We're friends, Noah. You're my friend, I'm yours. It needs to stay that way, so please don't wait for me. You need to go about your normal life while I'm gone. I don't want to be worrying about you."

That didn't stop the words I had said to him that day from replaying often in my mind, mostly when I was alone with my thoughts. Always seeing his face looking back at me with so much pain, it hurt my soul. He didn't keep me up to date with his life. I couldn't tell if it was because he thought I was genuinely ashamed of him, or if it was just too painful for him to discuss the traitorous acts and betrayal. Either way it sucked. I hated the distance that seemed to be growing between us. Getting bigger as the days went on.

I missed him.

I missed him more than I could have ever imagined.

"You have ten minutes until you're needed in makeup again," Keith prompted, pulling me away from my hounding thoughts. "Feeling better?"

I nodded.

"Good. I'm going to make a few calls. I'll see you on set." He stood and left.

The second he closed the door to my trailer, I pulled out my phone wanting, needing to talk to Noah. Longing to hear his voice, knowing it would ease the worry in my mind.

"Shit," I breathed out. Noticing there were four missed calls from him, he never called back to back like that. The unease in my stomach intensified as I instantly returned his call. It rang four times and went straight to voicemail. I hung up and called three more times, my anxiety radiating with each ring on the other line.

"You reached Noah, you know what to do," his voicemail beeped.

"Hey, ummm… I just saw that you called a few times earlier, and I'm worried about you. I hope everything is okay. I uh… I had a bad day, and I would love to be able to talk to you for a minute. But uh…"

The demanding knock on my trailer let me know that I had to get going.

"I just uh… I miss you, Noah. Hope we can talk soon." I hung up, feeling like a piece of shit for not being there for him when he obviously needed me.

Knowing he was going to feel the same when he saw my missed calls

and listened to my voicemail, realizing…
I needed him too.

NOAH

Sixteen

My instincts and sensory perception kicked into overdrive, switching to high alert as my fist collided with Mateo's face. His head whooshed back, taking half of his body with him, practically losing his footing. Blood splattered through the air between us, flinging in all directions as he staggered to remain upright.

"That's right, boy! You show him what you're fuckin' made of!" Pops hollered, standing nearby with some brothers beside him.

Mateo snarled, charging me. Ramming his shoulder into my torso and taking me to the ground behind the clubhouse. My back skidded across the rough grass beneath me, rocks cutting into my bare skin.

"Gotcha, motherfucker," he snarled, thinking he pulled a fucking fast one on me, but there was no element of surprise. I was prepared for his attack and instantly fought back.

Punching.

Kicking.

Blocking.

Using all of my strength to buck him off of me. The end goal was always the same, knock the opponent out before they knocked my lights out. This wasn't my first fucking rodeo, not by a long shot. I was used to the pain that accompanied the victory. The challenge to succeed, to win at something in my life. Leaving me with all the power, control, and the will to keep going. I lived for moments like these. Even though they were wrong, they still felt so fucking right. At the end of the day it was all I had.

Violence on my mind.

Blood on my hands.

Scars on my body.

"Noah, you fuckin' prospect! Get your head out of your fucking ass and put him to ground! Now!" Pops seethed, stirring my fury.

This motherfucker should've known better, stealing money from the club and thinking he could get away with it. No one ever got away with shit, but the truth was… it didn't matter. He could be innocent, or he could be guilty, and I still would've had to fuck him up. Proving myself to my old man time and time again.

For what?

One fucking thing.

The peace fighting gave me.

It became my source of adrenaline, the air I had to have to keep breathing, my wants and needs. Silencing the memories I didn't demand, and the future I couldn't fucking stand. It was a vicious cycle I was wreaking havoc in, savoring every second of it while I could. Because deep down, my worst fear had become my reality—

I was just like my father, and he knew it too. We were one in the same. It's why he kept using me to fight his battles. He was conscious of the fact I craved it—the blood, the glory, the calm before the storm—and he used it against me and to his advantage.

Right hook.

Left upper cut.

Right hook again.

Mateo and I wrestled around for a few minutes, each of us trying to gain the upper hand on the other. Elbows, fists, and legs flew everywhere, intermingling together as we threw the fuck down. I hit him in the gut, causing him to fall to the side in pain, and used the momentum from my punch to flip him over onto the concrete patio, locking him in with my weight. He immediately guarded his face, but he was fucked… I preferred laying into an opponent's body. It was easier to take someone down when they couldn't fucking stand to begin with. I struck him in the ribs, the stomach, getting a few good hits to his chest.

"Prospect, what dafuq is this? You tryin' to piss me the fuck off?!" Pops raged with the same cold and detached tone.

But my desolate, brazen eyes never wavered far from the man I was fucking up. My chest heaved and my nostrils flared, looking like a rabid fucking dog with a mixture of our blood and sweat slithering down my face and body. Mateo's battered frame rolled on the ground, recoiling from my brutal and malicious assault. I didn't stop, I never could. Blinking away the haze, sweat, and blood gushing from the severe gash above my left brow, I went full force into laying him the fuck out.

Pops' voice started to sound muffled as he repeated, "Do it, boy! Do it now!" and everything around me started to fade away till it disappeared. Exactly the way it always did when I was fighting. It was just Mateo and me, where nothing else mattered but the freedom from being buried alive.

Fight or die...

Fight or die...

Fight or die...

With every ounce of drive I had in me, I gripped onto Mateo's head, following the evil that lived inside of me.

My father.

And I savagely slammed his head onto the concrete ground.

Crack.

Blood and brains splattered and gushed everywhere.

Lights fucking out.

Game fucking over.

I won.

Making him, *Mateo*, my first...

Kill.

The rest of the night went by in a blur. I was there, but I wasn't. My mind was still in kill or be killed mode, and that never happened in the aftermath. Each time I blinked something else was going down in front of me.

Blink.

Pops handing me money.

Blink.

The brothers congratulating me.

Blink.

Women and music everywhere.

Blink.

Drugs and booze in front of my eyes .

Blink.

I snorted another line.

Blink.

Grabbing a bottle of Jack from the bar.

Blink.

I was on my bike.

Blink.

The wind on my bloodied face, the breeze on my raw knuckles, the river right ahead of me.

Blink.

Blink.

Blink.

Now, I was hallucinating because my girl, who still haunted my dreams, was staring right at me. Opening my eyes to yet another one of my worst fears, she was witnessing the man I was destined to be. The one I became. After she left me…

Over two years ago.

Skylar

Neither one of us said a word, not one damn word for I don't know how long. I could barely form any thoughts, let alone words. Even with the soft lighting shining from the lamp post near the bridge, I could still see his bloody, bruised face and body. The deep cut above his eye with fresh blood seeping out. The five o'clock shadow taking over his masculine jawline, and the way his wavy, distressed hair moved in the breeze. It was much longer than I remembered, slightly hanging in his face, inhibiting me from seeing his blue-green eyes that I yearned for so much.

My boy was gone, and in his place stood a hardened man on a motorcycle with intricate tattoos on his arms, along his neck, down his legs and I knew more ink had to be covering his chest and back. He was wearing a black leather vest that said Prospect, Devil's Rejects embroidered on it with several patches stitched all over.

When did he join?

My eyes shifted from one place to another, trying to take it all in. Take *him* all in. Noah was always tall and bulky for his age, but now he was almost seventeen-years-old and he looked so much older, broader, muscular. His arms and chest were chiseled and defined, exuding dominance. If I thought he towered over me before then, now he would consume me, and I meant that in every sense of the word.

When I couldn't take it anymore, I longingly stared back up at him, needing to look into his eyes. See the boy I missed with all my heart and soul. Instantly noticing his intense stare never lingered from my face, almost like he thought I was just a figment of his imagination.

I wasn't.

I was there.

Here.

Finally.

With him.

"Noah," I coaxed in a tortured, thick tone, showing him every emotion inside of me.

With wild, dark, dilated eyes he shook his head. "You ain't real."

I winced, frowning. My heart breaking for him, little by little, inch by inch, until my feet started shuffling forward on their own accord toward him.

He didn't move.

He didn't flinch.

I don't even think he was breathing.

Our profound, deep gazes never wavered from each other, our connection pulling me closer to his sadness and despair. Not thinking twice about it, I reached up to caress the uninjured side of his face with the backs of my fingers. Needing him to feel me.

"Skyler," he murmured so low, replicating the tone in my voice.

I nodded, smiling. Trying to hold back the tears. "Yeah, Rebel. It's me, I'm here."

He jerked back with watery eyes, and the next thing I knew, I was gasping. My body colliding with his chest as he pulled me toward him. His arms wrapped around me so tight, so warm, so everything. I swallowed hard, hugging him back just as firm, just as sturdy. Inhaling his scent, feeling his sorrow, battling his demons for him.

Snapping out of whatever was holding him down, he muttered, "I missed you. I missed ya so fuckin' much," into the side of my neck.

"Me too, me too," I repeated with tears slowly falling out of my eyes. "So much."

"Fuck." He shook his head, pulling away from me. "I'm gettin' blood all over you."

I threw myself on him, bringing his love back toward me. "I don't care. I don't care, Noah. Just hold me, please… just for a little while. I just want you to hold me. Don't let me go. Please… just don't let me go."

He didn't have to be told twice, he held me like his best friend, his *only* friend. Like *I* was home, like *he* was my home. I couldn't remember the last time someone just held me, just curled me against them. I didn't realize how much I needed it, needed *him*, until right then, until that *very* moment. Where nothing else mattered but his arms around me, where we were in our own little world, just the two of us.

Noah and Skyler.

Rebel and Cutie.

Lost boy and found girl.

Where I wanted to stay, for who knows…
How long this time.

SEVENTEEN

I walked into an old rundown warehouse on Clark Street that had been turned into a boxing gym just after noon. It was a huge, wide-open space with white industrial ceilings and fluorescent lighting buzzing overhead. Though that wasn't what caught my attention the most. It was the large boxing ring in the middle of the place, reminding me of the movie *Rocky*. I couldn't help but look around the vast room as I made my way further in, inhaling the smell of disinfectant and sweat.

My fingers lightly skimmed the rusty, well-used workout equipment that lined the old brick walls, picturing Noah all sweaty, lifting weights. Hoping he wouldn't catch me thinking about the way his muscles flexed with each rep, before I even saw him that day. I'd been home for over three months, and we'd been spending every single day together, making up for lost time.

I never imagined my movie *Chicago* would run another two months late, and by the time it finally hit theatres across the world, I was beyond exhausted. I spent weeks catching up on sleep at Keith's L.A. home, and reading every last review that was published in magazines or on the Internet. Never expecting the amount of success it would bring into my life. I didn't even have time to dwell on my television show being canceled, because I was thrown into a whirlwind of auditions, interviews, and paparazzi. Directors, producers, screen writers, everyone came out of the woodwork asking me to read their scripts for roles that they always insisted were only made for me.

In the last year alone, I'd been on every magazine cover from *Vogue* to *People* to *Entertainment Weekly*. Jumping headfirst into another movie where I was the lead actress, acting alongside Hollywood's elite. But thank God that movie didn't run over the scheduled six months of production. *The New Yorker* had proclaimed it one of the best movies of the year, stating I was the reason. Declaring me a natural born talent. Claiming I was ahead of my generation.

Keith's phone never stopped ringing, blowing up with inquiries, interviews, and movie deals, but he was well aware I needed a break. Not worried in the least I'd be forgotten if I came home for a minute, but I'd be lying if I said I wasn't either. Of course it lingered in the back of my mind. I'd worked so hard to get where I was in this hardcore industry, and I didn't want to lose it. Keith reassured me that I wouldn't, and he scheduled photoshoots, interviews, and small press stuff that I could do from home instead. Insisting it was the right decision for me.

"Skyler, you've been going full force for over two years, you need a break. Go home, spend some time with your dad. I've only flown him out here three times since you've been gone. Maybe make some friends. Just take a breather, and for fuck's sake, get some sleep," Keith suggested, smiling at me with a sincere expression on his face.

"You know I want to go home more than anything, but I don't want to jeopardize my career. I love what I do, my fans mean everything to me. I just want to perform, it's all I've ever wanted to do."

"I know that more than anyone. Please let me take care of you. It's my job to look after you, Skyler. I don't want you to burn out. Besides, most of the new scripts coming in are for next year. It's a good time for you to go home."

I wanted to argue with him, but I wanted to see Noah more.

Noah Jameson.

My lost boy who never strayed far from my mind. On set, I always pictured it was him I was kissing, touching, being intimate with during those type of scenes. For some reason, it made it easier for me to envision his face, his hands touching me, his lips on mine. Our phone calls became less and less, more voicemails than anything else. Our emails were few and far between, most of them going unanswered. We were both too busy. I was caught up in the limelight, and he was doing God knows what.

My heart was in my throat the entire private flight home, I didn't even tell Noah I was coming back. Terrified he wouldn't care, or he wouldn't believe me. Adding to the countless times I told him I'd be home soon, only to end up disappointing him. I couldn't wait to get back to him and my dad, finally sleep in my own bed versus the hotels and trailers I'd been living in.

I'd spent the whole day with my dad, catching him up on life. Finding out how he'd been living these last two years without me. He had an arsenal of magazines with my face on them, bragging to everyone I was his daughter. He was so proud of who I'd become.

I'd tried to stay in the moment with him, but my mind still wouldn't stray far from Noah and wanting, needing to see him. As soon as my dad left for work that night, I'd jumped into my rental car and drove to the river, praying he'd be there. I must have waited for hours, thinking every sound, every car, every light was him. But he never came. Just as I was about to give up and call him, search the streets if I had to, I'd heard a loud rumble of a motorcycle, and I just knew…

It was him.

Knowing in my heart he'd show up that night. Searching for me amongst the darkness too.

My thoughts drew back to the present, and I called out, "Noah?" not finding him anywhere. Considering he was the reason I was in this gym in the first place.

He shouted, "Back here, Cutie!" from the far corner of the warehouse.

I smiled, walking on the light hardwood floors that were partially covered with foam mats. Making my way around the black punching bags and boxing ring in the center. I turned the corner after the lockers, coming face to face with Noah.

A very naked, wet Noah.

Wrapping a thin towel around his waist as he strode out of the shower. I should've looked away, turned my back and given him some privacy, but there wasn't a chance in hell that was happening. My mouth dropped open at the sight of him standing in front of me. The steam filling the air behind him like those body wash commercials where a hot guy steps out in slow motion, whipping his wet hair around, flexing his lickable abs.

I shook off the vision, concentrating on *my* hot guy. I'd never seen him this exposed, this vulnerable, this bare. His muscles were strained from working out, accentuating the veins in his arms. Showing off his broad, sculpted, tattooed chest, down to his carved abs, emphasizing his eight-pack, and the V right above his happy trail.

Which, in itself, did all sorts of things to me. His tattooed arms were defined, toned, and bulky, only adding to his tall, husky frame.

He was a real-life bad boy.

I. Couldn't. Breathe.

He followed my intense, captivated stare down to his exposed body before looking back up to my face. Pursing his lips, trying not to grin. My cheeks felt flushed, burning against my heated skin as my heart raced, rapidly thudding against my chest, making me weak in the knees and fuzzy in the mind.

With a cocky smirk, he baited, “Like what you see, baby?”

And I swear I fucking died, right then and there.

“No!” I squealed in a high-pitched tone I didn’t recognize. Clearing my throat, I shook my head and stood taller. Trying to act unfazed on the outside, when internally I was flipping the fuck out.

“No, huh?”

Shit! Even his rough, raspy voice was doing things to me. The somersault feeling in my belly returned for the first time in over two years, doing the ultimate floor routine.

“I’m going to wait—” I abruptly turned, slamming face first into one of the lockers— “Ow! Fuck!”

“Skyler—”

“No!” I held my hands out in front of me, stopping him from coming any closer like I was suddenly a magician.

“You alright?” he asked, nodding to the bump that was probably forming on my forehead.

“Yeah.” I shrugged. “You’re fine, I’m fine—wait, what?”

He hid back a smile, biting his bottom lip.

My eyes widened, and I swallowed hard. “Oh my God! I can’t be here with you when you’re not wearing any clothes. Okay? There. I’m going to go wet.”

He cocked an eyebrow with a predatory flicker in his gaze, like he could smell my arousal.

“What? Did I say wet? I meant wait! I’m going to go *wait.*” I pointed somewhere behind me. “Out there. While you’re wet in here. Right?” I nodded to myself. “Yeah, that makes sense.” With that, I abruptly turned again, slamming into the same locker. “Goddamn it! How does this locker keep coming out of nowhere?!”

“Cutie…”

I bowed my head, walking away. “I’m going to go try not to hurt myself.”

He chuckled. “I’ll bring ya some ice, yeah?”

“Yeah, whatever. I’m fine.” I stalked back into the gym, whispering to myself, “You’re an idiot, Skyler. What the fuck was that? You didn’t even act like that when you met Brad Pitt.” I sighed, grabbing a pair of boxing gloves hanging from the ring, and started hitting one of the punching bags. A sequence of right and left hooks that barely budged the massive bag. It made me feel better, so I hit it again and again and again. Losing count of how many times I struck it.

Until I overheard Noah chastise, "Your form is all wrong."

I spun and glared at him. "Hey, I know how to fight. I can kick someone's ass too."

"Is that right?" he drawled, sidling up next to me. Placing a bag of ice against my bruised forehead, causing me to hiss.

I ignored his sly grin and answered, "Yeah, that's right." Cocking my head side-to-side. "I'm a badass bitch, *mothafucka,*" I mocked in an arrogant tone.

"Don't call yourself a bitch, and don't fuckin' cuss."

I put my hands on his chest, giving him a little shove. Spewing nothing but attitude, "You want a piece of me? Is that it, *Prospect*?"

He hadn't said much about his new role in his MC life, and to be honest, I was too scared of him to ask. We didn't talk about our time apart, we just lived in the moment like we always had. It was easier falling back into the refuge and comfort we sought out in each other in the first place. Making our time together more memorable, personal, life changing.

More *everything*.

His eyes zeroed in on me, amused with my performance. "I just saw you get your ass kicked by a locker. That answer your question?"

I snidely eyed him up and down, staying in character. Shoving the ice away from my forehead to get right up in his face. I mimicked the way he talked, "You scared of me? 'Cuz I ain't scared of you." And to really prove my point, I dramatically threw off my gloves and started jumping up and down, from my left foot to my right, holding my fists out in front of me like a real boxer. "I can take you raw." Referring to my bare knuckles.

"Those are fightin' words, little girl."

"I'm a fucking ninja." With that, I went to punch him in the face with my right fist, but he caught it.

"What I tell you 'bout cussin'?"

"You ain't the boss of me," I sassed, trying to hit him with my left fist, but he caught that one too.

"Didn't ya say you were gonna try not to hurt yourself," he taunted, spinning me around so fast that my back collided with his solid chest which felt like a steel wall. His sculpted arm snaked around my neck, holding my tiny frame captive against his massive physique. "Whataya gonna do now? You're at my mercy," he rasped in my ear, thrusting his groin into my ass. "Ya feel that? That's not me scared of you, baby, that's me fuckin' hard for you. Wantin' to take *you* fuckin' raw."

My eyes widened, and my heart started to race a mile a second.

"Not so tough now, yeah? Not when my cock is in between your ass cheeks. Ya said you wanted a piece of me, is it everythin' you imagined back there in the locker room? Huh? Or is it too fuckin' big for your pretty little pussy?"

My mouth suddenly felt dry, battling my mind over what my body yearned for. I hated losing, but Jesus he felt huge, and I wanted to see just how big it was. Needless to say, my mind trumped my body, and when I felt him loosening his hold around my neck, I sprang into action. Choosing to win, I crouched low to the ground to break out of his hold and gripped onto his arm before swiftly stepping behind him. In one quick motion, I kicked his legs out from under him, and he instantly fell backward onto the mat with an oomph.

I smiled, hovering above him. "The bigger they are, the harder they fall." All proud of myself, I straddled his waist, leaning forward until I was close to his mouth. Breathing out against his lips, "Not so tough when your ass is on the ground."

He scoffed, "Where'd ya learn how to do that?" mirroring the proud expression on my face.

"My last movie." I smiled wider. "I do all my own stunts. I told ya, I'm a fucking ninja."

The last word barely left my mouth before he rapidly flipped me over, and now I was the one under him.

I gasped, surprised by the turn of events. His body was in between my legs, pressing his cock into my core. His right leg was hitched against my ass and the other stretched out behind him. He had one hand gripping my left thigh up to his hip and the other around the back of my neck, locking me firmly into the mat with his weight.

Looking deep into my eyes, he spanked me, hard.

"What the fu—"

"Cuss one more fuckin' time and it'll feel twice as hard, and I ain't talkin' 'bout my cock," he murmured. "I let you take me down." His thumb started to caress my cheek as he rubbed the tip of his nose against mine. The scent of mint and Noah mixed together assaulted my senses, causing a wave of sensations I had never felt before.

I smirked, despite the heady urgency running at lightning speed through my body. "Oh yeah?"

He leisurely nodded, never letting up on grazing my nose with his. "Fuck yeah."

"Why is that?"

"'Cuz I always follow my dick, I mean my heart." He mischievously grinned. "And it wanted to be on top of you, feelin' you beneath me."

I didn't have a clue how he could say something so dirty, but make it sound like he was reciting poetry. My thighs clenched and my face felt on fire, igniting his flame to keep going.

He pointed out, "I really do fuckin' love that shade of red on you."

Blushing more, my eyes shifted toward the door. Thinking someone could walk in on our compromising situation.

"I locked it," he replied, reading my mind. "I don't ever fuckin' share, Cutie. Why? Are you ready for me, Skyler? You think you can take me?"

I wasn't sure if he was still talking about fighting or if he meant it in a sexual manner, but either way, my body responded for me. Loudly moaning, rolling my hips into his rock-hard cock.

He gripped onto my thigh harder, huskily groaning, "Fuck me…"

"Wha—"

He. Kissed. Me.

Cutting me off.

My eyes shut tightly, my breathing hitched, and my hands went to his back. This was the first time he truly kissed me because I was the one who kissed him in his room years ago. This embrace was much different than the last. His lips were rough but smooth against mine, his touch firm yet gentle. My heart drummed so fast, I swear he could hear it, feeling it against his chiseled chest. He pulled me closer by the nook of my neck as if I wasn't already close enough, pinned beneath him.

My body molded perfectly against his like I was made just for him, *only* him. It was the most overwhelming, mind blowing, consuming feeling I'd ever felt in my entire life. There would be no coming back from this.

From him.

From us.

Ruining me for any other guy. He slowly parted his lips, beckoning me to do the same. I followed his lead, imitating the same rhythm he set. His tongue traced my swollen lips, and it left the craziest sensation in its wake. A tingly fire that only he could put out. I'd never be able to lick my lips and not think of this very moment. It would be lodged next to my heart where he belonged.

I pulled back my tongue, and he took it as an open invitation to gently push his into my awaiting mouth. Seeking mine out, turning this kiss into something more than I could've ever imagined it could be.

No words came close to describing what was happening between us. The feelings he stirred deep within my mind, my soul, matching my emotions with each stroke of his tongue and lips. This push and pull was as uncontrollable as wherever it was fate wanted to take us. I never wanted him to stop kissing me.

Not for a second.

A year.

A lifetime.

Noah's lips were meant to be on mine. My body was meant to be beneath his. Our hearts were meant to be together.

I was his girl.

I had always been *his* girl.

A soft moan escaped my mouth as he pecked my lips one last time, gradually pulling away from me. Leaving me breathless and wanting more. Soooooo much more. Incoherent thoughts ran rapidly in my mind with no end in sight. My eyes fluttered open, instantly locking with his hypnotizing blue-green stare that answered every question I needed to know, every emotion I needed to feel, every expression I needed to see.

But I still found myself asking, "Why did you kiss me?"

He pecked my lips a few more times, rasping in between, "I wanted to know what Heaven felt like."

My heart melted, beating only for him.

Taking breaths in between, he added, "I wanna lose myself inside of you," kissing me again. Deeper, more urgent and demanding.

His hand moved from clutching my thigh and began roaming. It started in my hair and traveled down to my face as I writhed and moaned beneath him, enticing him to go further. Wanting to feel his callused fingers on every inch of my tingly skin.

"Fuck… you feel good. How do ya feel this fuckin' good?" he growled, gliding his hand toward the top of my breast. I could feel my nipple hardening through my flimsy cotton tank and bathing suit top underneath.

I pushed my chest further into his hand and he immediately gripped it harder, using his knee that was still holding up my thigh as leverage. He started thrusting his dick against my core, earning him another whimper. My hips moved on their own accord, rubbing against his cock with the same momentum of his thrusts. His thin gym shorts and my cotton ones made it easy to feel the friction that ignited between us. His dick relentlessly grinded against my clit, stimulating my longing to come felt fucking amazing.

He painfully groaned, knowing exactly what he was stirring inside of me. Kissing me with all the passion and hunger of a starved man while his hand slid under my tank. Demanding a response from me that only he elicited. He caressed the top of my bathing suit, and it didn't take long for him to push the material aside and knead my warm, perky breast. My sweltering skin felt fucking incredible in the palm of his hand, exciting me in ways I never thought were possible. With that one touch, my nipples hardened, my stomach clenched, and shivers coursed down my spine.

Our movements became headier and more urgent, both of us searching for something, anything. My back arched off the mat when he pushed my shirt up and kissed his way down to my breast. His lips sensually pecked from the side of my neck to my collarbone. He was slowly savoring the burn of my body coming apart against his rugged frame. Getting hotter with each caress of his tongue touching my flesh.

The desire…

The ache…

The need for relief…

Was right there, wavering and waiting to go off.

My hips rocked faster against his cock with him keeping up the same momentum. Both of us wanting to come down from the high that we were rousing with dry fucking each other. My breathing picked up as did my arousal, engulfing him in nothing but my want for us to keep going and have him claim what had been his for so long.

"Fuck… Skyler. You're so fuckin' wet. I can feel your come on my shorts against my cock."

"Please… don't stop… please…" I shamelessly begged, swaying my hips faster against his dick with much more force than before. "Please… I'm… almost… there…" I panted all in one breath.

He released a growl from deep within his chest, vibrating against my core. His mouth slammed back into mine and our tongues did a sinful dance, colliding as one.

His lips.

His tongue.

His hands.

I felt him everywhere and all at once.

"Skyler… give it to me, baby…" he roughly muttered in between kisses. Biting my bottom lip and sucking it into his mouth.

I surrendered to it, I surrendered to *him*. My legs quivered, my core pulsated. I breathlessly gasped, sucking in air and falling over the edge so fucking hard I saw stars. Coming undone from the inside out. Throbbing, shuddering, helpless beneath him. My panties were drenched. I was motionless from his touch. He could do whatever he wanted with me and I'd mold to his every desire. Just to feel like I did right now.

Loved.

So very loved.

It wasn't until I heard Noah whisper into my ear with a seductive regard, "Can you imagine how much harder I could make you come wit' my cock actually inside of your soaking wet cunt?" that my eyes snapped open. Connecting with his intoxicating stare.

Knowing, he meant every last word and I was royally screwed. If things were complicated and confusing with us before, well this just added a whole new dynamic to our relationship. Where I prayed neither of us would get hurt because now we were playing with fire, just waiting for one of us…

To get burned.

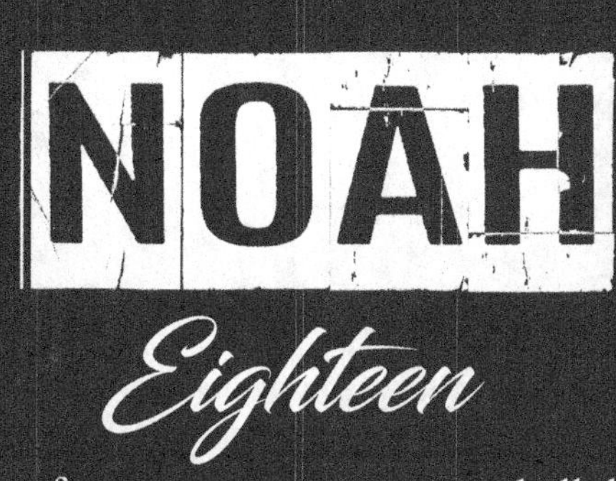

NOAH

Eighteen

It didn't take long for my name to get around all the MC chapters in North Carolina, maybe even across the states. Not that I expected it to, but I guess it went along with never losing a fucking fight for my old man. I honestly couldn't tell you how it all started. One thing led to another, and before I knew it, I was taking bets on the side for matches between rival clubs. Laying motherfuckers out left and right. One fight alone could make me a shitload of money. Anywhere from a couple hundred to several thousands of dollars. It just depended on if it was a kill fight.

But I wasn't fighting for the money. I fought for the peace the act of vengeance provided in my mind. The control of having someone's life hanging from my fingers like a goddamn puppeteer.

Fight or die.

Fighting was my outlet, an act that allowed me to take out life's frustrations I'd gathered over the years. More of a punishment than a relief, but I deserved it. The last words Luke spoke would forever haunt me.

"I wanted to crash, but I don't wanna be around you right now. So thanks for not only ruin'n my day, but for ruin'n my night too."

Every punch came from Luke's words, and everything that followed was from seeing his dead, lifeless eyes bearing into my soul. I fought for him now because I couldn't fight for his life then.

The only thing that had changed in the last six months since Skyler came home was I had to be more fucking careful on how and where I got hit. She didn't know about the life I led, the life I fell headfirst into while she was off being a fucking movie star. The fights were always scheduled well into the wee hours of the night, when fucking outlaws could come out and play.

With me.

They were always in different locations, mostly underground in abandoned warehouses. Places where it was neutral territory between the clubs, and cops wouldn't give a shit if we wanted to try to take one another out. Making their jobs easier for them, one less 1% MC member in the world. With only a few brothers on each side of the line during the fights.

Skyler Bell, my sunshine and happiness, was still the only other thing in my life that silenced the demons on my back. When I was with her, when we were together, nothing else mattered.

Not the past.

The present.

Or the future.

Just her.

She was my main focus, as if no time had passed between us, drowning out all the pain and all the sorrow in my soul. Except, when she'd leave me for the night, or when she was too caught up some days with work-related shit, I needed the fight.

The peace of mind.

Feigning for blood like a fucking wolf in the night. It didn't help that my mother was getting worse as the days went long. My father relied on me more to make things right in his world of nothing but wrong. I was like a caged animal salivating to be set free, waiting for the moments I was either with Skyler or fighting. Using my fists to suppress the memories of the life I lived.

Everything was going great until one night, two weeks ago, I fucked up. Fighting was never about how hard I could fucking hit. It was strictly about how hard I could get hit. And my last fight fucked me up pretty bad. The motherfucker fought dirty though, flinging sand in my eyes, throwing me off kilter for a few seconds, maybe a minute. That was all it took for him to lay the fuck into me. It was the only fight in the last five years, since I started picking fights with random people, that I almost lost.

Almost.

If he was going to fight fucking dirty, then I was going to fight dirtier.

I blinked and shook away the haze, sweat, and blood gushing from my face, laying there in a pool of my own blood.

"That's right, you fucking prospect! Know your place! You ain't nothing but a little bitch trying to be a real man! A real fucking outlaw!" he spewed, spitting on me. Standing above my battered body. "Time to go to sleep for good, boy! And I'm gonna be the one who puts your fucking ass to ground!"

I tried to get up on my hands and knees, but the son of a bitch kicked me in the stomach with his combat boot.

"Ugh!" I groaned, falling on the dirt. Recoiling in pain.

He didn't stop there, repeatedly kicking me all over my torso. Causing my body to roll until he finally decided to stop.

"You fucking pussy! I'm gonna love the glory of killing Jameson's son!"

I waited, always waiting, for the right moment to strike. Number one rule of fighting—always be aware of your surroundings because it might save your life.

Fight or die.

Fight or die.

Fight or die.

Right when he was going in for the kill, I swiftly rolled over and grabbed ahold of a chain that was near one of the rusted, broken down machines, and I whipped it against his knees. Instantly hearing the loud crack of his kneecaps shattering as he crumbled to the ground that I was still laying on.

"You piece of shit!" he screamed in agony, holding his legs in a fetal position.

Without hesitation, I slowly stood up from my hands and knees. Ignoring the crippling pain, knowing it was my fucking turn to make myself known. Put him in his fucking place.

Six feet under.

Cocking my head to the side, I spit in his face. Spewing, "Night, night, motherfucker."

Using all the strength I had left, I whipped the heavy, metal chain over my shoulder, striking his face. Over and over. Ruthlessly not letting up until he took his last breath. His face unrecognizable from my wrath.

Bottom line.

I won.

There were no bullshit excuses I could give Skyler when she saw my face the next day. It wasn't as bad as the night at the river when she came back, but it was damn near close. She didn't say a word about it, although she didn't have to. Her eyes expressed everything she couldn't say with words while trying to fix me up. Making me feel even more like shit.

I couldn't continue down this path of keeping my two worlds apart. As much as I didn't want to, I had to show her she had nothing to worry about when it came to me and fighting. I could handle my own, proving to her I was made to battle. Hopefully, silencing the panic in her mind the same way she always had for me.

Once and for all…

I needed to let her in.

I cut the engine of my sleek Harley Davidson Sportster motorcycle my pops gave me for my sixteenth birthday like he did for Creed. A sick-looking bike with all matte black components, custom fenders, seat, and gas tank with the club logo painted on it. The killer engine and exhaust system were visible on the sides. A set of shortened handlebars and a massive front headlight completed my badass bike. Pops more than likely stole or won her in a bet, but I didn't fucking care. She was my other girl, I loved her like I did my cock.

I parked a few houses down from Skyler's. It was late, and I didn't know if her dad was awake or asleep, or even home for that matter. Pulling out my cell phone, I called her.

"Hey you," she answered.

"Happy seventeenth birthday, Cutie."

She giggled, "Happy seventeenth birthday, Rebel."

"Were you sleepin'?"

"No. Just trying to unwind from the photoshoot for *Cosmopolitan* today. Twelve grueling hours of being told to smile, then to look serious, then to smile again. I don't know how models do it. Not to mention the wardrobe changes, and I haven't been dieting and most of the shots were in revealing bikinis—"

"It's fuckin' August. Summer's over."

"Not for Hollywood. Sex sells, no matter what."

"The fuck?"

"Noah—"

"And don't give me that dietin' shit. You're fuckin' perfect. I can throw you around and put you where I want ya, yeah?"

"Yeah, and where's that?"

"Legs spread wide on my face."

"Noah!"

I chuckled, I couldn't help it. She was too fucking adorable. "Then don't ask questions ya already know the answers to."

"Anyway," she changed the subject. "I don't think I've ever had anyone call me at midnight on my birthday. You may be my first."

"I love bein' your firsts."

She laughed. "How was your day?"

"Better, now that I'm talkin' to you." I hadn't seen her in almost two days. She was busy with publicity shoots or some shit. Apparently, in revealing fucking bikinis for dickwads to jerk off to. I didn't like it, not at all, but I bit my tongue because what could I do about it?

Not one damn thing.

"Look out your window, Skyler."

"Why?"

"Just do it."

"So bossy," she mumbled. "Okay, I'm looking. What am I looking for?"

"Your knight in shinin' armor."

I saw her smile big and wide before she looked to her left and found me. "What are you doing sitting there all by yourself like a stalker?"

"I prefer number one fan."

She giggled again.

"Come ride wit' me."

"What?"

"You heard me."

"Noah—"

"You got five minutes." I hung up. I could see her rolling her eyes and shaking her head before she backed away from the window.

It didn't take long for her to come outside, walking toward me with the helmet I gave her years ago in her hand. She was wearing those tight black pants that framed her ass perfectly, a long sleeve shirt, and her own black combat boots she bought in L.A. Saying she saw them window shopping and had to have them to go riding with me.

The cool breeze picked up, causing her to shiver, and without thinking twice about it, I took off my cut and pulled my hoodie over my head, throwing it at her. North Carolina was hit with a cold front out of nowhere for it only being August, so nights required sweatshirts especially when riding.

She smirked, bringing it up to her nose for a second before slipping it on. Wanting to inhale my scent, always telling me it was as addicting as her favorite blueberry bubble gum.

I grinned, eyeing her up and down. "You look good in my clothes."

She beamed. "Alright, Romeo. Where are we going?"

"I wanna show ya somethin'."

She arched an eyebrow. "*Something*, yeah?"

"Getcha mind out of the gutter, Cutie. 'Cuz I can show you somethin' right now, but I don't want your old man to kill me. 'Cuz I sure as shit would kill a motherfucker like me if he was sittin' on a Harley near my house, showin' his huge somethin' to my baby girl."

"Huge, huh? Don't brag, Noah."

I grabbed my cock. "Ain't braggin' if you can back it up."

She busted out laughing. We hadn't done shit since that day at the gym, where I had her losing her shit beneath me. Our relationship wasn't like that. It wasn't built on sex or any of that other shit, it was more than that.

It was everything and in between.

Not that I didn't want to sink balls deep into her pussy, I just didn't need it.

I only needed *her*.

My girl.

"Besides, he's not even home. He works nights as a highway construction worker."

This was the first time she'd shared anything about her dad, and I'd be lying if I said it didn't mean more to me than what I was about to show her.

"You ready to ride?"

She nodded, putting her helmet on and jumping on the back of my bike where she belonged. I threw my cut over my t-shirt and wrapped her arms around my waist, pulling her snug against my back where she always felt like home to me.

I was still anxious as hell on the ride to our final destination, silently praying I was doing the right thing. What felt like an eternity later, I pulled up to the abandoned school on Parkston and turned off the engine, kicking out the stand.

"Where are we?" she asked, still sitting on my bike as I got off. Looking around the old, dark lot with an apprehensive expression on her beautiful face.

"Hey…" I grabbed her chin, making her look at me. "Baby, I'd never let anythin' happen to you. Tell me you know that."

She nodded, frowning. "Of course, but that doesn't answer my question."

"You scared?"

"No. Should I be? What are we doing here, Noah?"

"I told you. I wanna show ya somethin'."

She narrowed her eyes at me.

"This is my life, Skyler. And I need ya to understand that. I want ya to know everythin'. No more hidin' the truth from you. It's our birthday, no more fuckin' secrets between us, yeah?"

She winced. It was quick, but I saw it. "I don't understand. What does your life have to do with us being here?"

I pulled off her helmet and kissed the tip of her nose, leaning my forehead against hers. I peered deep into her eyes, murmuring, "You will."

Nineteen

The hesitation was written clear across her face as I helped her off my Harley. Not letting go of her hand, I walked in front of her, leading the way inside of the old, vacant building toward what appeared to be the gymnasium.

I nodded at Diesel when we walked through the rusty double doors, grateful as fuck he was there for me. Well, not me, but for Skyler. He knew the shit I was involved in, all the brothers did. My old man didn't hide it from anyone other than Creed. The brothers knew the consequences if they didn't keep their mouths fucking shut and it got back to Creed. Our bastard of a father was fully aware that my oldest brother would shit a fucking brick if he found out what my life had become. Ma was too shitfaced to notice anything besides the liquor bottle that was permanently glued to her hand, so there was no need to worry about her finding out.

I wasn't scared of my brother, he could eat shit for all I cared. In my eyes, we weren't on good terms. He still wrote me letters, and I still read every one, but never wrote him back. I had nothing to say to him, although the selfish fuck had plenty to say to me.

Diesel, on the other hand, he minded his business. It wasn't his place to tattle on me, no matter how close he and Creed were. His loyalty was to the club and each of his brothers, including me. Which was why he was here to begin with, knowing I needed him to watch over Skyler.

Besides, this wasn't one of my usual fights. It was just another prospect from another MC we didn't have beef with, who for some reason challenged me. He probably wanted to make a name for himself amongst the clubs, having the balls to go against the undefeated motherfucker.

Me.

Bets were placed and here I was, ready to make him regret his fucking words. Knock him out and walk away with thousands of dollars in my pocket.

We came face-to-face with the six-foot-two man standing on the other side of the gym, looking me up and down with a menacing regard. Noticing he showed up alone, wanting to prove a fucking point I assumed. Only making him look like more of a pussy.

Skyler stopped dead in her tracks, jolting me back with her. "Noah…" she coaxed in a cautious tone, eyeing only him.

I grabbed her chin again, connecting our stares. "Imma buy you somethin' really fuckin' nice after I kick his fuckin' ass."

With wide eyes, she jerked back. Understanding my subtle response. "I don't need you to buy me something fucking nice. What I need is for you to take me the hell out of here. Now," she gritted through a clenched jaw.

I smiled, trying to break the unexpected tension between us. "Don't fuckin' cuss, Cutie."

"Don't fucking do this, Noah. Please. Don't do this. I am fully capable of buying my own shit."

"It ain't 'bout that. I just want ya to be part of my life."

"You won't have a life to be part of if you fucking die."

"Ain't gonna die."

"Because you're suddenly invincible? I haven't said a word. Not one single word to you about what I saw when I first got back, or what I saw two weeks ago, so please… don't do this. You don't have to prove anything to me. I know you can fight. I've seen it with my own two eyes, remember? There's nothing you can show me right now that will make this okay with me."

"Skyler—"

"Please. Don't do this. For me, Noah. Walk away, for *me*."

There was no choice to be made. Not when she was looking at me as if her whole world was standing in front of her. I did the only thing that made sense, the only thing that felt right over all the wrong in my life. I reached up, holding her face in between my hands, caressing her cheeks with my thumbs, and kissed her.

Long.

Hard.

And deep.

Before pulling away, I angled my forehead against hers. Stating, "Let's go."

She smiled, breathing out a heavy sigh of relief. Pecking my lips one last time, she replied, "Lead the way."

So I did, holding my girl's hand. I walked away from a fight for the first time in my life, but not for me.

Just for her.

In the end, she was all that mattered.

"You gotta be fuckin' shittin' me, you pussy-whipped motherfucker!" the prospect spewed from across the room.

My jaw clenched and my hand twitched in Skyler's. She didn't waver, stepping out in front of me and leading the way.

"But fuck it, look at that ass. I guess I can't blame you. I'd like to go a few rounds with her pussy instead."

She walked faster, her stride hurrying out as quick as she could, dragging me behind her.

"Oh, come on, sweetheart! The party was just getting started. How about you turn around, come bend over, and take it like the whore that you are! Like you do in all your movies! Jameson here got himself a fucking movie star! How many cocks have been in her already? Can she even feel yours?"

His voice began to sound muffled, and everything around me faded. I cracked my neck, my feet weighing heavy toward the doors while Skyler picked up her pace to get me out of there as fast as possible.

"Don't worry, motherfucker! I'll even let you fucking watch. Or better yet, how about we both just tag team her! Diesel here can even partake!"

"Fuck you!" Diesel hollered, following behind us.

"Hey! She's got three fucking holes for reason! Let's see who can make her come first. I bet you it'll be my cock up her ass that really makes her fucking scream when I'm making her bleed!"

I saw red.

Nothing but fucking red.

"No wonder your brother died, the pussy gene runs strong in you Jameson men!"

Rage quickly overtook every last fiber of my being as the words,

"Noah, no!" flew out of Skyler's mouth.

It was too late.

I was too far gone.

Fight or die.

Fight or die.

Fight or die.

And in the end, I was wrong. There was a choice to be made by me, and I instinctively chose.

Fight.

I took off, hauling motherfucking ass like a possessed man toward the piece of shit in front of me. Hearing the faint sound of Skyler's shouting muffled in the background as I charged him. Ramming my shoulder into his chest, forcefully slamming his back into the brick wall.

"Noah! It's not worth it! He's not worth it!" she yelled, and I already knew Diesel was holding her back from running over to me. Protecting the beauty from her fucked-up beast.

The cocksucker's hands immediately went to my vicious hold, trying to pry me off, but I didn't give him a chance. I went full force, yanking him away from the wall and slamming his body back into it. Gripping onto his hair, I spun him around so his back was to my front and crashed his face into the window beside us. It shattered, sending glass in every direction. Blood instantly gushed from every inch of his battered skull.

Skyler screamed and her voice echoed off the walls.

Shards of glass carved into my fists and arms, slicing into my face too. I didn't pay any mind to the blood dripping from my body as he stumbled to remain upright. Using his momentum, my fist connected with his jaw before he even saw it coming. His head snapped back, taking half his body with him. I was over to the piece of shit in one stride, grabbing ahold of his cut and punching his fucking face repeatedly.

Delivering blow after blow to his stomach, his ribs, his chest, and back to his fucking face. Hearing hasty cracks in my fist's wake.

"Jesus Christ, Noah! Stop! You're going to fucking kill him! Stop!" Skyler begged for his mercy.

I let the pussy go and he fell to the ground, covered in blood, whimpering in pain.

"Get up!" I snarled, kicking him repeatedly in the kidneys. Making him recoil, feeling more of the agony I was spitefully delivering. "Get the fuck up and come at me like a man!"

"Noah! Enough! Stop! He's had enough!" Skyler demanded, her voice still sounded so far away as I heard her struggle to break free.

It didn't stop me in the least. I continued my assault on the motherfucker's face and body. Hitting him until my knuckles felt raw. When suddenly, it was as if Skyler appeared out of thin air. I felt her hands on my cut, trying to desperately pull me off of him.

"Stop!" she yelled with despair in her tone. "You're killing him! You're fucking killing him!"

I instinctively spun around, and she slapped me across the face, snapping me back to reality. Instantly making me realize what the fuck I had just done.

"Holy shit," she breathed out, immediately falling to her knees on the floor to tend to his knocked-out body. I halted her attempt, clutching onto her wrists. Roughly yanking her to her feet and turning her to face me instead.

She didn't back down, using all her strength to shove me away. "Don't fucking touch me! What the fuck is wrong with you?! You didn't have to do that! You could have walked away! You could have walked the fuck away! For me! With me!"

I stepped toward her. "Cutie—"

"Don't 'Cutie' me! I can't believe you just did that! Why would you?!" she bellowed, tears falling down the sides of her face as she started to slam her fists into my chest.

I let her take her aggression out on me. Her adrenaline was pumping through her veins at full force, blowing through the abandoned school's roof. She was now in fight-or-flight mode because of me, and I hated myself a little more for what I was putting her through.

This didn't go as planned. I shouldn't have brought her here. Shown her this aspect of my life if I knew things would have turned south, becoming something it wasn't intended to be. I allowed her to scream, hit me, do whatever the fuck she needed to calm her ass down and come back to me.

Taking every blow to my bruised ego and my tattered soul.

"Is this what you do?! Is this who you are?! A fucking killer?!" Her words hit me as hard as my fists hit that motherfucker on the ground. She stumbled back, trying to catch her footing. "I don't know you at all, do I?"

"Don't say that! Don't fuckin' say that! You know me more than anyone!"

She fervently shook her head, scowling, "Not like this! I don't know this person standing in front of me! Who the fuck is he?! Not *my* Noah." She pointed to herself. "I don't even think you know who he is! It's like you're not even here, Noah! Like you don't even know what you're doing!"

"Fuck, baby… I'm sorry… I don't know why I would think this was a good idea. To show you this. I just wanted you to see my life, 'cuz this is who I am… this is what I do…"

"For who?"

I opened my mouth to say something, but nothing came out.

"For who, Noah?"

"My father."

She jerked back, winded. All the fight in her gone. "Oh. My. God. This is what you do for the club?" she asked, her mind trying to process the reality of my life. "How long has this been going on?"

"Skyler—"

"How long?" she repeated in a harsh tone.

I shook my head, answering, "All my life."

Her lips trembled as she backed away from me, slaying my heart a little more. Fear evident on her face.

For me?

Or because of me?

She stopped once she was standing beside Diesel, breathing out, "Please take me home."

His eyes shifted over to me, and even though it killed me to think about my girl on the back of another man's bike, I reluctantly nodded. Giving her the space she obviously needed.

"I'll let his club know to come get him," Diesel informed, mostly for her. Knowing I didn't give a fuck about him. "He ain't dead," he added, glancing at Skyler. Trying to ease the strain between us.

"So that makes it okay?" she countered, locking eyes with him.

"Just sayin'. You got your panties in a bunch, and you shouldn't, 'cuz he ain't dead," Diesel voiced, wanting to help but failing fucking miserably.

She scoffed, "I see. But he would have died had I not been here, right?" She peered back at me. "Is this how it works, Noah?"

"Somethin' like that," I implied, at a loss for words.

She took one last look at me with so much uncertainty in her gaze, digging the dagger deeper into my fucking heart before she unwillingly turned and left.

Leaving me there with nothing…

But my shame and regret.

Twenty

"Motherfucker!"

My fist collided with the old, tarnished lockers as I walked toward the exit. The sound of metal crushing echoed down the vacant hall with each strike, seeing images of Skyler's face looking at me with so much disgust. Her hurtful words ringing in my ears as my knuckles took another beating that night. But I didn't care, I welcomed the fucking sting. I deserved it tenfold.

Why did I think this was a good idea?

Punch.

I'm such a fucking idiot.

Punch. Punch.

Worthless piece of shit.

Punch. Punch. Punch.

I turned, sliding my back down the steel, banging my head against the locker a few times. Trying to knock some sense into my mind. Listening to Diesel's bike roaring to life, whisking away my mistake. My chest was heaving for my next breath, and my vision began to tunnel. I was still in fight mode with no one to fight but myself.

She was gone.

I didn't stay absorbed in my own self-pity for very long after they took off. I waited until they were gone because there was no way in hell I was going to just watch her leave on the back of another man's bike. Even fucking Diesel's. She was mine, and I already had to share her with the world, which fucking killed me inside. I jumped on my bike around two o'clock in the morning and drove around for I don't know how long, aimlessly wandering the streets of Southport. Hoping this was all just a nightmare I'd wake up from. I was never that fucking lucky, though. It was damn near sunrise by the time I found myself smoking a cigarette on the bridge over the river. Nothing else in the world compared to seeing life just come awake right before your eyes.

I thought about Skyler.

About the life I wanted with her, and the one I'd have to live without her.

What could I fucking do at this point? She'd seen my true colors, flashing bright and bold in front of her eyes. My truths were like a warning in the night, telling her to steer clear of the jagged rocks. Like the current of the river that almost took her life. I was the force of gravity trying to drag her down the stream right along with me.

See her beauty in my pain.

Hear her voice in my nightmares.

Feel her love in my death.

"Is this what you do?! Is this who you are?! A fucking killer?!"

Question after question plagued my thoughts as I sat there on my bike chain-smoking. Each thought more unforgiving than the last, tumbling around in my mind. Fighting every bone in my body not to go to her, make her understand, to see the guy I was with her, and the one I wanted to be when I wasn't. Throw her over my shoulder if I had to, and take her and the pain I caused away. She was the only person who could bring me to my fucking knees without even trying. Without so much as a breath or a word.

I inhaled deeply, finishing off my cigarette, and flicking it off the bridge into the rough waters below. Waiting for the black Lincoln hot rod, driving up onto the bridge, to pass so I could take off and most likely go drink my weight in a bottle of Jack.

However, the car abruptly stopped. The driver's side door opened, and out came the last person I ever expected to see.

"Noah?" Doctor Aiden Pierce addressed.

I nodded at him. "Nice wheels, Doc."

I probably saw him a handful of times since our last encounter when Ma had a seizure. Each time needing to have her stomach pumped after a night or two of binge drinking. And every time we showed up in his ER, he was still on my ass about getting her into rehab. He was a good fucking doctor, I'd give him that.

He narrowed his eyes at me, cocking his head to the side, taking me in. "Jesus, man, you look like shit."

"You should see the other guy, but nice to see you too. Might wanna work on that bedside manner."

His gaze shifted from one cut to the other on my face, hands, and arms before his concerned stare met my eyes. "Have you been to the hospital?"

"If I had, they sure as hell did a shitty job fixin' me up," I chucked, lighting another cigarette. Noticing he was wearing scrubs, I asked, "You on your way in?"

He shook his head. "No, I'm actually on my way home. Are you going to go to the hospital?"

"You always this bright-eyed and bushy-tailed at the ass crack of fuckin' dawn?"

"Noah," he coaxed in a straightforward tone. "Just by looking at you from over here, I can see you need stitches."

I shrugged. "A little blood ain't ever hurt anybody."

"Yeah, well that shard of glass lodged in the left side of your head is a lot more than just a little blood."

I touched the glass he was referring to. "Well, that explains the killer fuckin' headache."

"You need to go to the ER."

I grabbed it, hissing, "Nah, I can take it out."

"Noah!"

I halted.

"Your hands are covered in blood, which I'm guessing isn't yours. So not only are you fucking stupid for fighting, that person's blood is going to give you an infection if it hasn't already. You need a doctor."

"For fuck's sake, Doc, you always this big of a pain in the ass?"

"According to my wife, yes, but you can ask her yourself after you follow me home. I live right up the road about two blocks. I'll get you stitched up and you can be on your way." He didn't give me a chance to reply, stepping back into his car. Nodding at me through the rearview mirror to follow him, and I simply nodded back.

It was late, yet too fucking early, and I was too exhausted to refuse. Besides, he was right. I didn't need an infection on top of all this bullshit. Taking one last drag of my cigarette, I flicked it to the ground and followed the good doctor to his house. He was right, he lived only a few blocks from the river in a fancy gated community, where I pictured a bunch of country club sons of bitches having BBQ's every Sunday after church. With a bunch of Suzy homemakers or Betty fucking Crocker's or some shit that they were married to. Living their perfect lives, with their perfect kids and their perfect pets that didn't shit in the house.

As he pulled into his three-car garage, I parked on the side of his driveway out of the way. Deciding at the last second to take off my cut and leave it on my bike. Not that I gave a flying fuck what people thought about me, but I was already covered in dried blood, and he was doing me a solid by fixing me up. The least I could do was have some respect for his wife. I was probably going to scare the shit out of her as it was with my being there. I didn't need to add to it by showing her I was just one of the outlaws that I called my family.

I took a deep breath and met him in the garage, trying to wipe some of the dried-up blood off the back of my hands on my jeans. He took another look at me from head to toe when I was standing in front of him, and this is when I knew he was too good to be fucking true.

I scoffed, shaking my head. Mentally chastising myself for letting my guard down for even one fucking second. I was about to turn my ass around before he had the chance to tell me he changed his mind. Not wanting him to see the disappointment in my eyes for believing in someone who bought me a cup a coffee a few times. Trying to pretend like he gave a fucking damn about my life.

When he said, "Tell my wife whatever you want, but don't tell her the truth, alright? She'll worry about you," almost knocking me on my ass.

I jerked back, caught off guard by his statement. "She don't even know me."

"That won't matter to her."

My cautious gaze moved to the tattoo on his neck, the three crosses were now on full display, but his solely black ink didn't stop there. More religious pieces followed all the way down his left arm, ending with a dove on his wrist.

I peered up at him through the slits in my eyes, locking them with his knowing stare. "So she the reason you're such a good doctor?"

"No. She's the reason I'm a good man. I told you, I know what it's like to be—"

The garage door opened, cutting him off. Pulling both of our attention to who I assumed was his wife.

"Hey! I thought I heard you," she greeted him with a huge smile on her pretty face.

He walked up to her. "Hey, baby." Kissing her before they both peered back at me. "I picked up a stray. Want to feed him?"

She giggled in a Skyler sort of way, making me miss her even more. Playfully smacking his chest. "Don't mind him. I picked him up as a stray too. Fed him once and he never left my side."

I scoffed out a laugh despite myself.

"I'm Bailey."

"Noah."

"I'd give you a hug because I'm a hugger, but uh…" She eyed me up and down. "What happened?"

"He walked into a sliding glass door," Aiden replied for me.

She regarded him for a few seconds and then returned her stare to me, glancing down at my knuckles before returning her perceptive expression to him. Sassing, "And I was born yesterday?"

I chuckled, I couldn't help it. I instantly liked her, she called him out on his shit like Skyler did with me.

Without another word, she shook her head. Opening the door wider, motioning for me to come inside.

I did, immediately realizing how nice their house was. Not a thing out of place, except me.

"Take a seat," Aiden stated, pulling out one of the chairs at the island in the kitchen. "Give me a couple minutes. I'm going to go grab a few things I need to fix you up." He kissed his wife again, looking at her adoringly, and walked out of the room.

"Noah, how do you like your eggs?" she asked, opening the fridge. Making me feel like I was a guest in their home, and not the trash they needed to take out.

"Don't need ya to cook—"

"Don't even try me, boy," she chimed in with a teasing tone, setting the eggs on the island. Never breaking her stare from mine. "I know a hungry guy when I see one, and you are definitely starving. I don't need two hangry men in my house. Besides, I love cooking. It's a good distraction, keeps me busy while Aiden's working mostly nights for his residency at the hospital. I find it brings me a sense of peace, since I have a hard time sleeping without him," she freely shared, as if I was just an old friend and not a random guy covered in blood, sitting in her kitchen that probably cost more than anything I'd ever be able to afford.

Knowing I wouldn't have a chance to win this fight, I muttered, "Sunny side up."

"That's how I like my eggs too." She smiled at me, cracking an egg on the bowl. "So how do you know my husband?"

I hesitated, because for some reason, I didn't want to lie to her. There was just something about the Pierce's that fucked with my mind. Wanting to let my guard down after having it up my entire life.

"My ma, uh…" I rubbed the back of my neck in a nervous gesture. "She's umm… a drinker and… uh… an ambulance brought her into the ER."

"Oh, Noah… I'm so sorry."

I shrugged, not used to the sincerity and sympathy pouring out of her. The only other people that ever showed any concern for me were her husband and Skyler.

"How old are you?"

"Seventeen."

"You look a lot older than that."

"Feel a lot older too."

"Yeah, I understand." She nodded. "Don't you wish we could just choose our families. It would make life so much easier. Aiden was—"

"Alright, you ready?" Aiden walked back into the kitchen with a black bag in his hands. Cutting her off without even knowing it.

"You got any Jack?" I questioned, wishing that she would have finished what she was going to say.

The look in Aiden's eyes every time he saw me at the hospital, the look in hers from the moment she saw me in her garage. It seemed so familiar yet foreign, almost like they were looking at me from the inside out, and not just my appearance like everyone else. As if they knew who I was and what I'd been through because they were once there themselves. Like they were looking in a mirror, making a connection brought on by pain and suffering. Sensing maybe I needed exactly what they did back then.

"Not for a minor," Aiden remarked, pulling me away from my thoughts as he set up his medical shit on the island in front of us. "But I have something better."

"Doubt that."

He held up a needle. "Lidocaine. It will numb you, but it's going to burn like a bitch before it does."

"So does Jack."

They laughed, and for first time since Ma started drowning in a liquor bottle, I felt like I was with a family that actually wanted me in their home. Which didn't make any fucking sense, but it didn't change the fact I wanted to be in their home too, making even less fucking sense.

Bailey tried to distract me by getting to know me a little better while Aiden went to work, stitching more cuts than I thought I had. Pulling out shards of glass from not only the side of my head, but my arms and knuckles as well.

"Where do you live, Noah?" she led on.

"Over on McMullen Street, but my Ma, you know… so… mostly I stay at the clubhouse."

"Clubhouse?"

Fuck.

Apparently, letting my guard down made me have no filter. "Yeah, my old man is uh… he's the president of an MC."

"Oh, really? Which one?"

Aiden and I locked eyes.

"Devil's Rejects," I simply stated, hoping she wouldn't kick me the fuck out of her house with this needle still in my arm.

"Oh…" she breathed out in a recognizable tone everyone had when they learned who my father was.

It pained me to see her expression change. Aiden wasn't lying, her face read nothing but worry for me. Which again, made no fucking sense. She didn't owe me any sympathy, she didn't owe me shit.

Neither one of them did.

By the time I was done with breakfast, the good doctor was done with me. Thank fuck too, I couldn't take his wife's kind, concerned eyes for me much longer. He handed me a few prescriptions for pain, and some other shit I didn't understand and wouldn't be filling anyway.

I stood, getting ready to leave. Pulling out my wallet to give him money for fixing me up.

"We're good," he said, nodding to the bills in my hand.

I shook my head, expressing the truth, "Don't want or need your charity."

"We're friends, Noah."

"Friends?"

"Yeah. Friends."

"Hey, Noah, what do you know about boats?" Bailey chimed in out of nowhere.

"They float, yeah?"

She chuckled, smiling. Trying to hide the unease in her eyes. "That's about as much as Aiden and I know about them, but his grandpa left us an old one in his will. We're not even boat people."

"Baby…" Aiden murmured, bringing her attention to him.

"What? It's the truth. It's been sitting at the marina for the last year, collecting more dust and God knows what else inside. You don't have time to restore it, maybe Noah does."

I shook my head again. "No, I don't—"

"It would really be a huge blessing and favor to us if you took it off our hands. It's actually a fifty-five-foot yacht, but I hate the way that sounds. So snotty, *I have a yacht.* Anyway, it has three bedrooms, a full kitchen, and living room. Looks like you use your hands a lot." She smirked, nodding to my knuckles. "Why don't you put them to good use, maybe you can fix it up and live on it."

Aiden sighed, looking at me. "I told you. She worries."

"I do." She nodded. "It would make me feel better, but like I said, we also don't have the time to put in the hours and days it needs to be restored. It would be beneficial for the both of us. Considering the slip is paid for and so is the boat. It's yours free and clear if you want it. As long as you take us out when it's done."

"Jesus, Bailey, I can't do that."

"Why not?"

"'Cuz… I mean… you don't even know me."

"Yes, I do. Your Noah, our friend."

My eyes shifted to Aiden who was just grinning at her with a gleam in his eyes, like what she just said reminded him of another place and time.

"She's not going to take no for an answer, Noah," he added, still only looking at her.

"I won't," she agreed, still only looking at me.

"Why are you doin' this?" I asked, needing to know.

"Because, Noah, *I can.*"

Both of them completely caught me off guard, I never expected to meet people like them. To have people like them in my life. Making me aware that good people did exist in this world, and that maybe I deserved to have them in my life too.

Even though…

That life wasn't in the cards for me.

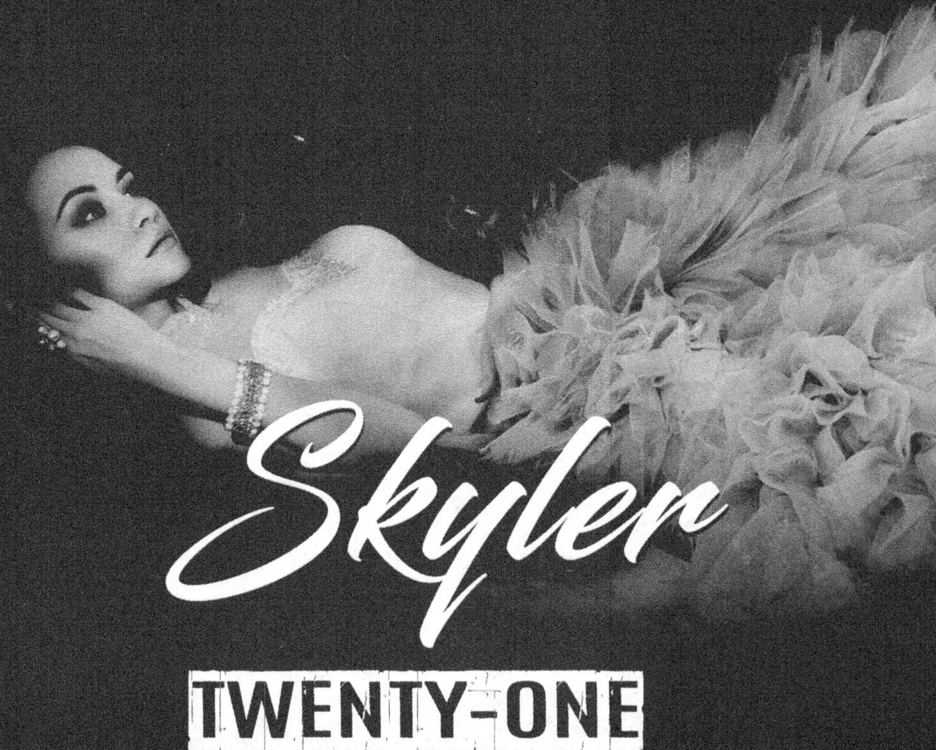

TWENTY-ONE

It had been a month since I'd last seen Noah.

Thirty days since I left home and flew back to L.A.

Seven hundred and thirty hours since I felt whole.

It didn't matter that I hadn't talked to him, that I didn't answer any of his calls or return any of his texts. I still listened to every last voicemail, read every last message, and thought about him every last second of the day. Missing him as if part of me was missing, as if nothing else mattered but him, as if…

I was head over heels in love with him.

Scaring the absolute shit out of me.

Love was something I never considered or even thought about for that matter. My life had always been about one thing and one thing alone—my career. It was a lonely life I created, where I had believed my own lies about not needing to rely on anyone other than myself. I was the source of my own sadness and possibly the destruction of my own happiness. It was easier that way, to drown out the chaos of the heavy load I carried day after day. Trying to find the meaning of life and the price I would pay for working mine away.

My mind was sometimes my own worst enemy. The memories were a constant reminder of the battle I fought every single day. They felt so real, so consuming, so life changing like they hadn't already changed everything. Like my life hadn't been flipped upside down and turned inside out, by the past, by my career, and especially, by Noah. At times, I felt our relationship was more than just wanting to seek refuge within each other, it was more than the classic boy-meets-girl story.

Our lives may have been completely different on the outside, but the sentiments of what we lived through and the internal scars they left behind were the same. Making our feelings for each other run that much deeper, that much harder, that much more real. It had been that way since the very beginning, and as the years flew by, the more I realized he didn't just want to know me…

He wanted to *own* me.

When my life already did.

Which was why I had said from the very start, I needed to stay away from the boy who had always meant more to me than words could ever truly express.

It was only seven in the morning and my thoughts were still looming in the back of my mind as I walked into my dad's house in Southport. Throwing my keys on the entryway table, I grabbed the stack of mail my dad let pile up and made my way into the kitchen.

"Junk, bill, bill, bill, more junk, magazine I want to read, magazine Dad would want to read, oh, and magazine with my face on the cover that I definitely don't want to read. More junk, more bills, and more shit to throw in the trash." And I did just that, making a mental note on paying the bills after I cleaned up the house and did some much-needed laundry. Living out of a suitcase was easier said than done, and it always took its toll when I'd eventually fly back home.

Although, for some reason as I stood there, gazing around the wide-open space I'd lived in all my life, it didn't come close to the feeling of when Noah's arms were around me. When he was kissing me, laughing with me, making me feel like I was his everything. Knowing in my heart that I truly was.

His presence.

His voice.

His love.

That felt like home to me.

He felt like home to me.

To make matters worse, my conversation with Diesel, after Noah decided to show me the very last part of him on our birthday, still weighed heavy on my mind.

"Fourth townhouse on the left!" I shouted over the engine of Diesel's Harley.

Riding on the back of his bike felt different than riding on the back of Noah's. Not that Diesel's driving skills weren't that of an experienced rider. It just didn't feel the same, only adding to my incessant thoughts of Noah and how everything between us had always felt so natural. As if we had known one another all our lives.

There was this huge sense of longing as we pulled up to my house, wishing I had someone to talk to about all these emotions and thoughts that were so controlling and confusing. Where nothing made sense but the fact that Noah consumed every last part of me, and he had since day one.

Relief washed over me as I jumped off Diesel's bike, handing him his helmet. "Thanks," I affirmed, wanting him to know that I was grateful he'd brought me home with no questions asked.

He didn't know the difference between me and a hole in the wall, and yet he took it upon himself to make sure I got home alright. Knowing I needed some distance from Noah and the violence that was their life. However, I was also thankful Noah had someone like him to help weather the storm he was adamant to stand in.

"You good?"

I nodded, smiling. "I'm Skyler, by the way." Pointing to the scratch I left on the side of his face, trying to get to Noah, I professed, "I'm sorry about that."

"No worries. Not bad for a girl, you can hold your own. That's a good thing to have in an old lady."

"Old lady? I'm seventeen."

He chuckled, and I couldn't help but notice how deep and husky it sounded. "Old lady means my woman, my wife, my girl. My whole fuckin' world. Ya feel me?"

"Yeah. So, you're a member of Devil's Rejects too?"

"I'm more than a member. I'm Sergeant at Arms."

"What's that?"

"Damn, Noah got himself a civilian, yeah?"

"A what?"

He laughed again, big and throaty. "I fuckin' like you. I can see why Noah does too. Sergeant at Arms means I kick fuckin' ass. Anyone gets outta line, I make sure they step back in."

"Oh. So that's like a big thing then? The fighting? You guys just don't know how to talk shit out, huh?"

He busted out laughing that time. "So what you sayin' is you want a fucker who's a pussy, not a real man?"

"By 'real' man you mean one who fights and kills for money?"

He shook his head with disappointment searing off him. "You gotta lock that shit up, Skyler. This is Noah's life, he's a biker. You wanna ride wit' him, then you stand beside him, and ain't no one gonna be there for him more than you. He don't need that shit, not from you. From everyone else, maybe, but never from you. Right or wrong, in the end, he's puttin' motherfuckers to ground who should be there regardless. This ain't no good cop, bad cop bullshit. He's doin' a fuckin' solid gettin' those motherfuckers off the street. They up to no good."

"So all the men he fights are bad? Is that what you're saying?"

"Would it make a difference to you if they were?"

"I don't know." I shrugged. "It's all so confusing."

"Only confusin' 'cuz you lettin' it. If you love him, then that's all that fuckin' matters. Noah's lived this life since the second he came out fuckin' screamin'. His old man is my Prez, but what he does to his sons is all sorts of fucked up. Noah was dealt a shitty fuckin' hand, and he don't need you makin' it worse for him. You either stand wit' him or you don't, but I'm hopin' you do. 'Cuz he don't have many people on his side. And every man, good or bad, needs an old lady standin' beside 'em."

I took a deep breath, not knowing how to reply or what to even think. I wanted to be there for Noah, but at the same time, what he was doing scared the ever-loving shit out of me.

For him.

For me.

For us.

What if he lost? Did that mean he would die too? Would they kill him like he would have killed them?

There were so many questions that swarmed my mind, and the truth was, the answers to those questions scared me just as much, if not more than the questions themselves. This life of violence was nothing I ever imagined I'd be involved in. And knowing that it came attached to the guy I was possibly in love with, was just as hard a pill to swallow as any of this was.

Listening to everything Diesel said made me realize I couldn't face Noah, not right now. I needed time to think, to figure out how I fit into this huge part of his life. A life I never wanted to begin with. A life that terrified me more than anything.

As his girl.

His best friend.

His one and only.

His old lady.

With one last curt nod, Diesel kick-started his bike, and I made my way inside. Doing the only thing that seemed natural to me, I threw myself back into work. Taking the first flight out the next morning, needing to clear my mind from the guy I thought I knew.

At least, for a while.

Keith wasn't surprised when I'd told him I was flying back to L.A. the next morning. He was used to me being a workaholic. It was just in my nature, all I'd ever known. But he didn't know the real reason I was running away.

Noah.

He had no clue what I had witnessed that night, what haunted my thoughts in more ways than one.

The blood.

The violence.

The aftermath.

I'd waited on pins and needles daily for the other shoe to drop. Anticipating my face on the cover of every tabloid magazine, and just waiting for Keith's wrath for how irresponsible I was. Fucking up my image and everything I'd worked so hard for, all for a boy covered in tattoos who drove a Harley and lived on the wrong side of the tracks.

I had convinced myself that the man Noah knocked out on our birthday was going to run to the press, informing the tabloids I was with Noah the night he almost died. The night *Noah* almost killed him. Then they'd dig like the cockroaches they were and air out all Noah's skeletons from his closet. Shining light on me and my involvement with him. Reporters would eat me alive along with the rise of social media platforms like Myspace and Facebook. They wouldn't hesitate becoming keyboard warriors, spreading their hate and more rumors behind computer screens. Fueling the fire and enjoying every minute of it.

I envisioned it all, expecting the worst. Trying to come up with ways to spin the truth, getting my stories straight for Noah's privacy and for my career. But the truth had yet to be exposed, and as the weeks went by with not so much as one nasty thing printed about me, I just knew Noah had something to do with that too. There's not a chance that man wouldn't have sought his fifteen minutes of fame. Not to mention the money for a story like that, if Noah hadn't put in his two cents on what would happen to him if he did.

As much as I tried throwing myself into work, filling my days with meetings, interviews, and everything and anything to keep my mind occupied, nothing worked. So after speaking to my dad a few times while I was in L.A., I decided I'd come home and hopefully spend some much needed time with him. Time I had craved for most of my life.

"Dad!" I called out, walking room to room through the house. Stopping every few feet to pick-up some sort of garbage or article of clothing he'd left sitting out. "Dad, I'm home!" Whispering under my breath, "Not that you care, obviously." But he was nowhere to be found. "Dad, you here?" I knocked on his bedroom door next, listening for an answer.

Nothing.

"I'm coming in!" And just as I thought, his bed was made like always and his room was a mess similar to the rest of the house.

With still no sign of him.

I deeply sighed, becoming more annoyed and frustrated. "How can one person dirty these many clothes?" I asked myself, treading through the chaos on the carpet and around the room as I tossed piles of work jeans and shirts into the laundry basket.

"Eww."

Beyond grossed out by the moldy food on his nightstand, but relieved he was at least eating. It was like he was the damn child and I was the adult in this household, and you'd think I'd be used to it by now.

But nope.

Not in the least.

I shook my head, collecting the rest of his dirty clothes and once I finished picking up after him, I threw a load in the washer and started separating the rest by colors and whites so I could move onto my own laundry. When the doorbell suddenly rang.

"I'm coming!" I announced, glancing at the time on the microwave as I walked toward the front door. "Who the hell is up this early?"

I should have known…

I should have felt it.

I should have done anything but open that door.

Unexpectedly coming face-to-face with the guy who never left my mind.

"Noah," I breathlessly mouthed, at a loss for words. Instantly gazing into his blue-green eyes that always did things to me.

He looked better than I remembered. His hair was a mess of waves, his skin tanner, highlighting his five o'clock shadow that was doing fluttering things to me too. His arms more chiseled, his chest broader. His whole demeanor read of a man who had been lost without me. Losing sleep, his mind, his heart to me.

How the hell did he look this good in the morning?

I immediately noticed he wasn't wearing his cut, like his instincts told him I wasn't ready to see it again. The silence between us was deafening as we just stood there, lost in each other's presence. Taking one another in, as if we hadn't seen each other in years when it had only been a month.

I watched the way his lips moved with each rapid breath that blew out of his mouth, knowing his heart was racing as fast as mine.

I watched the way his hair blew in the wind, framing his defined face and intense stare that was solely narrowed in on me.

I watched the way his solid muscular chest heaved up and down, mirroring mine as if they were in sync with one another.

I especially watched the way he was looking at me. No one ever looked at me like he did. I had engrained it in my mind, a memory and piece of him I took with me wherever I went.

When he casually brushed the hair away from my face, he still didn't say a word, only needing to feel my skin beneath his callused fingers and loving touch.

The way Noah affected my mind and my heart was just so petrifying, and it was just so real.

The emotion…

I could touch it.

Feel it.

Taste it.

It surrounded me. Engulfed me. Loved me.

And I never wanted to let it go.

I never wanted to let *him* go.

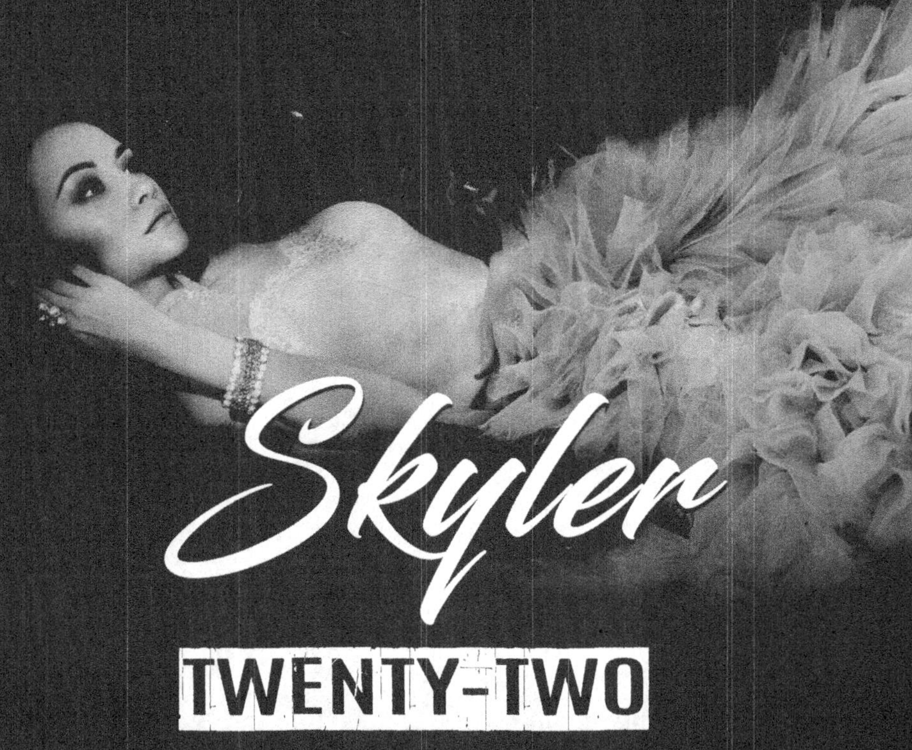

TWENTY-TWO

My heart fluttered, my stomach dropped, and my mouth parted the moment he rasped, “Hey, Cutie.”

I hid back a smile, unaware of how to proceed with him. Blurting, “What are you doing here?” instead.

He flinched from the sharp tone in my voice, not trying to hide his emotions, unlike me. Which had always been a consistent trait about Noah, he never tried hiding from me. Always showing me his true colors.

What you saw was what you got.

What he said was what he meant.

No matter what.

Whether I wanted to see it or not.

Proving my point, he stated, “Been waitin’ for you to come home.”

“So you’ve been sitting in front of my house for the last month or what?”

“Somethin’ like that.”

“That’s not creepy or anything.”

He grinned. “Number one fan, remember?”

I was never one to beat around the bush and, as much as I wanted to fall back into the constant safe haven of our relationship, I couldn’t. The fear of the violence in his life wouldn’t let me.

“Yeah, Noah, I do remember. I remember everything. Especially our birthday.”

"I'm so fuckin' sorry, Skyler. I never meant to scare you. The last thing I wanted was for you to run away from me, all the way to fuckin' L.A."

"I didn't run away. I had to work."

"Come on." He cocked his head to the side with a sly grin. "Who do ya think you're talkin' to? Just 'cuz I haven't seen ya in a month, don't mean I don't know when you're bullshittin' me, yeah?"

"What do you want me to say, Noah? Because I don't even know how to handle you. Jesus… what happened that night is *not* okay with me. It will never be okay with me."

"I know."

"Do you? Because I don't think you do. The guy who is standing in front of me right now, showing me so much remorse in his eyes that it hurts my heart, is the boy who ate shit trying to show off for me when we were eleven-years-old. Making me sing for him when we were thirteen. Who's been there for me without even knowing it every year since. That's—" I pointed to myself "—the guy I know. The one who's my best friend, my only friend. I don't know that person who fights and kills for money, and honestly, I don't think you do either."

He swallowed hard, taking in every last word that fell from my lips. By the look on his face, he knew what I implied was true. Which only frightened me more for him and the life he led when I wasn't around.

"I'm still that guy, Cutie. Nothin' has changed, not one single word I've ever said to you has been a lie. You are my sunshine and happiness, who has brought nothin' but dark fuckin' clouds over me these last few weeks. I need ya in my fucked-up life, Skyler, 'cuz you make it worth livin'."

My resolve shattered. He couldn't say stuff like that to me and it not.

"Come ride wit' me. I wanna show you somethin'," he coaxed, holding up three fingers with his hand. "You'll like it this time, Scout's Honor."

"When have you ever been a boy scout?"

"When I used to beat up kids who were."

I glared at him.

"I'm jokin'. Did my girl lose her sense of humor in Hollywood wit' all those fake-ass people?"

I rolled my eyes.

"There she is. There's my girl." Before I had a chance to reply, he grabbed my hand. Adding, "Let's put ya on the back of my bike where ya belong, yeah?"

"Verdict's still out on you."

He smirked in that Noah sort of way, pulling me behind him as he led me to his bike. Almost like he thought if he let go, I'd go running back to L.A.

But regardless of the uncertainties between us, there it was…

The second he wrapped my arms around his waist when we were on his bike, I felt it. What I had been missing for the last month.

Home.

I tried not getting emotional on the ride to wherever he was taking me, but it was difficult not to. Having his warm body wrapped up in my arms was Heaven on Earth. An endless stream of conflicting emotions spiraled through my mind, tearing at my heart. Confusing me even more when it came to him, but in a much different way than before. It wasn't just about my career anymore. It was about his life and how I fit in it. How we fit together when there was an overwhelming amount of reasons to keep us apart. When everything in my mind was telling me, screaming at me, that I needed to stay away from him.

Now more than ever.

I closed my eyes just for a second, too consumed with decisions I didn't know I'd ever be able to make. What was wrong sat right in front of my eyes, bared into the guy who felt so right. I tried ignoring the looming feeling in the pit of my stomach, focusing on the cutest little beach town with a quaint family-style restaurant, nestled on the ocean that we were driving past. Some good ol' boys were running around out front, and a beautiful young girl, wearing a yellow sundress, chased after them. Making me wish I could be that carefree, where nothing else mattered but being a kid and living each day to the fullest.

My thoughts never stopped racing as I desperately tried enjoying the fresh ocean breeze in my face, living in the moment with Noah, even if it wouldn't last. Seeking the refuge he always provided, with or without him even knowing it. Which was yet another thing about Noah…

He wanted to see the truths that most people tried to ignore.

It was a persistent struggle to let go of my guard that I had been holding onto ever since I could remember. To bring down the wall I'd built so high, so thick with everyone including him. The way he looked at me, the way he spoke to me, the way he listened. Every smile, every laugh, every word that descended from Noah's lips, meant something.

It didn't matter how big or how small.

It was there.

Etching its way into my heart where no one could ever come close to it.

Not that I had ever let them.

When he slowed down and took a turn onto a secluded road that read *Private Property Davidson Marina* at the entrance, I asked, giggling, "You kidnapping me, Rebel?"

With a predatory regard, he glanced back at me. "You'd love that, wouldn't you? Bein' tied up and at my mercy. You wanna be my bad or good girl, baby? 'Cuz either way you'll look fuckin' beautiful on your knees with my cock fuckin' that saucy little mouth of yours."

"Noah!" My mouth dropped open, and I slapped his arm. "Just-just—oh my god—just pay attention to the road before we crash."

He cockily smiled, pulling into a parking spot. Loving my response that only he stirred, fully aware of what he always did to me.

What only *he* could ever do to me.

Before I knew what was happening, he jumped off his bike, and I thought he was going to help me off like always, but instead, he pulled me closer to him by the nook of my neck, until our lips were almost touching and breathed out, "I ain't the one squirmin' at the thought of my cock in your mouth."

I whimpered when he abruptly pulled away and helped me off his bike. Hating and loving the effect his dirty mouth had on me. I clenched my thighs, clearing my throat, failing miserably with what he just called me out on. It didn't help that his hands were still gripped onto my waist.

"What are we doing in Oak Island? At a marina?" I questioned, changing the subject before my panties exploded at the thought of his huge, thick dick in my…

Oh my God, Skyler! Stop it!

As if reading my mind, he tilted his head to the side, tempting me with whatever he wanted to do. I could see, feel his heated stare on every inch of my skin, and the bastard was responsive of it too.

I licked my lips, my mouth suddenly dry. His mischievous glare shadowed the movement of my tongue.

Waiting.

Anticipating.

Rousing from the inside out.

So when he slowly backed away, taking his warmth with him, it was like a bucket of freezing cold water washed over me.

Did he just reject me?

He turned around and grabbed my hand, ignoring my question and my disappointed expression. Leading us over to a cemented walkway, he urgently tugged me toward him and kissed the palm of my hand. Looking at me with that blaze in his eyes and excitement on his face. He was barely able to contain it as we walked hand-in-hand down the dock.

Making me smile, his eagerness was contagious. I realized it had nothing to do with rejection, he just really wanted to show me something. I felt better as we continued strolling past one boat after another, all in pristine condition, until we reached the end of the boat slip and there was nowhere else for us to go.

"It's a surprise," he finally replied, grabbing the black rope tied to the dock. He stepped overboard onto the last yacht, trying to pull me along with him, but I hesitated. Snapping him back to face me again.

"Noah, my law-breaking days are over."

He beamed, simply stating, "Trust me."

So I did, stepping onto the side before jumping onto the deck, following close behind him. "Noah, what are we doin—" He rendered me speechless as soon as he opened the door, and I could see what he had been beyond excited to show me.

He walked in first, but I didn't waver in trailing in after him, stepping into a huge open space filled with tools and lumber.

"Holy shit," I whispered under my breath, gazing at the completely gutted interior of the massive yacht.

My eyes shifted from the large industrial fan next to the door, keeping the stale air circulating, to the big hole in the floor on the left side of the room that looked like it was an access area to the engines, to the ceiling that was entirely ripped apart with shop lights hanging down, sporadically lighting the cabin. The floors were bare planks of wood with sawdust everywhere. Cans of paint and varnish were spread throughout the open space with drop clothes pushed to the side.

It didn't look like much right now, but someone had already put in a lot of man hours restoring the inside, and once they finished this yacht, it would be every bit as stunning as I already imagined in my head.

"Wow," was all I managed to say as I slowly let go of his hand and turned in a circle, taking in everything from the freshly varnished wood in the kitchen to the unfinished floors in the living room. The smell of saltwater, sweat, and Noah filled the humid air.

"Whose boat is—"

He placed his index finger over my lips. "Shhh… you ask too many questions." Grinning, he gradually backed away toward the radio on the floor a few feet away from us.

"Noah—"

Silencing me again, he turned it on. And what proceeded next, happened so fast, I never had a chance to see it coming. In an instant, he wrapped his arms around me, locking me in place, flush against his hard, firm chest.

Murmuring, "Dance wit' me," into my ear before he swiftly brushed the hair away from my face with the back of his fingers. Leaving a trail of yearning in his wake, he allowed his eyes to speak for himself.

I nodded, unable to find my voice. Taking one of my hands, he spun me around and then placed it on his shoulder. Intertwining his other hand in mine, he promptly laid them over his heart while his face conveyed so many emotions in a matter of seconds, and I paid close attention to every last one.

He started moving and I instinctively followed, swaying as one to the beat of the music as he hummed the soft melody in my ear. We got lost in each other in the same way we always had, feeling *everything* and all at once.

"This is my boat, and I wanna make it a home, wit' *you*."

I jerked back with wide eyes, not expecting him to say that. Stunned, I only questioned, "This isn't a boat Noah, it's a yacht. How did you get it?"

I'd be lying if I said I wasn't nervous about his response. My initial thoughts were he either won it in a fight or he stole it, and neither reason sat well with me.

"It was a gift."

"From who?"

"Good people, like you."

"They just gave you this?"

He nodded.

"Why?"

"Been askin' myself that question for the last month, but it don't change the fact she's mine."

"She?"

"Oh yeah, she's definitely a girl."

"And I don't get a say in this?"

"You want one?"

Without thinking, I answered, "Yes."

He smiled big and wide, and it lit up his entire face. "Whataya want? I'll build ya whatever you want."

"What do you know about restoring yachts, Noah?"

"As much as I know 'bout you."

"Which is?"

"Not a damn thing, but I'll learn."

"Noah—"

He spun me around, tugging me back to his chest. His response hurt me in more ways than he could ever understand, knowing all along what he truly wanted.

Needed.

Couldn't live without.

Me.

All of me.

The expression on my face must have softened, giving him the push he needed to keep going with what he had to say to me.

Rubbing his nose against mine, he groaned in an aching tone, "I wanna know everythin' 'bout you, Skyler Bell."

I opened my mouth to reply, but quickly shut it. Not knowing what to say or where to even start. There were things I wanted to say that Noah needed to hear. Things I wanted to express that he needed to understand.

Secrets needed to be shared.

Truths needed to be told.

Demons needed to be buried.

But as I looked into his eyes, standing in front of him…

Words failed me.

And I failed him because I casually just brushed him off. Questioning, "Where did ya learn how to dance?" instead.

Breaking both our hearts a little more, digging the knife a little deeper, where neither one of us would survive the repercussions of my daily battle of letting him into a life that didn't belong to me. I belonged to my career, and my career owned my life.

The good.

The bad.

The in between.

It was all mine.

Where there was no room for anyone else.

Even though I was only almost eighteen, an adult by legal standards, I felt much older than that. Much wiser, much more mature beyond my years. Having to grow up fast in a world that valued only youth will do that to a person.

You don't realize how much of your childhood affects the person you become, the person you are. How memories shape your life, your feelings, and most importantly your *love.*

The struggle between the things we couldn't change but wanted to versus the things we could change but didn't know how to.

Felt as if I was forever standing in the same spot.

Living a life of loneliness was simply the only way I knew how to live.

And as I looked into Noah's eyes, I saw it. Clear as day, big and bold and right in front of me, was a future I never thought I could have staring back at me.

But at what price?

I couldn't tell if Noah was trying to hide his disappointment from my response, for me or for himself, but either way, it killed me inside. Knowing in the back of my mind that it wasn't in his nature and he was more than likely doing it for *me*.

Allowing that little voice to repeat in my head, *"Stay away from him, Skyler. You need to stay away from him."*

I never expected that my guarded regard would make him want to open up even more. With so much pain in his eyes and regret laced in his voice, he shared, "My Ma, she wasn't always a drunk. She was a good momma once, taught me how to ride my first dirt bike, how to use my words instead of my fists, how to pray to God when I needed him. When *she* needed him." He twirled me around again before pulling me back toward his chest.

Smiling, "Taught me how to dance for my old lady. She did everythin' for us boys and never once fuckin' complained. Like she was born to be a mother, *our* mother. I was her baby boy, her last son, and I guess maybe that was the reason I had always been the closest to her. My momma was my best friend, and before you came along, she was my only friend. We had this unspoken bond, and we still do. 'Cuz even after everythin' I took away from her, everythin' she's put me through, I can't let her go. I won't let her go. I'll fuckin' die fightin' for her life that she don't wanna live, if I havta."

Overpowering tears brimmed my eyes, listening to more of his truths. Fully aware that I was the first person he was confiding them with.

"Skyler, don't cry for me," he stated, wiping away one of my tears.

Feeling so much.

So so so much…

"'Cuz ya see, Skyler. My older brother Luke, well, Cutie, he was put to ground 'cuz of me. And now Creed's off fightin' a fuckin' war within himself, and my old man doesn't give two shits 'bout her. He gave up on Ma years ago. So I'm all she's got left, and when you ain't around… she's all I got left too."

I whimpered, "Noah…" feeling his hurt and shame. It was swallowing me whole.

My mind instantly went back to our first date at the park where Billy implied it was someone in his family who took his brother's life. I just never imagined it would be him.

Anyone else but Noah.

He wiped away a few more of my tears, they flowed freely now. There was no stopping them. Not when he had the same distressed expression on his face from that night, when he walked back into his room. Thinking I was gone, that I had left him alone. Telling me he'd take me home after he realized I hadn't. It still sliced into my heart like it did then. As if over three years hadn't flown by, and we were still standing in his room.

Scared.

Alone.

Feeling hopeless.

"So ya see… I couldn't save Luke. I couldn't save my momma. I couldn't even save Creed. So I lost 'em all."

I stood there in shock, listening to the silence for a second. My mind was reeling, trying to grab onto something, anything.

That could help him.

It wasn't until he breathed out, "Baby, please say somethin'. I need ya to say somethin'. Please…"

My body moved on its own accord, and my mind didn't have time to doubt it. I grabbed the back of his neck and brought my lips up to his and kissed him. I couldn't help myself, I had to feel his lips on mine. I had to show him with actions, not words, prove to him he wasn't alone. That I was there for him. That nothing had changed between us, even though I knew about his worst nightmares.

His father.

His mother.

Luke.

The fighting.

The truth to his life.

My chest rose and fell when I pulled away, staring into his dark and dilated, mesmerizing but painful, stare. Burning with so much raw emotion that it was almost hard to breathe. Captivating every last part of me.

I didn't move an inch.

Not for one second.

I gazed profoundly into his eyes and exposed a huge part of me, whispering, "Thank you for saving my life."

Meaning it in more ways…

Than him just saving me at the river, over four years ago.

Twenty-three

It had been eight months since I shared my last truth with Skyler, and she had yet to share at least one fucking thing with me about her life. Not so much as a memory, or an invite into her house, or even about her upcoming work schedule. After all these years, and everything I'd openly shared with her, she wouldn't allow me into any aspect of her life. Except spending time with her.

And a man could only take so much.

She was still trying to keep both her lives separate. Like she was two different people, one for me and another one for the cameras. It was blatantly obvious to me now, or maybe it always had been, and I was just too blinded by my love for her to see it. She was spending more days in L.A. and less in Southport.

Away from me.

Avoiding me.

At this point, who the fuck knew, because I sure as shit didn't.

I knew her career was moving at full speed since her role as Roxie Hart. I saw her face everywhere, on magazines, online, on television with the latest celebrity news. Her picture was even on the side of a bus I rode past a few weeks ago. But the one that really fucking pissed me off was the billboard of her in the city. Where she was dressed in a revealing black bra that made her tits pop-out at the seams with matching panties that she was slightly pulling down with her thumbs. Sexually posing for some company, Victoria's Secret, with her lips pursed and her hair tussled like she'd just been fucked.

Every time I drove past it for one thing or another, mostly doing runs for the club, I resisted the urge to graffiti the fuck out of it. Until I finally decided on another route so I would avoid seeing it completely. Which didn't fucking help, I still knew it was there for all the world to see, when I had yet to fucking see her like that. Knowing dickwads were jerking off to her, and I was no better because I was fucking my fist to the memory of her beneath me…

Moaning.

Panting.

Screaming my name to make her come.

Regardless, there was no defining our relationship, considering I called her my girl and she called me her best friend.

Every time my mind went there, every time I allowed the unanswered questions to fester inside of me, just waiting to blow the fuck up and take over, my mind couldn't help but remember the words she'd said to me from all those years ago. As if she was saying them to me right then and there…

"I need you to promise me something, okay? Please, please don't fall in love with me."

They carved into my skin, slicing into my core. Leaving behind one hell of a fucking scar each time. Marking my soul, my goddamn patience, my fucking love for her. Whether I desired it or not.

Because at the end of the day, I wanted to love her, despite the fact she didn't want me to.

Nothing made sense, and as more time went on, it became crystal fucking clear it never would. Unless I took drastic matters into my own hands. But there was the catch…

She wasn't home enough for me to jeopardize the time we did spend together, and I think that was part of the reason she started working so damn much. She knew it because she knew me.

It was that plain and simple.

Only fueling my restlessness when it came to her.

I began fighting more for my old man and on the side, purely for selfish fucking reasons. My mind and body feening for the control beating someone's ass always provided for me. Seeing as though my refuge from my fucked-up life was off living her best one without me. Making me feel like she was leaving me behind, to eventually be forgotten like the rest of my fucking family.

I wasn't lying when I said I wanted to make a home with her, and as the weeks went on with the boat restoration, for the life I wanted with her, it started seeming further and further away.

Becoming just a fantasy from my reality.

A dream from my nightmares.

A refuge I sought out in her absence.

I couldn't go on with this uncertainty of what the future held for us. There was already so much of that in my life, and I needed Skyler to be my fucking anchor from the storm, residing inside of me. Yearning for her to be the stability of the home I never had and the family I always wanted. I even started sleeping on the boat just to feel close to her, instead of at the clubhouse or at the house with Ma.

It wasn't like Ma would notice I was gone. She started attending AA a few times a week a couple months ago. Sometimes she'd even spend the entire day there. Talking to other people about her problems seemed to help her through the jonesing of wanting and needing a drink. Though that didn't stop me from checking on her often, making sure she was still sober, or at least trying to stay sober. She'd relapse here and there, but she kept putting an effort in nonetheless.

I think it was a combination of her last seizure where she about flatlined and Aiden's persistence on her getting help. It finally made her see some sort of fucking light. Except, it was still hard for me to have faith in her sobriety, which only aided the lost boy inside of me.

Then there was Pops, who didn't give a flying fuck where I slept as long as I was there when he needed me. Which was more often than not. There was so much blood on my hands, no amount of holy water could cleanse my soul.

I was fucking damned.

Exactly how *he* always wanted me to be.

At times, it felt like Skyler was my only salvation, but even she might not be able to set me free.

I kicked out the stand on my Harley, shoving away my plaguing thoughts. I hadn't seen Skyler in about three weeks, and I missed the ever-loving shit out of her. I knew she flew back to Southport sometime last night, because she texted me when she was lying in her bed, *Home sweet home.*

I spent most of the night chain-smoking on the bow of the boat, chugging down a bottle of Jack. Numbing my mind and my heart. Allowing the darkness to take over, it was just easier that way. Feeling more lost than ever.

My sunshine was gone until she wasn't. I knocked on her door, expecting her to answer this early in the morning. Instantly taken back when an older man with her eyes opened the door. Locking up like a goddamn pussy as I stood in front of the man, I assumed was her father, for the first time ever. Grateful as fuck I wasn't wearing my cut.

Hastily shaking it off, I extended out my hand. "Good mornin', I'm Noah." Silently hoping I hadn't already fucked this up.

"Not interested," he snapped, trying to slam the door in my face.

But I was quick on my feet and wedged my combat boot against the doorframe, adding, "Imma friend of Skyler's."

"Oh." He jerked back, opening the door again. "I'm sorry about that. I thought you were a solicitor." He extended out his hand, making me feel a little more at ease. "I'm Daniel Morgan, Skyler's dad."

I nodded, shaking it. *I thought Skyler's last name was Bell?*

"She's not home right now. She's at a shoot over at the country club till late tonight. I'll tell her you stopped by, though. Noah, right?"

"Yeah, that's right." I waited for some sort of recognition in his expression from hearing my name. Like a lightbulb going off, knowing who I was and what I meant to his daughter. When it never came, I gave him one last curt nod. "Sorry to bother ya." Turned back around and started walking toward my bike. Not only was I disappointed she wasn't home, but her father had no idea who I was. She hadn't even mentioned me in passing.

Jesus Christ, Skyler... not even to your old man?

"Do you know her from work? You an actor too?" he hollered from the porch, bringing my attention back to him.

I grinned, wanting him to get a feel for who I was. "Naw. Why? I look like I gotta stick up my ass?"

He busted out laughing, throwing his head back. "Good." He smiled, looking me over. "She needs real people in her life. And those L.A. people are the furthest thing from that. I swear, they're a different breed out there. No substance. No loyalty either."

Her father shared more with me in the last minute than Skyler had in almost five years.

"I'm glad Skyler has you. She needs friends. I worry about her, you know?"

"Yeah, I feel ya. I been worryin' 'bout her since the first time I saw her swimmin' at Cape Fear River—"

"What?" he harshly blurted, narrowing his eyes at me. "Skyler was swimming at Cape Fear? When?"

"A few years back, I think we were eleven almost twelve."

"You must be mistaken."

"Nah, I was there. It was definitely that river."

"But that was only the first time, right? That's what you just said? That means there's been more? How many more times then?" He couldn't get his questions out fast enough. "How many times have you seen my daughter swimming in there since then?"

By the sharp tone in his voice and the drastic change in his demeanor, I knew Skyler hadn't breathed a word about what happened the last time I saw her in that river. And before I had the chance to reply, his phone rang. Breaking the sudden tension between us.

Never taking his eyes off mine, he answered, "Hey."

I used it as my excuse to leave, signaling to him that I was taking off.

"Give me a second," he said into his phone and then covered it with his hand. "Noah, I'll just be a minute. I want to know—"

"Actually, I have somewhere I gotta be. I'm sorry, maybe another time."

He wearily nodded, making me feel like a piece of shit for unintentionally sharing something that made him so upset.

But why?

I jumped on my bike and took off, avoiding the shit out of that situation. Knowing Skyler was going to have to deal with her old man instead didn't make me feel any less confused or concerned for what the hell just happened. I spent the entire ride back to Ma's house trying to force away the memory of the day I saved her life, but it held onto me. Exactly the way my love for her did.

Replaying over and over in my mind.

"I'm gonna take you home on two conditions," I stated.

"Is that so?" she countered, cocking her head to the side.

"Damn straight," I affirmed, cocking my head to the side too. "You gotta promise me you'll get checked out by your doctor, your parents, I don't give a fuck, but by someone who can make sure you're really okay."

"I'll tell my dad. What's the next condition?"

After all these years of wanting to know something about her, I thought when I finally did, it would make everything truthful between us.

I just never imagined…

It would be a lie.

Skyler

TWENTY-FOUR

"Keith, I already told you I still don't know," I reminded him for what felt like the hundredth time today.

I'd flown in late last night, and as soon as I got home, I took a warm shower and went straight to bed. Snapping a quick photo of myself for Noah first, hoping he'd reply to my text with at least a goodnight. I waited for as long as I could, but my eyes struggled to stay open.

The next thing I knew, my alarm was going off. Indicating it was five a.m. and I had to get my ass out of bed for my photoshoot. I must have passed out hard, though I still woke up as if I hadn't slept at all. Disappointed to find no reply from Noah.

It was evident the closer our relationship became, the further our friendship drifted apart. If that made any sense at all.

I'd been working nonstop. Between the grueling hours of prepping for my movie starting production in the next two months, to flying overseas to promote my new perfume launching in the fall, to photoshoots for Calvin Klein because I was the new face for their spring campaign. There wasn't much free time left for myself, not to mention all the back and forth from L.A. to Southport, back to L.A. and so on, and so on. It was taxing to say the least.

As much as I didn't want to admit it to Keith, *that* in itself was exhausting.

"Sky, what is keeping you in Southport?"

And now, I'm having to deal with him in my trailer, on my lunch hour. Instead of taking a much-needed break from yet another shoot that would be going into the late hours of the evening.

"Oh, I don't know… maybe my dad," I sarcastically stated the truth, knowing he wasn't the main reason I kept flying home. I brushed past him, walking over to the fridge to grab a bottle of water and some Tylenol. My head was already pounding from this exchange I didn't want to have to begin with.

Keith wouldn't drop this conversation. For the last three months, he'd been adamantly persistent on me permanently moving out to L.A. Particularly in the last month. It seemed like the closer the days got to my eighteenth birthday, the harder he kept hounding me to move. Especially now that my career was on fire and I'd been spending most of my time there anyway. From his point of view, it did make sense for me to go.

If Noah and I had never met…

If our lives had never crossed paths…

If he didn't mean so damn much to me…

I probably would have moved years ago.

My whole life seemed to be based off of *ifs*. If I got that role, if I shot that cover, if I did that interview, if I wore this or that, if I go here or there, if I… if I… if I…

There was an endless number of ifs with no certainties attached to them whatsoever. No one understood what it was like to be me.

Not my father.

Not Keith.

Not even Noah.

Sometimes, it felt as if I didn't even know what it was like to be me. I'd been so many different people for so long, and I wasn't referring to all the roles I'd played over the years.

"Oh, don't give me that shit! Your dad is never around. You see him here as much as you see him when you're in L.A. Nice try, Skyler."

It was true. He was right.

But what if I moved and stopped seeing him entirely?

Would it even matter to him?

Did I even matter to him anymore?

What if I did? Or worse… What if I didn't?

"Ugh! What does it matter? I'm doing fine commuting back and forth," I lied, expecting him to call me out on it.

Since in reality, *my* reality, Keith was more of a father to me than my own. And I wish I could tell you it hadn't always been that way, but then… I'd just be lying again.

"Oh, come on, give me more credit than that, Sky. Look at you." He gestured to me as I stood back in front of him. "You're exhausted. You think I don't notice these things? Like the amount of time the makeup artists have been spending trying to cover your dark circles and your hollow cheekbones. Or what about how the wardrobe department for your next movie keeps having your clothes taken in because you're losing so much weight. Those reasons alone should tell you something."

"That's not from me flying to and from L.A, Keith. But if you're so concerned about my eating habits and weight, how about you leave so I can eat lunch? Or better yet, call *Hollywood Reporter* since last week they said I was looking a little rounder."

"They photoshopped those pictures to sell their bullshit lies. Besides, when has it ever bothered you what the tabloids are fabricating this week?"

"It doesn't bother me now. I'm just stating facts. Because if it's printed online or in a magazine, then it must be true, right?"

I hated that we were arguing. Seeing as though, I couldn't just tell him the truth about who Noah was and what he meant to me. He wouldn't understand, I barely understood. He'd tell me Noah wasn't right for me, he'd go digging into his life, and there was no way the press wouldn't pick him apart and do the same. Everyone would find out about his family, all the illegal shit he was involved in, including the cops. The fighting, the killings, and God knows what else. His whole life would be turned upside down, for a life he knew nothing about. A life he didn't choose, never realizing it came hand-in-hand with me.

I couldn't do that to him.

I wouldn't.

He was mine and mine alone. Whether he knew it or not.

Keith sighed, getting frustrated with me. "Alright, I'll play it your way. I'll just move onto the next reasons on why you need to move to L.A."

"Oh goodie," I mocked, smiling. "I can't wait."

"Skyler," he coaxed in that fatherly tone I hated as well. "I've kept my mouth shut for as long as I needed to, but soon you're going to be an adult and you need to start making wise choices for your future. You're going to be eighteen in a few months, it's time you start using your money wisely like for investments. The real estate market in L.A. is a great place for you to start. You could buy a house, make it your own home. Where your dad can have his own room, and he can visit you as much as he wants. There's nothing here for you."

I rolled my eyes, not backing down. If I did, I'd lose him.

Noah.

"I can buy real estate here too, Keith. If you're so concerned about how I'm spending my money."

"For fucks sake, Skyler! It's like talking to a child!"

"I'm not a child!" I screamed back at him, getting just as frustrated as he was.

I wasn't a child.

I had never been a child.

My life didn't allow it.

"Then stop acting like one! You're missing out on a ton of opportunity as it is, because you're here and not there."

"Like what?"

"Events, parties, charities, socializing with your peers, sponsorships. Do you need me to keep going?"

"Why does that matter?" I questioned, already knowing the answer. Everything and anything in this industry counted. No matter how big or small, it all mattered.

"Come on, Sky. You know why. This entire business is based on who you know and what they can do for you. And you're missing out on all of that because you're flying back to Southport, North Carolina! As Queen B of this redneck podunk town to do a photoshoot for a fucking country club magazine cover. A place no one is going to travel to because it's out in the middle of fucking nowhere!"

"You're not listening to me!"

He wasn't, or maybe he was. I just didn't know what the right or wrong answer would be when it came to moving, and that scared me more than anything. It was as life changing as permitting Noah into my world to begin with. Knowing if I did, there was a huge chance he'd leave me after seeing what I desperately tried to hide.

Me.

And that if…

Wasn't worth it to me.

"Goddamn it! All I'm doing is respecting your mom's wishes! Looking after you like I always promised her I would! It's my job to take care of you! Because she's not—"

"Stop it!" I pointed at him. "That's a low fucking blow, and you know it!"

"It's the truth! I'm all you have! And I'll be damned if you fuck up your career thinking about a man who's never been there for you! The only thing your dad ever did right by you was saving your—"

Abruptly covering my ears, I sang, *"The sun'll come out tomorrow, bet all those dollars that tomorrow!"*

"Skyler, don't pull this shit!" He ripped my hands away from my ears. "You're not a little girl anymore! Enough!"

I reacted, enabling my demons to take over. "Who pays who here, Keith?! Because last time I checked, I was the one who signed your fucking paychecks! The goddamn ten percent of what I work my fucking ass off for!"

"And who gets you all that money?!" He tugged me toward him. "Those roles?! Those contracts?! The fucking publicity and the exposure! *Me!* So that you can pay me my goddamn ten percent. Because last I checked, Skyler fucking Bell, I was the one who made you a fucking star!"

Before the last word even flew out of his mouth, the door to my trailer slammed open, practically flying off the hinges. Snapping both our attention over to its source as the last person I expected to see hauled ass over to Keith with that murderous glare I was all too familiar with.

I instantly gasped, yelling, "Noah, no!"

He didn't hesitate, roughly gripping onto the lapels of Keith's suit jacket, getting right in his face.

Gritting out through a clenched jaw, "Raise your fuckin' voice to her one more time, and watch what I fuckin' do to you."

Fully aware, he meant every last word.

NOAH

Twenty-five

Skyler sprang into action as the son of a bitch in my tight grasp jerked back, spewing, "Who the fuck are you?!" His hands flew to mine at the same time Skyler's did.

"Stop! No, Noah! Please, let go of him! Now!"

"I'm the motherfucker who's 'bout to teach ya some goddamn manners."

"Please, Noah! Don't do this! Please, I'm begging you! Let go of him! Please, don't do this!"

It was her panic-ridden tone that made me defiantly let go by shoving him back, and he barely wavered.

Skyler instantly placed herself in between us with an expression on her face I'd never seen before. "What are you doing here?" she bit, almost knocking me on my ass again.

It wasn't enough that I overheard their entire conversation about her moving, and how this fucking bastard spoke to her. Now she was giving me shit for wanting to surprise her at her shoot.

What the fuck?

"Keep lookin' at me like that, motherfucker." I nodded to him. "And I'll make you fuckin' regret it."

She pushed me. "Stop it!"

"Who the fuck is this, Sky?! And what the hell is he doing here?! Security!"

She abruptly turned around, setting her hands on his chest. Giving him a much different response than the one she just gave me.

Again, what the fuck?

"Please, Keith! I'll handle it. I promise! There's no need to get security involved. I swear! Please! Just give me a chance! I'll take care of it!"

His threatening regard went from my face to my clothes, shifting to my ink in a matter of seconds. Taking in every last one of my tattoos with nothing but an expression of disgust spread across his pretty boy fucking face. Before he locked eyes with my murderous stare.

"Who the hell is this low-life?"

"Keith, please…"

"I should have your ass thrown in jail for trespassing!"

"Keith, you're only making it worse. Please…" Her hands were trembling along with the tone in her voice, making me feel like shit.

"He sure as hell isn't here to play golf, Skyler. So I'll ask you again, who the fuck is he?"

"He's… he's… he's…"

I resisted the urge to tell him who I was for her, simply for the reason of needing to hear it from her mouth. Wanting some sort of validation of who I was to her. Even if it meant I had to swallow my fucking pride and let this piece of shit tear into me. It didn't help that I could feel her nervousness, her turmoil, all her conflicting emotions radiating off her skin, burning into my core.

"Is he the reason you keep flying home every chance you get? The reason you're so fucking exhausted?"

"He's—I, please—just, he's—"

"Jesus, Skyler." He met her eyes. "If you were slumming it to see how the other side lived and he's turned into some sort of stalker, then you need to tell me. Now!"

She jolted, and my fingers twitched. Anger rose, but I swallowed it back down. Hesitantly moving my glare from his face over to the side of hers. Quickly noticing the sweat glistening on her temple, how her cheeks were bright red, and the way she moved her head back and forth, internally battling something.

Was it fear for herself or for me? Or was that embarrassment? Had I been right from the start? Was she ashamed of me all these years? Is that the real reason why she won't let me into her life? Why can't she just answer him?

Question after question tore through my mind at full force, like there was a fucking gun to my head, waiting to go off when she replied. I could hear the ticking of the clock, her accelerated heart beating out of her chest, her breath leaving her lips, her mind racing for the right answer that would clearly end it all for me.

"This guy is obviously affecting you. Look at you, you're shaking. What has he done to you? What has he got on you? Did he get you into something bad? Just say the word and I can make him go away for good. I'll throw his ass behind bars." He glared at me. "By the looks of it, he belongs there anyway. Who. Is. He?"

"He's—he's…"

"For fucks sake, I've had enough of this!" His eyes darted to the door. "Security!"

"He's no one!" she finally shot out, proving me wrong.

The gun wasn't pointed to my head, it was aimed right over my fucking heart. Digging into my skin where at any moment, I'd be a dead man, laying here in a pool of my own tainted blood, bleeding out all my truths and lies when I'd never get to discover hers.

With one shot, Skyler ended me.

Destroying us.

"He's nobody, alright?! He's no one to me! Now just let me handle him! Please, Keith! Just go!"

He reluctantly nodded at her before eyeing me up and down as he backed away toward the door. His stare spoke fucking volumes, and I learned right then and there that Keith was a fucking snake in the grass. He knew what he was doing by ramming Skyler into a corner so she would answer how he wanted.

Fucking killing me inside.

She may have been holding the gun, but Keith made her pull the trigger.

"You have twenty minutes or I'm involving the cops."

"Cops, huh? Ya that big of a pussy you can't do it yourself?"

"Noah!" She glared at me, pretty much pushing him out the door. Instantly locking it behind him.

I didn't waver, the adrenaline coursing through my veins wouldn't let me. "I'm no one, yeah?"

She didn't move, not one fucking inch with her back still to me. Her hands rested on the doorframe, like she didn't know how to handle me.

Or worse.

How to respond...

To *me*.

"Noah, please…"

"Turn around, Skyler," I snarled. "And tell me to my fuckin' face that I'm no one to you."

"Noah, please don't do this."

"Turn around, Skyler."

"Noah—"

"Fucking do it!"

She jolted again, except this time it wasn't because of Keith. This was all me. She still hadn't moved from the goddamn door, still hadn't looked into my goddamn eyes, and the last bit of my resolve holding me together fucking snapped.

It was loud.

Chaotic.

Taking ahold of me.

I was over to her in two determined strides, gripping onto to her arm, forcefully spinning her around to face me. Viciously taunting, "Do it, Cutie. Tell me… tell me I'm no one to you."

She fervently shook her head, not meeting my eyes. Knowing what would happen if she did. Trying to mask her truths. The pain she was inflicting was unbearable, and I couldn't take it anymore.

Not Keith.

Or her.

Without thinking, I grabbed her chin to make her look at me, but she jerked her face away, fighting me instead. Trying and failing to break free from my tight grasp, stabbing into her flushed skin. But in the end, I won. Our eyes locked. And hers were laced with so much remorse and regret, fresh tears threatening to surface.

"Tell me, Skyler, tell me I'm fuckin' no one to you."

"Please, stop," she whimpered, blinking her eyes. Allowing tears to slide down her beautiful face.

"Tell me."

"Noah, please…"

"Fucking tell me!"

"I can't!"

"Why? Why can't you? Say it. Fucking say it, Skyler!"

All I wanted was to hear her finally express those three little words, those three words that would make everything restored between us. Saving our future was in her hands. It had always been in her fucking hands.

The control I willingly gave her. Sacrificing what felt so fucking agonizing for me.

"Noah, please…"

It was now or never.

This was it.

The moment she would show me her true colors.

"Say it!"

She flinched, her lips trembling. Trying to find her voice, her mind, her fucking heart that I knew was mine.

"Please, Skyler, please…" I begged, ready to get on my knees if I had to. If that's what it would take to finally make her admit she was mine, then I'd do it over and over again. Proving myself to her until the end of time. "Please…"

I shut my eyes, swallowing the bile that rose in my throat. Leaning my forehead on her shoulder for support, I turned my face, laying soft kisses down her neck. I kissed all along her cheeks, kissing away her tears that belonged to me now. Savoring the feel of her against me, all while battling the urge to fall apart. I wrapped my arms around her, wanting her to seek the comfort she needed in my embrace. Return the love I always received from hers.

I held her quivering body in my shuddering arms, physically feeling her soul breaking piece by piece. Every last part of her felt as if it was slipping through my hold and my heart. I slightly inched back, barely brushing my lips along her cheek until our lips were almost touching.

Breathing out against her mouth, "Say it, baby. I know you want to. Please, just fucking say it *for me*."

She swallowed hard and rasped, "I'm sorry, Noah… I just can't."

Immediately making me let her go, her words were like acid on every inch of my skin. I stepped back, putting some much-needed distance between us before I manhandled her the way I suddenly wanted to.

While traitorous waves of betrayal rolled off me, I closed my eyes. Desperately trying to govern my breathing, my thoughts.

My fucking heart.

Fight or die.

Fight or die.

Fight or die.

Opening my eyes, I stared deep into hers. "I went to your house lookin' for ya this mornin'."

Her eyes widened, fueling my urgency to continue. Silently praying it would be the push she needed to let me into her life.

It was my last resort.

I'd have nothing else left in me after this.

"I know what happened to you, Skyler Bell *Morgan*."

Her demeanor quickly changed, and her guard swiftly flew back up.

As if nothing had just happened between us. “You don’t know shit.”

“I know it all. What happened to your family, to your mom. What your dad had to do, saving—”

“Stop it!”

“I read the articles online. Why you had to hide this from the press.”

“Stop! I mean it, Noah! Stop it!”

“No! I’m not gonna fuckin’ stop! After everythin’ I have told you and you know ’bout my life. Why couldn’t you have told me this? I coulda helped you, been there for you like you’ve been for me.”

“Don’t do this, Noah.” She intensely shook her head back and forth. “Please don’t do this.”

“When then, huh? When is a good time? After you move to L.A.? Were you even gonna tell me this time? Or were you just gonna leave me like you always do?”

“That’s not fair! I’m working. It’s my life. You’ve always known this is my life.”

“No shit! I’m just on the back burner for ya, yeah? Like your piece of shit agent said, you just been slummin’ it wit’ the guy from the wrong side of the tracks. Wanted to see how the other side lived?”

“That’s not true! You know that’s not true!”

“Is that right? How do I know that, Skyler? When you keep every fuckin’ thing from me! I don’t know shit ’bout you. Not one fuckin’ thing, when I wanna know everythin’!”

“What do you want from me, Noah?! What do you want me to say, huh? What can I tell you that will make things between us any less complicated than what they’ve always been!”

“The truth! How ’bout you fuckin’ start there? What happened that mornin’ at the river when I saved your life?”

“Stop it,” she gritted out. “I mean it. Don’t you fucking dare!”

I should have listened, I should have stopped, I should have done anything, something other than what I did. What I said. But I was too far gone and at my wit’s end. I couldn’t control my emotions, actions, words, especially when it came to her.

Skyler Bell was my sunshine and happiness.

Skyler Morgan was my darkness and despair.

And they were both attached to the girl who’d always own my soul.

“What were you doin’ in the river? What have ya always been tryin’ to do in that fuckin’ river?!”

“Please, don’t… please, don’t say—”

“Tell me, Skyler! What were you doin’ in the river where your mom fuckin’ died?!”

She instantly covered her ears, catching me completely off guard. Loudly belting the lyrics, "*Tomorrow! Tomorrow! I love ya all the days and nights of tomorrow!*"

Breaking my goddamn heart even more.

"Baby," I ached, reaching for her, but she slapped my hands away. Trying to fight me off. "Skyler, stop! Stop it! Please! Let me be here for you! Stop fuckin' fightin' me!"

"No! You didn't when I was begging you to stop! You didn't fucking stop!"

"Please, baby… I just want ya to let me in! I wanna know who you are! Your family! Your life! Why is that so hard for you to understand? To let me in!"

"I have let you in!" She shoved me as hard as she could, and I barely wavered.

"To what exactly? Your pussy? 'Cuz you comin' in your panties is the only thing I've ever been able to get outta ya." I didn't hesitate, even though the expression on her face told me this was my moment to make things right. To listen to her and stop, knowing this wasn't going to end well.

I didn't.

I couldn't.

I shouted, "I love you! You hear me?! I fuckin' love you!"

She abruptly jerked back as if I had slapped her. "Take it back! You don't mean that. Take it back! Now!"

I stepped toward her, and she immediately stepped back. "Goddamn it! I mean that with every fuckin' bone in my body, Skyler! I. Love. You."

She scoffed in disappointment, shaking her head. "I told you from the beginning not to fall in love with me. From the very start, I warned you! Why couldn't you just fucking listen to me?! You wanted something from me? Well here it is, fuck you, Noah Jameson! You hear me? Fuck. You."

And with that, she turned away and left me.

For what I knew would be the last time.

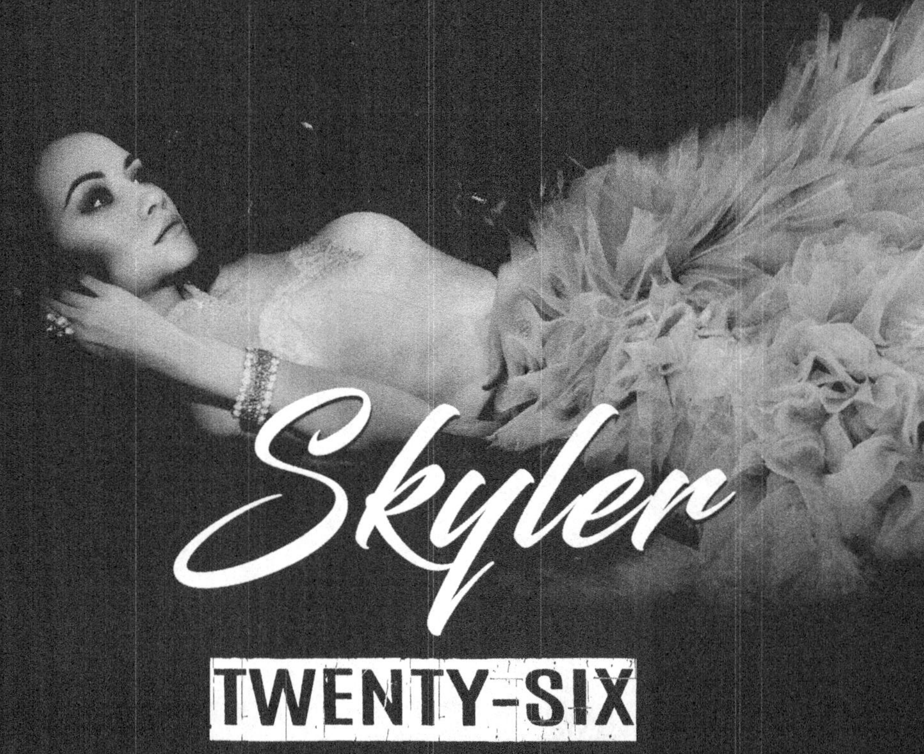

Skyler

TWENTY-SIX

Daddy buckled me into my booster chair in the backseat of his SUV and kissed me on the forehead. I was so happy he was at my Annie *audition today. He got to see me light up the room with my voice that was too big and powerful for my six-year-old body. At least that's what Keith said. Everyone's faces were smiling, all wide-eyed as they listened to me belt out the lyrics with everything I had in me. Like my expression the first time I heard Annie sing on the video the production people said I had to watch before my audition.*

They said it would help me get into character, and it did. Something in my tummy exploded, and I had to sing with all my heart just like Annie. I could tell everyone was super impressed because Keith gave me the thumbs-up, and that always meant I was doing a great job. He was proud of me. I loved Keith, he was my best friend.

My only friend.

He loved me too. He always told me he did. Saying I was like the daughter he never had. And because my daddy wasn't around a lot, always working like me, Keith felt like he was kind of like my daddy too. It was why I was so happy today, because I had both of my daddies there. Oh, and my mommy.

I love them all so much.

I was just so excited we were all together. Since it was usually just me and Keith and sometimes Mommy. But it didn't bother me as long as I wasn't alone, even though I missed them. I loved to work. It made me happy too. Really happy. I got to travel to places most six-year-olds wouldn't be able to go, meeting all sorts of new people at auditions. Get my hair and makeup done like I was some sort of princess. Wearing fancy dresses and costumes with so many sparkles. Living the best life.

All I ever wanted to do was sing and act. Mommy said it's what I was born to do. My God-given talent was to entertain others. It was my special gift, and I was meant to be a shining star.

Just like Annie.

Daddy gave me another kiss on the forehead and told me he loved me, and closed the door. He rounded the corner of the car and tried to give Mommy a kiss on her lips, but she pulled her face away. Mommy looked like she was sad. Why was Mommy so sad? Mommy was never sad. Maybe because I gave Keith a hug after my audition before I gave her a hug. Maybe I should give her a hug right now to make up for it. But Mommy loved Keith, so that couldn't be right.

I watched as she got into the driver's seat, and Daddy got into the one beside her.

"Mommy, what's wrong? Did I do something bad?"

She turned around and looked at me with so much sadness in her eyes, it made my belly hurt.

A lot.

"No, baby, you didn't do anything wrong. You're such a good girl. You're Mommy's angel. I'm so proud of you, Skyler Bell. So proud."

I smiled, feeling a little bit better.

She blew me a kiss. "I love you, baby, so, so, so much."

"I love you, Mommy, so, so, so much."

She lovingly smiled and turned back around, putting her seatbelt on, but Daddy didn't. He never wore his unless Mommy told him he had to. She didn't tell him this time, instead she just started driving.

Maybe I should tell him?

"Emma, talk to me. What's going on?" he asked her, and I pretended like I wasn't listening.

"I can't do this anymore, Daniel. I just can't keep doing this. I can't believe I let this happen. How did I let this happen? How did I do this to our family?" Mommy's hands were gripping onto the steering wheel so tight, her knuckles were turning white.

"Do what? What are you talking about?"

"You're never around. You're never home. I'm raising Skyler on my own. I've raised her on my own. Oh God, I just can't..."

"Emma, you're not making any sense. Calm down, you're swerving

all over the place. Pull over and let me drive."

The car shifted right and left in the lane, and a car horn sounded. I looked out the back window to see a very angry driver waving his fist at us, mouthing some words I couldn't make out.

"Skyler baby, can you do something for Mommy."

I nodded, smiling. Turning my attention away from the mean man, looking at her through the rearview mirror.

"Can you grab your cassette player from my bag and listen to Annie. The tape Keith gave you today so you could practice."

I nodded again, happy I got to listen to Annie so soon. Even though I didn't have to listen to her to know the words, her singing voice was already in my head. Locked in my memory.

Taking off my seatbelt, I slid down my booster and grabbed her bag from the floor. "Got it, Mommy," I said, sitting on the floor to look around for my cassette player.

"Emma, please just talk to me."

"I don't know what to say, I don't even know what to think. I'm so confused, Daniel. I just can't believe I let this happen to us."

I tried to ignore the pain in Mommy's voice, but it made my stomach hurt again. Maybe she didn't like my audition? Maybe I didn't make her proud? Maybe I needed to try harder, work harder, so I could be a shining star like she wanted?

"Skyler, please sit back down and put your seatbelt on," she ordered, making me feel like she was mad at me now.

I nodded again, finally finding my cassette player and tape in Mommy's Mary Poppins bag. The thought usually made me smile and laugh, but I couldn't because my tummy hurt so bad.

"Emma, you're scaring me. I love you. You know I love you. I work my ass off for you and Skyler. You think this life you're adamant Skyler is made to have is cheap? You think it pays for itself? Jesus, between the auditions, flying her back and forth to L.A. every other week, and everything else in between is what? Who do you think pays for all that? I can't keep up with all these bills for a vocal coach and acting classes, and a new outfit for every different audition. Not to mention, Keith. Skyler's jobs don't bring in that sort of money."

I was right.

This was all my fault.

I didn't work hard enough. I needed to work harder. Now they were both disappointed in me...

Bringing the headphones up to my ears, I pressed play on my cassette player. Wanting to hear Annie, hoping she would make me happy again. I would practice for as long as it took to get it right. To make them proud. To make them not be mad at me.

Her voice came alive in my ears, and the same fluttering feeling returned in my tummy. Replacing the pain and the sadness.

As Annie sang, "The sun'll come out tomorrow, bet all those dollars that tomorrow. There'll be sun shining bright and happiness. Just thinkin' about tomorrow."

"I don't know what to say. I just don't know what to say. I feel like I can't breathe, Daniel. I just feel like I can't breathe." Mommy sounded like she was crying.

Now I made her cry, I hated when Mommy cried.

Annie's voice vibrated deep in my bones as she continued singing, "Just thinkin' about tomorrow. Clears away the sadness, the rain, and the emptiness. 'Till it's not there,"

But Mommy's voice vibrated deep in my bones too, when she said, "Oh my God, I did this. I'm the reason you're not around. It's all my fault. I ruined our family."

The car shifted to the right and left again, and was going faster now. Throwing me around. I looked out the window seeing the trees blur by. Closing my eyes for a second to feel the warm sun on my face, hoping my thoughts would go away. My brain battling the song playing in my ears.

"Emma, enough! Pull over. You can't drive. We're going to wreck. Pull over, now!"

"I can't breathe, Daniel... I just can't breathe."

It was my fault. This was all my fault. I ruined my family, not Mommy. I was the reason Daddy worked so much. I was the reason Mommy was sad. I needed to get better jobs and make more money. I had to work harder.

To be a shining star.

With Annie, I belted out, "So just hang on 'til tomorrow and work through the pain!" Feeling better. Annie made me feel better. She was my happy place. She would forever be my happy place.

"Fuck! Emma, watch out!"

"Tomorrow! Tomorrow! I love ya all of the days and nights of tomorrow!" I sang with all my heart, feeling like we were flying through the air. "You're almost there! And only a... day... a.... way!"

"Sky!"

I jolted out of my skin, snapping back to the present. Instantly turning, I placed my hand over my heart. "Jesus, Keith, you scared the shit out of me!"

"I scared you? You should see your face. You look as pale as a ghost.

Are you alright?"

"Yeah." I swallowed hard. "I'm fine."

"What the hell were you thinking about?"

"Nothing."

"Skyler," he coaxed in that fatherly tone.

Though, it didn't matter. I could still hear the desperation in my mom's voice in my mind.

The urgency and fear in my dad's.

The river.

The freezing cold river.

It was as if I'd never left that place and time, where my whole world was ripped away from me in a matter of minutes. I couldn't breathe. Just like her… I felt like I couldn't breathe, because I had never been able to fully breathe again after that day.

I smiled, despite the cold chills coursing through my body. Despite the fact that it felt like I was constantly drowning inside. And up until I met Noah, swimming in that river felt like it was my only salvation. It was the only time I could breathe…

Steady and deep.

In and out.

Rise and fall.

The place that ended one chapter of my life, also started a new one with Noah.

The irony was not lost on me.

Oh, God, Noah.

Memories of our time together came flooding back, playing like a movie reel in my mind. Seeing every smile, every laugh, every sentiment. Feeling every stolen touch, every kiss, every last emotion he pulled out of me. The warmth his arms always provided, the sensation of freedom in his embrace, in his eyes, in each memory he ever shared with me. Hoping, praying, I'd do the same. I wanted to, more than anything.

I didn't.

I couldn't.

Not even for him.

When was the last time I felt any of this?

Would I ever feel it again?

I hadn't seen, spoken, or stopped thinking about Noah since our last encounter in my trailer three weeks ago. Knowing in my heart, in my soul, in every last fiber of my being that it was the end of us, and he did too. I could see it in his eyes, hear it in his voice, feel it in his heart, nearly killing me in the process all over again. I never meant to hurt him, he was never supposed to fall in love with me. *I* was never supposed to fall in love with him. But there was no going back, I did what I had to do. I saved him from the demons on my back, he already had too many of his own.

And now, I would forever be one of them.

Life was all about choices, and I chose mine a long time ago.

To be a shining star...

For everyone, especially my mom.

"It's nothing, I promise," I lied, not wanting to worry him.

I knew how to play this part, this role, this girl—she was a character I'd perfected over the years. One that survived and lived to tell the tale.

"Why are you out here by yourself?"

"Honestly," I shrugged, "I don't really know. I guess I just needed some fresh air. You know all of this is so new to me, and there's so many people in there. I just… it's a little overwhelming."

There I was, standing on the balcony at the home of one of the most powerful men in all of Hollywood. Surrounded by hundreds of people who were just as influential and yet, I'd never felt more alone. Even though my mom had been gone for over a decade, and my father may have physically stayed behind with me, he still died that day, right along with her.

Keith was all I had for years.

Until Noah came along, Keith was the one who had always taken care of me, looked out for me, did everything in my best interest. In my parents' absence, Keith just took over. He was there for me when no one else was. To hold me when I'd wake up from nightmares from that day. To tell me he loved me and wipe away my tears. To lie to me and reassure me everything was going to be okay.

That *I* was going to be okay.

Keith was my family, and I owed him more than I'd ever be able to repay.

"You've always been kind of a loner, Sky." He leaned against the railing, and I followed suit.

Staring back out at the Atlantic Ocean, looking over the city of Miami. "I have, haven't I?"

"You certainly have."

"Why do you think that is?"

"You're an artist, Skyler Bell. You were always meant to do more with your life."

I nodded, watching the waves roll onto the shore, breathing in the salty air.

"When that guy barged into your trailer, it's what surprised me the most. I was more caught off guard that you might actually have a friend," he chuckled, glancing over at me.

"Keith…"

"I know." He put his hands up in the air in a surrendering gesture. "I was out of line that day. I've already apologized to you."

"You have, and I apologized as well. I was out of line too."

"You know you've always been like a daughter to me, and any father would want nothing but the best for you." He brushed the hair away from my face, pulling it behind my ear. "Right now, living in L.A. is what's best."

I nodded. "I know."

"And I don't regret for one fucking second the way I handled that guy, he looks like trouble, Skyler. Go ahead and tell me I'm wrong."

"It doesn't matter. I'm moving to L.A., remember? You're right. You're always right. My career is the only thing that matters. It's what I was born to do."

"Your mom always wanted it that way, Sky." He smiled, "A shining star for all the world to see and love, remember?"

"Yeah. That's right."

"You don't need any distractions right now. Especially one that looks like he'd only ruin your life and everything you've worked so hard for. You don't want to let anyone down, or feel like your mom did with your dad, do you? All they sacrificed for you."

"I know."

"It's better this way. She would be so proud of how far you've come."

"You think so?" I wiped a single tear that escaped my eye with the back of my hand.

"I know so. You're still so young, and you have this amazing career ahead of you, Skyler. You keep listening to me, and we're going to make you the biggest name in the whole world. Everyone is going to know who you are. Exactly how your mom always knew it would be. We do it for her."

I smiled, nodding.

"Here." He handed me his glass of champagne. "It'll calm your nerves. You need to go back inside and mingle. There's a lot of important people in there—directors, producers, major executives. The real deal. You need to be your charming self."

"Okay," I simply stated, drinking down his champagne in one big gulp.

"Feel better?"

"Depends. Is there more of this?" I asked, handing his glass back to him.

"Skyler, you're a big girl. Go get a drink from the bartender. They won't card you."

He was right, they wouldn't. Most of the child actors and actresses in L.A. started drinking by the time they could see over the bar. I was never into that scene, not that it hadn't been there for the taking.

I needed to take the edge off and stop thinking about the things I couldn't change. I just had to keep working, keep busy, keep moving in the right direction of my career.

Keith always had a way of making me feel better, even when I felt at my worst. I nodded again, walking over to the double glass doors.

"Oh and, Sky."

"Yeah," I replied, turning to face him.

"I'm really proud of you too. I couldn't have asked for a better daughter."

I chuckled, "Now you're just being really corny."

"There she is…" He grinned, making me laugh harder. "There's my Skyler Bell. Now, go inside and be that shining star we both know you are."

"Good talk." I winked at him and then beelined it straight to the bar.

After drinking two more flutes of champagne, I started feeling more at ease, more like myself. It clouded all the memories and all the pain. Not allowing my heart to control my mind as I made my way around the room, talking, laughing, putting on the best performance of the night. Dancing with all the right people, schmoozing the rich and the famous. Proving what I could bring to the table.

Somehow, I ended up standing beside Christopher Anderson, who just happened to be one of the executive directors of the best production company in Hollywood. And the owner of this mansion. He was a major power player in the industry who I had suddenly been talking to for the last hour. As if it wasn't a big deal, when it was huge one.

"When does production start for your next movie?"

"I don't know, Anderson. When does production start for *our* next movie? You know, the one you're going to let me audition for and give me the lead role in. Because *I* was just made for the part."

He laughed, throwing his head back. "I like you." Pointing at me. "It's hard to find an actress who still has a personality and isn't trying to kiss my ass."

I lifted my glass in the air. "The booze helps."

He laughed again. "Steven!" Calling over another one of his executives.

"What's up?" he replied, standing beside him.

I tried to stay calm and collected, hoping they wouldn't notice the nervousness I felt inside. Playing it off like I wasn't fazed that now *two* of the most important men in Hollywood were talking to me.

Anderson placed his hand on the small of my back. "You know Skyler Bell, right?"

"Of course." He nodded at me before looking at me. "Your last movie was amazing. You knocked it out of the park with that amazing voice. You've made quite a name for yourself these last few years. And come to think of it, I can't remember the last time I heard a vocal talent like yours. You got quite the gift, Skyler."

"Oh wow. Thank you. It makes all the grueling hours and sleepless nights worth it."

"I bet."

"Skyler here was just saying how she was made for the role of Charlotte in our next movie."

I swear they could hear my heart hammering in my chest as I took another sip of champagne. Trying to calm my overly stimulated nerves. That was the thing about this industry, they could smell fear and thrived on power. At the end of the day, only those who faked it until they made it were ones who stood out amongst the rest.

Bottom line.

I was faking the shit out of my confident demeanor, because this was just another role I perfected over the years.

Steven smiled. "Is that right?"

"Absolutely," I boldly answered for myself.

"Well if Anderson says we need to give you a chance, then I definitely think we can work something out. We haven't worked with a new actress in quite some time. As I'm sure you know, we stick with what works. Same actresses and actors that we know will bring in box office numbers. But, with that said, it might be beneficial for all of us to bring in a fresh face. "

"I agree. I definitely think she has what it takes to play Charlotte. You're young, beautiful, talented. How soon can you read for the part?"

"Skyler, there you are," Keith chimed in, bringing our attention over to him. Handing me another glass of champagne, like he knew I needed it.

Thank God.

"Keith, good timing. We were just telling Skyler how we want her to audition for the lead in our next movie. How soon can we get her in?"

"Skyler's booked in Miami for the next week and then she's flying back home for a few days. She's actually moving out to L.A. and she's packing the last of her things. But once she gets to L.A., she's scheduled out through the month. Everyone wants a piece of Skyler these days," he replied in a proud tone, making me feel less nervousness, as if he knew I needed to hear that too.

"How about we step into my office and try to narrow down a date then?" Anderson responded, causing my heart to beat out of my chest.

"Sounds great," I reaffirmed, smiling.

As we all walked back toward his office, my heart now felt like it was in my throat. And I did the only thing that felt natural to me when I was this overwhelmed. I went to my happy place inside of me, where all I heard was, "*Tomorrow! Tomorrow! I love ya all of the days and nights of tomorrow!*"

Except, I didn't see my mom's face this time like I always did.

The only face I saw…

Was Noah's.

My lost boy.

Knowing, they were about to make me a shining star. Exactly the way my mom always wanted, costing her, her life.

Making me lose myself…

In the process.

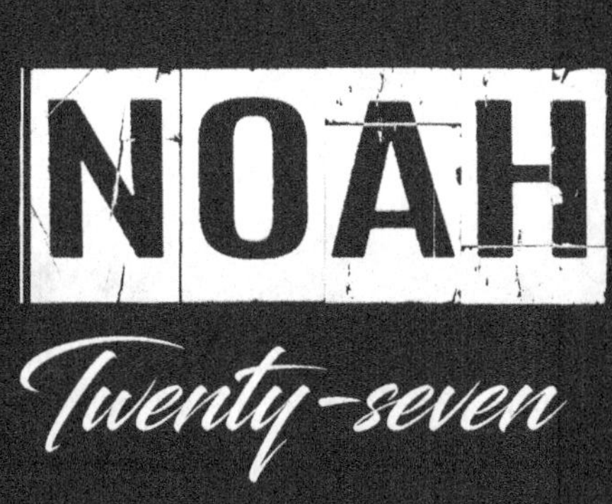

NOAH

Twenty-seven

"Noah..."

I groaned, shaking my head. Stirring awake beneath my white tangled sheets as I faintly felt someone's lips, laying soft kisses down the side of my neck.

"Noah, I'm sorry. I'm so sorry."

My eyes fluttered, trying to wake up, but my body wouldn't allow it, and sleep won out. I was beyond exhausted from spending the day in the hot sun, working on the boat, falling asleep fast and hard as soon as my head hit the pillow. Dreaming only about Skyler. Even in my deep slumber, I could still smell her intoxicating blueberry scent, feel her soft lips along my skin while she pressed her tits against my chest. Her wet mouth making its way down my torso.

"Noah, will you be with me? Please, can you just be with me?"

"Mmm hmm," I hummed, feeling her lips trail toward my stomach.

Kiss by kiss, she pecked every inch of my heated skin until she reached my happy trail. Making my cock twitch at the heady feel of her mouth so close to my dick. I fisted my sheets, wanting, needing, her lips wrapped around my cock.

When I felt her delicate fingers start to tug the waistband of my gym shorts down, whispering, *"Please, just be with me."* My breathing hitched and my eyes snapped open, big and wide. Coming face to face with the last person I expected to see, hovering above me.

Skyler.

There was no way I was still dreaming, but if this happened to be a dream within a dream, then I never wanted to wake up. In that moment, the world stopped spinning, stopped moving, and time just stood still for us. It had been over a month since I last saw her, a month since she walked out on me, leaving me in her trailer with nothing but my love for her.

Even with the dim lighting in the boat, I could still see her glossy eyes like she'd been crying. Her sunken cheeks and dark circles were only emphasized by the moon casting shadows on her distraught expression. Her disheveled hair partially covering her face didn't help.

She looked fucking beautiful and tortured all at once.

My demons may have been silenced by her presence, but Skyler's were very much alive and present in the space between us. She was willingly showing me what she had been trying to hide for so damn long. For so many years, I wanted to see this side of her, and now that I finally was…

All I could feel was her agony, blocking out all of my other senses.

I couldn't form words.

I couldn't think.

Not when she was looking at me like that, scaring the fucking shit out of me.

Intently staring into my eyes, searching for something in my stare. As if she was looking for some recognition of who I was, or maybe traces of who she was when she was with me. Skyler may have physically been there with me in my bed, but emotionally and mentally, she was somewhere else entirely. Somewhere deep inside herself. A place she visited often. And without words, she was confessing all the broken parts of her, all the deepest wounds, all the oldest scars. Sharing her sadness and despair, and above all else, the damage it left behind.

Down to the bottomless depths of her soul.

"Baby…" I muttered, my voice laced thick with uncertainty and concern.

"Shhh…" She leaned forward, placing her lips close to mine. "Just be with me, Noah. Please…" Her eyes watered, fighting back the tears. "I just want you to be with me. Can you do that for me? Please…" It was her pleading tone that shook me to my core as a single tear slid down her beautiful face.

The next thing I knew, she was kissing me. Beckoning me to do the same. "Sky—"

"Shhh..." she murmured against my mouth. "Just be with me, Noah. Please, just do it for me."

My mind battled my heart, raging a war I never had a chance to survive. It was her loneliness that was fucking eating me alive, swallowing me whole. Making me want to seek refuge within her, and that was when it clicked and I understood. She came to me for the same fucking reason.

So I did what I had to do, what felt right and so fucking true.

I kissed her back.

My heart breaking for her, piece by piece, crumbling to the ground as I made up for all the times I needed to feel my mouth against hers. For each tear, each regret, each moment we needed one another, but weren't there for each other. For the past we couldn't change and the future we so desperately wanted together, but there would forever be an endless number of obstacles in our way.

We kissed, and kissed, and kissed some more.

We kissed until none of that fucking mattered, until it felt like we were simply breathing for one another. Until all that was finally left...

Was us.

Noah and Skyler.

The way it was always meant to be.

Knowing deep down in the goddamn pit of my stomach this wouldn't change anything between us. I wanted what she would never be able to give me.

Her.

All of her or nothing. And yet, here I was...

Chasing away her demons while she was just becoming another one of mine.

I grabbed onto the back of her neck, bringing her closer to me as if she wasn't already close enough. Not having a fucking clue where this was going, but I was there for the ride nonetheless.

Sitting up gradually, I flipped our bodies over, so I was now lying on top of her, yearning to feel her beneath me. Resting my arms by the sides of her face, I started lowering my frame onto her petite, trembling body. Cherishing every second our lips moved against one another. Our mouths starving for affection, aching for warmth, longing to lose ourselves inside each other.

"Be with me, please, just be with me, Noah," she panted in between kissing, reading my mind.

I didn't have to be told again. Reaching for the hem of her dress, I slid it off her body, leaving her in nothing but her panties and distress.

So exposed.

So vulnerable.

So goddamn afflicting.

With a predatory regard, I devoured every inch of her bare skin. From her rosy colored nipples, to her perky, supple tits, down to her narrow, slender waist, and her luscious ass and thighs.

"Jesus, baby, you're fuckin' beautiful," I painfully groaned, slipping off her panties before crawling up her body. Spreading her legs for me, I laid in between them. Kissing her all over again.

Her lips, her cheeks, the tip of her nose, down to the sides of her neck. Kissing, licking, caressing my way toward her nipples, while my callused fingers coasted along her smooth, silky fucking skin, trailing all over her naked body. Following the moon's light shining in the cabin, casting shadows over what was really happening here tonight.

The addictive fucking sounds she was making.

The way her body kept shuddering beneath mine.

The smell of her fucking arousal.

Had me losing my goddamn mind.

I flicked, sucked, slightly bit her nipples, driving her wild with need. Working my way toward where I wanted to be the most, I peered up at her through the slits of my eyes.

Rasping, "I've wanted to tongue fuck your pussy for as long as I can remember." With a sly grin, I pulled down my gym shorts, freeing my hard, thick cock.

Her eyes widened, taking in the size of dick while I jerked it in my hand. Never once took my eyes off hers as I sparingly skimmed my lips over her bare heat.

"I been fistin' my cock for years, just thinkin' 'bout the way you'd taste, when I finally made ya come so fuckin' hard in my mouth."

She swallowed hard, her chest rising and falling, waiting, eager, ready…

"You gonna come for me, Skyler?" I taunted, drinking in her wet, pink flesh for the first time. "Prettiest fuckin' pussy," I breathed out against her clit.

Her thighs clenched and cunt ached.

Grinning, I nudged my nose along her folds, faintly blowing the entire time. Gradually, lightly, running the tip of my tongue over her clit. Hearing her breathe, heavy and deep. Feeling the sweat glistening off her roused body.

Her cunt was warm and so fucking soft.

I fisted my cock, faster and harder.

"I've barely licked you and your legs are already shakin' for me. This what you want, Skyler? This what you came for?"

"Please," she begged in a breathless tone.

"Here?" I baited, tenderly kissing her nub. Resisting the urge to growl when I tore my eyes away from her pussy to look up at her face. Huskily ordering, "Watch me, baby."

Our eyes connected, and I let go of my cock and gripped onto her thighs instead. Locking them in place at the sides of my face, putting her exactly where I fucking wanted her.

"You gonna watch me eat the fuck out of your pussy like a good girl?" I licked my lips. "Yeah?"

She rocked her hips, arching her back. Making my cock twitch for what felt like the hundredth time.

"Say it."

"Yeah…"

As soon as I sucked her bright red clit into my mouth, she moaned loudly.

"Good girl."

I savored the taste of her, the feel of her, as her legs tightened around me. Sliding my finger into her tight little hole, I gently, purposely, started finger-fucking her sweet spot. Getting her nice and ready to take my cock.

I devoured her, lustfully lapping up and down, side to side. She'd be nothing after this. Exactly like me.

So fucking wet.

Tasting so fucking good.

Her pussy throbbed.

Her body shook.

"Noah," she panted, over and over.

Coming in my fucking mouth, again and again.

"Noah, please…" she begged for mercy, but I didn't stop. I couldn't.

She consumed me.

From my mind, to my soul, to my goddamn cock.

A rumble vibrated from deep within my chest, fully aware that this would never be enough for me.

How do I forget about her after this?

How do I let her go? I was finally making her mine.

I was trying to save her from herself, but I was fucking destroying myself in the end. It should have mattered, but it didn't. Because I was taking what had always belonged to me.

Her.

"Noah… I can't… I can't come… any... more…"

"One more, give it to me, Skyler."

And she did. Squirting down my face and chest.

But even that wasn't enough for me. I was like a man possessed, licking her fucking clean. Thrusting my tongue into her opening, unable to get enough of her.

Craving it all.

Every last drop of her come.

I relentlessly kissed her overly stimulated clit one last time, causing her to shudder once more. Before I crawled my way back up to her lips, kissing her as if my life depended on it, making her taste herself. Needing her to realize that no other man would ever be able to claim her like this.

Snarling into her mouth, battling new demons. Conscious that these might actually have the power to take me under.

Finally put me to ground.

I imagined another man's mouth on her, his hands on her, his cock inside of her.

"Skyler." I placed my forehead against hers, gazing into her eyes. For the first time in my life, I couldn't fight them on my own. "I can't do thi—"

"Please, Noah… just be with me… please…" she urged, in the same yearning tone, with the same desperate look in her stare.

And I was a fucking goner.

There wasn't a chance in hell I could say no to her.

I belonged to her.

She owned me.

Every last part of me was hers.

Taking a deep breath, I peered deep into her eyes. Searching for my girl.

My sunshine and happiness.

"Please, Noah… please."

I hesitantly nodded. "I can go as slow as you need."

She kissed me, lifting her hips. Silently demanding me to keep going. When I didn't move fast enough, she reached for my dick and wrapped her hand around my shaft. Causing my breath to hitch against her lips and my dick to jerk in her grasp.

"Fuck me," I scoffed out, biting her bottom lip.

"Just be with me, Noah. That's all I want." There was no hesitation on her part, placing my cock at her entrance. I slowly inched my way in.

Sliding inside of Skyler's pussy was as excruciating as the realization that even after I claimed her innocence, there'd be no us.

"Stop thinking, Noah, and just be with me."

My plaguing thoughts refused to let me go. I tried like hell to just get lost in the sensation of her by just taking a moment once I was fully inside of her. Paying close attention to the expressions on her face and the responses of her body.

They were so blinding and almost unbearable.

She was on the brink of tears, and I'd be fucking lying if I said I wasn't there as well. Seeking the depths of her soul, I pleaded with no words for her not to go.

For her not to leave me behind.

I couldn't make her stay.

I wasn't enough to make her want to stay, and that hurt like a thousand fucking knifes slowly carving, *"He's nobody,"* into my flesh, slicing away at my skin.

"Skyler…" I started thrusting in and out of her. "I lov—"

"I know. Trust me, Noah." She kissed me again. "I feel it all too." Gradually rotating her hips, adjusting to the size of my dick. Shuddering in pleasure as I engulfed her body with mine.

She was so fucking tight.

So fucking warm.

So fucking perfect.

Something just took over me, my body completely moving on its own accord. Grasping that I was making love to someone for the first time, and a huge part of me knew it would be the last. Skyler mirrored my same thoughts, and our bodies began moving like we were made for each other.

While our new demons danced together in the room.

"My cock belongs inside of you. Promise me… please, baby… that no matter what happens or who comes along, you'll always remember that you're mine, yeah?"

Tears escaped her eyes, sliding down the sides of her face. She nodded, moaning, "Yeah."

Our mouths parted, both of us panting profusely, unable to control the thoughts that were wreaking chaos on our souls. Frantically trying to cling onto every sensation of our skin-on-skin contact.

Never wanting this moment between two broken beings, connecting as one, to end.

We were two sweaty bodies, swimming in a pool of emotions, of mistakes and regrets, of the pain of tomorrow and every day after that.

She gasped the second she felt my fingers rubbing against her clit. While I picked up the pace of my assault on her core. Thrusting in and out, biting, nipping, tonguing her neck. Driving her further and further to the edge, about to fall over…

For me.

"Noah… right there."

"Where baby, here?" I coaxed, my dick aching to come balls deep inside of her.

"Oh, God… yes… right there…"

Hitting her g-spot, her moans got louder and louder. I claimed her lips, muffling her screams as she came all down my shaft.

Squeezing the fuck out of my cock.

"You're so fuckin' wet," I groaned, thrusting.

Harder.

Faster.

Deeper.

"You okay?"

"Yes… don't stop… please don't stop."

"Come on my cock, Cutie. Come on my fuckin' cock like you know I love."

"Noah…" She pulsated, and her sweet pussy sucked my cock fucking dry.

I came so hard, I saw stars. My body shuddering right along with hers. Both of us going over the edge together, where I could barely see straight. Our pleasure didn't last nearly long enough until the pain took over. Feeling her silently break down, her body trembling in my arms with tears cascading down her face. Falling onto the sheets we just made love on.

"Shhh… Skyler… shhh…"

We stayed like that for I don't know how long, in our safe haven that may have turned into our hell. It felt as if an eternity had passed between us, and yet it still wasn't enough time with her.

Never enough time.

Kissing all over her face again, I slowly, unwillingly, pulled out of her, causing her to wince from the sting of my cock. "I'll be right back." I kissed the tip of her nose and got up, going straight into the bathroom.

Needing a minute to myself for what I wasn't prepared to face. My emotions held me hostage while I cleaned myself up. Failing miserably at trying to keep my shit together.

I took a deep breath, dampening a washcloth and made my way back into the room. She was in the exact same position I left her, staring up at the ceiling. Lost in her own thoughts with my white sheet wrapped around her naked torso. Before she knew what I was doing, I was in between her legs again. Except this time, I was cleaning her up.

She peered up at me with fresh tears in her eyes, biting her bottom lip.

Overwhelmed and disheveled. I closed my eyes, I had to. Unable to look at her any longer, even though she had always been my favorite fucking thing to look at. The next thing I knew she was kissing all over my face, wrapping her arms and legs around me, seeking the comfort she needed in my embrace. Before she broke the fuck down.

I kissed her, softly pecking her lips, taking my time with each stroke of my tongue as it tangled with hers.

I tasted her tears.

And she tasted mine.

Once I opened my eyes, I saw every goddamn sentiment I felt through her gaze. She was allowing me to see her again, her walls were down, her flag was up.

She surrendered.

To me.

To us.

"I'm sorry, Noah… please know that. Please know that I never meant to hurt you." More tears slid down her tortured face, and I kissed those away as well. "I wish I could be the girl you want me to be… the one I am when I'm with you, but I can't."

We locked eyes.

"I thought she died with my mom in that river. And for years, I searched for that girl in there, but I never found her. *You* did... instead."

I jerked back, never expecting her to share that with me. Learning right then and there that Skyler Bell was my beginning… And now the time had come for our end. I just didn't know what hurt more, the fact that this was our ending. Or the fact that she hadn't been…

A virgin.

TWENTY-EIGHT

"Happy twenty-second birthday, Skyler Bell!" my friend and fellow actress Melania exclaimed, blowing into her obnoxious party horn. Standing out in front of me, provocatively dancing to the beat blasting from the speakers. Springing up like she had just jumped out of a damn cake. Shaking her ass, singing, "Happy birthday to you," in a seductive voice.

I laughed, smiling as she continued her performance. Peering around her, taking in the suite full of people who were there only for me.

"Motherfucking Vegas, baby!" Eli shouted, kissing the side of my face. Taking a seat beside me on the couch, he pulled me into his side and kissed my forehead. Letting his lips linger for a second.

Eli was my on-again/off-again… whatever for the last few years. Someone I had fun with. Case in point, it was why he was in Vegas with me tonight.

Leaning forward, I grabbed the rolled-up hundred-dollar bill off the coffee table and brought it up to my nose. Snorting a line of cocaine up each nostril. Instantly jerking my head back, sniffing harder. Handing the bill over to Melania next, while I wiped away the residue with my index finger. The last thing I needed was the press snapping a photo of me with white powder on the tip of my nose.

Oh, the scandal.

I giggled at the thought, immediately feeling the drug drip flow down the back of my throat. Just another thing to add to the endless list of bad choices I'd made since leaving Southport. Since leaving… *him*.

The second it hit my bloodstream, I was alive and thriving. My heart rate accelerated, my face felt numb, and I was ready for a good fucking time, celebrating my twenty-second birthday at the hottest nightclub on the strip. Getting paid a shitload of money to party at their club with my entourage of celebrity friends. I couldn't ask for a better birthday.

Spending it with my fans meant everything to me.

"Baby, you should see your eyes right now. They're so fucking stunning," Eli rasped against my lips, grabbing my hand and pulling me off the couch to stand in front of him. Gripping onto my ass. "You look hot as fuck. You're not even wearing a bra or panties, are you, you dirty little girl?"

I cheekily smirked, "The sacrifices I make in the name of fashion."

"Fashion?" He started rubbing his goatee against the side of my neck, making me giggle. I tried breaking free, but he made it nearly impossible. Squeezing my ass harder, locking me firmly in place against his chest. His cock jutted to break free from his slacks, digging into my core. Causing my stomach to flutter and my pussy to throb.

Cocaine and sex always went hand-in-hand.

"You're wearing a jeweled piece of fabric that leaves very little to the imagination, Skyler Bell. I'd hardly call that fashion, more like a fucking cock tease."

"Tell that to Valentino then," I chuckled as he continued his shenanigans. "Eli, stop! You're going to ruin my makeup! And my glam squad already went down to the club!"

Biting the tender flesh at my neckline, he grinned up at me with mischievous dilated eyes. "Then you should have worn a different dress."

"Oh. My. God!" Melania chimed in. "Are you guys going to do this all night?"

"Yes!"

"No!" we answered at the same time. "Eli, stop! Please!"

"Baby, I love it when you beg."

"You're relentless!"

He bit me again. "Only when it comes to you."

"Oh yeah?" I jerked my head back. "What about every other model that's been seen on your arm in the last month while I've been overseas finishing up my album, huh?"

I'd spent the last few weeks in Europe, working alongside renowned composer Xander Brideau. Finishing up the last song on my debut album releasing next week. It was a dream come true to not only work with some of the biggest names in the music industry, but also have the chance to release an album on my own as a solo artist. Contrary to the movie soundtracks I was featured on in the past.

It had been years in the making. I spent hours upon hours in the studio, coming up with sounds, lyrics, vocals. Narrowing down the complete vibe I was aiming for. Recording each song over and over again, until it was absolutely perfect and felt just right. There was nothing that compared to the feeling of putting on a pair of headphones, stepping up to the mic in the sound booth, and belting out every word that came from my heart and soul. Purging my feelings in an almost therapeutic way. Most of the songs on the album were personal to me, in one way or another. From life, to growing up, to falling in love, to heartbreak. Writing became an outlet for me from…

Everything.

It was how I survived over the last four years, specifically the last two and a half. The way I coped after leaving a huge part of me behind. Music saved my soul after I destroyed it. I even titled my album *Safe Haven* for the refuge it provided, in place of the guy I hadn't seen or talked to in a very long time.

Noah Jameson.

With every year that passed, the more I thought about him. Particularly on our birthday. Turning into the second hardest day of the year for me, the first being the day my mom died. The third was every day after that.

Daily, I resisted the urge to call Noah. Though on our birthdays, the desire to hear his voice and know how he was doing intensified tenfold. Knowing in my heart and gut, down to the depths of my being, there was no future left for us. I lost any chance of reconciliation with him the day I chose a different path in life. The wrong one.

Without him.

Eli murmured in my ear, making me jump out of skin. Bringing me back to the now, "They don't count, because you're my favorite," tugging me away from the ghosts of my past.

"I'm not a model."

"You should be. Especially in this fucking dress."

I laughed again, I couldn't help it. He was adorable.

Eli and I met randomly at a Vanity Fair party about two years ago in Paris. I was standing by the bar, talking with some friends, when a man in his late twenties strutted up to me all James Bond like, cocky as hell. Signaling to the bartender for a straight bourbon, eye-fucking the shit out of me.

My breathing picked up when he suddenly stepped toward me, closing the gap between us. Using the back of his fingers to brush the hair away from my face as he took a sip of his drink. Before he seamlessly leaned forward, holding my hair behind my ear and whispered, *"Would you like to come?"* His intoxicating bourbon scent mixed with his musky cologne, lingered in the air.

Making me lock eyes with the first man that held my attention since Noah. Who no matter what, would always hold me captive. I was stuck in the past, with him.

With us.

"Where?" I'd breathed out, trying to stay in the moment with Eli.

He grinned, slowly licking his lips and simply stated, *"In my mouth."*

I had to give him props for originality. He made me laugh, and it was what I needed. Although, he wasn't the man I wanted, it still felt good to laugh, to smile, to feel lust in place of the pain. I knew it wouldn't last, but for the time being, it had been a distraction from the lonely world I'd created. Eli and I had a mutual understanding—no strings attached, no jealousy, no bullshit drama, and to only have fun together.

It worked.

We worked.

However, the press loved making us out to be something we weren't. It probably didn't help that anytime we were seen together, we appeared to be Hollywood's *It* couple. All the tabloid magazines claimed we already were.

"Eternal playboy and self-made millionaire Eli Ward, was seen vacationing with Hollywood's highest paid actress, Skyler Bell. Has she finally tamed the infamous player?"

"Is Hollywood's It Girl, Skyler Bell, just another notch on notorious bachelor, Eli Ward's belt? He can't seem to keep his hands to himself when she isn't around."

"Will Forbes most eligible bachelor, Eli Ward, ever settle down with Hollywood's shining star, Skyler Bell?"

Our relationship status was always the first question the paparazzi harassed and hounded me about. Reporters, on the other hand, didn't breach the subject due to my management team screening their questions prior to accepting interviews. I kept my life as private as I could, given the fact I was an A-list celebrity and soon to be double platinum artist. At least that's what Keith kept telling me.

"You ready, birthday girl?"

"For what?"

"To sit on my face."

"Eli!" I slapped his arm.

He laughed, "Alright later, *yeah*?"

I froze from that one word alone. Dragging me back to another place and time, where I was in the arms of the boy who stole my heart and never gave it back.

Not that I wanted it back either.

It was his.

I was his.

"Eli, let me go." I abruptly pushed off his chest, unable to breathe again.

"Skyler—"

"I mean it, let me go!"

He did, grabbing my face instead. "Hey… hey… hey… what just happened?"

Tearing my face out of his grasp, I grabbed the hundred-dollar bill off the coffee table and sat on the couch again. Snorting two more lines of blow up each nostril. Immediately finding the air I needed to breathe.

"Promise me... please, baby... that no matter what happens or who comes along. You'll always remember that you're mine, yeah?"

I did another line, and then another.

"Whoa, birthday girl." Eli snatched the money out of my hand. "I'm all for having a good fucking time, but that shits barely cut, Sky. Take it easy. You still have to walk the red carpet and deal with the press. You're the belle of the ball tonight, babe. Pace yourself, yeah?"

"Stop saying that! Where did you even hear that?"

"Hear what, baby?" He genuinely looked confused, and I immediately felt bad, but he'd never used the word *yeah* before.

How was I supposed to know it would trigger something inside of me to respond this way?

"Never mind." I shook it off. "I'm just overwhelmed. You ready to go?"

He crouched down in front of me, setting his hands on my bare thighs. "What's going on? Talk to me, Sky."

"No drama, remember? I'm fine."

"For the last two years I've known you, your birthday always seems to be a hard day for you. Did something happen? You can talk to me. We're still friends, baby. I care about you. You know that, right?"

I nodded.

But did I?

That was the thing about this industry, what fucked with your mind more than anything else. I never truly knew who wanted to be seen with me because of what I could offer, with notoriety, with money, with fame.

Everything in life came with a price.

And I found out what mine was two and a half years ago…

"Come on, we're good." I stood, pulling him up with me. The cocaine finally doing its job, numbing my emotions exactly how it always did. "Who's ready to fucking party?!" I shouted to the room full of people.

They screamed in response.

I winked at Eli and grabbed his hand. Not giving him a chance to continue searching for answers to questions I didn't want to discuss.

By the time we arrived, the entry line was around the building. Along with swarms of people standing out in the street in front of the club, waiting for my arrival. A two-block radius stacked with fans behind barricades, chanting my name as I walked up to the entrance with my arsenal of bodyguards surrounding us. There were people in every direction I turned, waving to all of them around me. Showing my appreciation to each and every one of them for coming out tonight.

Before someone on my team could stop me, I hurried toward the fans who were behind the waist-high gates. Signing autographs and taking pictures with as many fans as I could in a short amount of time.

"Come on, Skyler," my publicist Lisa coaxed, grabbing my arm.

I hated when my management team did this, pulling me away from my fans when they were the only reason each of them had a job to begin with.

"I'm sorry! Thank you so much for being here! I love you all so much!" I hollered, blowing kisses to the crowd.

"Sky, you can't keep running off like that. It's not safe for you or your guards," she chastised, shifting my attention over to her. "How many times has Keith told you to stop doing that? You're putting everyone's life at risk, especially yours."

I rolled my eyes. "Keith isn't here. Relax."

She shook her head, sighing in defeat. Quickly leading me toward the press junkets as the paparazzi unceasingly snapped photo after photo of me. Making it extremely hard to see with all the blinding, flashing lights coming from all directions. It was almost impossible to hear anything with the jumbled voices of photogs and fans, yelling over each other to get my attention.

"Skyler, are you and Eli back on?!"

"Skyler, Eli was cheating on you while you were in Europe! How do you feel about that?"

"Skyler! How does it feel to be twenty-two?!"

"Skyler, you look amazing! You ready for your album to drop?!"

"Skyler! Eli is using you! Can we get an exclusive?!"

I smiled, regardless of the persistent badgering from the paparazzi that I was used to by now. Everywhere and anywhere I went, they followed. Shopping, eating, the movies, the gym… it was endless and the fuckers had no boundaries. Everything was fair game to them, including causing car accidents just to get close to me when I was driving. I couldn't even go to the bathroom without it being turned into some headline news. They were borderline stalkers, with no laws in L.A. to stop them or protect us from them.

So, I just put on my happy face and waved to the crazed sons of bitches like a good girl, playing the role of Skyler Bell. Besides, if I showed my true colors and told them to mind their own fucking business like I always wanted to, they would just get the reaction they feen for. Like the bloodhounds they were. Selling the footage and pictures of my outburst to tabloids, media gossip sites, and so on. I'd end up making them thousands and thousands of dollars for the "money shot" of my meltdown.

"Alright, the only reporters you'll be answering questions for—" Lisa interjected, reading off the agenda in her hands "—are Access Hollywood, Entertainment Tonight, E News, the Insider, and Extra."

I nodded, and walked the red carpet. Stopping for more photos, more questions…

More.

More.

More.

Nothing was ever enough.

"How does it feel to be at the height of your career?" An E News reporter asked at my last interview of the night.

"I feel beyond blessed to be living out my dreams. I'm a very lucky girl."

"You're so young and you've accomplished so much already. What's next after your world tour for the album?"

"I actually have some scripts I'm reading over right now so I can jump back into film."

"Your tour is scheduled for over twelve months and you've been working nonstop for years now. You won't be taking a break? Some down time for yourself maybe?"

"No break for now." I smiled. "But it's better for me this way. I'm at my best when I'm with my fans. They're my home."

The female reporter beamed. "You're so lovely, Skyler Bell. Don't ever change. It's why you're Hollywood's shining star."

"Awe, thank you so much. I love what I do, it doesn't feel like work to me. It's what I was born to do."

"Can you give us some insight on your personal life? Your family stays behind closed doors. Any reason for that?"

"My dad's just a good ol' southern boy at heart. I see him often, but he doesn't attend events with me. He watches them if they air on television though," I lied, playing it off. It was easier that way.

The truth was I saw my father less now than ever. Phone calls were few and far between, and forget about emails, they were non-existent. I sent him money every month to help him get by without so much as a thank you. Sometimes the checks were cashed, other times they weren't.

It didn't matter how many plane tickets I'd send him on a whim, for birthdays, holidays, award shows, anything and everything. They'd never get used, and I hadn't flown back to my home since the last time I witnessed firsthand the consequences for my actions.

He wasn't even in the audience when I won my first Academy Award or my Golden Globe. On the rare occasions we did talk on the phone, it was mostly short, one-sided conversations. But at least I had peace of mind and could say I was checking up on him, not the other way around.

As the years gathered, collecting one by one, so did my resentment for him. Growing more and more each day. Every time I needed him and he wasn't there for me, and I wasn't just talking about the monumental moments.

Keith was still all I had in my life, even more so now. He was my only family and support system, and to this very moment, I'd *still* be lost without him.

I answered a few more questions for E News, finishing up the last round of pictures before we were ready to head inside.

The manager of the club greeted us and introduced himself, "Hi, Miss Bell. I am Andrew, the GM of the club. If you'd come right this way, I will personally escort you up to your reserved section." He took my arm in his and led my team and I through the back entrance away from prying eyes down a long empty corridor. My usual bodyguards fell in place, surrounding us, with some extras the club assigned solely for this event. We followed him into a private elevator, up to a reserved, secluded area that took up half of the second floor.

With crystal-clear vision, I scanned the open space from the plush, white leather sofas lining the entire back wall. Set further back from the prying eyes of fans were tables stocked with nothing but the best drugs and finest liquors and mixers money and fame could buy.

My entourage and Eli were already up there, awaiting my presence—drinking, smoking, mingling while I worked before I played. Getting the festitvies started and on their way as the bottle hostesses introduced themselves. Stating they were our exclusive hostesses for the entire night and would get us "anything" we wanted with a nod and a wink. I didn't have to worry about shit being leaked to the press, not when everyone associated with me had to sign a non-disclosure agreement, including my celebrity friends.

For the next hour, we danced, drank, and partied like we were in our own little bubble. Laughing and living life to the fullest. Money was no object. I had more than I knew what to do with. Thanks to my fame, I had the world at my fingertips and no one said no to me.

But even with all that…

I still felt more alone than I ever had before.

Money, fame, power, they couldn't buy happiness, love, or the life I really wanted beside the only guy who ever made me feel complete.

I did another two lines of blow, trying to forget about everything besides dancing. Swaying my hips to the beat of the music as I stood against the balcony railing, watching the people dancing below through dilated eyes. Riding the high for as long as I could.

Hours…

Days…

It all blended together.

The crowd in the club got louder, heavier, deeper.

It was warm, but I suddenly felt cold all over, chills stirring down my spine. Closing my eyes, I reeled in the emotions, the feelings, the unforgiving memory that had forever made a home inside my mind. Trying so hard to not let it takeover, but failing miserably at doing so.

I could never fight it and a huge part of me knew I didn't want to. I could still see it all as if it was happening right now in front of my eyes, right at this very moment, instead of two and a half years ago.

Where I lost everything I ever wanted, but didn't think I could have until…

It was too late.

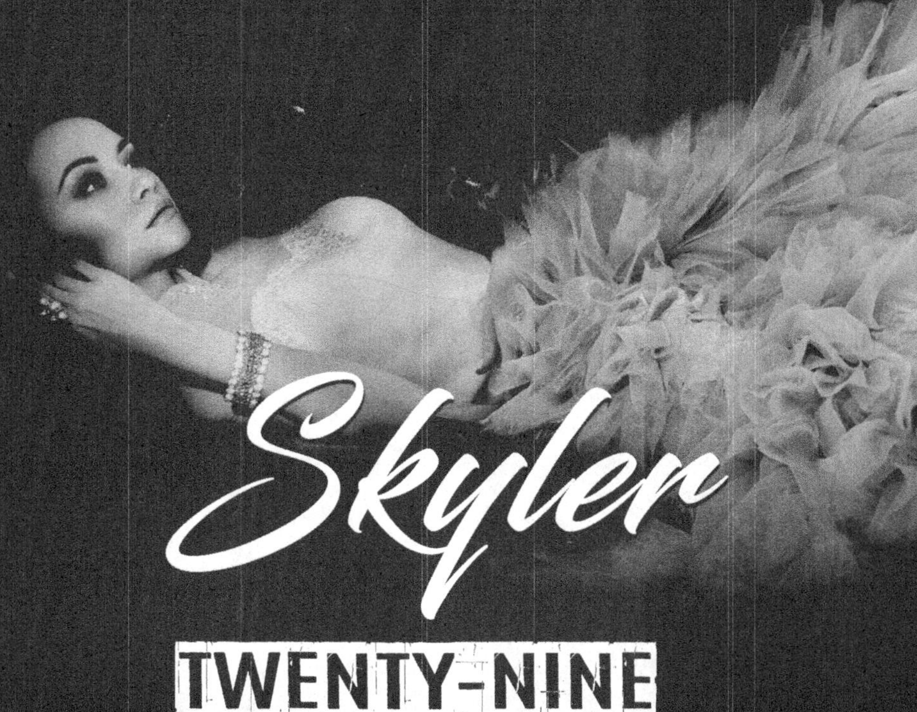

Skyler

TWENTY-NINE

I jumped in my rental car and sped the entire way from the airport to his boat. Swerving and veering through traffic with a heavy heart and a guilty conscience. Going over what I would say in my head, ready to plead for his forgiveness, for his love, for his heart that I felt down to my bones, was still mine. I couldn't live without him any longer.

Not then.

Not now.

Not ever.

I loved him.

I fucking loved him.

I was finally going to say those three little words he begged me to express over a year and a half ago. At nineteen years old, I finally let go of the notion that my career was everything, my life, but he was more. He'd always been more. I was ready to let him into my world, my secrets, give him everything he ever wanted from me. Praying it wasn't too late, I wasn't too late.

Every single day had been another day of sorrow and unrelenting sadness. Another day I had to walk through a life of chaos without him. My boy was gone, leaving nothing but a hollow shell of a woman, a lost girl trailing behind.

Since I left him and moved to L.A., I couldn't breathe, because he kept my last breath.

My last tear.

My whole heart and soul.

The closer I got to his boat, the more my head raced with thoughts of what to say and how to say it to him. Needing... wanting... to openly show him all my pain and my remorse. All the love I had for him grew with each passing day I'd spent without him. Whatever it took to make him look at me the way he always had.

Always seeing the girl I no longer thought existed.

I didn't care how we would make it work. Where there's a will, there's a way.

And he was my will.

He was my way.

I pulled in at Davidson's marina and was out the door before fully shifting my car into park. I bolted out of the driver's seat as fast as I could because all that really mattered was getting to him.

I ran.

I fucking ran for my life that was in that boat. Hauling ass through the parking lot, breathless and winded by the time I stepped onto the deck.

Ready to give him everything left inside of me.

"Noah! Noah, I'm here! Please tell me you're in there too?!" I questioned out in pure desperation, needing him to know I was finally emotional and mentally in the boat he wanted to make us a home.

Immediately sliding the door open, coming face to face with the damage I'd regrettably done when I left him behind. In two seconds flat, my whole fucking world, the life I yearned for, came crashing down on me.

"Oh my God," I breathed out, placing my hand over my mouth as I slowly gazed around the demolished space.

All the hours of hard labor he put in for months and months on end, was destroyed. Like he took a sledgehammer to the interior, taking out his anger the only way he knew how. With fresh tears in my eyes, I carefully walked through the destruction on the floor of what used to be his home, our home he was building us.

Trying to take in everything from the splintered wood floors, to the broken shards of glass, crunching under my feet. To the cushion stuffing thrown everywhere, and the fabric torn to shreds like he ripped it open with his bare hands. The light fixtures hung from their sockets with broken bulbs still attached. The kitchen cabinets swung from their hinges, practically falling to the floor. All the custom countertops were carved with unreadable script. Except the word...

Nobody.

Before I knew what I was doing, my fingers were tracing the big, bold letters. Smacking me right in the face. Remembering those hurtful words from years ago I once spewed in my trailer. "He's nobody, alright?! He's no one to me! Now just let me handle him! Please, Keith! Just go!"

"Oh, god, Noah. What did I do? What the fuck did I do?" I pleaded to no one but myself.

The place looked like a hurricane had torn through it, leaving Noah's havoc in its path.

It nearly brought me to my knees as I reached the bedroom, where he made love to me. The last place and time I saw him. The door creaked open, revealing the shambles of the room that we lost ourselves inside one another. The mattress was completely overturned, while the white sheets we were tangled in were ripped to shreds. The feathers from the pillows clung to every surface, cut open with a pocket knife by him. Clothes were thrown everywhere around the cabin, hanging from the broken closet doors, and blanketing the shattered mirrors on the ground.

Unable to hold it in any longer, I sobbed uncontrollably into the white shirt he always wore. Gripping onto the only thing that was left of his presence in this safe haven we'd created that night. I searched the cabin for I don't know what when my glossy eyes stopped on the tool responsible for it all. Just as I thought, there was a sledgehammer sitting on top of the devastation I created. Instantly making me realize this was the last room he destroyed and there might not be any hope for us after all.

I shook my head, feeling disgusted with myself for what I'd put him through. The bile rising in the back of throat with every unforgiving thought that crossed my battered mind. I didn't deserve his forgiveness, his love, him, but that didn't stop me from still wanting all of it.

Backing away from the wreckage, I sought refuge in his shirt that I took with me as I left. I drove to his home in a much different state of mind than I'd started with. At the last second, I decided to park my car a few houses down from his ma's when I noticed his motorcycle was in the driveway. Aware that he more than likely wouldn't want to see me, not after what I just saw. At this point, the only option I had was to catch him by surprise.

I swallowed hard with each step that brought me closer to his home, and possibly closer to my own demise. Praying he would at least talk to me. Hear me out. Give me a chance to make things right between us. I didn't care if he only wanted to be my friend, I just needed him to be in my life. My eyes wandered everywhere, trying to drown out the insecurities which had swiftly seized my entire core.

My feet moved on their own accord as soon as I saw him through the open front window and screen door. I hid behind a huge tree by the side of his house, closest to where I could see in, but nobody could see me. Just wanting a minute to take him in, powerless to take my eyes off of him as he moved about the living room.

I closed my eyes for just a second when I heard his husky voice resonate deep within my entire being. Causing old feelings to resurface, stronger than ever. Ready to take me under if needed.

Once I opened my eyes, I found him standing so close yet so far away. Looking out into the yard as if he could feel my heart beating for him. He looked as good as I remembered, standing tall with that mischievous smirk I fell in love with as a young girl. Covered in more tattoos, wearing his cut, and standard combat boots with jeans.

I smiled despite the way I felt inside. Missing him so much.

So, so, so much…

Except it wouldn't be his warm welcoming arms that wrapped around me this time, devouring me with his comforting musky scent, I loved more than anything.

Taking a deep reassuring breath, I breathed in through my nose and out through my mouth. Shaking off another insecurity. "You can do this, Skyler. Don't be afraid, you can do this. He loves you. He's always loved you." I went to step forward, stopping dead in my tracks when I heard a car door slam shut from the road in front of his house. Turning toward the noise, I immediately froze. A girl I'd never seen before, wearing a long white flowy dress, was walking toward the front door, with what looked like a picture in her hand.

"What the fuck?" I whispered to myself, trying to figure out what the hell was going on.

She knocked on the door, gazing back at the front yard. Like she was watching some sort of memory play out in front of her. I couldn't help but narrow my eyes and take her in. Instantly noticing how much she resembled me. Her bone structure, the color of her eyes, her pouty lips, her long brown hair, even her figure was petite like mine. This girl could be my sister.

Noah opened the door before I could give it or her anymore thought. Smiling big and wide at her. Showing her the same smile that he always had for me. No one else, but me.

My heart fucking dropped.

I swear I stopped breathing.

Everything played out in slow motion right in front of me. Though at the same time it all happened so damn fast.

He greeted, "Hey, pretty girl," moving aside to let her in.

Causing her to shyly smile, and look down at the ground as she walked by him.

"I like your dress." He grinned, eyeing her up and down with that familiar stare that was once only mine.

Is this what it feels like to die?

As soon as their eyes connected, his playful spark shined so fucking bright for her.

Killing me all over again.

"Thanks," she replied.

With that unforgettable Noah Jameson swagger, he cocked his head to the side and licked his lips. Baiting her. "You get dressed up for me—" A car drove by muffling the rest of what he said.

She smirked. "Don't flatter yourself, Rebel. I wanted to look nice for your momma."

I don't know what killed me more, her calling him Rebel. Him saying that same line, those same exact words to me once. Or the fact that she was meeting his mother. When he never introduced me to her...

After everything we went through together, everything he shared with me, everything I witnessed.

Not. One. Time.

In over four years.

My eyes shut on their own as I leaned my hands and forehead against the side of the tree for support. Feeling like my body was giving out on me. Trying to reel in the emotions that were ruthlessly breaking me.

Bit by bit.

Limb by limb.

Layer by layer.

Stripping me of everything...

Bare.

Exposed.

Vulnerable.

While hiding behind a tree, in front of the man's house I thought I knew. Now brutally questioning if what we had was real, or if I was just another girl to him. The thought alone made me sick to my stomach, my mind telling me one thing and my heart pleading to believe that I was his everything. Except I was the one who left him. I was the one who pushed him away, and now I was the one watching him move on.

This was my doing.

I did this.

No one else, but me.

"Don't need to put on a dress to accomplish that," I heard him say. Stabbing my heart harder.

Deeper.

Firmer.

Over and over again...

I opened my eyes, continuing to watch my worst fucking nightmare unfold in reality.

She bashfully smiled just for him, her cheeks flushing, replicating the very expression on my face when he would talk to me like that.

But it wasn't until she sassed, "Are you going to show me around or just stand there and flirt with me?" that I wholeheartedly knew, right then and there, he might be falling for her because he once loved my smartass mouth too.

Placing my hand over my heart, I desperately tried holding it together. Undeniably failing at doing so. The dagger wedged in my heart was twisting, refusing to let me go. The pain unbearable, merciless, never-ending. Swallowing me whole, but never spitting me back out. I couldn't breathe, gasping for my next breath he was denying me, without even knowing it.

Suddenly remembering my words from years ago, "I need you to promise me something, okay? Please, please don't fall in love with me," wishing I could turn back the hands of time. Warn my past self, tell her what she should have done in order to prevent what was happening now. Save myself from what I was witnessing right before my tear-stained eyes. Hoping things could have been different.

We could have been different.

There was a time and place for everything, and there was always that one instant, that one second, where time just stood still. Though nothing could have prepared me for what happened next.

Not him.

Not me.

Or our love.

He hammered the final nail into my coffin when he confessed, "It ain't flirtin' if you've already slept with the girl," Noah teased, but the joke was on me. Because he gently placed his hand on her growing belly, she was hiding under that beautiful white flowy dress this entire time.

Fucking killing me completely.

I thought I left him behind in the room we made love in, realizing for the first time that day, he left me there too.

Ending me.

Ending us.

That night I learned a cruel lesson. Love didn't come to me as heartbreak, it came to me as everything I've ever wanted. Where walking away wasn't an option, until it became the only choice I had. I made the wrong decision the first time I left him over four years ago when we were almost eighteen, but I sure as hell did the right thing the second time around, when I left him two and a half years ago with *her*.

Ultimately finding out what the price of fame cost me.

I lost the love of my life the moment he unknowingly showed me he was making a new one with her and their unborn child. Where walking away was the right decision, the only option.

For him.

For us.

For them.

Giving him the chance to have the family he always longed for, the future he always deserved, but never thought he was good enough to have.

Even after everything had been said and done between us, that life didn't include me. Becoming just another demon that lived inside of my heart.

"Skyler, baby," Eli whispered in my ear from behind, drawing me back to the present when my mind always seemed to be stuck in the past.

"Hmm…" I hummed, leaning into his embrace.

"It's almost midnight. The D.J. is calling you."

"Oh, right." I smiled, nodding to my guards who were waiting to escort me over to the stage. Snapping right back to the shining star I was always destined to be.

As soon as I was standing in the booth beside the D.J., he shouted into the microphone, "Skyler Bell is in the house! Who's ready to sing 'Happy Birthday' to her?! You ready?!"

The crowd went wild, and I breathed it all in. Feeling their energy, their love, their excitement for having me there, celebrating my birthday with them. Replacing the memory that would infinitely haunt me.

They all broke out in song, while the orchestra the club hired to play "Happy Birthday" performed along.

When they were done, everyone started chanting, "Sing! Sing! Sing!"

I laughed, throwing my head back. Appreciating that they once again saved me from myself without even knowing it.

"It's not in your contract to perform tonight," Lisa muttered from behind me. "You weren't paid for that, Sky."

I didn't pay her any mind. Grabbing the microphone from the D.J.'s hand, I yelled, "How are you doing, Las Vegas?!"

"Skyler! Skyler! Skyler!" they repeated, hooting and hollering with huge smiles on their excited faces.

"I'm so happy and thankful to be here, celebrating my birthday with you all! But what was that? I don't think I heard you correctly. Did you say you wanted me to sing to you? Is that what you were saying?"

"Sing! Sing! Sing!"

I caught Eli's expression from the balcony as they continued on, he was laughing and shaking his head. Fully aware I was going to give my fans what they wanted. Not giving a shit I wasn't getting paid for it. It wouldn't be the first time I performed with no pay, and it wouldn't be the last. I didn't sing for the money, I sang for my fans. For me. It was the air I needed to finally be able to breathe for however long it lasted.

Beaming from head to toe, and without any thought, I blurted into the microphone, "Alright! Who's a Radiohead fan?!"

The club went crazy, losing their shit as I walked over to the orchestra on the stage, behind the D.J. booth. "Can you guys help me out? You know the song 'Creep'?"

"Of course," one of them answered.

"Perfect! I want to give it a new spin. You think you can give me a bluesy beat and tempo for the song?"

Their eyes lit up, loving my idea.

I smiled, mouthing, "Thank you," and turned back around. Hushing the crowd with my index finger against my lips as the stage lights dimmed. Dragging me to a deep, dark, depressing place. The state of mind I needed to be in to pull off this song. I waited until my fans silenced and all that could be heard was the first verse of the song that I softly rasped a cappella. Recognizing immediately why I'd chosen this song.

It was always *his* favorite.

The orchestra quickly followed, making me close my eyes to the soft strum of the melody, getting lost in the lyrics and the power music always held over me. Soothing my tortured soul. My sensations running wild with everything that was going on around me.

The crowd.

The alcohol and drugs.

The memories that came rushing back at warp speed because of this song. Battling to keep my emotions in check and the thoughts that attacked the forefront of my mind at a rapid pace.

One right after the other.

Refusing to let me go.

I channeled it into my performance. Strumming out the harmony perfectly, allowing the sound waves from the band's instruments to bury themselves deep into my chest, into my vocal cords. Making itself at home inside of me. Contemplating how the words to this song reflected my life and how much I could relate to them. How much this song affected me, even after all this time.

All these years.

The emotions bleeding off of my voice, my God-given talent with no end in sight. Each word, each lyric, each high pitch, each low pitch…

Each.

Each.

Each.

I belted out the pre-chorus, my body shaking, shuddering, roaring to life. Becoming one with the ballad, expressing my agony, my mistakes, the past I could never change, no matter how much I yearned to or how much I prayed. Vanishing in the symmetry of the words and the rhythm of the tune.

The intensity of the stringed instruments pulled at my heart, mimicking my own sadness and despair, I conveyed it effortlessly through the microphone. The natural vibrations of my body guided me to the only other home I'd ever felt solace in.

Music was my peace.

I sang like it was my last show, as if my life, my happiness, my world depended on it.

For a moment, I was finally free from the demons that chained me beside Noah and his new family.

I instinctively opened my eyes, still singing to a jam-packed room of people. A faceless crowd, all except for the one person I'd never forget. The one soul that was eternally connected to mine.

Was I imagining him?

Was this really happening?

Was he here, for me?

Question after question flew through my mind with Noah undoubtedly…

Staring back at me.

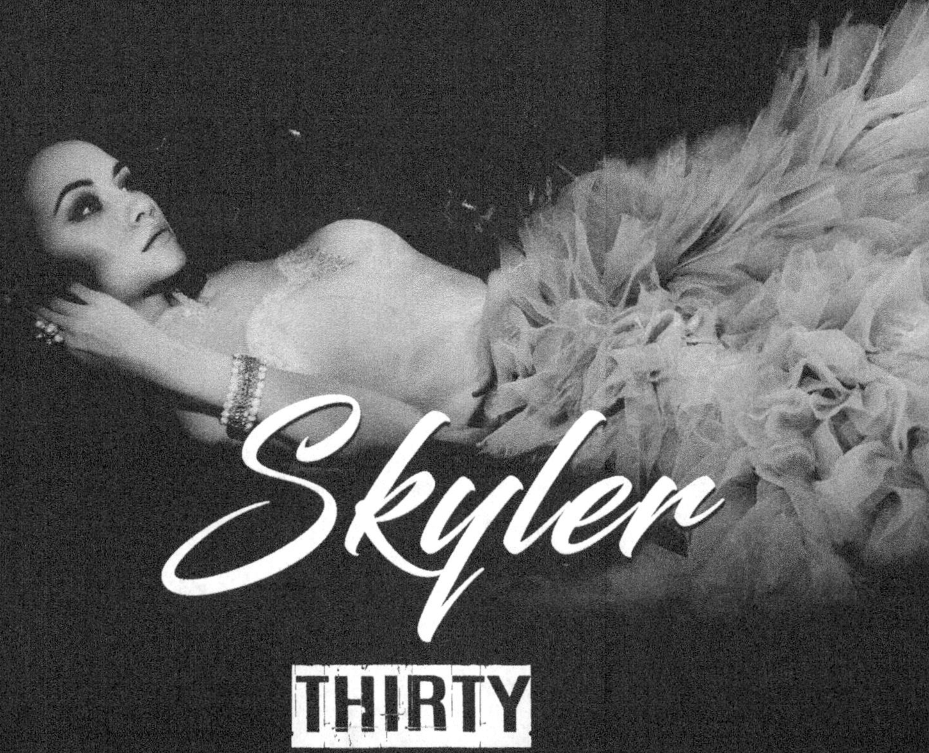

THIRTY

Before I knew what was I was doing, a familiar desire came over me. A magnetic pull, pushing me toward him. My feet started moving, abruptly making their way up the stage, to the long, narrow staircase. All I could hear was the music and my voice, and all I could see was him and nobody else. I didn't contemplate the repercussions of me stepping into the crowd, not when he was standing right there, right in front of me. Where I could feel him, breathe him in, finally see him up close.

He was really here.

For me.

Only for me.

The guards didn't waver either, clearing a path for me to walk through, ushering fans out of the way and holding them back as a sea of arms reached out to touch me. Never once breaking our connection, we gazed deeply into each other's eyes, as if the hundreds and hundreds of people around us simply disappeared into thin air. Everything faded out, the lights, the club, leaving only the music and us.

There was something excruciating about the way we looked at one another, from the way he watched me gravitate toward him, to the way I belted out the chorus with every last piece of my shattered heart. Fueled by an uncontrollable craze for the man I loved and lost. Each stride felt like it was burning a hole in the floor beneath me. Only adding to the longing to touch him, embrace him, be with him.

Not just now.

But forever.

And all the days in between.

I sensed it in my blood, throbbing through my veins, stirring a piercing sting in my mind, behind all the heartache and heartbreak.

Three steps…

Two steps…

One.

I hummed the jazzy verse, with an edgy rasp, *"You're so very special to me, I wish I was special to you."* My voice effortless and defined. Smooth like silk but so raw and so real, giving myself chills. *"Oh... oh... she cries, and she cries, crying out."* Reaching for his hand, I set his warm palm on the center of my heated chest, right below my throat. Placing mine over his, aching for him to feel me through the lyrics of the song. Knowing the only way he could was by touching the source, feeling my misery and distress seeping through my skin for all I had done to him.

His lips parted.

His breath hitched.

He felt it.

Because he finally felt me.

I projected the high pitch chorus from deep within my core, deep within my soul, *"But I'm a creep, I'm this weirdo. This fucked up person. I don't know what I've been doing here, what the fuck have I been doing here?!"*

We could see them, feel them, breathe them in, the memories of us. Where I pretended he was mine, knowing all along he truly was.

His face…

His eyes…

His body…

Recalling how they felt on top of mine.

His lips…

His tongue…

His arms…

Consuming me all over again.

The expression on Noah's face was somewhere in between pleasure and pain. His blue-green eyes burning into my flesh with a slight smile from feeling my pain. The two conflicting emotions going fist to fist, punch by punch, till one of them won.

Pain.

My voice dropped to a soft tone, as did the piano when I started singing the outro, *"Whatever makes you happy... I just want you to be hap-*

py… I don't care if it hurts…" My body fell forward, almost bringing me to my knees as my vocal cords strained to convey and exude the words that meant so much to him. Singing with everything I had left in me, *"I can't belong here, I'm not supposed to be here! Without you!"* hitting that high note perfectly. Breaking down all my walls. All my barriers. Everything I ever placed in between us, leaving only my love for him.

Quivering.

Trembling.

Shuddering.

Until there was nothing left inside of me.

Once again, staring deep into his eyes, I faintly rasped the last verse of the song. Lastly saying those three little words the only way I knew how, *"I'm a creep, I'm a weirdo, but I love you… I always loved you…"*

Noah didn't hesitate, he grabbed my hand that was still over his on my chest and tugged me toward him. Engulfing me in nothing but his whiskey, cigarette, and fresh, clean scent. Wrapping his arms around me, pressing me close to his solid, muscular frame.

He breathed out into my ear, "Hey, Cutie," causing shivers to course throughout my entire body.

My heart pounded against his chest, to the point I knew he could feel it because I could feel his too.

And finally, after all these years, after all this time, and all the memories… I felt him.

Felt us.

Home.

My eyes watered, soaking up this moment for as long as I could. But when the crowd began cheering, it was like a bucket of freezing cold water was poured on top of my already frenzied, heightened skin. Everything came back full force. The fans surrounding us, the bright, flashing lights above us, including the fact that I wasn't there alone.

My entourage…

Eli.

Noah didn't know this life.

I jolted as soon as I heard the D.J. shout into the microphone, "Now that was one hell of a fucking performance! Give it up for Skyler Bell and this monumental moment!"

In a matter of seconds, the guards sprang into action by grabbing me before chaos erupted and things turned crazier than they already were. Then *I* already made them. Ripping Noah away from me in the process.

"No! He's with me!" I shouted over the noise, panic rapidly taking over. "Let go of me! He's with me!" I broke free, running and grabbing his hand. Pulling him along as the guards did crowd control.

They steered us into the elevator, and the minute the doors closed, Noah and I locked eyes again. He was standing across from me, leaning up against the steel wall with his arms crossed over his chest. Silence filled the small space between us as his eyes drank me in and I couldn't help but do the same. He looked better than I remembered. Older and more defined. He'd always been big for his age, though now he was massive. Wearing his signature white shirt that emphasized every last muscle of his solid chest and sculpted arms, like he lived our years apart at the gym.

Gone was the boy I fell head over heels in love with, and in his place, stood the man he'd grown up to be. Covered in more tattoos, sporting fully colored ink from his neck, down to the sleeves of his arms and hands. Only accentuating his bad boy, I-don't-give-a-fuck kind of look that only Noah could ever pull off.

My mouth watered and my thighs clenched.

He grinned, reading my body language with that same predatory regard. Making me remember the last time I saw that expression on his face. It was geared toward a girl that wasn't me. Carrying his baby.

I winced. It was quick, but he saw it. I opened my mouth to say something, however shut it just as quickly. Terrified of what might come out. We hadn't spoken in over four years and there was so much I wanted to ask him, but I was too afraid to hear what he'd confess. So I forced a smile, adverting my gaze toward the guards leading us back to my table instead.

As we rounded the corner, I was completely side swiped when Eli rushed over to me and picked me up off the ground. "Goddamn, babe! Your voice never ceases to amaze me!"

"Eli—"

"Oh. My. God, Sky! You fucking killed it!" Melania chimed in, tugging me away from Eli. Handing me a drink. "I can't believe you didn't tell us you were performing!"

"I wasn't sup—"

"Who's that?" Her focus drifted toward Noah, who was now glaring daggers at Eli.

What about the girl?

His baby?

Are they no longer together?

Eli didn't even notice, he was too busy socializing with everyone around us. Always the life of the party.

"Hi, I'm Melania," she introduced herself, holding her hand out in front of her. "Sky's single best friend." She winked.

I rolled my eyes as Noah shook her hand before nodding over to me, he replied with a grin, "I'm her number one fan."

A sly smile slowly crossed my face. The memories of all the times he said that to me appeared in the forefront of my mind. "More like borderline stalker."

He let out a throaty laugh, making my stomach flutter. I couldn't help it. Him being here right now with me, brought back so many mixed emotions. Feeling like that teenage girl all over again.

"Oh, that's so sweet," Melania enticed, rubbing his arm. "Maybe you'd like to be my fan too."

"Melan—"

"Come on, birthday girl," Eli interrupted me, turning my body to face him. "Let's go celebrate your performance with you snorting a rail off my dic—"

"Eli!" My eyes snapped back to Noah, hoping he didn't hear him.

Fuck he heard him.

He stepped forward with his fists clenched at his sides, his nostrils flared, his jaw tense. I knew that look, and what was about to go down if I didn't stop him. I moved out in front of Noah's intimidating stature, towering over mine. Softly placing my hands on his broad, rock hard chest, halting his descent.

I shook my head, begging him with my eyes. "Please… the press. If you start something, it will be on the front cover of every magazine in a few hours. Not to mention all over social media. Please… *for me.* Do it for me."

After a few seconds, he reluctantly backed off, but his murderous glare shifted from me, toward the piles of cocaine on the table.

"Noah—"

It was his scrutinizing stare that rendered me speechless. Cocking his head to the side, he took me in again, except this time there was a baffled yet concerned expression spread across his face. Directed at the woman standing in front of him, who he still thinks left him behind.

I bit my lip, feeling his apprehension as he searched for the girl he once knew. The one he saved at the river all those years ago. The same one who stole his heart with her voice, singing about tomorrow.

His sunshine and happiness.

I held his gaze until the sensations became too much. Redirecting my attention back over to Eli, but it didn't matter. I could still feel Noah's stare burning into every inch of my body.

What happened that brought him to Vegas? Was his family here too? Did I get this all wrong? But why would he be looking at me like that?

Maybe he was just here for closure?

Countless questions rambled through my mind, and I wasn't going to get any answers still standing here with Eli.

Placing my hand on my stomach for effect, I lied to him, "I'm not feeling that well. I think I'm just exhausted and may have overdone it with the drinking and everything else. I'm going to call it a night and head to my suite."

"Fuck, babe," he exclaimed in a shocked but worried tone. "Let me grab my blazer, and we'll head on up."

"No." I shook my head. "Don't do that. I'm fine. I just want to be alone. Stay, enjoy the night. Go find some aspiring model or actress to sleep with," I nervously chuckled, saying it more for Noah's sake than his.

Although, in Noah's eyes, nothing would make having a fuck buddy versus a boyfriend any better, but I still chose the first one. Hoping it would at least derail his pissed-off demeanor aimed at Eli and me.

Nope, not even a little.

If anything, it only intensified.

I should have known better. Eli was as perceptive as they come, it came with the territory when you were a jack of all trades. His eyes wandered toward Noah, and the tension was suddenly so thick, you could cut it with a knife. But without any hesitation whatsoever, Eli walked over to him in three confident, determined strides. Making my eyes bulge out of my head.

"I'm Eli." He held out his hand. "And you are?"

My heart started beating its way up to my throat. The pulsating red, blue, and green club lights blurred by while the house music muffled in my ears as Noah took one look at his gesture and scoffed at him. Through the slits of his eyes, his lethal glare deliberately zeroed in on me, like we were the only two in the room.

He spitefully answered him, speaking with conviction, *"I'm nobody."*

Knocking the fucking wind right out of me.

Skyler

THIRTY-ONE

"Who *are you* to her?" Noah followed up, nodding over at me where I stood as frozen as ice.

"What I am to Skyler is none of your business."

Noah maliciously grinned, stepping up to him. "Is that right?"

"No!" I jumped in between them, placing my hands on Eli's chest to back him away. Feeling Noah's fury now geared toward me.

This was déjà vu all over again, except we weren't seventeen, and Eli wasn't Keith.

"He's Noah. *My* Noah," I simply explained for him. Loud enough for Noah to hear me.

The expression on Eli's face quickly softened, recognizing the name I called out in my sleep sometimes. Usually when Noah haunted my dreams, turning them into my worst nightmares.

"Jesus Christ, baby, he looks like a fucking serial killer."

I scoffed out a chuckle, "I gotta go, okay? Cover for me."

"Sky—"

"Please. He doesn't know anything about this life, Eli. I just want a few hours alone with him. No bodyguards, no press, no *Skyler Bell*, alright? Please," I whispered with pleading eyes.

After a long, exaggerated pause, he sighed and hesitantly nodded. "If you don't text me before dawn, little girl, I'm going to assume he fucking kidnapped you or killed you. Because he sure as shit looks like he wants to do one or the other."

I shook my head. "He won't hurt me."

"Then you better make sure I know you're alright, or I'll have no choice but to involve Keith. Understood?"

I nodded.

"Let me hear you say it, Skyler."

"Yes, I will text you when I'm back in my suite, *Daddy*."

"Fuck me… I could get used to you calling me that."

I smirked.

"Now get out of here before I change my mind, and look at my phone to make sure he's not on America's Most Wanted list."

I laughed, I couldn't help it. "Thank you."

Noah's demeanor hadn't changed as I made my way back toward him. He stood taller, crossing his muscular arms over his chest. His eyes void of any emotion, never wavering from mine. Pulling me in with an invisible chain, shackled to my heart. This must have been what his opponents saw right before he went in for the kill. A snake about to strike his prey at any second, quivering from his venomous stare.

With each step, I felt more vulnerable and exposed, unsure of how to proceed or where to even go from here. Our relationship had always been complicated, and if tonight proved anything at all, it still was. Distance didn't make the heart grow fonder, it stopped time, making you relive the years apart at dangerous speeds. I met his stare, wanting to believe my boy was still in there, hiding behind the bad choices I'd made.

My eyes didn't wander from his as I reached over and grabbed his hand, trying to ease his thoughts that were wreaking havoc on both of our minds. "Noah—"

"Not here."

"I know, but—"

"Not. Here," he gritted through a clenched jaw and turned around, taking me with him.

There was no uncertainty in his stride, as if he knew the protocol for how to escape unnoticed. Making me question what the hell he'd been up to since we last spoke. Once the coast was clear, he led me into a private stairwell located at the back of the club, I didn't know existed.

"Noah, I can't—"

He jerked around, getting right in my face. "What, Skyler? Can't be seen wit' me? Can't leave your coked-out crew? What the fuck can't you do now?"

I grimaced, feeling the years of his pent-up aggression firing shots at me. Just another thing to add to the list of faults. He wasn't making this any easier with how to advance from the past. Not that I could blame him.

"I was just going to say I can't walk down those stairs in these heels."

He glanced down, taking in my six-inch stiletto pumps I angled to the side for him to see. "I'll break my ankle."

Relief washed over his features, and without another word, he let go of my hand, leaned forward, and picked me up by my waist. Throwing me over his shoulder like I was a ragdoll.

"Noah," I huffed, pressing my hands on his upper back so I could look around. His strong hold tightened behind my knees to keep me locked in place. My ass right in his face. "You can't carry me down all those flights of stairs."

"Watch me." He started down the steps. "I ain't no pussy like your fuck buddy back there."

"It's not what you think."

"Keep tellin' yourself that, Cutie. Guys like him only snort coke off whores' asses and tits. He must think pretty fuckin' highly of ya, yeah?"

"Wow." My mouth flew open. "Well, you must think pretty fucking highly of me too. Now put me down!"

He spanked my ass, hard.

"What the fuc—"

He did it again, harder. "Don't fuckin' cuss."

"Are you kidding me?! You can throw low blows my way, but I can't swear? That's bulls—"

His hand shot up in the air, instantly silencing me from another slap I didn't want on my ass.

"Once upon a time, I fucked Skyler Bell too. Along with hundreds of other dicks. And the funny thing is, I wasn't her first. So now, I call it how I see it."

My eyes widened, winded and dismayed. "Jesus Christ, Noah," I breathed out, unable to form words. "I- it wasn't- I- just- wow…"

"You didn't think I'd notice? Oh, come on, baby. I've always noticed everythin' 'bout you. Includin' the fact that you're not wearin' any fuckin' panties right now. But I wasn't the only man to notice that, we could all see your cunt from the stage. Quite the cock tease these days, yeah?"

They say vengeance doesn't make you feel better. It was a lie. Noah was getting off on this.

"It's not what you think."

"You keep sayin' that. So why don't ya tell me the truth then? Cuz I'd love to finally fuckin' hear it."

Letting out the breath I didn't realize I was holding, I murmured, "I've made mistakes. I have regrets, but you were never one of them. I...

damn... I don't know what to say that will make anything okay between us." I shook my head, frazzled. "Put me down! I want down now!"

I couldn't think straight being held captive. I needed some space to clear my head. I wanted to see his face, read his expressions, watch his lips move, but he didn't budge. Instead, I felt his breath and nose begin to skim up the back of my thigh, lifting my dress.

He inhaled deeply. "Why would I do that? When your pussy is so close to my mouth?"

"Is this why you're here?" I blurted, not holding back any longer. "To humiliate me? Insult me? Fuck me? Are you for real?"

"Stop pretendin' you don't like it. Your pussy is already so fuckin' wet *for me*. I can practically taste you on my tongue."

"You arrogant bastard! Put me down now!"

"You mad cuz you didn't get to celebrate by snortin' blow off your fuck buddy's cock?" He abruptly set me down, holding me upright in front of him, while I regained my footing. Baring his gaze into mine, he eyed me up and down before stopping at my pursed lips. "I'll make it up to you." Peering up at me through the slits of his eyes, he spewed, "I'll let ya snort it off mine."

I thrashed around, trying to get away from him. Never imagining the pain of seeing his face again would be far worse than when I left him. His words were like a fist to my heart. The worst part of it all, was he intentionally wanted to hurt me and was fully succeeding at tearing me a part.

"I'll put ya—" he backed me up against the wall, caging me in with his arms "—where I fuckin' want ya."

I stood taller, not backing down. "So what, Noah? You haven't been with anyone since I left yo—" I halted, I couldn't bring myself to say it, knowing this was all my fault.

He was being this coldhearted bastard toward me because I made him that way. I did this to him. Breaking my resolve a little bit more.

"Finish that fuckin' sentence, Skyler, and you'll have your answer."

I wanted to scream at him, yell I came back for him, that I'd made a mistake and tried to make it right. But it was too late, *I* was too late. It was resting on the tip of my tongue, to shout at him I knew about her, about their baby. That I witnessed him starting a new life without me and it killed me inside…

That *he* killed me.

And up until I saw him in the club, until he held me, until this very moment with him standing in front of me with so much hate and so much love at the same time, I started living again.

Though it wasn't until he viciously stated, "It's alright, baby. I don't know 'em, but I fuck 'em like they're *you*," I snapped.

With my heart pounding and my ears ringing, I forcefully shoved him as hard as I could. He staggered away far enough for me to pull back my fist and cold-cock him across the face. His head whooshed back as I cried out, "Fuck!" Instantly shaking my hand. "Oh, shit… I think I broke my hand. Ow…" He went to grab me, but I moved. "Don't touch me! You made me break my goddamn hand!"

"Cutie—" He paused to rub his jaw from the sting of my unexpected blow, and for some reason it made me feel better. "Let me see."

"Oh! Now, I'm Cutie again? A second ago I was just a whore."

"I just wanted to feel your lips wrapped around my cock. It's the least you could do on my birthday, don'tcha think?"

My chest heaved when I raised my other fist to punch him, but he caught it mid-air. Tugging me toward him. "How 'bout you use this hand for the only thing it's good for. And I don't mean fightin'.

"Do you want me to use it to take off my stiletto and shove it up your ass?"

He let out a low laugh, grabbing my injured hand. "Open and close it for me."

I reluctantly did what I was told, hissing the entire time. It throbbed. He carefully bent my fingers back and forth, and then slowly flexed my wrist up and down before he cupped my entire hand in his to form what looked like a proper fist.

"You punch like a girl. You gonna come at me like a man, then learn to hit like one."

I glared at him.

"It ain't broken, it's just sprained." With that, he simply stepped back and picked me up by my waist again, throwing me back over his shoulder.

"What the fuck—"

Smack.

Smack.

Smack.

Smack.

The son of a bitch had the balls to spank me even harder. Not once, but four damn slaps to my bare cheeks in the same spot.

"Keep cussin', and you will have a permanent reminder on your ass."

"So this is how it is now, Noah? You treat me like shit and manhandle me?"

"Why? Is it makin' your sweet pussy wanna come on my face? Cuz I could eat, I'm fuckin' starvin'."

"Are you kidding me?!" I pounded on his back as he carried me through a long, dark, narrow hallway that led to an emergency exit. The house music bumping on the other side of the wall. "I would never let you touch me again!"

"Is that right?"

"Yes! You're an assho—"

My legs wrapped around his waist, and I was backed up against the solid wall before I even saw it coming. My back collided with a hard thud, knocking the air out of my lungs. With one firm grasp, he had my wrists pinned above my head and the other gripped onto my ass. Pressing his dick into my bare core with his mouth so close to mine. Immediately feeling as though I was about to be in a wreck, waiting for the impact.

"I could *fuck you* until you begged me to stop right now," he rasped, slowly licking his lips. Grazing my sensitive skin in the process, sending a cold shiver straight down my spine.

Get it together, Skyler.

"So tell me, baby… how many cocks have been inside of you, makin' you come like mine?"

My chest rose and fell with each word that fell from his lips. Only making him hold me tighter.

To feel him…

"Not nearly as many pussies you've made come with yours."

He grinned, rubbing the tip of his nose with mine. Purposely bringing back all the memories this loving endearment provoked in me. My stomach somersaulted like old times, making me weak in the knees and heavy in the heart. If he hadn't been holding me up, I definitely would have fallen hard to the ground.

This was his chance to tell me about the girl and their baby. I waited on pins and needles for him to say something, silently praying they weren't together or even worse…

There was no baby.

Feeling like the worst piece-of-shit for wishing an innocent life away.

What if they were still a family? Would he be talking and touching me this way? Was I now the other woman?

"Hey, baby, baby, baby… where'd ya go?"

I shook off the aggravating thoughts. "Why are you here, Noah? What do you want?"

My breathing hitched and my lips parted when he started lightly grazing the crease of my inner thigh and cheek with his fingers. Palming my ass with his warm calloused hand, right next to my pussy.

"What I've always wanted. *You.* Do you wanna piece of me too?" Up until this point, his anger had been attacking me in waves, but it wasn't until he added, "Cuz, sweetheart, that's all that's left of this man since you left him behind," that he completely pulled me under his riptide with him. Hearing pure misery and desperation in his tone. His voice was trying to tell me the story of the past four years of us being a part.

Leaving me wanting more.

Craving everything.

Lingering in my mind.

In my heart.

In my goddamn soul.

"That's not fair, Noah."

His jaw clenched as he stared deep into my eyes. "Or you can just get on your knees and show me how sorry you are… but, if ya wanna talk to me 'bout fair, Skyler? I'll tell you what's not fuckin' fair, yeah?"

Swallowing hard, I braced myself for the bullet firing at full speed toward me.

"As much as I wanna fuckin' hate you with every bone in my body, I can't stop lovin' you just as much."

I bit my lip, battling the tears as he continued to lodge bullet after bullet into my chest.

You deserve it, Skyler. This and more.

"I've had to watch ya live your happy, perfect fuckin' life through magazines, on the TV screen, the newsstands on every fuckin' corner. See you travelin' all over the world, hangin' on other men's arms when it shoulda been mine. Flauntin' your tits and fuckin' ass in movies and more goddamn magazines that I ripped the fuck a part! Wishin' it was you my hands were destroyin'! You have no fuckin' idea how much I hate you, and still fuckin' love you!"

His eyes glazed over, and I saw it clear as day. He was no longer the boy I fell in love with since day one. He was now the man who killed for money. Leaning back to look at me with nothing but that murderous glare and those dark, seedy eyes. Seeing this side of him emerge was like being dragged back in time to when I was a young girl and he showed me all his demons.

Noah was out for blood.

My blood.

"Please, Noah, I can't… just please, stop…"

It was all for show! It's my persona! I've been dead without you! Don't you see? Can't you see me?

"You have no fuckin' idea what you did to me," he snarled in an eerie tone, causing my body to tense, and I swear I stopped breathing. He felt it too, his taut grip on my wrists tightened to the point of pain.

I winced, and for a second, my pain broke through his uncontrollable rage, but he shook it off, simply blinking it away.

"Skyler, you ripped my fuckin' heart out and shit on it. I gave you everythin'. All of me, every fuckin' ounce of me. I woulda done anythin' for you, but that wasn't good enough. Was it?!"

I shuddered, fueling the wrath of his fury.

"I was never good enough, was I?!"

"That's not true."

Tell him, Skyler! Tell him you went back for him! Tell him you love him! Just fucking tell him!

"You wanna know what's so fuckin' real? How much I truly fuckin' hate you for makin' me fall in love wit' you. Manipulatin' me into thinkin' I was your world, your best friend, when I was nothin', yeah? Remember, I'm *nobody*."

"Noah, please just—"

"What, baby? What else can I fuckin' give ya? Huh? What does Skyler want now? What does she need this time? Wit' you cryin' those worthless fuckin' tears, they mean shit to me now. The same way I wish you did too."

No! He doesn't mean that! He's just trying to hurt you! You know he doesn't mean that!

I was the first to break our connection, shutting my eyes. My heart, my mind, my sanity couldn't take it anymore. He was pulling every sentiment from my body, every last emotion out of me I didn't even know I had. I strained, locking up, staying firmly rooted to the happy place in my head.

"The sun'll come out tomorrow, bet all those dollars that tomorrow." Surrendering, seeking refuge within myself for however long I could.

He didn't stop.

He wasn't mentally there with me anymore, and a huge part of me wasn't there either.

"I never imagined a life without you, Skyler. Not for one fuckin' second. After you left, I broke down, and all I wanted was to just be forgotten. I wanted to lay in my bed and fuckin' disappear, cuz at least there'd be no more fuckin' pain. You broke my goddamn heart beyond repair. You took away the one thing I never thought I'd live without… *you*."

More tears streamed down my face, I didn't even try to stop them. They were his now. *"Just thinkin' about tomorrow. Clears away the sadness, the rain, and the emptiness. 'Till it's not there."*

"My girl, my best friend, the only fuckin' family I had for so long. I lost it all. You may have left, but your presence stayed inside of me, in our safe haven, and it never left me alone. Not for one fuckin' day. Your scent still lingers there even after all these years. You might as well have ended me that night, put a gun to my heart and pulled the fuckin' trigger. You coulda put me out of my fuckin' misery." He finally let go of my wrists, but his grip went right for my face. "Open your eyes."

I didn't let his firm grasp deter me from my safe place. *"So just hang on 'til tomorrow and work through the pain."*

"Open your fuckin' eyes, Skyler!"

"Tomorrow! Tomorrow! I love ya all of the days and nights of tomorrow!"

"I shoulda let you drown in that river!"

My eyes snapped open.

"Cuz, it woulda saved me from the path of destruction you left behind."

And just like that…

My resolve fucking shattered.

NOAH

Thirty-two

"Fuck off!" she roared, her body shaking uncontrollably.

I grinned, cocking my head to the side. "But, baby, I'd much rather fuck you." I let go of her face as if her skin burned into mine. Adding more scars to my already marred flesh. "I've lost count of how many times I've thought 'bout stickin' my cock—" I slapped her ass, thrusting my erection against her bare pussy "—in that tight, little fuck hole since I first saw you tonight."

She gasped, but stood taller, angling her chin up. Challenging me. A hint of amusement passed through my eyes from her thinking she still held all the power over me.

I wasn't the pussy-whipped boy she left behind.

My eyes never wavered from hers as I began gliding my fingers along her collarbone to the sides of her breasts, and over to her rapidly beating heart. Causing her body to quiver, creating goose bumps all over her skin. She sucked in a breath, her mouth suddenly seemed dry.

I wanted to fucking break her, as much as she broke me.

"Cutie, you didn't answer my question… how many cocks have been inside of you, makin' you come like mine? Huh? Does Eli know how much you love to be fucked raw?"

"Stop it," she gritted out.

"It's our fuckin' birthday, baby. How many men were you plannin' on blowin' tonight? Just Eli? Or you fuckin' half of Hollywood too with your pretty little pussy?"

Her walls were caving in on her, one by one, so I leaned forward and whispered in her ear, "Give it to me, Skyler. Tell me? How many guys fucked you before I did? Is that why you came to me that night? You wanted to feel a real man in between your legs? My girl wanted to come, yeah?"

Her eyes dilated in a way I'd never seen before, triggering something inside of her. It was like her head finally caught up with the feelings, I was brutally inflicting for my own peace of mind. She couldn't process it fast enough. Showing me everything through her eyes.

Only adding gasoline to my furious, out of control fiery blaze, and I was burning her alive with me.

"Why ya playin' hard to get, baby, when you know you're already hard for me to want. Cuz any person who has ever loved you, Skyler Bell, was dead fuckin' wrong."

More tears erupted from her eyes and her nostrils flared.

"What doesn't kill you, only disappoints me."

She shuddered, softly humming a vaguely familiar tune.

"Are you gonna sing for me now, baby? Cuz you know that *Annie* song only gets my cock hard."

The chain I had around her fucking broke.

All the blood drained from my face, and my stomach dropped when she hastily screamed, "I went to you that night because I needed you! I fucking needed you! I still need you, you fucking bastard!"

I flew back from the impact of her words, instantly letting her go.

She didn't hesitate, it was her turn to come for me. "You have no idea who the fuck I am, Noah! You never fucking did! Because if you had, you'd have known I came ba—" she paused, the pain of our past taking over.

"Oh fuck no," I seethed. "Finish what you were 'bout to say."

"Why? It's not going to change anything. The damage is already fucking done! You would have never talked to me like this before! Look at you! Jesus Christ, who are you?"

"I'm the man you fuckin' created! Is he everythin' you wanted? Cuz I sure as shit can't stand who you've become." I took a deep breath, gesturing to her. "This movie star who dresses like a fuckin' whore and expects me to treat her like a lady. Go snort some more rails off guy's cocks so you can get the fuck outta here wit' your goddamn bullshit. You want me to believe you gave a shit 'bout me, then just fuckin' admit it already, Skyler." I was over to her in one long, determined stride, getting right in her face. "You. Are. Ashamed. Of. Me."

In the blink of an eye, her expression changed to utter disbelief and devastation. The air suddenly so fucking thick, I could choke on it. Especially when she started scanning my eyes, searching for the man who once loved her more than anything in this world. Proving it time after time. I didn't know who that man was anymore.

Too much had happened.

Making me remember why I hated her so fucking much.

I bit back the bile rising in my throat. Briefly blinded by her remorse, her presence, my goddamn love for her. Slicing me open all over again.

With tears blurring her crystal blue eyes, she finally revealed the truth I'd always known wasn't a lie, "I love you. I've always, always fucking loved you."

Almost bringing me to my knees.

"There, you got what you came for, *yeah*?" she mocked. Her lips trembling, "Is this what you wanted?"

She started shoving me, and I let her.

"To hurt me."

Push.

"To belittle me."

Push.

"To make me feel worse…"

Push.

Push.

Push.

"Then I already have over the last four years!"

My back hit the concrete wall with a thud.

"You got what you wanted, so you can go now. Because I can't stand fucking looking at you any longer!"

I reached for her on pure impulse. "Skyler—" As soon as she felt my strong arm's wrap around her waist, she kneed me in the balls.

"We're even now, because I hate you too."

Push.

I groaned in pain, and in her fuck-me heels, she took off running toward the exit. Breathing through the discomfort for a moment, I hauled ass after her. My boots pounding the wet pavement, chasing her in the pouring rain. Catching up with her outside the back of the dark building.

I gripped her arm and roughly turned her toward me, never expecting what happened next.

"No!" she shouted bloody murder, once again shoving me as hard as she could. She didn't falter, losing her fucking shit on me. "I loved you!" She ignored the sting I knew her hand must have felt every time it connected with my face and body. Hitting me anywhere she could.

I tried blocking each and every blow, driving her further to push and hit me harder. Taking out every malicious word I'd said to her, and years of pent-up anger with herself, on me.

"I fucking loved you!"

"Cutie, calm the fuck down," I ordered, trying to grip onto her wrists.

"Fuck you!" she yelled, punching and shoving me more, the closer I came toward her. "You don't know anything! Nothing!"

"Skyler, enough!"

Raising her hand up to slap me across the face, I gripped onto her wrist and spun her around before she could react. She lost her footing which only made it easier for me to carry her up into my arms. Striding over to the nearest car that appeared abandoned in a secluded corner of the alley.

"Stop it," I warned, controlling her body from thrashing around. Pissing her off even more.

"You stop it! Put me down!"

And I did, slamming her ass on the hood. Taking ahold of both her wrists with my hand and placing them above her head. I pinned her down, and still she fought with every ounce of courage she had left in her.

"For fucks sake, stop!"

"No!"

"Well then, I'm just gonna havta fuck the fight right out of ya."

"Don't you dar—"

My lips crashed onto hers, slipping my tongue into her mouth. Demanding complete and utter control. She weakly thrashed around, and I held her tighter against my chest, kissing her fucking senseless.

Groaning against her lips, "Fuck… I missed you…"

Her frustrated screams were muffled by my mouth, knowing she wasn't going anywhere unless I wanted her to. And the only place she was going was on my fucking cock. Loosening my grip, I slowly brushed my lips against hers.

Breathing out, "Say it again, Cutie."

She turned her face away from my attack, but I gripped onto her chin forcing her to lock eyes with me. Needing her to see she wasn't going to win this power struggle between us.

We were both panting profusely, drenched from head to toe from the storm that had only just started.

"Say it."

"Why? It's not going to change anything."

I rubbed her bottom lip with my thumb, needing a minute to touch her. Aware that an eternity could have passed down the middle of us, and it still wouldn't have been enough time.

To look at her.

Hold her.

Fucking feel her.

I missed her so fucking much, and she was right in front of me, right in my arms where she always belonged.

"It's already changed everythin'."

We stared at each other for what felt like hours, both of us lost in our own demons. Even after all these years, she still took my goddamn breath away. She was so fucking beautiful, so painfully fucking breathtaking. Laying there beneath me with her wet hair stuck to the sides of her face and her black eye makeup sliding down her red cheeks. Her pouty lips already swollen from my assault made her look like a gorgeous disaster, and I was just getting started.

"Please… baby, for me. Just say it for me," I begged.

Her hands dug into my hair and her legs wrapped around my waist as she murmured, "I love you. I've always loved you."

I growled, slamming my mouth onto hers again.

Claiming her tongue.

Her mind.

Her heart.

Every last part of her body and soul.

She met each and every push and pull I expressed through my core, blanketing hers. I clutched onto the sides of her face, devouring her lips, her neck, her perfect fucking tits.

It was intense.

It was needy.

It was everything and so much more.

In an instant, I stripped off her flimsy fucking dress, tossing it on the wet hood. Making a mental note to throw it the fuck away later. My cock throbbed against my zipper, seeing her naked and helpless below me. Excruciatingly aching to empty my balls deep inside of her.

I groaned, my memories of her didn't even compare to this.

To her.

She forcefully gripped onto the front of my soaked white shirt, yanking me closer like we weren't close enough. Trying to mold us into one person, kissing me as if her life depended on it. She moaned into my mouth, frantically trying to gather her bearings from my tight hold. While both of our bodies shook with undeniable fucking desire. Every part of our reserve hammered all around us.

I slapped her ass, making her whimper before lifting her up to straddle my waist as I sat on the hood of the car. Our mouths collided again, unable to get enough of each other.

"Pull out my cock."

Her hand immediately undid my belt, working my button and zipper, her fingers slipping from the downpour of rain washing away our sins for just one night. Unable to get them open fast enough. Finally, freeing my hard cock, she stroked it.

"Fuck," I huskily snarled, biting her lip.

When she suddenly stopped and pulled away from me, my eyes popped open. Seeing her gazing down at my dick in her hand.

"You're pierced?" she asked, entirely caught off guard.

I scoffed out a chuckle, I'd forgotten about that.

"Did you have this before?"

"No."

"When did you get it done?"

"A few months ago."

Her fingers slid up and down the three piercings on my shaft and then grazed the one through the head of my cock.

"Can these get lost inside me?"

"The only thing that's going to get lost inside of you—" I kissed along her neck, gripping onto her ass, and in one hard thrust, I was balls deep in her pussy "—is my cock."

She loudly moaned, her eyes rolling to the back of her head.

"Don't close your eyes. I want ya to look at me while you ride my dick," I throatily rasped, sucking her tongue into my mouth. "Ride me, Skyler, ride me long and fuckin' hard."

She slowly rocked her hips until she got used to the feeling of my cock and piercings inside of her. Wrapping her arms around my neck, using me as leverage, she swayed her hips faster and harder. Causing her head to roll back, giving me access to her tits. I took her nipple into my mouth, kneading the other one, unable to get enough of her. Another moan escaped deep down in her throat. All I could hear was desire, as I fondled her breasts and sucked on her nipples.

"Noah..."

"Yeah, baby. Just like that. Fuck me. Fuck my cock like my good girl."

Moving one of my hands to her clit, I worked her bundle of nerves, sending her over the edge. Her breathing escalated, and her cunt tightened, gripping my dick like a fucking vise. Vaguely feeling her shiver all around me as the rain picked up, pelting off the metal frame beneath us. She leaned in, kissing me more aggressively than before. I grabbed the back of her neck, wanting to bring her closer, needing her body to cover mine. Our lips moved on their own accord, no longer having control over our demanding movements.

"Fuck, you feel so goddamn good," I groaned loudly against her parted lips as she hissed into mouth. Crying out but not saying a word.

I dug my fingers into her ass, rolling her hips to fuck me harder and faster, for her pleasure and mine. There was nothing sweet about what we did to each other. I kissed her jawline, to her neck, and deliberately made my way back to her lips. Thrusting my hips upward, feeling her g-spot on my tip of my cock.

My fucking sweet spot.

Her mouth dropped open.

"Right there, baby? That feel good, yeah?" I taunted, knowing damn well it fucking did.

"Noah… yes… right there… please… don't stop… right there…"

Every thrust inside her, she felt the mass of my body's movement, inching her a little higher each time. Savoring the velvety feel of my mouth claiming hers, her pussy throbbing against my shaft, and her g-spot pulsating along the head of my dick. Over and over again.

"I'm going to come," she panted.

"So come, come on my fuckin' cock."

We were spiraling out of control in a heated frenzy from the feel of our mouths and bodies colliding. Coming together for the first time since she left me behind. She could feel it as much as I could. It was lingering in both of our chaotic minds.

Each thrust.

Every moan.

Brought back memories both of us could never forget. She fucked me harder and with more determination. I kissed her passionately with everything left inside of me, needing her to understand my agony of when she'd left me alone.

"Give it to me, Skyler."

"Ah, Noah! I'm coming, I'm coming, I'm coming..."

Her knees buckled as her body fell forward. Her pussy squeezing the fuck out of my dick as she rode out her orgasm. I kissed and bit along her neck, leaving more marks on her perfect creamy skin. Never once letting up on my ruthless thrusts. She cried out some more, compressing her thighs with her release and clamping down on my cock again through another wave of ecstasy.

I drove in and out of her a few more times before I pulled away, needing to look into her eyes. Our bodies smacking from the skin-on-skin contact and rain that wasn't letting up. Thunder crashing above us, mimicking our stride. My pace increased as I made her fuck me as hard as she could. I couldn't help it, I loved taking her raw, and from the sounds escaping her, so did she. Both our mouths parted, breathless, riding the high, wanting to prolong her coming on my dick as long as I could.

"Say it."

She breathlessly smiled and it lit up her entire face. "I love you, Noah. I've always loved you."

Those eight words were my undoing, exactly the way I always knew they'd be.

Another growl escaped from deep within my chest as I came so fucking hard. Taking her over the edge with me. Our bodies went lax in the pouring rain, feeling the eternal connection, nothing could ever break.

Not the past.

Or the present.

Not even the future.

Not even the future.

We stayed like that for I don't know how long before we went back to her hotel suite. As soon as we walked through the doors, she grabbed her phone and texted her fuck buddy that she was alive and well. While I tried like hell to pretend it didn't bother me, I couldn't help but rip her phone out of her hand and turn it off.

Possessively growling, "Mine" into her ear.

Once I was done proving my statement by fucking her mouth with my dick, we took a nice, long, hot shower together. Where I continued my lesson, getting on my knees and eating her pussy until she repeatedly squirted down the sides of my face. Begging, pleading, for me to stop.

I didn't.

"Little girl, where did ya learn how to come like that?"

"You."

We made love all over her suite, from the couch, to the kitchen counters, to the window that overlooked Sin City until we both passed the fuck out. Wrapped in one another's arms with my cock still inside of her.

When she stirred awake the next morning, I had already been staring at her beautiful peaceful face for what felt like hours.

"Mornin', Cutie."

"I could get used to waking up to you every morning."

"You were dry fuckin' my leg in your sleep. Were you dream 'bout my pierced cock?"

"Maybe." She smirked. "What made you pierce your dick anyway?"

"The pain."

She bit her lip, not expecting me to say that.

"I ain't got much bare skin left for more ink."

Her eyes went to the name tattooed right over my heart, which wasn't there before she left me. I caught her staring at it several times during the previous night.

"You got your nipples pierced too. Same reason?"

I nodded, grabbing her chin to look into my eyes instead.

"Maybe I should get my first tattoo? What should I get?"

Skimming my fingers over her lower stomach, just above her pussy. "Property of Noah, right here."

She laughed. "Don't I get my own cut with that on there or something?"

I arched an eyebrow, knowing she didn't know shit about club life before.

"I love *Sons of Anarchy*."

"Is that right?"

"Yes." She blushed.

"Still my favorite color on you, Cutie. So, *Sons of Anarchy*, huh? Why is that?"

"You know why."

"Tell me anyways."

"Jax reminds me of you."

I smiled. "I fuckin' love you."

"What?"

"You heard me."

"Say it again."

"I. Fuckin'." I got on top of her, caging her in with my arms. "Love. You."

"So last night's insults didn't mean anything?"

"Do you honestly think it did?"

She shrugged, and I began rubbing my nose against hers, wanting to ease the pain I'd purposely caused. Not wanting to start another argument, I didn't tell her that I did mean some of the shit I spewed last night. Mostly, about the part of hating and loving her so goddamn much.

"You've never treated me that badly before."

"You've never pissed me off that badly before. Besides you had help."

"Eli isn't—"

I kissed her. "You think I wanna talk 'bout another man when you're in my arms and I'm 'bout to fuck your pussy?"

She didn't say shit, but I could tell she wanted to ask me something, and she was holding back.

Fuck it.

I asked for her, needing to know. "Now what, Skyler? What happens now?" Dreading her answer.

There was a hint of hurt in her eyes as she peered into mine. "Do you need to go back home for anything?"

"No."

Smiling from ear to ear, she flipped me over. Her demeanor quickly changing as if I had just imagined it all. Sliding her pussy down my dick. "Right now, you can fuck me until I come and then… you'll come home with me."

"Home?"

She nodded, swaying her hips back and forth. "In L.A," she moaned. "We're there for a few days," she moaned again. "And then I'm going to show you my world. Have you be part of it, if you still want toooo?"

"You're goin' on tour, yeah?"

She beamed, realizing I'd been following her career. Leaning forward, she kissed me and simply stated, "Yeah. And you're coming with me."

Meaning it in every sense of the word.

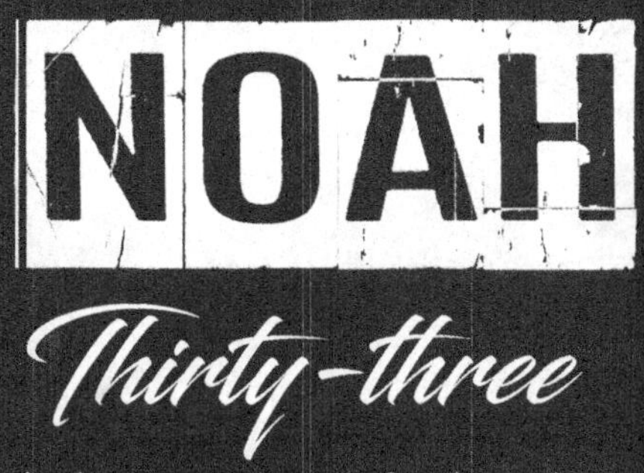

Thirty-three

We'd only been in her L.A. home for less than twenty-four hours and I think I spent that whole time inside of her. Making up for lost time, enjoying each other's company as much as possible.

"You know what I want?" I groaned, kissing her neck. I'd just finished fucking her against the glass in her encased shower.

"Hmm…"

"I wanna see you on your knees wit' my cock in your mouth."

She giggled and it was still the sweetest sound I'd ever heard. "Noah, you're still inside my pussy. How can you want in another hole already?"

"Cuz my dick belongs inside you."

"Well… if you put it that way then—"

"Sky!" a man's voice abruptly echoed off the walls.

"Shit," she breathed out against my lips as I set her down.

Instantly making me see fucking red.

"No! It's not what you think."

"Say that to me one more fuckin' time, and I'm gonna let my fists show him what I think."

She fervently shook her head. "It's Keith."

"Even fuckin' better."

"Noah, please."

"Does he know I'm here?"

"No."

"Does he know 'bout us?"

When the expression on her face answered my question, I stepped passed her. "I'll go tell him then."

She grabbed my arm. "Noah. Come on… don't do this. I didn't want to tell him over the phone."

"Is that right?"

"Yes."

"Sky! I know you're here! Where are you?" he called out, pissing me off even more.

"Jesus Christ, doesn't he know how to fuckin' knock? How many men have the key to your home, Skyler?"

"He's like my dad. Please don't make this out to be something it's not."

"You didn't answer my question."

"Just Keith."

"Any particular reason for that?"

"Sky! Where are you?!" his shout was getting closer, testing my fucking patience.

"I'm out of town a lot, sometimes he checks on things. My PA has my house key too. Would you like to know why as well, so you can stop being an asshole?"

I slapped her ass, hard.

She yelped.

"Don't fuckin' cuss."

"Sky! You in there?"

"So I can see he also barges into your bedroom. You better answer him, Skyler, before he bursts in here too, and I finally show him some goddamn manners. Or has the motherfucker already made himself a home in your bed?"

She opened her mouth to say something, but the son of bitch hollered her name again. Turning her attention toward the bathroom door instead, she yelled, "Yeah! I'm just finishing up in the shower! Give me a bit!"

"Hurry up! I have great news!"

"Okay!"

I snidely mocked, "I'm sure he's gonna be just as thrilled to hear our news too."

"Oh no. You stay in here, and I'll go tell Keith by myself."

"Fuck n—"

She put her hand over my mouth. "I'll come get you when I'm done. Just let me tell him first. *Please.*"

I reluctantly stepped back, letting her handle business as she deemed fit. "You got twenty minutes." And with that, I turned to finish up my shower.

After five minutes, maybe ten, I lost my fucking patience, barely hanging on by a thread. Deciding to make my presence known on my own, I walked out of the shower soaking wet and made my way toward their voices in the living room. Forgoing a towel.

"Sky, you can't be fucking serious!" he roared, really trying my tolerance when it came to him. Even after all these years, I still fucking despised the motherfucker.

"Keith, calm down. It's not that big of a deal."

"Not that big of a deal? He looks like white trash! The press is going to tear him a part!"

"You didn't care about Eli's reputation."

"Eli Ward owns multimillion dollar corporations. His name helped your career, not hinder it."

"You're being dramatic."

"Fuck him," I murmured to myself, striding into the living room, dripping wet. "Baby, I used your razor to shave my balls. I know you like 'em smooth when you deep throat my cock."

They both instantly jerked back, caught off guard that I came out butt-ass fucking naked.

"Noah!" she exclaimed.

"What? Better on your razor than in your mouth, yeah?"

Skyler's jaw dropped open and her face instantly turned five different shades of red.

I caressed her cheek with the back of my fingers. "Still my favorite color on you, Cutie."

Her eyes widened, trailing up my body.

I grinned, facing Keith. "I didn't know *we* had company. You sure-as-shit know how to make yourself right at home when you're not invited?" I didn't wait for him to answer. "But just so ya know, I sorta am a big deal." Gesturing to my dick. "And you wouldn't think so low of me, if you knew how many times I'd made her come today alone," I paused for effect, far too satisfied by the 'what the fuck' expression on his face. "Get used to seein' me, motherfucker. I ain't goin' nowhere without her by my side."

"Oh my God, Noah… you couldn't have just let me handle this."

We locked eyes.

"That's like askin' you to stop screamin' out my name when you're beggin' me to take mercy on you and stop makin' you come." I glanced back at him. "I never do." Rendering him speechless before I left the room.

If there was one thing I learned very fucking quickly, it was that Keith was still a snake in the fucking grass.

In order to prevent unwanted bullshit in my life and Skyler's, he was adamant we keep our relationship behind closed doors until we figured our shit out. At first, my initial reaction was to tell him to eat shit, but after giving it some thought, I realized it was for the best.

At least for the time being and foreseeable future.

I didn't need pieces-of-shit prying into my life, exposing my shit to make a buck. I had too much to lose.

Including Skyler.

So I played along for everyone's sake, and we made the press think I was just another one of her bodyguards. It wasn't like I didn't fit the role. Things were just easier that way, seeing as the next few months proved to be anything but easy.

They flew by, and before I knew it, I'd been with her for over four months.

Another day, another fucking city.

I groaned, not feeling her body wrapped around mine when she pretty much slept on top of me every night. My eyes fluttered open, stirring awake from a heavy deep sleep. Searching for her through the darkness of our bedroom suite, only to find myself alone.

"Babe?" I called out to no avail, blinking away the sleepy haze.

My gaze shifted toward the clock on the nightstand, partially covered by a pair of Skyler's panties I'd thrown over there this morning when I ate her for breakfast. Before she had to leave for what felt like the hundredth press junket bullshit on this fucking tour, at the ass crack of dawn.

"Fuckin' three o'clock in the mornin'."

Between the concerts in different locations, traveling on a daily basis, the interviews, parties, something or another, it was never ending. It was fucking exhausting, seeing her less and less over the last few months.

I rubbed my face, trying to gather my bearings. To wake-up enough and go hunt her down, failing miserably at remembering where the fuck we were. All the suites, penthouses, private planes, and tour buses started blending together. Along with whatever state, city, or continent we were in. I shook off the confusion of my state of mind, kicking away the silky sheet that made me fucking sweat like crazy. I sat up yawning, bare-assed with middle of the night wood.

Grabbing my half-hard dick, I walked over to the bay window, looking at the miles and miles of lights shining through, but not seeing one star in the sky.

"Oh yeah, fuckin' Chicago," I mumbled to myself.

I hated this place, and it had only taken me one day to figure that out. As much as I loved Skyler between my legs, I'd be lying if I said I didn't daydream about riding out of here with a Harley between them instead. In an instant, my hate for the city was replaced with a frown and then a smile when I heard her. Walking toward the dim light cascading across the white marble floor, I stayed hidden behind the crack in the bedroom suite door.

God she was fucking beautiful.

There in the middle of the living room floor, wearing nothing but a guitar, sat my whole world. One side of her hair was tucked behind her ear and the other side hung over her face, while she held a pencil in between her teeth. She was humming a lulling tune, softly throwing in words here and there. Bits and pieces of a song I knew she was writing from her heart.

For a good twenty minutes, I listened to the words falling from her lips that stung, knowing they were stinging her too.

"Toxic me, hmm hmm… toxic you, hmm hmm… wild me, wild you, hmm hmm… am I hiding my light from you… or are you hiding yours from me, hmm hmm…"

I stepped out of the shadows and went to her, wanting to ease the pain in her voice and in her heart. The more I was around her, the more I realized how truly lost she was. To the world, she was Skyler Bell, but that girl wasn't the deepest part of her. It was who she wanted everyone to think she was.

Including me.

Over the past four months I'd traveled all over the United States and twelve different countries with her, seeing things from my own perspective. Sure, she lit up a room with her smile, but sometimes I wondered if it was forced. It was no doubt different with me by her side. That smile wasn't forced. That smile was all for me and I knew it. As genuine as they come, making me feel guilty as fuck for wanting to back out of this tour.

And for wanting her to come with me.

Although, as much as I fucking hated all this shit, I couldn't take her away from this life she built for herself. Especially now that she was finally involving me.

What was that saying though? Be careful what you wished for…

Her eyes slowly climbed up my naked body when she heard my footsteps approaching her. Briefly resting on my half-hard shaft before reaching my eyes.

"I'm sorry. Did I wake you?" Her eyes once again dropped to my cock.

"You were gone." I looked down at her. "My eyes are up here, yeah?"

Beaming with the smile I'd just been thinking about moments ago, her eyes lit up. "Want to hear something funny?"

"Not if it's about my dick."

She let out a loud laugh with a giggle that made my cock twitch. Moving her guitar to her side, she teased, "Fine, I won't tell you how cute it is." With one finger waving, a seductive smile, and a look that no one but me was capable of stirring in her, she added, "Come here."

I didn't have to be told twice. I sat right in the middle of the floor beside her, picking up her notebook only to have it pulled from my hands.

"Whatcha writin' 'bout, Cutie?"

She shrugged, straddling me. "Just messing around." Pushing me with her hands on my chest. "Scoot back."

My hands went to her ass and I obeyed, moving us until I felt the sofa against my back. "People always do what you say?"

"Yeah."

Kiss.

"They."

Kiss.

"Do."

Kiss.

Brushing her hair behind her ear, I cupped her tits and kissed both nipples. Staring up at her through the slits of my eyes, I noticed the expression on her face had changed as she stared at my chest lost in thought.

"Hey… where'd you go?"

Her eyes connected with mine, but her thumb didn't stop tracing the name tattooed right over my heart. Every time she saw it, I could see it in her stare. Hidden among all the questions eating away at her that she hadn't brought herself to ask me, *yet*.

I knew eventually there'd be a time and a place we'd have to face each new demon we acquired through the years we weren't together. Though, I'd be lying if I said it didn't make me hate her just a little bit more every time I saw *that* name inked on my chest as well.

It was a permanent reminder of the destruction she caused in my life when she decided not to be part of it anymore.

She was getting restless though with the lack of sharing my personal life with her the same way I used to. She never used to have to ask, but now, I didn't tell. I just couldn't. In the past, I always voluntarily shared my demons with her, except I wasn't that guy anymore, and there was no trying to find him.

At least not…

By me.

It wasn't easy to hide my indiscretions, specifically what I was doing when she wasn't around.

"Sky—"

"Yeah, I'm good," she played it off, shaking her head. "Just couldn't sleep."

"Yeah that's what coke does."

Her eyes held mine with a glare I knew all too well. Putting me right in my place, she narrowed her eyes and I gave it right back at her.

"Did you come out here to be an asshole?"

Pulling her lips to mine with my hand on the back of her neck, I smiled against her mouth and then parted them with my tongue. Not wanting to fuck up this moment between us any longer. We already had enough of that since the first night I laid eyes on her in Vegas. Our years apart proved one thing and one thing alone, time had changed her, but it had also changed me. We weren't the kids we were back then, too much shit had happened in between.

My sunshine and happiness had her new demons and they came in the form of fame, money, and literally having the world at her goddamn fingertips.

Everyone knew who she was, we couldn't walk down the street together without someone flashing a goddamn camera in our faces. There was always someone asking her for an autograph or a picture, and Skyler loved her fans so fucking much, she never said no. The press, the paparazzi, her team, motherfucking Keith, they were always up her ass in one way or another. Invading her privacy and controlling her every move and thought.

But it was the drugs that scared me more than anything. She didn't do them often since I only allowed it in my presence, making sure she was safe while under the influence. But when she did, it was for "work-related" shit. How could I reason with her when it was her own goddamn team who were handing the shit to her?

To help her stay up so she could finish whatever the fuck needed to be done.

To help her fall asleep so she could rest for whatever the fuck else they excused it for.

You name it… she could get it with the snap of her fingers. We'd gotten into so many arguments about her using, it was pointless trying to tell her that the shit wasn't normal, when everyone around her was doing the exact same thing. And the people she trusted were giving it to her like fucking candy. I resisted the urge to knock Keith the fuck out every time he permitted it. Saying some shit about he'd never let anything happen to her. Even after the trash was thrown to the curb.

Referring to me.

For the first time, I picked and chose my battles and Keith, father figure or not, I would ultimately fucking defeat.

My girl fell down the rabbit hole of the fucking Hollywood cliché and all I could do was be there for her when shit hit the fan. Because what goes up, must come down. I learned that the hard way. At the end of the day, who the fuck was I to tell her what she couldn't do? I'd done my fair share of drugs, way before she even knew what the hell they were.

Our private moments were few and far between, and we did the only thing that ever came natural to us.

We sought refuge within each other.

Playing fucking house like we were still two kids, trying to be a family. Time would stop for us when we were together like this. It wasn't about sex, it was deeper than that. It had always been deeper than that.

We kissed, losing ourselves in one another. As I caressed her back, she slid my dick gradually inside her.

"Fuck, baby," I rasped, pulling her hips to go deeper. Feeling the unbreakable connection I'd always had with her.

Skyler rocked her hips back and forth into mine to the tune she'd just been humming. Moving my thumb to her swollen clit, I circled it to the same melody. Her head fell back effortlessly and she softly moaned as I gripped onto her hips. With the way the Chicago horizon was displayed right behind her, the way her hair hung to the side, her naked body, I swear she was the definition of fucking breathtaking. Our lovemaking was quick, but so damn impactful.

I felt all of her and she felt all of me.

We went to bed shortly after, crashing fucking hard against the mattress. Fucking exhaustion catching up with the both of us. Lulling us into a deep somber, intertwined in each other.

Even in my dreams I wished for her to be with me…

And I wasn't talking about Skyler.

It wasn't until the next morning, I got the call I was expecting, where I had to disappear from her once again…

To take care of the person I just couldn't seem to leave behind.

Not even with Skyler by my side.

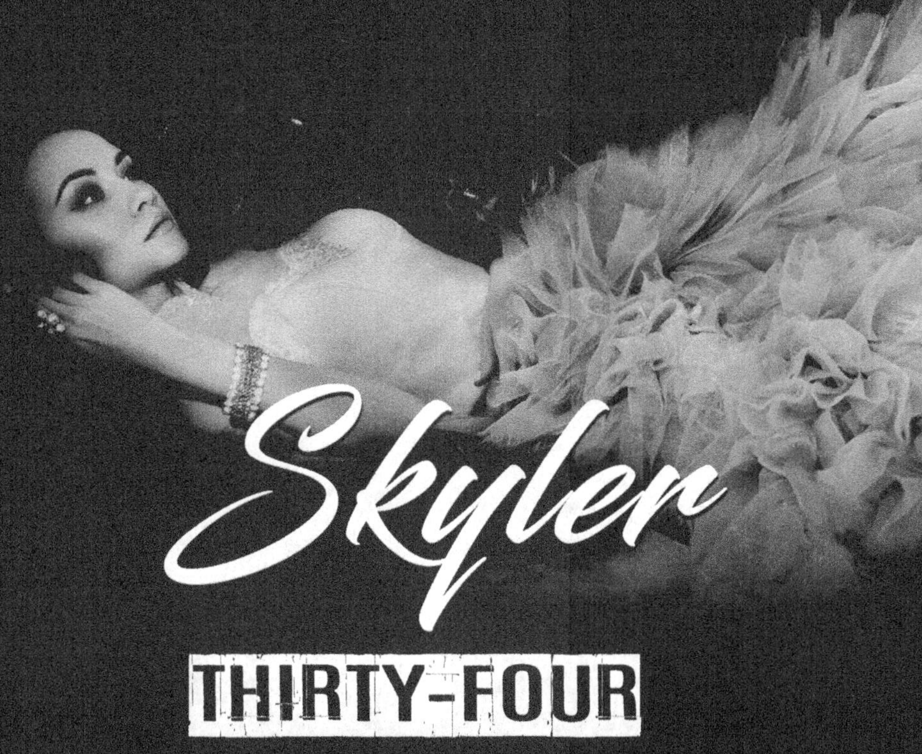

THIRTY-FOUR

Maddie.

A six-letter name.

Two syllables.

One bullet to my heart every time I saw the girl's name in small cursive writing tatted over Noah's heart.

Mocking me.

Maddie. Maddie. Maddie.

For the last eight months, he'd been with me on tour, the name constantly tormented my thoughts. I relentlessly racked my brain, sorting through the years of memories. Trying to remember every tattoo on his body, knowing for a fact that name wasn't there before I left him.

Maddie. Maddie. Maddie.

Noah's hand on her pregnant belly…

Was that girl's name Maddie?

Noah smiling at her…

He smiled at me like that, right?

Noah flirting with her…

Did he love her more than me?

Noah making love to her…

Was he thinking of her when he was with me?

Kissing me…

Touching me…

Fucking me…

Maddie. Maddie. Maddie.

Every thrust…

Every groan…

Every I love you…

I frustratingly snarled from deep within my throat, waking Noah up beside me in bed.

"Mmm," he groaned, his eyes fluttering open. Blinking away the sleep-induced haze, catching me for what was probably the hundredth time staring at the name of a woman who wasn't me.

Maddie.

"Mornin', Cutie."

Ask him Skyler! Ask him whose name is over his heart!

I just couldn't take it anymore, not my thoughts, or my questions, or my patience, so I blurted, "Whose name is that?"

If he was shocked by my question, he didn't show it in the least. Which was something I wasn't used to, this man who didn't display any emotions or even share any information about his life.

This was not my Noah.

I didn't know a damn thing about what he did during our time apart. Other than what I saw with my own two eyes when I went back for him. He didn't tell me about his mom, or his brother who I assumed made it back from war safely, or his piece of shit father who I still hated for everything he put him through.

Nothing.

It was as if our roles had reversed and Noah was now the secretive one, and I was the one who shared my life with him. At least parts of it for now. Failing miserably at trying to get him to open up to me again. Making me understand why he'd spent so many years beyond aggravated with me. Anytime I asked about his family or anything personal, he blew me off like I used to with him. Usually reverting back to sex, and I was fully expecting him to do the same with the question I'd just asked him.

He reached for me. "Come here, baby."

I pulled away. "No."

I never rejected him, and based off the expression on his face, he didn't fucking like it.

"Who is she?"

He didn't waver in replying, "She's *nobody*."

"Bullshit! You wouldn't have her name tattooed over your heart, if she was nobody."

"Skyler, don't fuckin' try me." He abruptly sat up in the bed, tearing the sheets off his naked body. Grabbing his gym shorts off the floor before throwing them on. He let out a heavy sigh, sitting on the edge of the bed, placing his elbows on his knees. Raking his hands through his unruly hair like he wanted to tear it out.

I scooted closer to him, laying soft kisses along his shoulders. Wanting him to feel my misery, my insecurities, my heart and soul. "Then tell me who she is. Please…"

"Why?"

"Why not? You used to tell me everything. Without me even asking, and now… now it's like I'm not even… it's like… you don't even want to include me in your life… anymore."

There, I said it. I finally fucking said it.

He turned his head to look at me with a familiar glare in his eyes. "How's it fuckin' feel, Cutie?"

"Oh my God." I staggered back, holding onto my heart from yet another bullet he just shot at me, out of nowhere. "Is this why you came back to me? To teach me a lesson? Give me a taste of my own medicine? Is that all this is to you?"

"Do you honestly think that?"

"What the hell am I supposed to think when you say shit like that?!"

"Don't. Fuckin'. Cuss."

"That's what you're concerned about?!" I jumped off the bed before I got the last word out. Wrapping the sheet around me to leave him there, but he was up in my face before I could even take another step.

"You don't fuckin' walk away from me, Skyler. Not. Ever. Again."

"Watch me." I moved passed him, but he did what always came natural to him. He manhandled me, backing me into a wall.

"Un-fuckin'-believable. I spent years tryin' to get you to tell me one goddamn thing 'bout your life. One! It's been eight months. Eight fuckin' months, and you're losin' your shit cuz I won't share what's none of your fuckin' business. Jesus Christ, you can't be this fuckin' selfish."

"Selfish?" I scoffed out. "Excuse me for wanting to be part of your life. I thought we were past this. Why won't you let me in like you used to? It makes no sense unless it's because of h—" I hesitated, unable to say it.

"Skyler." He narrowed his eyes at me. "If you know what's good for you, you'll finish that fuckin' sentence."

"Fine! Is it because of the gi—"

The sound of his phone ringing on the nightstand, cut me off, and both of our eyes darted toward it as if it was a bomb about to explode. I expected him to go answer it and leave the room, the way he always did.

But he didn't.

He stayed firmly rooted in front of me and as soon as it stopped ringing, I interrogated him, "Who is that?" Wanting to lay out all our cards on the table.

His eyes once again locked with mine, but he didn't say one word. Not one fucking word.

"Who. Is. That?"

Silence.

"They call every few days at the same exact time, Noah. You think I'm stupid? Who is it, and what do they want?"

"None of your fuckin' business, that's who."

It rang again.

Taunting me.

"Go answer it then," I sneered. "Don't want to keep them waiting. It's obviously someone important. Someone who means something to you, or else why would you hide it from me? But what do I know, maybe I'm not the important one, considering you never even introduced me to your mom."

Caught off guard, he jerked back. "My ma? What the fuck does she have to do wit' this?"

"Everything! Why didn't you ever introduce me to her?"

"Cuz she was always fuckin' drunk, remember? Or did ya leave all your memories in Southport behind when you fuckin left? Cuz you're hittin' me wit' some bullshit right now."

"Was?"

"What?"

"You just said was? Does that mean she's not always drunk anymore? Is she sober now? Why wouldn't you tell me that?" I couldn't get my questions out fast enough, months of holding back flew to the surface, continuing to fuck with my mind.

And exactly like clockwork, his phone rang again.

"Third time, Noah. How many rings is it going to take for the person on the other end to catch a fucking clue?!"

"For fucks sake! You're givin' me fuckin' whiplash! Is it that time of the month or somethin'? Cuz you're never this much of a pain in my ass!"

"Then just tell me who it is?!"

"Fuckin' Santa Claus! There, you happy? Cat's out of the bag. Two days ago, it was the fuckin' Easter Bunny, and before that, it was the fuckin' Tooth Fairy. Don't believe me? Cuz no matter what I say to you right now, it won't be good enough. Nothin' ever is wit' you."

"Then just tell me the truth!"

Ring, ring, ring...

"Fuck this!" I ducked under his arms and hauled ass to his phone, ready to answer it myself and figure out the truth hidden behind his blatant lies.

As soon as I hit the accept button, Noah roughly ripped it out of my hands and chucked it across the room. It shattered against the wall, falling to the floor in broken pieces.

"Goddamn it!" he angrily roared, making my skin tingle and the hair on my arms stand straight up. "When are you gonna fuckin' learn not to push every one of my goddamn buttons?!"

My eyes widened, and my heart started beating profusely, anticipating what he was about to say. Knowing I would barely survive it.

Causing me to step back as he stepped forward.

"You just keep goin' and goin' and goin'! Naggin' the shit out of me! When I already told ya it's none of your fuckin' concern! So lay the fuck off me!"

This time he stepped forward and I stepped back.

"You lost my respect when you fuckin' left me! I don't owe you shit! Not to tell ya who I fuckin' talk to! Not to share any part of me, but my fuckin' cock! Cuz, sweetheart, that boat sailed away a long time ago wit' all my fucks given on board!"

Another step forward, another step back.

"Just cuz everyone else gives you anythin' you fuckin' want at the drop of a dime, doesn't mean I'm gonna answer to you or I ever will again!"

With his steps forward, my back hit the wall. Instinctively, my hands went on his chest. My left palm right over his heart which was beating as fast as mine.

Leaning in close to my lips, he spoke with conviction, "That's on you, Skyler fuckin' Bell... Cuz *you* left me. *You* broke us. And *you* never looked back."

I stood taller, staring deep into his eyes. "Yes. I. Did. I went back for you!"

"Bullshit!"

"I saw you, Noah. I saw you with *her*!"

Instantly, his eyes glazed over with nothing but agony and anguish for what I wanted to know so badly. He didn't try to hide it, or maybe he just couldn't control his emotions when it came to *her*.

Like he couldn't control them when it came to *me*.

"I heard you call her pretty girl. I heard you tell her the same line you once used on me, about getting dressed up for you in her white flowy dress."

"That's enough, Skyler," he gritted out, hanging on by a very thin thread, exactly how I'd been for the last eight months.

Only inciting me to keep inching my way across it, hoping it wouldn't snap.

"I heard her reply she just wanted to look nice for your momma. The same Mom you never introduced me to."

As if we were both reliving that day all over again, his hands fisted at his sides.

"Shut ya goddamn mouth, Skyler. You don't know shit 'bout shit."

"I saw you flirting with a girl that looked just like *me*. She had *my* round face, *my* light eyes, even her lips were pouty like *mine*. Down to her petite body and her sassy little mouth. '*But it ain't flirtin' if you've already slept wit' the girl, yeah?*'"

Noah's jaw clenched and his body tensed, locking up to the point I could feel his pain.

"I'll tell you what else I don't know."

"Don't fuckin' say it."

"I saw you touchin'—"

"I'm warnin' you, Skyler… don't you fuckin' breathe a word 'bout it."

Cocking my head to the side, I did exactly that. Breathing out, "Your baby through her pregnant belly."

"Motherfucker!" His fist hit the wall beside my head so fast I never saw it coming, making me scream and immediately shudder.

He backed away slowly, his chest heaving, his nostrils flared with his murderous glare directed right at me. My second offense in what felt like a short amount of time.

"Congratu-fuckin'-lations, Cutie." Placing his hand over the tattoo on his heart, he finally responded to my deepest fear and my seediest demon, "You just answered your own fuckin' question."

"Noah—"

With that, he turned around, grabbed some clothes off the floor, and walked out of the bedroom. It wasn't until I heard the door to the suite slam shut, making me jump out of my skin, that I realized for the first time he left…

Me. Behind.

Skyler

THIRTY-FIVE

As much as I dreaded the day ahead of me, I had obligations I needed to fulfill. Except, I couldn't stop thinking about Noah's last words to me.

"You just answered your own fuckin' question."

Which only meant the name over his heart was either the girl's or their baby's. And even though every fiber in my being already knew that answer, it still hurt more than anything he's ever said to me.

Of all the insults.

All the belittling.

All the hate.

Those seven words were my means to an end.

"Sky!" Keith hollered, walking through the double doors of the suite.

"Keith, you know you can't barge in here like that anymore. Noah would shit—"

"I saw your boy-toy hauling ass out of the building as I was stepping into the elevator. Is the honeymoon phase finally over?" he questioned, placing his briefcase on the coffee table before making his way over to the mini-bar.

"Don't say that."

"Get real, Sky. When are you going to open your eyes and see him for what he really is? He's white fucking trash." He walked back over to me, handing me a drink. "You're too good for him, and I'm fully convinced he's using you too."

hundreds of responses for him.

Noah talks to me.

Noah confides in me.

Noah needs me.

If you took away the obscene amount of sex we were having, what was left?

Some light conservation.

A few laughs.

More fighting.

More arguments.

More secrets.

More. More. More.

"That's what I thought," Keith replied for me, reading my mind.

"I work all the time. I'm constantly doing something, I can't even remember the last time I had an entire day off. We barely see each other as it is. Don't act like you know anything about us, Keith. Because you don't."

"Alright, I'm game." He opened his suit jacket and sat down on the couch, getting relaxed and comfortable. "Then tell me, what does he do all day while you're out working your ass off to provide a life he'd never have a chance of living without you? Huh?"

I swallowed hard, his words tearing into my insecurities in a way they never had before.

"For someone who claims to be so in love… you don't know shit about the man you're sharing a bed with. Do you?"

"Keith—"

"It's alright. This is why you have me." Opening his briefcase in front of him, he threw a file on the coffee table between us.

"What's that?"

"The truth on your biker trash boyfriend."

"You had him investigated?" I exclaimed, with an expression of pure disgust.

"Of course. I always have your best interests at heart, Skyler, and don't ever forget that."

Before I went off on him, I abruptly walked away. Pissed as fuck he was invading Noah's privacy, but I'd be lying if I said a huge part of me didn't want to open that file.

"You wasted your time. I'm not looking at that."

"Sky, I'm going to assume you knew his father was the President of an outlaw motorcycle club, but did you happen to know he was murdered about two years ago as well?"

I stopped dead in my tracks like I was suddenly glued to the ground.

"Ah. I didn't think so. There's a photo of a girl in his file who looks a hell of a lot like you, Sky. Did you know she was missing?"

I snapped around. "Missing?"

"That's what the file says. Look for yourself. The truth can literally be in your hands." When I didn't move from the place I was standing, he added, "Or how about the fact he has money… a lot of money. Where do you think he acquired that?"

Fighting?

Killing?

But he never had bruises, cuts, or even blood on his clothes. Could he be involved with the missing girl?

"I can see your mind spinning."

"Where's the girl? Is she still missing?"

"I didn't get that far." He shrugged. "I asked for the bare minimum, but could you imagine what the press would find? Considering I barely did any digging and struck fucking gold. These are just some interesting details I'm sure slipped his mind to tell you, *yeah*?"

Oh, god...

Reporters.

Magazines.

Social media.

Everything I ever feared about his past could come to light.

Destroying him.

"In his own words," Keith emphasized, now standing in front of me, "he loves you so fuckin' much, but he doesn't give a shit about ruining your reputation, your career, what you've worked so hard for… Jesus, Sky, what would your mom think? She'd be so disappointed in you."

"There has to be some sort of mistake. Noah, wouldn't—"

"The only mistake is you let him into your life to begin with. But, here's your chance to make it right. All you have to do is leave him behind."

I shuddered back. "What?"

"He has plenty of money to get where he needs to go. You never have to see him again. I'll take care of it. He won't even be able to look at you without getting his ass thrown in jail. And from the looks of that file—" he pointed to the scattered papers on top of a vanilla envelope "—it's actually where he belongs. I guarantee you it won't take long for him to end up there on his own. I should have had him locked up years ago, but I gave you the benefit of the doubt. You're going to leave me no choice but to take matters into my own hands to protect you. And don't think I won't, Skyler. I'd do anything to keep you safe."

"You can't do that." I frantically shook my head. "You can't do that to me, Keith."

"So then what? You're going to throw away your life for someone who hasn't even told you about his? You're smarter than that, Sky. Don't let your infatuation with him blind your reasoning. I raised you better than that."

"I'm sure there's an explanation for everything. People make up lies all the time. Just because it's on a document, doesn't mean it's the truth. You know that as much as I do."

"Skyler—"

"No!"

His stare narrowed in on, giving me one hell of a stern look. "What did you just say to me?"

"I mean… I just… there's… I know… but I… I love him, Keith. I fucking love him."

The expression on his face quickly changed from rigged to concerned before pulling me into his arms to hug me. "I know, sweetheart. I know. But I love you too. More than anything, Sky. I've always considered you my daughter. My responsibility. I'd hate to see everything you so worked for be flushed down the toilet for a piece of trash from Southport, North Carolina."

"I'm from Southport, North Carolina."

He chuckled, "Yes, but you were always meant to shine, Skyler Bell, regardless of being born in a podunk town. He's no good for you." He pulled away, holding my face in between his hands. "You want to be thrown in jail by association? Who knows what he'd involve you in. Pretty girls like you don't mesh well in prison, sweetheart. He's dangerous. You want to end up like the last girl?"

I felt myself about to breakdown, so conflicted with what he was saying. My mind processing it, but my heart screaming for me not to believe a word of it. Shaking off the plaguing thoughts, I fell right back into his arms, I'd never been more grateful to have Keith there for me. He was my only family. He'd always been my only family.

So I simply repeated the truth, praying he'd understand. "Keith, I love him."

He took a deep breath, wiping away my tears with his thumbs. "Alright, we'll talk about this again later, okay? In the meantime, how about you go get ready for the charity event at the hospital in a few hours. I will send your glam squad up here shortly with a selection of dresses you can choose from. It will do you some good to be reminded of how impactful and important your life is for others once you are there visiting some patients."

I nodded, and he hugged me one last time. Before, grabbing the file and placing it back into his briefcase. "I'm going to make some calls, but I'm ready when you are."

I nodded again, and for the rest of the day I moved around in a daze. Like I was on autopilot, my body moving on its own accord. Talking when I was supposed to, smiling for the cameras, nodding when it was expected of me. I was the epitome of Skyler Bell. From an outsider's perception, I had the world at my fingertips, everything I ever wanted, my life was perfect in every single way.

No one knew the real me.

No. One.

Not even Noah.

Sometimes it felt as if I didn't know her either. Everyone expected something from me, and somewhere along the years, the line of who I truly was got blurred. My persona took over.

I missed my mom.

My dad.

The life I thought I wanted turned out abandoning me instead. Leaving that lost little girl alone in the river, where she lost her whole world to more mistakes that could never be change.

No matter how many times she prayed.

I held a constant fake-as-fuck smile, trying to concentrate on the event, instead of wondering whether or not Noah would ever show up for me. He was supposed to be there by my side, pretending to be my bodyguard. Standing next to me, protecting me, loving me, eternally being my one and only. I waited for him, keeping my attention on the entrance as best as I could as I mingled with hospital executives and billionaires who were advocates for the cause. Forever contemplating the worst.

Maybe he wasn't coming back? Maybe he ran? Maybe he truly did leave me behind?

A sadness washed over me as I waited to present the big cardboard check to the hospital, and for a brief second, I let myself forget who I was. My smile plummeted, along with my heart, my soul, every bone in my body. I stared at the entrance throughout the entire speech the mayor of wherever the fuck we were for the next few days, rambled on.

"Ladies and gentlemen, Miss Skyler Bell."

I turned my attention to the sound of my name echoing through the ballroom while applause erupted over the vast space. Walking on stage, I smiled at the lady thanking me, unsure of what I was even being thanked for. Handing over the check and posing for what felt like a thousand pictures, blinding me with flashes of light. It all felt so fake and phony, I felt like a fraud with real life feelings.

My emotions Noah was putting through the ringer, day after day.

Did he have something to do with the girl missing? Was she still gone? What about their baby? How the hell was his father murdered?

I practically bolted to the SUV once the charity event was over, trying to be courteous to my fans and quick at the same time. Noah not showing up, only added to all my plaguing insecurities, and I worried I'd be getting on the private plane alone in a few days to wherever the fuck I was going next.

"You look tired, Sky. Please get some rest when you get back to your suite," Keith chimed in, pulling me away from the overwhelming devastation in my mind.

"I won't be able to sleep without him."

With a heavy sigh, he opened his briefcase as I continued aimlessly gazing at the trees flying by the tinted window. Thinking about how my mom loved trees, especially during the fall. All the colors they changed into, and the aroma they stirred in the air.

"Here."

Glancing down, I looked at the pill bottle in his hand.

"Take two, they'll help you sleep."

I nodded, not bothering to ask him what they were. I never did. It felt as if I blinked and I was walking toward the door to my suite with my arsenal of guards surrounding me.

"We'll be out here if you need anything, Miss Bell."

"Thanks, Tony."

Anxiety set in as the double doors closed behind me, wondering if Noah was inside waiting for me. Half expecting him to be there with open arms and an apology, ready to tell me everything and anything to finally make things right between us.

"Noah! You here?"

Silence.

The suite was spotless, his suitcase was still in the bedroom, the scent of his body wash and cologne lingered in the air, but the only trace of him was the hole he left in my heart.

I made my way into the bathroom, changing into a nightie, making myself more comfortable. I stripped the makeup off my face and pulled the pins out of my hair, allowing it to fall over my shoulders. Remembering how Noah loved to stand behind me at bedtime and watch me transform into the girl he fell in love with.

For a second, I blankly stared at my reflection in the mirror, trying to find that girl.

For him.

For me.

Was there an us?

With new thoughts of Noah, beating the hell out of my mind, I walked back into the living room and took three of those pills Keith gave me before snuggling into the sofa. My hand reached up, pulling the soft ivory blanket from the back of the couch over my chilled body, missing his warmth. Feeling like maybe I could just pass the fuck out. At least in my dreams I knew he'd be there, haunting me.

Only this time, it was another nightmare I hadn't dreamt…

Since Noah found me in Vegas.

Freeing the darkness to seep to the forefront of my mind, stirring memories, not even my subconscious could ever run from.

Flying.

Screaming.

Lost.

Always, always lost…

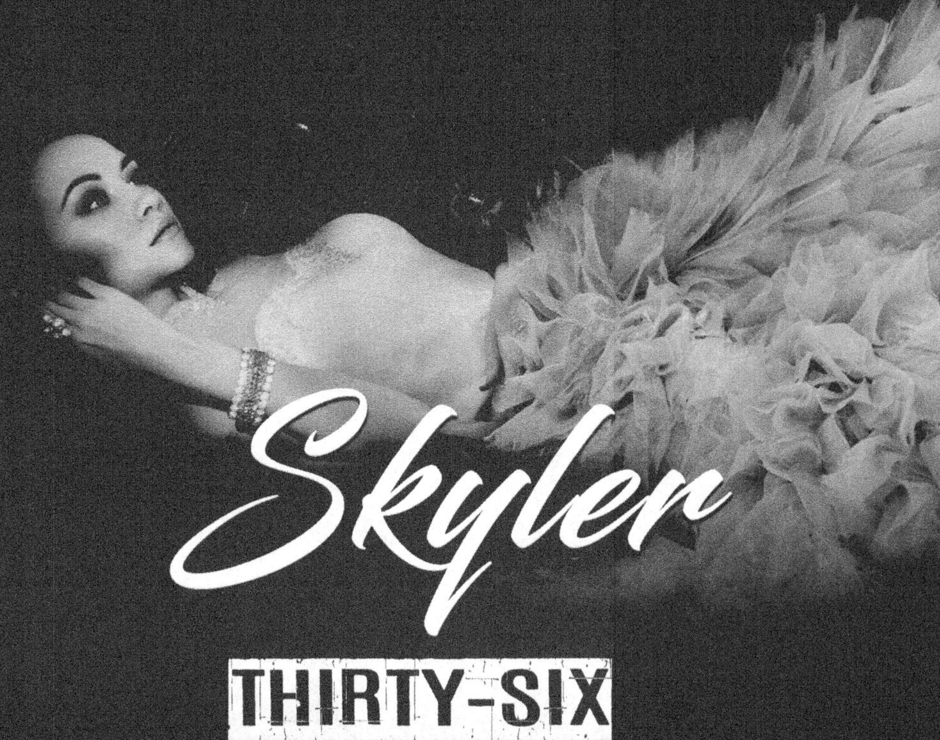

THIRTY-SIX

The car shifted to the right and left again, and was going faster now. Throwing me around side to side as Momma sped down the open road. I looked out the window seeing the trees blur by. Closing my eyes for a second to feel the warm sun on my face, hoping my thoughts would go away. My brain battling the song playing in my ears.

"Emma, enough! Pull over. You can't drive. We're going to wreck. Pull over, now!"

"I can't breathe, Daniel... I just can't breathe."

It was my fault. This was all my fault. I ruined my family, not just Mommy. I was the reason Daddy worked so much. I was the reason Mommy was sad. I needed to get better jobs and make more money. I had to work harder.

To be a shining star.

With Annie, I belted out, "So just hang on 'til tomorrow and work through the pain!" Feeling better. Annie made me feel better. She was my happy place. She would forever be my happy place.

"Fuck! Emma, watch out!"

"Tomorrow! Tomorrow! I love ya all of the days and nights of tomorrow!" I sang with all my heart, feeling like we were flying through the air. "You're almost there! And only a... day... a.... way!"

I didn't know what was happening, but for a second, I thought it was fun. The clouds were massive and bright white against a Smurf blue sky.

It was so pretty, when all of a sudden, my body flew up off the floor. Slamming so hard into what I thought was the roof of Daddy's SUV.

"Mommy!" I cried out, instantly feeling pain all over. From head to toe, inside and out.

My head was dizzy, my eyes were blurry, and I kept screaming, "Mommy! Mommy! Mommy!" Over, and over, and over again.

"Skyler! Baby! Hang on!" Daddy shouted from somewhere in car.

I couldn't see. Why I couldn't I see?

"Daddy, I can't see! I can't see you! Where are you?! Where's Mommy? I'm scared! I'm scared! I'm scared! Someone come get me! I hurt all over!"

"Calm down, Skyler! I have to get your mom free! Just hang on, baby! Hang on for Daddy!"

I did the best I could, thinking about Annie in my head. Her song, her words, how they made me feel.

Happy.

Safe.

Loved.

But freezing cold water started touching my skin, creeping higher and higher up my body.

"Mommy!" I shouted as loud as I could, finally starting to see again. Making me scream even louder when I saw her panicked eyes staring back at me.

Daddy was yanking at her seatbelt, but it wouldn't come lose. He couldn't get it to come loose. Why couldn't he get it to come loose?

"Mommy!"

"Skyler, baby! Hold on!" Daddy ordered in a tone I'd never heard before.

"Daddy, I'm cold! I'm so cold! Please come get me! I want to be with you and Mommy! I just want to be with you and Mommy!"

"Come here, baby! Come to me! Please just come to me!" he replied, finally looking over at me for a second before he went back to yanking at Mommy's seatbelt.

The water was filling the car more and more, faster and faster. And I suddenly realized I was all the way in the very back seats of his SUV. How did I get all the way back here? What was going on?

"I can't! I can't do it! I just can't do it, Daddy!"

"Yes, you can! You can do anything, Skyler! Anything! Be my brave girl! Come on!"

I warily nodded, wanting to be his brave girl. Carefully, I I pushed my body over the seats, the water touching me more and more. Causing shiv-

ers all over my body that I felt in my bones. Splashing through the rising water, I passed my booster seat and toys that had flown along with me. Mommy's purse spilled everywhere and I worried she'd blame me, since I was the last one in it.

Even my Mary Jane shoes filled with water, weighing me down. My clothes stuck to my skin, making it hard to wade through the seats to get to my daddy.

Until finally I was there.

"I did it, Daddy! I'm here now! I'm your brave girl!" I shouted over all the noises the car and the water were making. The crackling sounds, like a soda can being crush as the water filled the car. The sounds of the windows starting to crack.

It was almost hard to hear myself, even though I knew I was yelling really loud. Looking back and forth between them, Daddy kept trying as hard as he could to pull off Mommy's seatbelt while she was just sitting there in shock.

As hard as my daddy tried, he couldn't break her free, and I didn't understand why. Just push the button. Just push the button. It was easy. I did it all by myself all the time.

"Mommy, what's going on?! Someone tell me what's happening? I'm scared! Please, I'm really scared!"

"Skyler..." her voice was filled with so much pain, it hurt my stomach so much just hearing it.

"Oh, God, please, please!" Daddy prayed for I don't know what. Shaking so bad. Jerking Mommy's seatbelt harder, his eyes filling up with tears.

I'd never seen my Daddy cry, not ever. He was so strong, like all the princes in my Disney books. It made everything that was happening much scarier because if he was crying, then this was bad.

It was very, very bad, and that scared me more than anything.

"Emma!" he shouted, but Mommy wouldn't stop staring at me with those painful eyes. She'd never looked at me like that before.

Why was she looking at me like that?

It hurt my heart so much, I thought it was going to burst because of the pain.

"I'm sorry, Skyler baby, I'm so sorry. I should have never—"

"Emma!"

She finally looked over at Daddy as he pulled her seatbelt back. "Squeeze out! Now!"

"Daniel..."

"Mommy, squeeze out! You can do it! Just squeeze out! Please, Mom-

my, please!"

It was like she had already given up, and I didn't understand why. She wasn't even trying. Why wasn't she trying?

"Emma, do it now!"

She finally tried to do what Daddy said, holding onto the steering wheel, trying to lift herself free. But he couldn't get the seatbelt back far enough for her to squeeze through.

It was too stuck.

She was too stuck.

"Mommy, no!"

"Son of a bitch!" he yelled, his body shaking as hard as mine.

The water was touching Mommy's stomach now, only getting further and further up her chest.

"What's happening? Mommy get out! Please just get out! I want to go home! I want to go home now!"

Her panicked expression changed to one that looked like something bad was about to happen. Worse than what was already happening. The windows cracked some more. The crackling sound became louder and louder causing me to scream.

"Take her! Daniel, take her out now!" she ordered, but Daddy just kept yanking the seatbelt harder and harder.

"Goddamn it! No! Don't do this to me!" he yelled, pulling and pulling and pulling.

"Get her out, Daddy! Get Mommy out!" I grabbed onto the seatbelt with him, helping him. Pulling it back with all my strength. But it was no use, I couldn't help him. Making me feel so much worse. I couldn't help my Daddy for my Mommy.

I couldn't do anything right.

Not work hard enough.

Not make enough money.

"Daniel, get her out!" she screeched so hard from deep within her chest, causing my body to jump and shudder.

A fear I'd never seen before took over Daddy's face until he screamed out like he was in pain, once again yanking the seatbelt back until his face turned bright red and the veins in his neck were showing.

"Please! Please! Please!" she begged, looking at him with pleading eyes. So many tears were streaming down her face, I couldn't even count them all if I tried.

"Mommy, please! I want to go home! I'm so cold! I want to go home! Please take me home! I just want to go home! I don't want to be here anymore!"

Closer and closer, the water was up to Mommy's chest now. And I was treading through more water.

"No!" Daddy roared like the beast from Beauty and the Beast. He wrapped his arms under her, trying to yank her out of the seat. "Please, God, don't do this to me! Don't you do this to me!" Holding onto her so tightly like he never wanted to let her go.

"Get her out, Daniel! Please, just get her out!"

"Daddy!" I cried, watching as he frustratingly pulled away and grabbed Mommy's face to look into her eyes. Crying so hard, so, so, so hard. The water was now to her chin.

"Please... Emma... don't make me do this... I can't live without you... I just can't do it. You're my everything. Do you hear me? You're my world. There is no me without you. Do you understand me? I'm nothing without you. Nothing."

"Me too, Mommy! Me too!" I added to make her understand that everything Daddy was saying was true. Nodding my head with more tears falling down my face. I couldn't feel my body. The water was completely sinking me, with little room to breathe.

"Get her out, please, Daniel! Get our baby out! You're her father! Do you understand me? Your job is to protect her! Because I didn't—"

"Emma... goddamn it, I love you."

She nodded, her lips were turning blue and Daddy kissed them.

"I know... I love you too. Forever and forever. It's me and you."

He nodded, kissing her lips one last time before pulling away and I didn't think twice about it. "NO!" I screamed, crying hysterically, throwing my arms around my mommy. "NO, MOMMY! NO!"

"Please, Skyler baby, please," she begged in another voice I didn't recognize. Like she was saying goodbye to me. Like she was never coming back to me. "You be a good girl, okay? You be Mommy's good girl. You take care of Daddy, no matter what you always take care of Daddy. I will always, always be in your heart, Skyler Bell. You're my shining star."

"Mommy, I won't be a bad girl! I promise I will work harder! I'll get more jobs and make more money! Please, just get out, so we can go home!"

"Oh, Skyler... I'm so sorry, baby. I'm so sorry for everything... you're Mommy's good girl. You will always be my good girl. Through everything in your life, all those big moments, your first kiss, the first time you fall in love, your wedding, when you have babies of your own one day, I will be there, in your heart. I've been so blessed having a baby girl like you, so, so blessed. I love you. I will always, always, love... so, so, so mu—"

The water went to her lips, cutting her off.

"NO! MOMMY, NO!" I grabbed onto her chin, trying to hold her face up, but I couldn't. She couldn't breathe. Mommy couldn't breathe. "DADDY, DO SOMETHING! MOMMY CAN'T BREATHE! MOMMY CAN'T BREATHE! SHE NEEDS TO BE ABLE TO BREATHE TO STAY WITH US!"

Out of nowhere, I heard a loud pop and glass flew past my face. Feeling like it was cutting me open. Daddy's arms wrapped around my stomach, but I held onto Mommy harder as he roughly tried to pull me away.

"NO! NO! NO! DADDY, NO! I WANT MY MOMMY! I WANT MY MOMMY! NO, DADDY! NOOOOO!"

With one hard tug that took my breath away, he yanked me from her. Kicking and screaming. I fought him. I fought my daddy for my mommy. I fought the water. I fought for my life that was sinking to the bottom of the water. Without me.

Without us.

All I wanted was my mommy.

"DADDY, DON'T DO THIS! DON'T TAKE ME AWAY FROM HER! SHE NEEDS ME! I KNOW SHE NEEDS ME!" I screamed bloody murder, and my lungs started to burn. Even though I reached back, I couldn't touch her. Making me so angry, so mad.

Why was he doing this?

Why couldn't he get her?

Why was he taking me away!

Why! Why! Why!

"DADDY I HATE YOU! I HATE YOU SO MUCH!" I exploded, I'd never said that to him before, but I couldn't help it. I just couldn't help it.

"Mommy... Mommy... Mommy..." I cried out by the last thing I saw of was face rippling in the murky water through the windshield as she slowly blew me a kiss. The SUV sinking till I couldn't see her anymore. I was being pulled further and further away from her.

Gasping, when we hit the surface. I sucked in air, coughing out water that I swallowed along the way. Gagging and choking, I screamed out in pure agony and pain. Slicing and tearing at my insides, at my heart, at every inch of my skin.

"Mommy! I want my mommy! Please, Daddy, please! Just get her! Just go get her!"

"I'm sorry, Skyler... I'm so sorry," he voiced in a tone that would forever haunt me. Watching as the bubbles shot out of the water, praying every time it was my mommy. That at any second, she would break free and come up above the water. That this was just a bad dream, a nightmare I'd wake up from.

This wasn't happening.

This couldn't be happening.

I huffed and puffed, coughing out more water, unable to catch my breath. Unable to breathe.

"Noooooo!" I screamed again, feeling like I was dying too. I wanted to die.

I just wanted to die.

Please, God, let me die. Please...

"Skyler, Cutie, baby! I'm here... baby, I'm here..."

Noah?

"Come on, baby... wake up... I'm here... Cutie, please wake up...."

Was he in the river too? Why was he in the river? I don't want him to die. Please, God, I don't want him to die.

I couldn't breathe.

I couldn't fucking breathe.

No... No... No...

"Skyler, I'm hangin' on by a fuckin' thread here, and you're scarin' the shit out of me... WAKE UP!"

I loudly gasped, shooting straight up off the couch at lighting speed. Hyperventilating for my next breath, my heart feeling as though it was on fire, my lungs burning, my body profusely shaking. Every inch of my mind, my body, my soul was still in that river.

I just couldn't breathe.

"Shhh... baby, baby, baby."

With wide, wild eyes, my gaze flew to Noah's, instantly holding my hands out in front of me. Stopping him dead in his place with his arms still reaching out for me.

"Don't touch me. Don't fucking touch me," I panted, not knowing if this was just another dream or real life.

"Skyler..." His voice sounded so close, yet so far away. Almost like he was trying to talk me off a ledge. "It's me, Cutie. *Me*."

"Don't touch me." I uncontrollably shook my head. "Don't fucking touch me."

He surrendered his hands. "Baby..." Never taking his eyes off mine, he just started humming the tune to *Annie* for I don't know how long, until he rasped, "Sing for me, Skyler." Before continuing the lulling melody. "Come on, baby, you can do it. Sing wit' me, yeah? The sun'll come out tomorrow, bet all those dollars that..."

"Tomorrow..." I whispered, loud enough for him to hear.

He cautiously smiled, slowly inching his way closer to me. "Just thinkin' about..."

"Tomorrow…"

"Clears away the sadness, the rain, and the…"

"Emptiness…"

"'Till it's not…"

"There…"

"Good girl, baby. That's my good girl… So just hang on 'til…"

"Tomorrow…"

"And work through…"

"The pain..."

"Tomorrow… Tomorrow… I love ya…"

"Noah…"

"All of the days and nights of…"

"Noah…"

"I know, baby… I know…"

"My mom… my mom… I just want my mom…"

With tears pooling his eyes and an expression on his face that mirrored mine, he repeated, "I know, baby… I know…"

I didn't hesitate, throwing my arms around him and sliding myself onto his lap.

"There's my girl. There she is," he soothed in a soft, gentle, comforting tone. As he kissed away all my tears, tenderly whispering sweet words into my wet cheeks, nose, lips. "You're okay. I've got ya, baby. I'm here now and I ain't goin' anywhere."

"Please…" I begged, trembling in his arms. Trying with all my might to talk my six-year-old self-down. It was my fault. It was all my fault, and nothing could ever change that.

"Noah, please…"

"I'm here, I'm right here."

"I need you. Please, I just need you."

Grabbing the sides of my face, he peered deep into my eyes.

"Please… just make it go away… just make it go away…"

"I love you. I fuckin' love you, Skyler." In one swift move, he started kissing me as I frantically unfastened his belt. Making me remember my dad trying to unfasten my mom's, seeing flashes of that day in front me. I shook it away, whimpering.

"Baby, stay wit' me," he urged, kissing me all over again. "Just stay right here wit' me. You're in my arms, you're safe, I promise. I gotcha. You're mine, baby. No one can hurt you. No one."

He was right.

No one could hurt me.

Not as much as I would forever hurt myself.

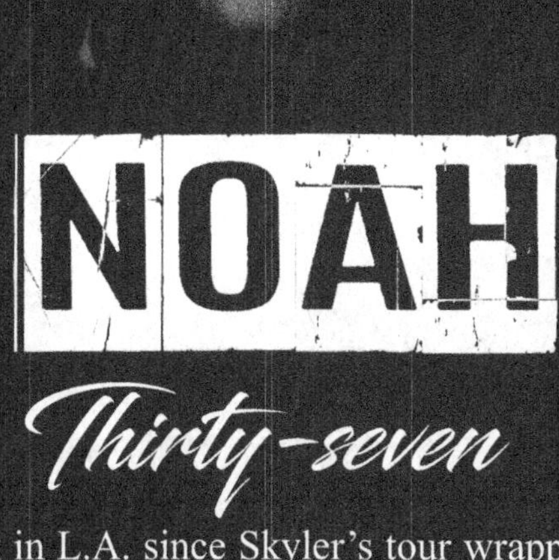

NOAH

Thirty-seven

We'd been back in L.A. since Skyler's tour wrapped up about three months ago in Europe. And I couldn't have been more fucking grateful settling down in one place versus living out of a suitcase for twelve months straight. I'd left Southport, North Carolina over a year ago and hadn't gone back, cutting all ties except for the occasional phone call with Ma to check in on her. She was still sober and attending AA meetings regularly.

Finally taking control of her life, genuinely sounding happy for the first time since Luke died. I hadn't talked to her since the last voicemail she left me while we were in Paris six months ago, inviting me back home for a special occasion, that at the time made me spiral down a bottle of Jack Daniels. Disappearing for a whole day alone, wondering the streets of Paris. Missing a black-tie affair, I was supposed to attend with Skyler.

"Hey, Baby, it's your mother. Just calling to check on you and make sure you are alright. I wish you'd tell me where you are and what you're up to these days, so I can stop worrying about you. Anyways, I called to tell you Creed is getting married this Saturday at one o'clock and I... we would really like it if you came. Now, before you get all pissed off like I know you are, hear me out. He is your brother, your blood. I know there is a lot of animosity between you two, especially after everything that hap-

pened, but, baby, it's time to move on and maybe try to forgive each other. He is with who he is meant to be with and something tells me you might be too. I will text you the details, please put your hatred aside for a day and come home. Please Noah, for me. I miss you, baby. I love you. Talk soon."

Needless to say, I was a no show. Selfish or not, I couldn't bear to witness them get married. Not after the fucking history we all shared.

Skyler and I were living together in her twenty thousand-square-foot mansion in Bel-Air. Even though I fucking hated L.A., I was here on my own accord.

I was here because *she* was here.

This city was just a big waste of space in the world, filled with pretentious motherfuckers left and right. Who had nothing better to do than wipe their asses with hundred dollar bills simply because they could. Everyone was rude as fuck, and they all thought they were better than each other. There was absolutely zero fucking substance to these rich bitches, and all they cared about was what they looked like, what you could do for them, or how much money you made.

The better looking you were, the more money you had, the higher you were considered on the fucking food chain. It was disgusting. And I was smack dab in the middle of it. If I had to meet one more stuck-up celebrity, arrogant producer, self-absorbed entrepreneur, I was going to lose my fucking shit. I couldn't believe this life even existed. It was like an alternate universe where Skyler was Queen fucking B.

When my girl walked into a room, everyone shut the fuck up and turned to look at her. If I thought she got attention while we on tour in different locations constantly, it didn't compare or come close to the amount of attention she got in L.A. Everywhere we went the paparazzi followed. Every newsstand, grocery aisle, fucking billboard had her face sprawled across it. There was no getting away from the cameras. In the last three months alone, I lost count of how many reporters tried to sneak into her private, guarded estate unnoticed to get a picture and exploit her.

It was fucking ridiculous the shit she was put through on the daily, and the worst part was, it didn't even faze her. She was so used to it. People were constantly coming in and out of her house for one thing or another, from her marketing team, to her PR bullshit, to her glam squad, to her wardrobe assistants, and who the fuck knows else. I was so over waking up to a house full of motherfuckers who needed something from her.

Especially Keith.

The son of a bitch manipulated the shit out of her, and I couldn't understand for the life of me how she didn't see it. He was a piece of shit Skyler considered a father figure, when in reality, he was anything but that. Anytime he was around, I started visualizing how easy it would be to put him to ground. Causing me to be around less and less.

It was all becoming too much.

Skyler hadn't stopped working the entire time we'd been together. She jumped right into a new movie as soon as we flew back to L.A. My girl looked fucking exhausted, relying more and more on whatever the fuck her team and Keith was shoving down her throat to keep going. At this point, I didn't even know anymore. She was on set so goddamn much, or at an event, or a photoshoot, or an interview, everything and anything in between.

There was no pause button to make her slow down.

The further I saw into her life, the more I hated it. Not just for me, but for her as well.

The night I witnessed firsthand the truth of her past fucking broke me. I knew her mom had died in Cape Fear river, but I had no idea Skyler watched it all happen. Or that her old man had to choose between his kid and his wife, making me realize we had more in common than I ever thought possible.

It made me sick to my fucking stomach just thinking about it. Knowing exactly what that felt like and how much it destroyed you inside. Leaving a shell of person, you thought you were. I despised where our lives had taken us, her killing herself with her career to feel alive while I…

Lost myself the only way I knew how.

Skyler threw herself into more obligations because of me. Trying her best to avoid the catastrophic war that awaited us just around the corner.

Lurking.

It was a ticking time bomb.

With her never-ending questions and thoughts I could blatantly see in her eyes every time she fucking looked at me.

Our love was saving and killing us at the same time.

Even with the mounting tension between us, we still sought refuge within each other through our love making. It became its own entity. Where we literally tried to fuck our demons out of one another. As if we were going into combat, and neither one of us knew if we'd make it out alive.

With every thrust.

Every moan, groan, pant.

Every *I love you*.

Our past made itself known through the heady movements of our bodies.

And our safe haven, now included parts of our Hell.

"Babe?" I called out, stepping into her bedroom, freshly showered with a towel wrapped around my waist.

She wasn't in bed anymore, so I threw on shirt and some gym shorts, and made my way through the house until I found her outside by the pool.

Walking up behind her, I wrapped my arms around her waist and kissed her bare shoulder. "You smell so fuckin' good."

She leaned into my embrace. "So do you."

I loved my girl best like this. Hair messy, face make-up-free, she was breathtaking with her natural beauty.

"Pepper will be here in a few hours to drop off your tuxedo for tonight."

"I thought that was tomorrow," I replied, turning her to face me.

"No. It's tonight. I reminded you a few days ago."

"I must have got the days confused."

Eyeing me up and down, she replied, "Don't look so excited or anything, Noah."

"Babe… ya know that's not it. I love spendin' time wit' ya, but the thought of another black-tie event, where I can't even fuckin' touch you, doesn't sound that appealin'."

We still hadn't told anyone who we really were to each other, and I was beginning to think we never would.

"You haven't gone to an event with me in like three weeks."

"I think I just answered why."

"Fine." She shrugged. "Don't come."

"Skyler, don't be like that."

"Be like what?"

"Don't fuck wit' me, Cutie. It's too early for this shit. I just made other plans for tonight, that's all."

"For what?"

"To ride out. You know my other girl just got here from Southport." I grinned. "I haven't had a Harley between my legs in months, the only thing I've been ridin' is you." Diesel had my bike brought out to L.A. for me a few months back. No questions asked.

She let out a low laugh. "I'm being replaced for a bike."

"Baby, don't be jealous. You know you'll always be my number one girl."

"Can't you just go this afternoon and come back to go with me to the event? It doesn't start till seven."

"Travis can't ride out till ten tonight."

"Travis? Who's Travis?"

I kissed her lips. "Your slutty best friend's bodyguard."

"You're my best friend."

"Tell that to Melania."

"You made friends with her bodyguard? When?"

"Skyler, you're on my ass to make friends out here, and when I do, you're on my ass 'bout that too? Make up your mind, yeah?"

"Yeah. You're right. I'm sorry. I just don't want to go to another event without you."

"Baby, you barely talk to me when I'm there."

"But you're still there with me. You help me relax."

"When are you ever nervous?"

"When you're not there with me."

I swear she was the most beautiful girl in the world, especially when she was looking at me with big eyes and pouty lips.

"I'll go to your next event."

She smiled, kissing my lips. "My next three events."

"Now you're just pushin' it."

"Mmm hmm…"

"I love you," I whispered in between kissing her, before I turned around to walk back inside. Knowing I'd be getting a call, silently hoping it wouldn't ring until I was out of her sight. Though when had I ever been that fucking lucky.

As if on cue, my phone rang as soon as I stepped away from her.

Adding more secrets to our mound of bullshit lies.

Skyler

Feeling exhausted, I quickly got dressed in the black fitted gown my stylist picked out for me. Trying to use my fatigue as a distraction for the night ahead. I spent all day on set, and now I had to get ready for yet another event. Unraveling with every minute that passed since Noah told me he wouldn't be attending it with me this morning. Although, I had a million reasons not to trust him, I had a million more why I should.

Of course, my mind went right to the worse. Noah was hiding more shit from me, I could feel it. His phone going off at ten o'clock precisely wasn't helping. Mumbling a hello, walking away from my prying ears. He still refused to tell me who it was. Just saying it wasn't something to worry my pretty little head over. And at this point, I had to pick and choose our battles. I didn't know what else I was supposed to do. I tried with all my strength to make him feel welcome, included, part of my life, but I knew he wasn't happy. As hard as he tried, he just couldn't fit in. He hated my world which was why I spent so many years keeping them separate.

In the past, we were part of the same world. Out here we were on the same planet, but galaxies apart.

For the next couple of hours, I mingled with all the "so-called" right people. Pretending to be there in the moment with them when I was miles and miles away in my own mind.

"Where's your hot tattooed bodyguard?" Melania questioned, winking at me. I hadn't told her how important Noah was to me, but she wasn't stupid. She saw the way we looked at each other, even from across the room. She could feel the chemistry radiating off of us. She knew something was up. Though she never called me out on it.

"He's out riding with your bodyguard, Travis."

"Travis? What? He's here with me."

My eyes shifted toward the direction she was pointing, and I couldn't resist. I excused myself and was over to him as soon as I made it through the crowd. Normally I wasn't one to be shy, but how the hell was I supposed to ask a total stranger why he wasn't out riding with my boyfriend like he was supposed to be?

"Hey," I nonchalantly greeted, smiling.

"Yes, Miss Bell, can I help you with something?"

"Umm… yeah. So… Noah tells me you ride."

"Noah?"

Nervous anxiety caused my stomach to churn, but I kept going, trying not to sound like a complete idiot. "Yeah, my bodyguard."

"Oh yeah. Noah. Right. We've talked a few times, nice guy."

Relief washed over me, and I let out a breath I didn't realize I was holding. "He said you guys were going to ride out tonight. Did those plans change?"

"I'm sorry, Miss Bell. I think you might have me confused with someone else. I mean we've talked about possibly going riding one day, but we've never actually made plans to do so. Are you sure he said it was me?"

My heart dropped, feeling all sorts of emotions.

Hurt.

Betrayed.

Angry as hell.

"Yeah, I must have. Thanks, Travis. Have a good night."

I fought with each sentiment as I went back to the event.

He lied to me.

He fucking lied to me.

How many other things had he been lying to me about?

As much as I wanted to, as much as I tried, I couldn't focus on anything other than Noah's lies. I told my team I wasn't feeling well and excused myself before they could question me any further. My heart was in my throat the entire time my chauffer drove to my house. I was done pretending we could continue sweeping things under the rug.

I needed answers.

And I needed them right fucking now.

"Pull over here, please."

He gave me a confused look through the rearview mirror.

"Miss Bell?"

"Please, Paul. I can walk from here."

He did as he was told, pulling over to the curb in front of my house. Thankful as fuck the paparazzi still thought I was at the event, giving me time to escape unnoticed.

It was a little past nine by the time I walked through my gates, praying that Noah was still there and I could confront him. He wasn't getting out of this one, not with how I was feeling.

He'd never lied to me before.

Or had he?

As soon as I saw him backing out of the garage on his Harley, I hid. Deciding to follow him instead, I grabbed the keys off the holder on the wall and jumped into my SUV, tailing a few cars behind him. Preparing myself for I don't know what, or maybe I had known all along and didn't want to come to grips with it. My heart just kept racing as the seconds ticked by, watching the lights on streets blur in the distance. Taking a deep breath every so often, trying to steady myself.

Was he going to the girl?

Their baby?

Is that what he'd been doing all this time?

Was she the one calling?

Did he kidnap her?

But why?

After what felt like an eternity later, I was parking my SUV furthest away from his bike in a dimly-lit lot just off Hollywood Boulevard. We were in the seediest neighborhood in all of L.A., and I was suddenly questioning why the fuck I decided to follow him here of all places. Especially when I was dressed in thousands of dollars' worth of clothing and jewelry, basically asking to get mugged. It wasn't until I looked at my surroundings that I noticed there where expensive sports cars parked along the side of the place. Lamborghinis, Ashton Martin's, Ferrari's and so on.

I watched Noah walk into what appeared to be some sort of abandon warehouse from the lot. Once again ignoring the looming feeling in the pit of my stomach, I waited lost in my own thoughts. Gathering the courage to follow him wherever the hell he was going, already feeling like I knew where that was. Although, I had to see it with my own two eyes. There was no way around it, not when I'd made it this far.

I took another deep breath before slowly stepping out of my SUV. My hands shook so badly, I had to place them under my arms. Holding myself together from crumbling into pieces. My whole body felt like it was giving out on me with each step that brought me closer to his truths. There were too many emotions happening all at the same time, and I couldn't control any of them.

Not a single one.

The warehouse was eerie and silent. The only light came from a few bulbs that weren't broken, hanging above my head as I walked down a long, narrow hallway. The closer I got to the end of what seemed like a road leading the way to Hell, the more I heard loud beats of techno music.

Something was not right.

This wasn't right.

Making my way toward the sound of the heavy vibrations thumbing and echoing off the walls…

Ten steps.

Twenty steps.

Forty steps.

"I got thirty grand on Noah!" I heard a voice shout. "Vlad, I got forty!" Another followed.

What the fuck? Who's Vlad?

Fifty steps.

Sixty steps.

Several crazy amounts of bets were hollered before a thick husky accent stated into a microphone, "Ladies and gentlemen."

I should have stopped.

I should have turned around and left.

But I couldn't get my feet to stop moving.

Seventy steps.

Eighty steps.

"Choose his fate," the same voice announced, at the exact moment I walked into what I could have never been prepared for.

To feel.

To see.

Noah Jameson chose his fate that night, and it didn't include me.

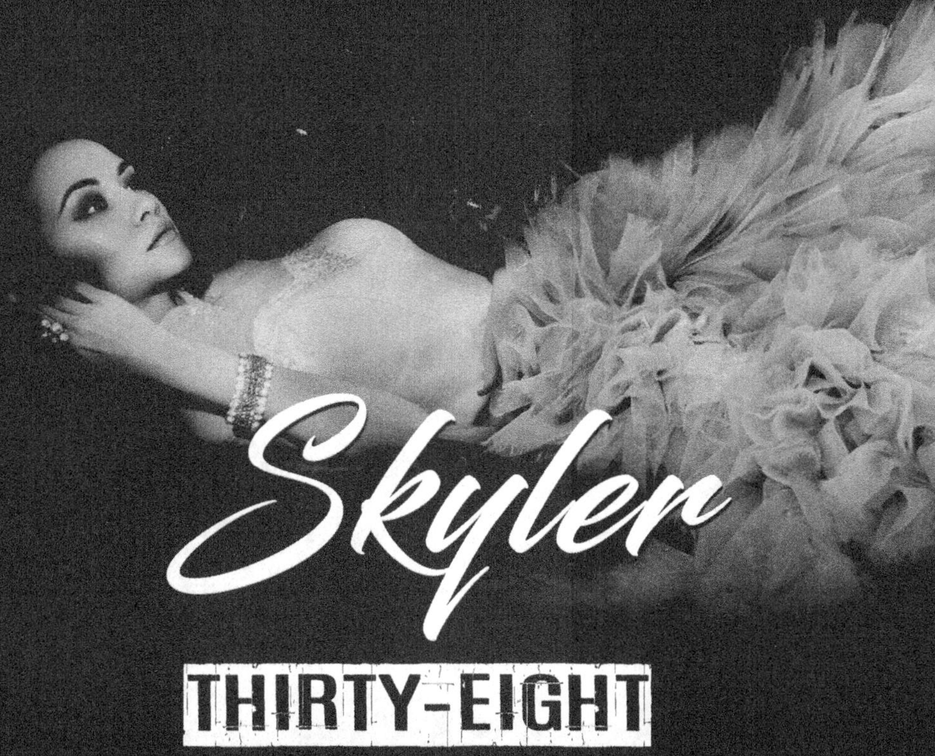

THIRTY-EIGHT

The smell of mold with a distinct trace of sweat and copper instantly assaulted my senses.

The crowd didn't hesitate in chanting, "Death! Death! Death!" over the deep beats of the music. Feeling the high adrenaline pumping in the atmosphere from that alone.

The intensity.

The ambiance.

The depravity of it all.

However, it was the man who was wearing only gym shorts, beating the life out of his opponent, who had my undivided attention.

Noah.

The two men were surrounded by people who were dressed exactly like I was, waving wads of bills in the air, yelling out obscene amounts of money for Noah to divide and conquer his victim. I'd heard of events like this taking place around the world. When you lived in Hollywood, in the midst of millionaires who already thought they were God, it was only natural they'd want to prove it by taking lives without any consequences or repercussions.

I just never imagined it would be Noah who crucified the victim.

Even with the dim lighting of the spacious, grungy warehouse, I could still see Noah's cold, dark, murderous glare. Sucking all the air from my lungs, taking my heart. The heart he owned and shattered it into a million pieces.

It was raw.

Excruciating.

Downright fucking torture.

As I watched the love of my life take another man's soul, for blood money. I spotted the man, who I assumed was Vlad, standing in the back with his arms crossed over his chest. His concentrated stare solely focused on Noah. There was another man standing beside him, keeping tally of the bets placed with chalk on the bloody wall behind him.

My attention snapped back to Noah while my mind urged me not to watch, to look away, to run, but it also willed me to stay in place. My feet glued to the goddamn dirty floor beneath me, suffocating in his demons.

In his lies.

In the lives he'd taken purely for some sick fuck's satisfaction and entertainment. He was as fucked-up as they were.

Noah's fists moved in the same momentum as the adrenaline coursing through my veins, flowing through the degenerate and voyeuristic air. Their bodies were covered in dirt, sweat, and blood, and just by looking at his opponent's mangled face and body, I knew the blood on Noah's skin wasn't his own.

His desolate and brazen eyes never wavered from the man he was tearing to shreds with his blood-infested hands. His chest heaved, his nostrils flared. He looked like a rabid fucking dog.

"Noah! Noah! Noah!" they cheered, only spurring him on more.

Blinking away the sweat and blood, he gripped onto his opponent's head, and used all his strength to knee him repeatedly in the face. Brutally pushing and pulling the guy's skull toward his knee, mercilessly connecting them at the same time. Enough to make me sick to my stomach. Bile rose in the back of my throat as I leaned forward and threw up, heaving everything from my stomach.

My food.

Alcohol.

His lies.

His demons.

Our love.

Panting for my next breath, I looked up and instantly locked eyes with Noah. Through the chaos exploding around us, he found me. As if he felt me through the pain and torment he was slamming into my body, using the same forceful blows he delivered to his opponent. Our eyes stayed connected for several seconds. Fuck, it could have been hours. Time just sort of stood still. It wasn't until my eyes shifted to the lifeless body on the ground that I took one last look at Noah…

And hauled ass like a bat out of hell, running to safety. The furthest away from him.

The boy who once saved me.

Killed me in the end.

Again. And again. And again.

NOAH

She wasn't getting out of this that easy. I wouldn't let her. Like a lion after his prey, I chased her. I hunted her down, ready to destroy anyone in my path to get to her.

My sunshine and happiness.

Turned out to be my biggest demon in the end.

"Skyler!" I ran behind her.

"Get away from me!" she shouted back, sprinting barefoot down the uneven street as if her life depended on it. Her heels firmly in one hand while the other held up her black gown.

"Skyler, you're gonna hurt yourself!"

"Not as bad as you're hurting me!"

"Jesus Christ, slow the fuck down!"

"Fuck you!"

"For fuck's sake, just talk to me!"

"Eat shit!"

And she did exactly that, she biffed it. Falling headfirst onto the jagged road. Piercingly yelling out in pain as her body tumbled in circles once it landed.

"Fuck," I breathed out, running faster. Darting until I finally got to her. Sliding on my fucking knees, ignoring the sting as my own skin torn. "Baby, baby, baby," I coaxed, carefully sitting her up as she weakly shook off the daze. Her forehead was split wide open, and there was no way in hell she wasn't going to need stitches. Blood was gushing down the side of her face. "Shit!"

"Mmm…"

"It's alright, I gotcha ya. I gotcha, Cutie."

I carried her back inside the warehouse, heading straight to the one person I knew could fix her up immediately. Calling out his name right when I saw him, sitting in the next room from where the fight was going down.

"Aiden!"

He peered up from his phone.

"Help me!"

"What the hell? Who's that?"

"My girl."

"That's Skyler? What the hell is she doing here?"

"Stop askin' me questions I don't know the fuckin' answers to and help my girl." I laid her on the table and she whimpered, half conscious. "I know, baby, I know. Aiden's gonna fix you right up. I'm right here, I'm right fuckin' here."

He shook his head with disappointment written clear across his face.

"Aiden, don't fuck wit' me right now."

"You know." He pulled his gloves out from his medical kit, putting them on. "When you first came to me a year and a half ago and told me you were going to start fighting for this motherfucker Vlad, I had no choice but to try to be here for you when I could, so you wouldn't fucking die! Taking me away from my wife, my patients, my life to try and save yours!"

I didn't say anything because what could I reply to that.

"I told you, Noah. I fucking warned you this guy was going to ruin your life, but you were adamant you had it under control," he stressed, injecting Lidocaine into Skyler's deep wound on her forehead. "And after what happened with Maddie—"

"Don't," I gritted out.

"Don't what? Tell you the truth. I'm sick of this shit. You are your own worst enemy, Noah. You have been since the moment I met you as a punk ass fifteen-year-old kid trying to be a man. No one can hurt you as much as you hurt yourself, and now you've dragged this innocent girl into your bullshit!"

Bowing my head in shame, I squeezed Skyler's hand while Aiden quickly went to work, stitching her up.

"What the hell were you going to do if I happen to not be here for a medical conference in L.A. this week, huh? What? You think you could just walk into an Emergency Room with her? She's Skyler Bell, the press would've torn you apart, and all of your secrets would have been exposed. Probably landing your ass in jail!"

"I didn't know she was gonna fuckin' follow me. Do you honestly think I wanted this to happen?"

"Yes." He glared at me. "I do, Noah. You've been holding a gun to your own head for as long as I've known you. It's like you want to die, and I'm fucking exhausted from trying to save you from yourself, but I do it because I wish someone would have done that for me. I do it because you're like a son to me. I have told you time after time, Vlad doesn't give a shit about you. You're just another fighter he stumbled upon during a bar fight. Where you were fighting anyone to feel anything but your daughter's de—"

"Aiden," I warned through a clenched jaw.

He shook his head, finishing up Skyler's wound. Before slamming a bottle of pain pills and antibiotics into my chest for her. "Make sure you watch her all night, she probably has a concussion. If she's still out in the morning, call me. Immediately."

I nodded. "Thanks, man. For everything."

Aiden wasn't just my friend, he became the father I never had. I'd be forever grateful and indebted to him for being there for me whenever I needed him.

No questions asked.

"Vlad is using you, Noah, and you're letting him. Why? You have her." He nodded to Skyler. "You finally fucking have her, and you're just going to end up losing her like you lost Madd—" he stopped himself, shaking his head again. "Get your shit together, man, because you're going to lose everyone who loves you. Including *me*."

I don't know how long I stood there just looking at Skyler after he left. Fucking dreading what was still to come between us, knowing it didn't end here. If anything, her falling only delayed the inevitable shit storm that awaited me when she'd fully come to the next morning.

Vlad didn't give me shit when I asked him if he could deal with my Harley and I'd pick it up from him later. Aiden was right, he didn't give a shit about me. Bottom line, all that mattered to Vlad was that I'd win fights and make him money.

End of story.

I drove Skyler's SUV back to her house, and for most of the ride she was in and out of consciousness. Spending the rest of the night in that state as well. I held her in my arms for as long as I could. Whispering how much I loved her, how sorry I was, how much I truly couldn't live without her. I must have fallen asleep sometime during the early hours of the morning. Letting my exhaustion take me under.

I woke up to the sound of her shower running, and I resisted the urge to go to her. Touch her, kiss her, make love to her, like I had done too many times to count in that exact shower. Simply waiting for her to walk out like I was a man on trial…

Awaiting my fucking death sentence.

NOAH

Thirty-nine

When she emerged wearing her short black silk robe, I almost gasped at the sight of her.

In the broad daylight shining through the French doors, I could see her legs and arms were covered in cuts and bruises. Wounds I didn't see last night when I took off her dress and laid her in bed beside me. The nasty gash on her forehead was swollen with a deep purple hue outlining the twenty small stitches, looking much worse than it did the night before as well.

But she was still so fucking beautiful, and that in itself took my goddamn breath away.

"How ya feelin'?"

"Like shit. I had to cancel my entire schedule for the next few days. Telling everyone I slipped in the pool and hit my forehead on the edge. Oh! And where did you take me to get stitched up? Did the paparazzi—"

"No one saw."

"Are you sure? What about the person who stitched me? Did you make them sign an NDA? Because I guarantee you they'll go to the press—"

"I handled it. Trust me, yeah?"

"Trust you? You can't be serious. Look at me." She held her arms out at her sides. "I look like I've been in a car accident."

"Cutie, I'm sor—"

"Don't, Noah. There's nothing you can say that's going to make anything okay between us. You lied to me. You fucking lied to me."

"Can you please come here?"

"No."

"Skyler, you had a helluva fall last night. You need to rest."

She glared at me, standing across the room. "Whose fault was that, Noah?"

"Technically, yours."

Jerking back from my blunt response, she instantly grabbed her ribs and hissed.

"Shit." I was over to her in three long strides.

"Don't touch me."

"Baby—"

"I mean it, Noah. Stay away from me. All you do is hurt me."

"You know that's bullshit. I fucked up, alright? I shouldn't have lied to ya, and for that I'm really fuckin' sorry, but I ain't the only one who's fuckin' shit up between us."

"Are you kidding me? I've done everything in my power to try and make up for what I did to you, for what I put you through. I've included you in *my* life, *my* home, every last part of *me* is *yours*."

"Is that right?"

"Absolutely."

I backed away, slowly shaking my head. "I ain't doin' this wit' you. Not when you need to rest."

I'd barely taken a step away from her when she stated, "Of course, you're just going to leave. It's your answer to everything now. Go ahead, Noah. Go kill more people to fucking feel better."

I snapped around. "What the fuck did you just say?"

"You. Heard. Me. You think I'm stupid? I'm not a kid anymore. I may have bought your bullshit story about fighting for the money when we were teenagers, but it couldn't be further from the truth. You don't give a shit about the money. You fight to fucking feel. Why? I'm right here. I've been here for over a year now, and you still don't tell me anything about what's going on with you. Why did you come back to me if you were just going to keep—" Her eyes widened, the realization of the answer to that question, slapping her right in the face.

"Skyler," I coaxed, stepping toward her.

Causing her to step back. “Oh my God,” she knowingly breathed out. “I’m such a fucking idiot. How did I not see this until now?”

“Skyler, please… don’t—”

“You weren’t in Vegas for me at all, were you?”

“Baby—”

“Were you?!”

I shook my head. “No.”

She grimaced, her heart breaking right in front of me. “Then why were you there?”

“Cutie—”

“Why?!”

When I didn’t reply, she did for me. “Oh…” She warily nodded. “I get it now. You were there for a fight. Weren’t you?”

“Skyler—”

“Weren’t you?!”

“Yes.”

“I see… so you just stumbled upon the club?”

“Somethin’ like that.”

“Tell me!”

I scoffed, “For fucks sake. I was walkin’ through the casino and when I passed the club, I heard you singin’. Alright? There. Feel better now?”

“You fucking bastard! This whole time! This whole fucking time I thought you were there for me! You’re nothing but a fucking liar!”

“I didn’t fuckin’ lie to you. Not once did I ever say I was in Vegas for you, Skyler.”

“But you still made me think you were! Not once did you say why you were really there! Not one fucking time in over a year!”

“You need to calm the fuck down and stop screamin’ at me, I’m standin’ right fuckin’ in front of you!”

“All this time… all this fucking time I thought… oh my God...” she muttered, expressing so many conflicting emotions on her face that it was hard to swallow. “This all makes sense now. All those phone calls, they were Vlad, weren’t they?”

“Skyl—”

“Weren’t they?!”

“Yes.”

“So you’ve been fighting this entire time?”

“Jesus Christ, why do you keep askin’ me shit you already know the answers to?”

“Because I want to hear it come from your mouth, so I’m done assuming shit! Like you being in Vegas for me!”

"What does it matter? It doesn't change anythin', I'm fuckin' here, aren't I? Wit' you, for you. You think I wanna be here for anyone or anythin' other than you? I fuckin' hate it here, Skyler! The pretentious motherfuckers, the goddamn press, you're career! It's all fuckin' bullshit! Between that and the fact I barely see you, and when I do you look like you could pass the fuck out just from standin'! I'm over it! All of this! It's not me and I swear it ain't you either!"

She got right in my face. "I have worked my ass off to get to where I am right now! How dare you say that to me?!"

"Cuz it's the fuckin' truth! You wanna talk 'bout more truths, Skyler fuckin' Bell?" I growled, eyeing her up and down. "How 'bout this one? You give me shit for not bein' honest wit' you, but when have you ever been sincere wit' me? Huh? You never introduced me to your old man, you never let me into your house in Southport, you never even told me 'bout your mom. I found out on-fuckin'-line, and then the actual details came out through your nightmare you had cuz you were fuckin' high on Quaaludes!"

"They were sleeping pills!"

"That most people use to get fuckin' high! You don't even bat a fuckin' eye or care to look at the shit your so-called father figure fuckin' hands you, like it's goddamn candy! But last time I fuckin' checked, most people just drink coffee and not snort rails of blow to stay the fuck awake, when their bodies are tellin' them their fuckin' exhausted!"

"Everyone. Does. It," she gritted out.

"In what fuckin' part of the world do you live in, that you think it's normal to pop pills and snort blow to fuckin' pass out or be coherent?!"

"I don't know, Noah! Maybe the same part of the world you think it's okay to kill people for the sick pleasure of your own piece of mind?! How many lives have you taken? How many people have you killed, or have you lost count?"

I looked away, I had to.

"Did you kill your piece of shit father too?"

We locked eyes.

"Been readin' up on old news, baby? I had nothin' to do wit' that, but I sure as shit wish I had."

She frowned. "It was on the news?"

"Yeah, how the hell else did you find out 'bout it?"

"What about the girl… she was missing. Did you have something to do with that?"

"Skyler, how the fuck do you know any of this if you didn't—"

"That was on the news too? When?"

"Over four years ago, when it happened. I didn't have shit to do wit' either of those, it was all my brother Creed."

"Your brother? What does he have to do with this?"

"Everythin'."

"Noah—"

"I ain't talkin' 'bout my brother. It's his fuckin' story to tell. But let's just say we were on the road to nowhere and his ended here." I held up my ring finger. "Wit' a happily fuckin' after."

"Fine."

Even though my responses were short, they were to the point and seemed enough to appease her. She reluctantly gave in, moving on. Believing that I didn't have shit to do with any of those questions.

There was no need for me to ask her again on how she found out this information, I knew.

Motherfucking Keith.

"Then answer this. How the hell did you never have any bruises, or cuts, when you've been fighting the whole time we've been together? Do they even hit you?"

"I had too much to lose if they did."

"What about your knuckles? They've never looked—"

"I always wrap them up wit' gauze and medical tape, to protect my fists from showin' you the truth."

"Wow..." she rasped, her mind trying to process everything I just shared for the first time. "I can't even look at you right now."

"Yeah? Well the feelin' is fuckin' mutual."

"We don't know each other at all, do we, Noah?"

"Bullshit. Don't fuckin' say that. Don't you ever fuckin' say that to me." Looking deep into her gaze, I murmured, "I know how you love to be touched, kissed, fucked... I know every smile that spreads on your face, every laugh that flows from your lips, every emotion you feel just by lookin' into your eyes."

Her chest started to rise and fall with each word I sincerely expressed.

"I know the sound of your voice from a mile away... every pant, every moan, every expression you possess when I make you come on my cock, wit' my mouth, my tongue, my goddamn fingers... every part of you is *mine*. From your heart, to your soul, to your pussy. It all belongs to me, cuz *you* belong to me. So don't ever fuckin' say I don't know you. Cuz you're a part of me, like I'm a part of you. And nothin' is ever gonna change that, do you understand me?"

"If that's the case, then tell me who Maddie is?"

My jaw clenched and my body seized up. I expected her to ask this, but it still didn't make it any easier to hear. Her name alone brought me to my goddamn knees.

"I'm sorry, Cutie. I just can't."

"Why?"

"Cuz you'll fuckin' hate me if I tell you."

"You don't know that."

"I do."

"How?"

"Cuz it's part of the reason I fuckin' hate you too."

Her body locked up as bad as mine. "I thought you said you didn't mean any of those things you said to me in Vegas. I guess you just lied about that too."

"I never said I didn't mean 'em, Skyler."

"Right… then I guess I just assumed that too."

Neither one of us said anything, we didn't have to. I think we both knew what was coming. I said it before, and I'll say it again. What goes up, must come down. It was simply the way the world went around.

With trembling lips and tears in her eyes, she whispered, "You need to leave, Noah."

Tearing at my insides, ripping my heart from my chest with her bare hands. "Cutie…"

"Please," she paused, trying to gather the strength to continue. "Because I can't leave you again."

When I blinked, it was only then I realized I was crying. Instinctively reaching for her, I grabbed her face in between my hands. Weeping, "I love you. I fuckin' love you," against her lips.

"I know." She held onto my wrists as if she needed to feel me as well. "I love you too. But sometimes, love just isn't enough."

I pulled her into my arms, wrapping my body around her tiny frame, letting all our demons go. Crying in each other's, mourning everything we ever had together, grieving for the love we lost.

The one we fought for.

That destroyed us both in the end.

Being the first to pull away, I gripped onto the sides of her face again. Kissing her like it was the last time. She was gasping, trying to breathe, so I did for her…

Carrying her to the bed, I made love to her for the rest of day, over and over again till the sun fell behind the horizon of the hills. Darkness settled over us, taking away our last hours as a storm rolled by. Mimicking our minds. We watched the droplets of water running down the windows with the eerie moon, peaking through. The sound of the rain took both of us under, falling asleep in one another's arms, but whenever she woke up I was gone.

It was simply the only way, I could ever leave her behind.

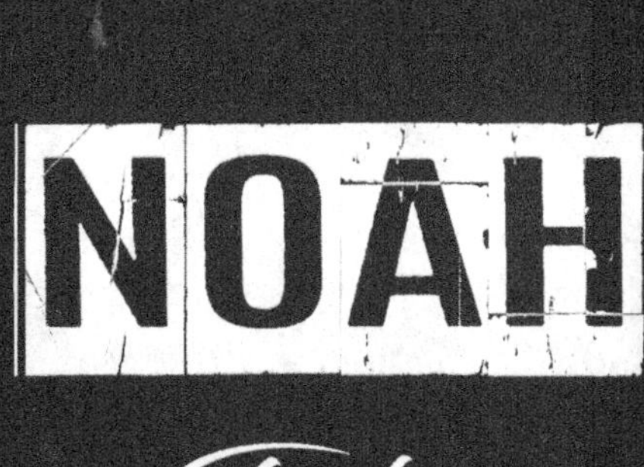

Forty

Walking in unannounced, I called for her. "Ma, you ready?"

"Just about. Give me five more minutes!" she shouted from her bedroom.

"You have the air on in here, damn."

It was hot as Hell outside. North Carolina was always humid as fuck during the summer, but I swear in the last four years since I moved back to Southport from L.A., it was getting hotter and hotter every season.

Using the back of my arm, I wiped the sweat off my forehead and made my way into Ma's kitchen. Knowing she'd have some sort of fresh pitcher to drink, sitting in her fridge. She always did. Chugging half of the iced tea I found right from jug, I reached over and grabbed the remote off her counter. Turning on the TV in the living room.

Hollering, "Ma! Hurry up! You said you'd be ready at six. It's six-twenty."

"I know, honey! But don't give me grief! Your momma's just getting all dolled up for you!"

I smiled, chuckling, but it was quickly replaced as soon as I caught her face from the corner of my eyes on the television screen. Even after all this time, all these years, she still haunted me every fucking day from the moment I left her.

"And if the weather isn't catching your attention then this definitely will. Hollywood's shining star Skyler Bell is back in the spotlight this week," the news reporter announced, stirring emotions deep down in my core.

Just the mere sound of her name caused an adrenaline rush to course through every inch of my body. I stood there in a frozen state of shock with my heart in my fucking stomach, hoping she was okay.

Feeling as though she wasn't before the reporter even revealed, "It seems Skyler Bell has checked herself into a rehab facility for, "exhaustion," apparently," she exclaimed, using finger quotes in the air.

"What the fuck's that supposed to mean?" I said to myself, sitting on the couch. Turning up the volume, needing to know what the hell was going on.

"Skyler Bell was reported, exiting a private plane at the Kahului Airport last Friday. Upon wrapping up her latest movie which is due out sometime around Christmas. The twenty-seven-year-old renowned Oscar winning actress and triple platinum artist, has more than made a name for herself in the industry for over a decade. Since her breakthrough role as Roxie Hart in the remake of the movie *Chicago*. Directed by legendary producer, Martin Addington. From there she went on to make several more movies that smashed box office records, her top grossing one brought in over forty million dollars on opening day. Nothing can stop this actress/singer."

I nodded, "No shit, lady. Not even me," adding my own commentary.

"When she wasn't on set, she was off recording her next hit album. Between her world tour, promoting her first album and returning to the studio right after, she had little to no downtime. Immediately starting on her next album which is due out in the fall. We can clearly see why she'd be exhausted."

"For fuck's sake, Cutie. You haven't even takin' a second to breathe."

"In the last year alone, Skyler has been honored with her own star on the Hollywood Walk of Fame. No one deserves the recognition more than her, it's been a long time coming that's for sure. Skyler Bell is the hardest working woman in the industry. Her Forbes magazine cover alone proved that, stating she's the youngest celebrity in history to have a network over a billion dollars at the mere age of twenty-seven-years-old."

"Goddamn, baby. I wonder how much Keith has acquired from you workin' your life away?"

"The young entrepreneur has also started her own charity for children who have lost a parent, donating hundreds of thousands of dollars of her own money to get it started. Raising over two million dollars the first year it was up and running. This charity is very near and dear to her heart, and she personally handles the funds, along with knowing who has contributed to her cause. If you'd like to donate, the link is on our website or call the number on the bottom of the screen. We'll be back with Ryan after the commercial break, he has more on the story as it uncovers."

Without giving it a second thought, I dialed the number on the screen and donated a very generous amount under the name Rebel. At the end of the call, her voice came over the receiver and it was the sweetest fucking sound I'd heard in a long time.

"Thank you so much for your donation. You have just helped one of many children around the world, struggling to follow their dreams. Thank you again, and have a blessed day."

The line went dead, and I fought the desire not to call again, just to torture myself a little more. Instead, I throw my phone on the coffee table, resting my elbows on my knees, focusing back onto the TV screen for what they had to share next.

The man I assumed was Ryan appeared. "I've known Skyler Bell for years and she's never been anything but lovely, courteous, professional. It's no wonder she's Hollywood's shining star. We absolutely adore her here at E, as do millions of you watching at home. I truly wish I had better news to report, Kat, but that's not the case as of right now."

Pictures of Skyler took over the screen as the male reporter continued with more developing information. A few of her posing with her Hollywood Star, smiling big and wide at the cameras. More pictures surfaced from her tour, singing on stage and shots with random fans, signing autographs. Video footage of her walking the red carpet, stopping every few seconds for pictures.

But the one that caught my eye the most, was her sporting fake as fuck long blonde hair, cascading down the sides of her petite body. Wearing a tiny white bikini with huge sunglasses that almost took up her entire face as she walked the beaches of Hawaii. Instantly making my fucking cock twitch at the sight of her.

She looked older, thinner, different...

But still took my goddamn breath away.

"Sources say Skyler hasn't been seen since wrapping up her latest movie in Hawaii. Though unidentified sources also say she was seen being transported to a secret retreat on one of Hawaii's small, secluded islands. Away from where the press could find her. As Kat was just saying, we all know this young superstar is a workaholic and hasn't taken time for herself in who knows how long. Skyler Bell is known for putting her career before anything else. Including, her on and off again self-made millionaire boyfriend, Eli Ward."

More pictures of her and that motherfucker filled the screen, and my fists clenched in front of me. This was exactly the reason I stayed away from anything concerning Skyler. I ignored every photo I saw of her on magazines, every interview with her on TV, every awards show, every corner I knew that would have a billboard of her.

Not to mention, every movie she had a role in. Anything that pertained to her, I avoided like the goddamn plague. It didn't help that she was probably one of the most famous people in all the world. Only making it that much harder to stay away from seeing or hearing shit about her.

Case and point, what the fuck was happening right now.

"Now, of course." The reporter appeared back up on the screen. "This is all hearsay, her team has yet to confirm any allegations. Although, our team and several other reporters caught up with her longtime manager/agent, Keith Kayes in the Hollywood Hills."

The fucking snake appeared on the screen, pushing cameras out of his way.

"Keith, is it true Miss. Bell has checked into a rehab facility?"

"Keith, are the allegations that drugs played a major role to why she's in rehab?

"Keith, is it true she almost overdosed filming the last scene in her upcoming movie?"

These questions the reporters were hounding him with, only reminded me of how much I fucking hated her life. They were vultures, firing question after question as Keith tried to wade his way through them with men I recognized as Skyler's bodyguards, shoving them out of the way.

Shouting, "No comment!"

"This just in," Ryan exclaimed, once again taking over the screen. "Her team has just announced there will be a press conference later today at eight P.M PST. Concerning the mental and physical state of Skyler Bell. As always E News will be live streaming the coverage and I will be there along with an endless list of media attention for Hollywood's shining star. If the young celebrity has taken a turn down the rabbit hole of Hollywood, it would be such a shame. She wouldn't be the first or the last celebrity to allow Hollywood's demons to outshine her obvious God-given talent, especially with that powerhouse of a voice she has."

One of her songs started playing in the background, her vocals almost bringing me to my fucking knees.

"Toxic me, hmm hmm... toxic you, hmm hmm... wild me, wild you,

hmm hmm… am I hiding my light from you… or are you hiding yours from me, hmm hmm…"

I recognized the song immediately, she was writing it the night I found her in the living room with her guitar in Chicago. Dragging me back to another place and time.

When nothing was right with our worlds, except that we were together.

"We will keep following this story as it develops," Ryan added. "And, Skyler Bell, if you are listening, you're in our thoughts and prayers. As always you heard it here first on E News live. Back to you, Kat."

"Oh no…" I heard Ma mutter from behind me.

"I'm so sorry, honey. When was the last time you talked to her?" she asked, jerking me away from the screen.

Narrowing my eyes at her, confused. "What?"

"Skyler, honey. When was the last time you talked to her?"

"Ma, how do you know I knew Skyler?" I grabbed the remote, muting the television.

"You mean, aside from the fact that anytime we're together and you see a photo of her, you lose all sense of everything. Your whole body tenses, your jaw clenches, even your eyes and the expression on your face gives you away, Noah. Pretty much like they are now."

"Damn." I was blown away from one thing to another. "Why haven't ya ever said anythin' then?"

"Why haven't you?"

I shrugged not know what to say, my mind couldn't process all of this fast enough.

"My baby boy." She lovingly smiled, sitting next to me on the couch. "There's so much I wish I could change in your life. So much I wish I'd done differently. I'll never forgive myself for everything I put you through. I love you more than anything in this world, Noah Jameson. You and I have always had this special bond. From the first moment I held you in my arms, I felt it." Holding my chin in her hand, she used her thumb to caress the side of my face. "But, Noah, you have always been so stubborn and hardheaded. Always thinking you were right when you were wrong, always fighting to feel… I can't tell you how many pairs of bloodstained clothes I've washed when you were a child, because you couldn't express yourself with a few simple words instead of your fists."

Blatantly unaware that old habits never died.

"When you first came back to Southport, I knew whatever you were running away from was destroying you. As much as you pretended to have yourself together, I knew it couldn't have been further from the truth.

I let you be, simply because things were finally settled between you and Creed. You quickly became a partner at his motorcycle shop which you boys and Diesel are making a killing at restoring bikes, doing something you love. You're VP of his MC, *End of The Road.* Godfather and the best uncle to their baby girl, Harley. She adores you, Noah."

Despite how I felt inside, I smiled. Knowing she was right. Creed and I would probably never see eye-to-eye on a lot of things, but at the end of the day we were brothers, blood, fucking family. He had his faults and I had mine. He was happy, living the life he always wanted.

With her.

And as the years flew by, I realized we were more alike than I ever cared to admit. Particularity when it came to our taste in women, his wife had always reminded me so much of Skyler. Since. Day. One.

From her pouty little lips…

To her round face…

To her light eyes and petite frame…

They both even had that saucy fucking mouth on them. Knowing all along, why I loved his wife to begin with.

For the first time in a long fucking time though, I was happy for him. He deserved it, and they deserved each other. No matter what we all went through together.

"I know you and Creed are in a good place, and I couldn't be happier about that, but baby, I still know a part of you blames him and especially yourself for Maddie… but honey, she just wasn't meant to be."

Pulling my chin out of her grasp, I coaxed, "We ain't talkin' 'bout Maddie, Ma."

She nodded, understanding. Being the only person who ever did. "I know, baby… I know. I lost a child too. Trust me, it kills you inside and I spent years trying to kill myself at the bottom of a liquor bottle, when I should have been taking care of you. Instead of you trying to take care of me."

"I'd do it again if I had to."

She beamed, her whole face lighting up. "I know. You saved me, Noah. More times than I even remember. You and Aiden. I will forever be grateful to that man and his wife Bailey for being there for you when your own parents weren't. So please, tell me. It's my turn to try to save you. When was the last time you talked to her?"

"Before I came back home."

"Ah. So I was right. You were with her the entire time you disappeared on us?"

"Somethin' like that."

"What happened?"

I took a deep breath and stated the truth, "I wish I knew, Ma. There was so much bullshit between Skyler and I. There's always been so much bullshit between us."

"She's a lovely girl, and she loves you so much, Noah. And I could see that within the first few seconds of meeting her."

"Meetin' her?" I snapped, caught off guard. "When did ya meet her?"

"She never told you?"

"No."

"Oh gosh, it was such a long time ago… I was barely staying sober for a few months back then. But I guess it was maybe sometime before you turned eighteen. I only remember that because she told me you guys had the same birthday. What are the odds of that, huh?"

"Ma," I warned, my patience slipping with each second that past.

"It was really late when she knocked on the door, looking for you. But the poor thing appeared to be exhausted, like she hadn't slept in days. Her eyes were red and swollen, and I more than recognized that look. She'd definitely been crying for just as long. I couldn't help but invite her to come inside. Try to do my best to console her, she was just so sad."

My mind instantly shifted to the night she was remembering. Thinking the same exact thing when I woke up and saw Skyler hovering above me. I may have chased away her demons the night before she left me behind, but over five years later, when it was my turn to do the same, they ended up chasing me away as well.

The irony was not fucking lost on me.

"After I made us some tea," Ma added, once again tearing me away from my persecuting thoughts. "We sat right here and she told me all about her moving to L.A. How you were her best friend and how much she'd miss you. Wishing you could just understand. Saying something about how there was so much she needed to tell you, but truly didn't know how. I don't know, baby, she was mostly just rambling incessant thoughts. I could literally see her mind spinning the entire time she was talking to me, and all I did was try to listen to her. Feeling like there weren't many people in her life who did. I mean, I may not have known firsthand the pressure of Hollywood, but the things they put these kids through is heartbreaking. I just felt bad for her, Noah. She reminded me so much of you. I could see why you gravitated toward each other. And I truly believe God was responsible for that. It was obvious she needed you as much as you needed her."

"Jesus," I breathed out, shaking my head. "She never told me she met you, let alone talked to you 'bout all this."

"I'm sorry, honey. I thought you knew. When I hugged the poor girl, she hugged me back like I was her family and not someone she just met. Like I was her—"

"Mother?"

"Yeah. Just like that."

Breaking my fucking heart a little more.

"Anyways, I told her you'd been staying on your boat, and she took off shortly after. That was the only time I ever saw her. Although, I have kept up with her career over the years. She's made quite a name for herself, but I can only imagine what she's had to give up in order to accomplish all that."

"Well, you can see for yourself, Ma. I'm here, aren't I? And she's what? In rehab for *exhaustion?* Fuckin' Keith," I growled, abruptly standing. Wanting now more than ever to put him to ground. "I knew it." I started pacing. "I fuckin' knew it. I coulda stopped this from happenin' to her." Resisting the uncontrollable urge to go fight, and take my frustrations out on someone's face. Like I had for as long as I could remember.

Itching to call Vlad, even though I had a new brawl in a few days in Miami. Nothing had changed with Vlad and I's relationship, if anything I fought more to fuckin' feel less. Making him a very rich man in the process. I was to this day, undefeated. Obviously, since I was still fucking breathing.

No one knew I was fighting.

I'd become an expert on how to hide that too.

"Maybe you should try to reach out to her. I'm sure she'd love to hear from you. Especially with what she seems to be going through right now."

I swear to fucking God it didn't matter how many years had gone by. One wasn't enough, two wasn't enough, three wasn't enough, and now we were at four years, and I could still say it wasn't enough.

The old saying about time healing all pain, was filled with nothing but fucking bullshit and lies.

"I have, Ma. Several times. Her numbers changed, her email too. The letters I've written and the gifts I've sent on our birthdays, get returned every single time. There's no way I could even try to get to her at this point. Keith wouldn't allow it, and he sure as shit is behind everythin' I just said as well. He'd have my ass thrown in jail before I'd step off the plane to see her."

"Keith? Her manager?"

"Yeah."

"Honey, are you sure? She spoke so highly of him. Saying he was her only family until she met you."

"Of course she did. He was only part of our problems. The son of a bitch has her wrapped around his manipulative finger. She doesn't see it, it's like her mind is protectin' her from the truth of who the man she's always seen as a father-figure really is. The only thing he wants from her, is control. And she willingly hands it to him. Havin' blind faith he loves her and has her best interest at heart. He feeds her drugs, Ma. And she don't question it cuz everyone in that Godforsaken industry is doin' the same thing. L.A. is filled wit' empty people, who only care 'bout what they look like and the almighty dollar. It's disgustin'."

"Oh, wow…"

"It makes me sick just thinkin' 'bout it, Ma. And she's at the center of it all. So if she's in rehab right now, it's only cuz that piece of shit put her there."

"Speaking of rehab, let me call my sponsor and tell him I'm not going to make tonight's meeting."

"No, Ma. Don't do that. You're gettin' your eight-year sobriety chip. Let's just go."

"Baby, you sure? I can get my chip another night. We can rent some movies and I can make you your favorite dinner."

I shook my head. "Nah, Ma. I wanna be there for ya. I'm proud as all hell of how far you've come."

She smiled. "Thanks, baby. I love you, Noah. I'm will always be here for you. I promise."

"I know. Come on."

By the time we walked into her meeting, we were fifteen minutes late. The room was filled with people all sitting in chairs, listening intently as one of the members was talking up at the podium.

Immediately catching my undivided attention.

"I wasn't always like this, but for over two decades now, I've struggled with my own demons. Dragging me under, more and more each day I've lived without her."

I stopped dead in my tracks, tugging Ma back with me.

"What's wrong?" she whispered.

The room abruptly started closing in on me, making it hard to breathe. A ticking time bomb suddenly taking over every fiber of my being.

Just waiting to go the fuck off.

Tick, tick, tick…

"I want to stay sober, I pray to stay sober. Knowing my wife wouldn't want this for me. For *her*. She's probably rolling around in her grave seeing the man, the father… I've become. Or rather lack of."

My heart began beating its way up to my throat. I could hear it my ears, feel it in my temples.

Three…

"Today was a huge wake-up call for me. After all these years, I finally hit my rock-bottom."

It all made sense now.

Why she never let me into her house.

Two…

"My daughter, my baby girl I love more than anything in this world. The one I was supposed to protect, take care of, be there through everything. Especially after being the only family she has left. Well now, my baby girl is fighting her own demons. And it's all my fault. I have no one to blame but myself."

Why she understood my pain when it came to my mother. Right from the start, when anyone in their right mind would've run away, she stuck by my side.

But the answer that made the most sense at this precise moment, was primarily the question I always had.

On why Skyler never introduced me to her old man.

One…

"My name is Daniel Morgan and I'm an alcoholic."

Motherfucking BOOM.

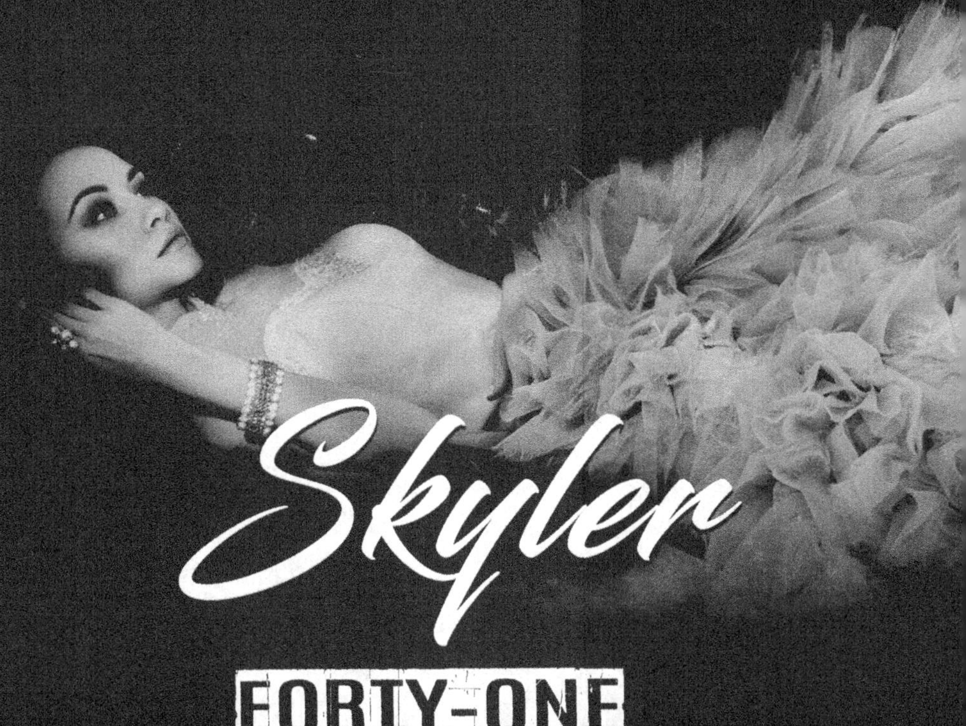

FORTY-ONE

Keith's name and face lit up the screen of my phone, as soon as I sat down in the limo, driving me to a Billboard Music Award after party in Miami. Where some filthy rich man hired me to perform for his guests. Saying he's a big fan and wouldn't take no for an answer, no matter what it'd cost him.

Before I even said a word, Keith greeted on speaker phone, "That was quite the perform, birthday girl."

"You had Pepper facetime you?"

"Of course. I had to watch you closing the Billboard Music Awards. Sky, you killed it, and I couldn't be prouder seeing you up there in your element like a natural shining star, you are. You were the only performer who got a standing ovation tonight. Not to mention you won Best Female Artist. That in itself should tell you something."

"Yeah. That I'm beyond exhausted," I chuckled, leaning my head back against the seat. Wishing it was my bed.

"There's a vile of cocaine under your seat, consider it your birthday present. I had Pepper leave it there for you."

I bent down grabbing the small vile, twirling it between my fingers.

"She's in the SUV behind you, handling your schedule for this week, while you're still in Miami. She thought you'd want to rest after your performance and have some privacy, so you can clear your mind and gear up for the rest of the night."

"I appreciate that, but I'm good. I really don't want to do blow tonight, Keith." I waited, silently anticipating his lecture on how he knows best. Bringing me back to my time in rehab.

Since I was discharged from the facility in Hawaii over a year ago, I'd been back for another round of *treatment* five months later. Seeking solace after yet another one of my fucking movies wrapped. I wasn't surprised in the least when it was leaked to the press both times by who I assumed could only be a money hungry employee. Knowing it was bound to happen, everybody was watching my every move.

It came with the title of being *Skyler Bell.*

Besides, in the eyes of fame, if you weren't being gossiped about, you weren't really famous to begin with. Even the biggest stars in Hollywood with the most private lives, had some sort of gossip reported about them. Rumors were what made this industry stand-out, and so many celebrities start a lot of their own gossip.

If not them, then someone on their team. Purely to have their face on highly publicized tabloid magazines or online media and blogger sites, but most importantly, the goal was to have their name blasted on the television screen. Where the potential to gain an excessive amount of exposure was remarkable and underestimated.

Because there is no such thing as bad publicity.

Though in my circumstance, the media made it out to look like I had a problem with drugs and alcohol. Which wasn't the case. Sure, I did my fair share of drugs occasionally, but everyone in this industry did. My recreational drug use wasn't even that bad, compared to most of the celebrities I knew and hung around with.

If I wanted to quit using, I could without any repercussions in view of the fact that I definitely didn't have a drug or alcohol addiction.

My father on the other hand was an addict. He was what you called a "functioning alcoholic," and had been since my mom died when I was six. It gradually began with a drink or two every night to cope and forget. Two drinks became four, four developed into six until eventually, he was downing liquor bottles on the daily.

I hated it.

I hated *him*.

Regardless, I promised my mom I'd always take care of him, no matter how many times throughout the years he'd let me down. Over and over again.

"Sky," Keith coaxed in a familiar tone I'd been expecting. "You have to perform as soon as you arrive to the party. This man has paid two million dollars for you to sing one goddamn song for his guests tonight. Guests that include some very important people, including, Jackson Ellis."

I bit my lip, concealing the squeal coming from my throat. He was the director every actor dreamed of working with, and I was no different.

"Oh my God! How do you know he's going to be there?"

"Because I know everything, Sky. It's part of my job description. You want the role in his next movie, right?"

"Yes!"

"Then you need to be on point, at your best. I need you to work that *Skyler Bell* charm that lights up a room. It's your twenty-eighth birthday, you've come so damn far. You don't want to start letting anyone down now, do you?"

"No," I sighed, knowing he was right. I quickly unscrewed the vile before I changed my mind. Using the tiny spoon attached, I brought the cap up to my nose and snorted a bump up each nostril. Closing my eyes, letting the coke work its magic.

"That's my girl."

Swiftly feeling the drip in the back of my throat.

Waiting.

And just like that, I wasn't tired anymore.

"So, tell me. Who is this guy? The one who's hosting the party."

"Some Albanian mogul. He's apparently your number one fan."

"...borderline stalker." I subconsciously internalized, thinking only of Noah.

"What's his na—"

"Shit! I have to get going. I'm dealing with another client's crisis over here in L.A., why can't they all just be perfect like you?"

"Hardly."

"I wish I could be there with you right now, but have a great time to-night. Call me tomorrow and let me know how things went with Jackson. I already know you're going to knock your performance out of the park. Happy birthday, sweetheart."

After he hung up, I couldn't help but think about the past year of my life. Our birthday, always triggering our time apart. Setting the wheels in motion to trudge through all the other endless bullshit. Seeing as, just because I'd gone to rehab for exhaustion twice, didn't mean I'd slowed down by any means. My career was my life, and no amount of time in facilities would ever change that.

The trickiest part about fame no one tells you about, no one prepares you for, was how easy it was for society to forget that you were a hu-man-being. A person with real feelings and real emotions.

If you cut me, I bled.

If you hurt me, I cried.

If you left me, I just… felt dead inside.

Life in the public eye, was by far one of the hardest lives to live. It made society think you were a super-human, above everyone else. A role model, an example, a goddamn target to judge, and criticize, and knock down.

When in reality, I was just like anyone else.

The worst part was, I never asked to be any of those personalities. I never claimed to be perfect, I never wanted to be put on a pedestal, I never wished to fall in love. All I ever wanted was to sing and act, except it all went hand-in-hand. Making me live out my life in front of a camera, was not something I was ever ready for.

And now, I had the added pressure weighing on my shoulders to prove the media wrong. Shut down their false accusations that were at an all-time high.

With Keith being Keith, he immediately started damage control. Using my exhaustion as a stepping stone to further my career. Humbling my persona to the press and my fans. Making everyone realize that I was actually a real person, who was flawed and made mistakes.

Landing me more jobs…

More roles…

More interviews…

More. More. More.

Which was why Keith was still the best manager/agent in the business.

The only real problem I had was that I was genuinely fucking exhausted in every sense of the word. Rehab became my only escape from the life I thought I always wanted to obtain and lead.

Island Waves Rehab & Spa Facility was more like a five-star resort than a treatment center. Both of my stays lasted for a little over two weeks, and by the end of it I started wishing I could stay longer, but I had obligations to fulfill. I needed to get back to whatever Keith had booked for me months in advance.

My first couple days at the facility were the worst, I didn't want to be there. I didn't want to attend group meetings and hold hands with random strangers who had it much worse than I did. Alcoholics, drug addicts, sex addicts, anger management, eating disorders, depression, everything a celebrity could possibly have, was treated there.

However, as always Keith knew what was best and pretty much hauled my ass into going. For the first five days of my stay, I did absolutely nothing but sleep. Hard. Only waking up to use the bathroom, drink some water, eat some food, and pass the hell out again.

On the sixth day when I finally came to, it was as if I'd been reborn or something. I felt amazing, refreshed, alive. Feeling like I'd been dead since Noah left me over four years prior at that point. I spent the next few days enjoying the resort, exploring the nature paths, walking around the remote beach. Savoring the sensation of the soft white sand beneath my feet and the hot sun beating down on my face.

Sunshine and happiness.

I even attended some mediation sessions and yoga classes to learn balance. Find my center and all that jazz.

Completely loving and relishing in the fact that after all these years, I finally had some privacy. A foreign feeling I couldn't remember the last time I felt. For the first time in well over a decade, there were no lights flashing in my face, no paparazzi hounding me, no one asking for my autograph or a photo, no prying eyes, no noisy ass people, nothing but peace and quiet.

Although, I stuck to myself most of the time, I was never alone. There was always someone close by, offering me refreshments, food, and support, but none of that was what I needed. I spent a lot of my time on the beach alone, staring out at the endless ocean lost in my memories, feeling mostly hopeless and utterly lonely.

Thinking about Noah Jameson. From songs that reminded me of him, to the people who reminded me of him, to motorcycles that reminded me of him, to *me* who reminded me of him. Even the treacherous waves of the ocean reminded me of him. He was everywhere I went, and no amount of time could ever change that.

One year didn't matter.

Three years didn't matter.

Five years later, and it still didn't matter.

I went to rehab to get away from it all, and Noah still unremittingly followed me there. Instead of focusing on myself like I'd came there to do, I found myself staring out at the ocean, analyzing everything. Knowing all along, Noah and I had always shared a deep connection, and I started to wonder if it could ever be broken. He had the power to make me feel the same way I did when I walked on stage and sang to a sold-out arena.

Without the stage or my fans.

Just him and I.

Noah and Skyler

Our love acting as the fire that burned so profoundly there was no way or chance of ever putting it out. Even with us being apart, it still burned further and further into my heart.

Only inflaming me with our memories.

By the last couple of days of my first stay, I realized it'd been a blessing, and I couldn't wait to go back.

How fucking sad is that?

"Sky, you ready?" my PA, Pepper questioned, holding open the limo door for me to exit.

I nodded, shaking away my drug infused thoughts. Now was not the time, nor the place, to be reminiscing about the hold he'd always have on me.

"That gown, Skyler. It's breathtaking, you look absolutely stunning. I think this might be my new favorite look on you. That peach color accentuates your eyes."

"Thanks, babe."

"I swear, one of these years you will not be working on your birthday. Even if it kills me, I will make it happen."

Smiling, I welcomed the cool breeze as I stepped out of the limo, picking up the hem of my dress. With my guards surrounding us, we made our way through a well-maintained courtyard full of greenery that went on for miles. Enclosing the immense property where I assumed the party was being held. We treaded over two sets of stair pathways, arriving at the main entrance, where several armed men were checking guests in at the gates.

They nodded at us, stepping aside. Signaling toward the large doors of what appeared to be a nineteenth century gothic-style mansion.

"Cecilia, the property manager is waiting for you inside. She will lead you toward the room where Miss. Bell is performing tonight," one of security detail informed.

"Thank you," Pepper replied.

The closer we got to entering the mansion, the more my eyes drifted over the domain. I'd never seen a place quite like this before, other than in the movies. Peering up to the heavens, where two high pointed peaks joined together to form a steepled roof. Practically touching the night's sky. I counted four stories of windows upon more windows, each giving off a soft glow with a burning candle illuminating in the night. You couldn't see where the acres of land started or ended, they went on and on with the rolling hills.

The whole ambiance of the estate gave off an eerie vibe before you even stepped foot inside. Leaving me to wonder what was in store for us once we crossed the threshold.

"Pepper… what the hell?" I muttered under my breath.

"I know, right? This estate is so beautifully creepy. We're in the right place though, because one, the guards recognized you and two, I've already talked to Cecilia, so she's definitely waiting for us."

"Well Keith said the man who's hosting this party is a big fan of mine but judging by his taste in homes, I can't see why."

She laughed, shrugging. "Maybe he's into BDSM or something.

"Awesome. Not only is this place creepy as Hell, now it seems like this guy might be as well."

"Could be worse."

I looked at her.

"You could be here without your bodyguards."

"Good point. Stay close and don't wonder off like the girls do in horror films."

"And always, always turn on the lights when entering the room."

We both laughed, stepping through the double iron doors of the mansion. Into a huge open foyer with floor-to-ceiling walls lined with beautiful intricate hand-carved woodwork. Showcasing the most dramatic grand staircase I have ever seen that split at the top. Reminding me of the Titanic set replica I got to visit in Hollywood, but much creepier. There was a massive wrought iron chandelier hanging above our heads with real burning candles, illuminating the dark alluring space. Reminding me of medieval times when King Arthur ruled.

What the fuck?

"Miss. Bell, it's a pleasure to finally meet you. I'm Cecilia," a busty woman in her thirties announced in a thick accent, shifting my attention from the two sculpted eagles perched on their own pillars, guarding the stairs with intense regard.

Again, creeping me the fuck out.

Only fueling my rampant thoughts of where the hell Keith sent me.

"Thank you, I'm happy to be here," I lied through my teeth, shaking her hand.

"I know this place looks intimidating." She gestured around. "But Mr. Jasari has a particular taste in architecture, as I'm sure you can see."

"It's definitely interesting to say the least."

"You're not the first to be alarmed, and I swear he loves doing that to people. But if you'll just follow me, I'll show you where you'll be performing. The guests are already waiting for you, including Mr. Jasari."

She led the way up the staircase to the third floor, down a narrow hallway with portraits of men and women in compromising positions.

Maybe Pepper was right, this had BDSM lifestyle written all over it. I chuckled at the thought as we made our way into a makeshift dressing room.

"You can freshen up in here if you need to. There is some food and drinks all set up for you, so you help yourself over there." She pointed to an elaborate set-up that was just for me. "Mr. Jasari will be giving a toast shortly and will announce you. All you have to do is walk through those double doors right over there and you will enter the stage. You have about ten-fifteen minutes. Please let me know if you ladies need anything at all."

"Thank you," we replied.

With that Cecilia exited the room, and Pepper handed me my glam bag. Touching up the dark circles under my eyes, I sat at the elegant vanity. Preparing for my last performance of the night.

Keith was right, I sang one song, and I was done. Only envisioning the man I'd written it for, like I did every time I belted out those lyrics. It ended with yet another standing ovation from the crowd.

"Sky! That was amazing!" Pepper exclaimed, closing the door to my makeshift dressing room, after I signed a few autographs and took a few pictures. Talking to me while I fixed up my makeup for the rest of the party ahead. "Every time I think you can't beat your last performance, you prove me wrong! Oh my God! Look! I have goosebumps!"

Ignoring her ass-kissing enthusiasm, I asked, "Did you happen to see Jackson Ellis?"

"Yes! He says he wants to meet with you."

I smiled, looking at her through the mirror. "Okay, give me a minute." I finished reapplying my lip stick and freshened up my hair.

Keith's words repeating in my mind, *"I need you to work that Skyler Bell charm that lights up a room,"* as I snorted a few more bumps of cocaine from the vile he left me. Ready to put on my best performance of the night, for none other than Jackson Ellis.

Fully aware this was an opportunity of a lifetime.

From the moment I crossed the threshold, I knew what I had to do. Confidently striding over to the director, I beamed big and wide.

Once again showing him…

Why I was Hollywood's shining star.

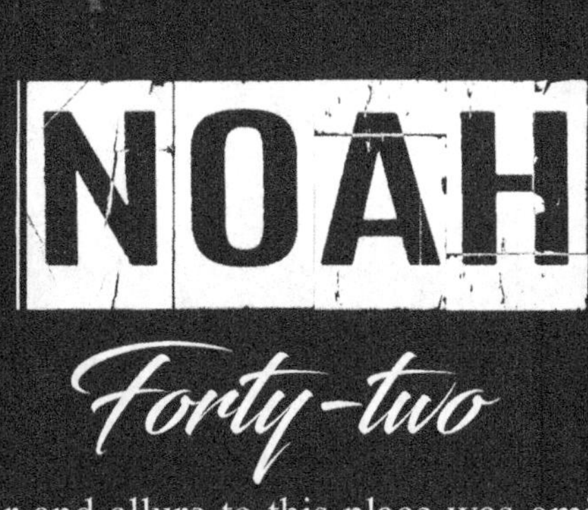

NOAH

Forty-two

The whole décor and allure to this place was ominous and disturbing. This was the first time I had been to this property, considering Vlad owned more estates than the fucking richest man in the world. Whoever the fuck that was. Every room had the same vibe throughout—giving you the feeling you were being watched, and I don't mean by the security cameras everywhere you turned, but by death looming around every goddamn corner.

Especially in the underground basement where I was fighting.

A heavy presence filled my lungs, making it hard to breath. Feeling the tortuous brutality these walls have seen for over a hundred years of existence. Which I'd be adding to after tonight.

I walked around the underground, piece of shit basement, mentally preparing myself for another fight to kill or be killed on my birthday.

Our birthday.

Trying not to think about Skyler, although it was pointless. Today was always the day I thought about her the most. Hoping, praying, she was thinking about me too.

Deep down knowing she was.

I felt it.

Grabbing my bag Aiden had prepared for me for every fight, I set out the gauze and medical tape on the table. Wondering where his ass was. And just as I was about to pull my phone out to call him, I heard a faint sound of a woman's voice. Singing in the distance over at the estate.

It couldn't be.

Like a moth to a fucking flame, I followed it.

Bolting through the door, taking the uneven cement stairs two at a time. Rushing past the dark stone walls lined with moss, outside to the back of the manor.

It wasn't until I walked back inside Vlad's mansion that the familiar voice echoing off the walls became louder and clearer. Inciting me to think I was fucking hallucinating. My head began spinning, one memory, one thought, right after the other.

"Toxic me, hmm hmm… toxic you, hmm hmm… wild me, wild you, hmm hmm… am I hiding my light from you… or are you hiding yours from me, hmm hmm…"

Each lyric that fell from her lips pulled, tugged, heaved me toward her. Dragging me further into the abyss of my own persecuting mind.

"I loved you then, I love you now, I'll love you forever and ever… because I'm the Cutie to your rebel…"

Ten steps…

"You were mine and I was yours… no matter what… we had each other… but now you're gone… and here I am… lost and alone… missing you… forever praying… you're missing me too…"

Twenty steps…

"Toxic me, hmm hmm… toxic you, hmm hmm… wild me, wild you, hmm hmm… am I hiding my light from you… or are you hiding yours from me, hmm hmm…"

Thirty steps…

"You left me behind because I begged you to… but first… you made love to me… relentlessly… always ruining me… for every other man…"

Each of my steps were precise and calculated, each stride more alarming than the last. I was a man possessed, wearing my goddamn heart on my sleeve, holding my breath, ultimately waiting till my soul found hers.

Forty steps…

"What we had… would eternally be, with you, with me, with us… for all infinity… because I was you're sunshine and happiness… and you were mine… up to… the end… of time…"

And then I saw her, right there in front of me.

"Toxic me, hmm hmm… toxic you, hmm hmm… wild me, wild you, hmm hmm… am I hiding my light from you… or are you hiding yours from

me, hmm hmm..."

I narrowed my eyes to the vision before me, she had this aura around her. It glowed, illuminating her with that same magnetic pull she had toward everyone in the room. No one stood a chance on resisting her God-given talent, born to perform on a stage.

She was still fucking breathtaking. I caught myself gasping at the sight of her. From her long, natural colored hair that was curled and cascading down the sides of her face. To her peach colored corset gown accentuated every curve of her petite body that I knew like the back of my hand. Losing myself inside of her for so many goddamn hours. Her dress had what appeared to be feathery material from her waist down, spreading out all around her.

She looked like the only angel in the spacious room, filled with nothing but blood thirsty voyeurs.

Before I knew it her performance was over and everyone was standing, cheering, and clapping. Causing me to lose sight of her through the crowd of party goers. Quickly realizing she disappeared.

Did I just imagine this? What would she be doing here of all of places?

I turned, looking for Vlad. Rushing my way through the party, needing to find her, feeling as though my life depended on it. The rooms were already swarming with endless amounts of people, feeding off the depravity of each other. While music played loudly through the speakers as everyone mingled and carried on, waiting for the main event.

Me.

I fucking hated Skyler being in this environment, she didn't belong in this world. She never did. In the blink of an eye, I remembered what happened the last time she stumbled upon my betrayal. Memories of that night clouded my intuition to just feel her through the seedy air. Recalling the look in her eyes when they locked with mine after she heaved the contents from her stomach. The act of violence delivered through my fists, physically made her sick.

Of me.

Of us.

Of everything.

I needed to find her. She couldn't bear to witness me fighting… killing another life, taking another soul, dragging them right down to the depths of Hell with me. She barely survived it last time, more than likely baring the scars to prove it.

My blood boiled to the point of searing pain, blinded by craze and madness looking for her, only to repeatedly come up empty. Unable to control the inner turmoil or the wave of emotions making themselves known, holding me captive in the prison staged in the forefront of my mind.

Panic set in.

Dominating every one of my actions, every one of my thoughts, every one of my senses.

Growling in frustration, I stopped in the middle of the foyer by the grand staircase. Tugging my hands through my unruly hair, my eyes darting in every direction as I did a three-sixty around the large, open space.

Tearing apart at the seams when I suddenly felt someone tap on my shoulder, I whipped around.

"Cuti—" Confronting Vlad face-to-face instead.

"Where the fuck have you been?" He grinned, "Did you happen to watch the performance from your birthday present?" Almost knocking me on my ass. "What?" He cocked his head to the side. "Did you think I didn't know about her? About the two of you? Oh come on, Noah, I knew way before she ever stepped foot into that warehouse in L.A.. Despite what your Dr. Pierce thinks, I do give a fuck about you. You fight for me, and your loyalty has spoken for itself over the years. A man like me can appreciate a man like you. Fighting to forget the lost boy inside of him."

Instantly, I jerked back stunned.

"You know, when I first saw you walk into that bar in the Bronx with that swagger and the weight of the fucking world on your shoulders. I just knew you were waiting to rip someone to shreds. Provoking anyone to step up to you. Until someone finally did, and you didn't hesitate on laying them the fuck out. Fucking feigning for their blood like a two-bit hustler."

"Is this the part you tell me you saved me from a life of corruption?" I mocked, arching an eyebrow. Curious of where he was going with this.

Scoffing out a chuckle, he ignored my question. Stating, "Over the years I've had a lot of men fight for me, but you're the first one that's never lost one fucking round. Why do you think that is?"

"Cuz I'm just that fuckin' good."

"You are, but that's merely because the only man you're fighting and killing every time you fuck someone up, is yourself, *yeah?*"

I didn't know how to reply or what to even think of that, knowing deep down he was right. Confusing the fuck out of me over the drastic change in his demeanor. Vlad was as corrupt as they came, so who the fuck was this man standing in front of me? He'd never spoken or taken an interest in my life, in any shape, way, or form.

Why now?

"Are you gonna tell me where the fuck Skyler is? Or are ya just gonna keep standin' there, pretendin' you actually give a fuck 'bout me?"

"Relax. I'm not kidnapping her and selling her to the highest bidder. She's far too famous for me to get away with that, Rebel."

I glared at him.

"Don't bite the hand that fucking feeds you, motherfucker," he spewed in a thick Albanian accent. Stepping closer to me, getting right up in my face. "It's your birthday and you've made me a lot of money, so how about you just say thank you."

"I find it hard to fuckin' believe you did this for me."

"And why is that?"

"Cuz you have me kill for money."

"I don't have you do shit. You do that on your own. I made you an offer years ago and you didn't refuse it. At any point and time, you could have walked away. You chose to kill people, Noah. I simply made it easier for you, but how much longer do you think you can fight without dying, eh? Might want to think about that when you find her."

"You gonna make things even more awkward between us and hug it out? Cuz I'll tell you right now, if you touch me, you'll leave me no fuckin' choice but to lay you out, old man. Now tell me where the fuck she is?"

He laughed, "Believe it or not, I have a soft spot for women who own men's balls, you pussy-whipped son of a bitch. But last I saw, she was talking to Director Jackson Ellis, in the library. Third floor, fifth room on the right."

Before he had the last word out, I was sprinting down the hallway.

"Don't wear yourself out, fucking her! You fight in an hour!" he called out behind me.

I ran the entire way there, dodging people, veering through the crowd. Sticking out like a sore fucking thumb. All his guests were dressed to the nines like they always were, and here I was wearing gyms shorts and a shirt with no sleeves.

I hauled ass, feeling as though forever flew by until I was finally taking the stairs three at a time. Each step faster than the last, trying to get to her through the mayhem of this goddamn party. My senses kicked into overdrive as soon as I made it to the third floor.

What do I say to her?

I'm sorry?

I love you?

I need you?

But you gotta leave, so I can kill someone first?

All those questions were pounding around in my mind as fast as my heart was pounding through my chest, I didn't waver, roaring down the hallway just as fast. Nothing could stop me, not even our past.

Ready to talk to her, hug her, feel her, for the first time in over five years. I'd been dreaming about this moment for just as long. More emotions consumed my mind, but it didn't stop me from reaching for the door handle and turning it.

When all of a sudden, I heard a man say, "You want the role, don't you, Skyler?" abruptly restraining my decent. "Then audition for me, sweetheart. Prove to me how bad you want this part."

My hand let go of the knob and the door slowly started to open on its own accord. Displaying by far my worst fucking nightmare.

Barely having a moment, a second to even contemplate what was happening, before I was standing in the open doorway.

Greeted by a whole new set of her demons, fucking possessing me to watch.

Him spewing, "Be the best actress you can be. Go above and beyond what you usually do for other directors."

It was as if I was reliving Luke dying.

Ma's seizures.

Creed and Pops burying my brother's body out in the woods.

All. At. Once.

I stopped breathing.

"I'm harder to please than most producers, I make my actresses audition all night for a role."

My fists balled up.

"Show me what makes you so goddamn special. It's my turn to experience Hollywood's shining star."

My body clenched.

"How far are you willing to go to get a part? All the way?"

My mind went to that dark place inside myself.

Fight or die...

Fight or die...

Fight or die...

As if my glare was shooting fucking bullets, my eyes went from Skyler laying on the couch with her peach colored gown spread out all around her.

"You're going to have to do better than that, sweetheart. Let me feel you."

To the man dressed in a black fucking tuxedo, his left arm placed on the back rest of the couch by her head, while his solid frame hovered over her body.

Fight or die…

Fight or die…

Fight or die…

With his hand up her fucking dress…

In between her spread fucking thighs.

Fisting its way to my fucking heart, replicating that feeling in my chest.

"You need to get wet for me, baby. It's a requirement for the role. Now let me feel your pussy come on my fingers, or else you're just wasting my time."

His vulgar words slammed into me like a thousand fucking daggers with no end in sight. My glare shot up to Skyler's face for the first time, needing to see her get off on the pleasure from another man like she always did for me.

Never expecting her to already be staring back at me, like the scene unfolding in front of her was by far her worst nightmare as well.

Our eyes locked, and she barred it all…

Her pain.

Her sorrow.

Her reality.

For the second time in over a decade, she revealed her truths. Showing me the girl who sought refuge in me by making love to her, before leaving me behind.

Exposing her other life.

The one I wanted to be a part of so badly when we were kids, but she just couldn't let me in, because she couldn't show me this part of her.

I grasped right then and there, I had been right all along. From the very beginning of our fucked up love story. Skyler truly was two different people.

One for me who owned her heart.

And another for her career who owned her body.

When all they really wanted…

Was. Her. Soul.

Forty-three

The words, "Noah, no!" flew out of Skyler's mouth right when I sprang into action with fury coursing through my veins.

I forcefully grabbed ahold of the motherfucker and ripped him off the top of her, as soon as the last word left her lips. Using the fuel from my rage to throw his solid body across the room, watching as his back connected with the adjacent wall with a loud, hard thud. Practically knocking him the fuck out as he tore through the shelves of books. Thankful no one was around to witness me snapping his fucking neck.

In two strides, I bent down and picked him up off the ground by his hair as he instantly surrendered his hands out in front of him.

"I don't want any trouble, she consented to this!" he let out in one breathe, shaking like a goddamn pussy. Nearly pissing himself.

Halting my vicious assault that I wanted to inflict by crushing his fucking windpipe, I crudely shoved him away instead. Making his back roughly collide with the shelves again.

My chest heaved, my nostril flared, and with my murderous glare, I narrowed my eyes at him. Snarling, *"Run before I fuckin' kill you."*

He took one last look at Skyler, and bolted out of there like a bat out of Hell. Slamming the door behind him.

After he left, she breathed out, “It’s not what you think,” loud enough for me to hear.

Unable to turn around and face her, I growled, “It’s exactly what I fuckin’ think.” Feeling like the room was caving in on me. “How. Long?”

“Noah—”

“How. Long?”

“Let me explain… please just let me explain.”

“Explain what exactly? How you whore yourself out for movie roles?”

“No! I… I just don’t… I can’t…”

“Here we go again wit’ your ‘*I can’t*’ bullshit.”

“Noah, please… Can you just turn around and look at me? I need you to look at me, please...”

“Skyler, if I look at you right now, it’ll fuckin’ destroy me. I’m hangin’ on by a thread. A very thin fuckin’ thread. And if you don’t start answerin’ my goddamn questions, I’m gonna find Keith and I’m gonna to do to him, what I was just ‘bout to do to that motherfuckin’ director, finger fuckin’ you. Do you understand me?”

She broke down and started crying, mutilating my heart a little more. “It’s not what you think… I swear it’s not what you think…”

“Then fuckin’ tell me!” I roared, slamming my fist into the mangled shelves. Causing her to let out a small scream, flinching away with her arm’s cradling her head.

Never expecting what she was about to say…

Ever.

“It’s just the way it is, Noah! It’s the way it’s always been! It’s how everyone gets roles!”

I snapped around so fucking fast, it almost gave me whiplash. “Bull-shit! Why the fuck woulda even think that?!”

Please… I just…” She frantically shook her head, stumbling over her words. “It’s just… I mean… just… let me explain.”

“Then fuckin’ explain, Skyler, cuz all I keep hearin’ is more fuckin’ bullshit!”

“I know how it looks, okay? But you don’t know a damn thing about this industry, alright? I’ve been in it my whole life. I know what I’m talking about, this is just how things are.”

“How. Long?” I shuddered from the brutal impact of her words.

“Noah—”

“How fuckin’ long?!”

Time stood still, everything around us stopped. Except my merci-less thoughts, as I impatiently waited for her to answer, knowing it was only going to intensify my chaotic state. I desperately tried governing any ounce of control I had left. My impulses were seething violently through my body.

I was shaking, every part of my resolve hammered throughout my core. I could hear it ringing in my ears, feel it in my blood. Producing a debilitating pain that made my eyes water, and my teeth grind.

Anticipating for her to kill me all over again.

"Skyler," I warned in an unnerving tone, with my thin fucking thread about to snap the fuck off.

"Noah, please… what are you even doing here?"

"How. Long?"

"I honestly don't know how to answer that."

"What the fuck does that even mean?"

"It means it's always been happening in one way or another."

My eyes widened, instantly brimming with tears. "Please don't tell me… Jesus Christ… was this happenin' when you were a child?"

"Sometimes."

"Cutie…"

"Don't look at me like that. Please, Noah. This is why I never told you. This is why I couldn't let you in… because of that look on your face right now. I knew you'd never be able to look at me the same ever again, and I couldn't risk losing you. Or having you look at me as anyone other than your sunshine and happiness. It's just the way Hollywood is. I accepted that a long time ago, so please stop looking at me like that. It's only killing me."

"Baby…" I blinked, and tears slipped from my eyes down to the floor between us. And before I knew it, I was standing in front of her, pulling her into my arms. Holding her close against my chest. Needing to feel her, in order to survive this. "I'm so sorry, Skyler… I shoulda known… I coulda protected you, baby… I'm just so fuckin' sorry…"

She melted into my embrace, like she was trying to sink into my body. Her shoulders trembled from the sobs wreaking havoc on hers. My arms tightened around her as a million more questions ran rapid though my mind.

Blurting, "How old were you when you first got molested?"

"Noah, it's not like that."

"Baby, yes, it is… you just didn't know any better…"

"No… I consented to it. I let them do it. It's just the way things are. That's what Keith has always said, he—"

"I'm gonna fuckin' kill him."

"No!" She pulled away from me. "He hated it too. He's always hated it. But it's just the way it is! He's been there for me, through it all, consoling me after. Telling me everything was going to be alright. Talking me through all the confusing emotions. Assuring me it was normal for girls in this industry to get ahead. Helping me understand that we couldn't change things! It's just how Hollywood is. You don't get it!"

"No, baby…" I shook my head, wiping the tears from her face. "It's you that doesn't fuckin' get it. He's your goddamn pimp, Skyler. Has he raped you too?"

"No! He's like my dad! He would never hurt me! You don't know anything about this life! Nothing!" Uncontrollable tears streamed down her beautiful face. "He loves me! Do you hear me?! Keith loves me!"

"For fuck's sake, Cutie! That's not love! It's pure manipulation! That's how he gets you to sell yourself! By makin' you believe it's normal! By relyin' on only him! By controllin' you're every move! Why can't you see you're only dollar signs to him?!"

"That's not true! It's just not true!"

"Does your daddy know? Huh? Tell me? Does he know what he's been puttin' you through?"

The expression on her face answered my question.

"Right… let me guess why. Cuz he's already grievin' his wife at the bottom of a bottle. No need to give him anymore shit, yeah?"

"How do you know that?"

"Cuz I saw him at a meetin' over a year ago. He had hit his rock bottom the same day the press announced you were in rehab for the first fuckin' time."

"Oh my God, does that mean he's sober?"

"He's tryin' to be," I paused, allowing my words to sink in.

"How did I not know this? I know I haven't been home to see him in a long time, but why wouldn't he tell me?"

"Looks like keepin' secrets runs wild in your family."

"That's not fair."

"Not fair? You wanna talk 'bout shit that's not fair again? Cuz I'll tell you what's not fuckin' fair. Havin' the girl, who I love more than anythin' in this world, crawl into my bed in the middle of the night, upset… torn… fuckin' devastated, while I chased away her demon's wit' my goddamn cock."

She winced from the shock of my abrasiveness.

"Only to be slapped in the fuckin' face that she wasn't a virgin. So tell me, which one of your precious fuckin' directors took what was supposed to be mine?"

Backing further away from me, her eyes intensified, with one hand over her heart. As if she was trying to hold it together.

A man could only take so much and I had reached my wits end. I wanted answers and I wanted them right fucking now. Even if it meant I had to pry them out of her, fighting tooth and nail to get her to just open up the flood gates and let her sins wash over me. They would be our burdens together.

Unable to control my patience and temper any longer, I went at her. Needing to hear all her truths once and for all.

"Where you goin', Cutie? Can't handle the truth? Goin' to run just like you did back then?" I stepped toward her and she stepped back.

"Stop!"

"Stop what? I'm just gettin' to know the real Skyler Bell. The one who thinks older men touchin' her pussy is okay, considerin' she was only a child. Cuz what did ya say? It's normal, yeah? That's just the way it is in Hollywood? Pedophiles, hidin' behind a title of bein' a fuckin' director, so they could molest and rape little girls."

"Noah, stop it!"

"No! I'm not gonna stop it! Not until you understand that Keith isn't anythin' but your goddamn pimp!"

I could see her resolve crumbling as fast as mine was. I was getting through to her, and as much as it was killing me to continue pushing her over edge. I had to. It was the only way, I could save her from this motherfucker who's been using her body like it belongs to him.

"Is that how you got your first big break? Did you fuck the producer into hirin' you as Roxie Hart? Which seems fittin' now, seein' as Roxie was a whore. How many directors are married? Wit' little shitlins running around? Cuz you're claimin' some mighty big words, you consented to it all, right? Then that would make ya one too.

She shut her eyes when I clung onto the back of her neck, tugging her to me. She came over to me naturally, and I hugged her tight against my body. Fitting me like a glove.

"What's wrong, baby? Is my girl realizin' that she might have it all twisted? That her father figure is just a snake in the fuckin' grass? Cuz the man who'd fuckin' die for her has known that since the first time he laid eyes on him."

"Noah, please… please… I'm begging you. Just stop… I can't breathe. I can't fucking breathe."

With my face on the side of hers, I glided my cheek along the crevice of her jaw and then along the side of her neck. Moving my lips to her quivering pout.

I kissed her lips for the first time in what felt like forever, murmuring,

"Then I'll just breathe for you." Finding the strength I needed to endure what I was about to bare. Realizing that if I wanted Skyler to share her demons with me than I had to do it as well.

Reaching for the hem of my shirt, I pulled it over my head, taking it off. But it wasn't until I grabbed her hand and placed it over my Maddie tattoo that she immediately opened her eyes. Connecting with my intense stare.

Not hesitating, I confessed my biggest demon. "She was my daughter."

Blowing her fucking resolve.

Her glassy eyes widened as her hand covered her trembling lips. "Was?"

I nodded. "Yeah, Cutie. Was. She died minutes after she was born, a month early."

Memories of that night hit me like a bucket of freezing cold water. Blistering my heated skin as I continued my story.

"Honestly, everythin' that happened prior to Maddie dyin' don't matter, cuz it won't bring her back." Wiping away the tears in my eyes with the back of my hand, I took a deep breath, finding the will to resume. "Shit went down with my old man's MC. Long story short, instead of stayin' wit' her and our baby, I ran after the motherfucker's wit' Diesel and some other brothers. Leavin' them both to fight for their lives wit' Creed and the MC doctor, Doc. By the time I got back, Maddie…" I paused, reeling in the emotions her name alone caused. "Was already gone."

Every emotion came flooding back as if I was still standing there, staring at my baby girl's lifeless body. This was the first time I was telling anyone about what happened, about what I went through.

All in the name of Devil's fuckin' Rejects.

Wishing more than anything, I was the one who put my old man to ground. My mind wondering to all the things I would have said and done to him, before putting a bullet between his eyes. I may have physically been there with Skyler, but mentally I was gone just like Maddie.

I was there, but I wasn't.

My mind dragged me back to the past, where I lost everything I've wanted.

A family.

Except, I'd always known in the back of my mind it was with…

The wrong girl.

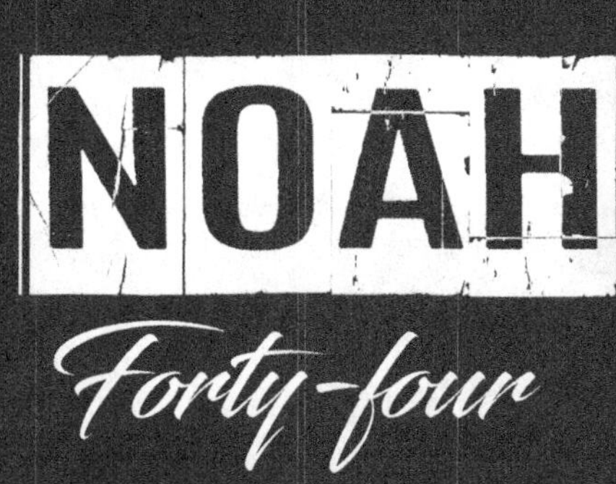

NOAH

Forty-four

"Creed," I whispered in an eerie tone. Cautiously walking around him. Taking in the scene in front of me, from all the blood on everyone's clothes, to the sullen expression on their faces, until my hesitant stare settled on my older brother.

He mouthed, "I'm sorry," for what, I understood.

My eyes widened, my jaw dropped, and all the life drained from my body. Fervently shaking my head, I breathed out, "No," peering down at my baby girl who was in his arms. "NOOOOO!" I screamed bloody murder, an ear-piercing scream that resonated deep in my bones.

Eternally etched in my mind, forever branding my soul. Tears swelled up in my eyes as my chest heaved and my body trembled.

"Give her to me!" I stepped toward him, but he stepped back.

Profusely shaking his head with fresh tears rolling down the sides of his face. "Noah... please..."

"GIVE HER TO ME!" I yelled loud enough to break fucking glass.

It echoed around the small room, lingering in my ears. I reached for her, causing him to take another step back. In spite of the devastating agony I was feeling, I knew he was trying to salvage what was left of my heart. Protecting his baby brother the only way he knew how. Knowing if he let me hold her, it would completely destroy me.

But, it wouldn't change the outcome. Letting me see her up close. Feel her.

Fucking love her.

"Noah, we did everythin' we could. I swear to you," he uttered, but I didn't catch the rest of what he said. Because despite the fact, I knew Creed would never purposely hurt me. It still didn't stop the feelings, the emotions, the sentiments of what I blamed him for.

Maddie…

"Fuck you!" I seethed through gritted teeth, murderously glaring at him. It was the first time I had ever felt so much fucking hatred for him. More now than when he left to play G.I. fucking Joe. More than leaving me with our alcoholic mother and piece of shit father. More than killing our brother, Luke.

This was unforgiveable.

Without giving it any thought, I lunged forward, roughly ripping my daughter's lifeless body out of his grasp. Cradling her in my hands, immediately unwrapping the blanket from her face. Needing to see her with my own two eyes.

She was so beautiful.

So small.

So perfect.

So. Dead.

"NO! NO! NO! PLEASE! PLEASE! DOC, DO SOMETHIN'! PLEASE FUCKIN' DO SOMETHIN'!" I bellowed, holding onto my daughter. Falling to my knees, I held her close to my chest rocking her back and forth. "It's okay, baby girl. It's okay, Daddy's here… I'm here now… Everythin' is gonna be fine. I'm gonna make it all better. It's okay," I choked on my words, setting her on the floor in front of me. My hands shaking over her, not knowing what to do.

Desperately wanting to resuscitate her.

"Please… Maddie… please… don't do this to me… please don't fuckin' do this to me… I can't lose you… you're all I ever wanted… please…" I suddenly looked around the room. "Why are you just fuckin' standin' there?! Why isn't anyone doin' anythin'?! PLEASE! FUCKIN' HELP ME!" Sucking in air, I hyperventilated. My heart fucking breaking into a million pieces.

"How could you let this happen?! I shouldn't have fuckin' left! She would be alive, if I hadn't fuckin' left!" I grabbed ahold of her again, taking her in my arms, pressing her up against my face. "I'm sorry, Maddie… I'm fuckin' sorry I failed you… Please… please… baby girl… for-

give me... I love you more than anything... I'm sorry," I repeated over and over again, kissing all over her tiny face, her tiny arms, her tiny chest.

My body gave out on me, hunching over from crying so fucking hard. Losing the battle I never had the chance of winning. After this day, my life would be forever changed. There was no coming back from this.

Everyone watched in silence as I mourned the death of my daughter for I don't know how long. Struggling to hand her over to Doc, who delivered her. Needing to hold onto her for a few more minutes, a few more hours, when a lifetime wouldn't have been enough time with her. I cradled her for as long as I could. Having a hard time letting her go. I couldn't do it, I just couldn't say goodbye to my baby girl.

Not now.

Not ever.

I huddled over her tiny frame, grieving her death. The life she should have had. The happiness she should have brought into this world.

Into my life.

Not the devastation that occurred.

I cried into the nook of her neck and broke the fuck down. Whispering more apologies in her ear before turning my face away, unable to look at her any longer. Doc helped me, by grabbing ahold of her, gently pulling her out of my tight grasp. Causing me to reluctantly let her go from my arms.

"I know, man... I know..." he mourned with me, letting me hold onto his shoulder for support.

I could barely fucking stand.

But I needed to keep going, keep moving, even though I was now fucking dead inside. Everything that proceeded was one big giant clusterfuck and blur.

Until I heard Creed holler, "Noah!" as I was making my way toward the front door.

I didn't answer or stop, not that he expected me to. When I felt him grab onto my shoulder, I didn't fucking hesitate in pulling out my gun and firmly pressing it right against his chest. Digging it right into his heart.

He jerked back, his eyes widening. Never fucking expecting that.

I gritted out, staring deep into his eyes, "If you know what's good for you, you'll let me walk out of here. I've killed men for far fuckin' less than what you just did in there, Creed."

He was no longer my brother standing in front of me.

My family.

My blood.

He was just the man who killed my daughter.

Taking away my whole fucking world, the one thing that made me feel whole after Skyler left me.

With my finger still firmly over the trigger, I cocked my gun to the side. Spewing, "But you ain't worth the blood. You ain't worth the fuckin' effort. Bein' a part of your life is a guaranteed fuckin' death sentence." I nodded behind him. "Maddie's death... her blood... it's on you. You're the reason she's dead."

The sincerity of my words were like taking bullet after bullet, after fucking bullet to his heart. Far worse than any shot could have delivered from the barrel of my gun.

I backed away slowly, still aiming my gun at his chest. Taking one last look at him with disgust and hatred evident in my eyes, before I turned and left. Slamming the door behind me.

Instantly seeing Skyler's face, knowing in my heart that this never would have happened. If she hadn't left me.

Immediately making me hate her just as much as I would eternally fucking love her.

Skyler crying out was what brought me back to the present, standing right there in front of her. She looked as devastated as I felt. Noticing that I was crying as well, more tears streaming down my face.

"Oh my God, Noah… I'm so sorry. Please… please forgive me…"

"I know, baby. I know."

"I had no idea…" She uncontrollably sobbed into my chest. I can't begin to imagine what you went through, losing a child. I'm so so so sorry. I wish I could go back. Change everything, take away the pain I've caused."

More shuddering.

More shaking.

More sobbing.

"I can't believe this, it's all my fault, Noah. If I wouldn't have left… you would have never… Jesus, now I understand why you hate me. I hate me too."

"Look at me." I grabbed her chin, making her look up at me through her tear soaked lashes. "For a long time I blamed you, Creed, and even myself, but the truth is it's no one's fault. My brother was placed in a shitty situation that night, and in the end, he did what I probably woulda done, if I'd been in his fuckin' boots. Creed and I are on good terms, we worked through our shit. But it don't matter, cuz—" I placed my hand over her name "—Maddie will forever live in my heart. I may have only gotten that one short moment wit' her. But I was there for every ultrasound, every doctor's appointment, tryin' to be the best father I could. Not wantin' to miss one damn milestone throughout her pregnancy. I got to feel my baby girl kickin' in her momma's belly, I got to see her tiny, beautiful face even if it was only brief. What still fuckin' kills me though, is that I never got the chance to say goodbye to her. But I'm prayin' that maybe I'll get to see her again one day, you know… before God tells me to get the fuck outta there."

She giggled, sniffling.

"Baby, no more secrets, yeah?"

Her eyes locked with mine, knowing it was her turn to share her demons with me. The mere thought of what she was about to tell me was almost too much to handle on its own.

Before she could give it anymore thought, she finally replied to my plaguing question with, "I went to you that night because for a week prior, I couldn't live with what had happened to me."

In an instant, it felt like I was standing in quicksand, and it was rapidly taking me under. Skyler must have felt it too, she shuddered and shut her eyes, cascading down the wall behind her. Reminding me of a waterfall, plunging into a pile of nothing when she hit the bottom. I willingly went with her, we could drown together.

Swallowing hard, she muttered, "I attended a party at a director's house in Miami. For most of the night, I drank away my sadness from having to leave you. Mingling around the room. Being *Skyler Bell*. When at some point during the night I just happened to be standing next to the owner of the estate. We talked, I charmed him, luring him in with my false confidence. Portraying the shining star, I was always meant to be. One thing led to another and he called over another executive producer…"

It was my turn to shut my eyes, leaning my forehead against hers. "Cutie, no more. I don't need to hear the rest." Aware of where she was leading with this.

Not making it any easier when fresh tears started flowing freely down her face, confiding, "They took my virginity, Noah," in a distressed voice that would forever haunt me.

Quickly realizing she was no longer there with me, her mind went right back to that night.

"They passed me around like I was nothing but a whore. Not caring that they were hurting me, not stopping when they made me bleed. Cry, breakdown…"

"Baby, baby, baby…" I wept against her lips. Placing my hand on her cheek. "Open your eyes. I'm here. You're wit' me. No one can ever hurt you again. Do you understand me?"

She hastily fought, trying to shove me away but it didn't faze me. I knew it wasn't me she was trying to battle, it was her recollection of that night. Where she lost what had always belonged to me.

Her soul.

I didn't move an inch though she wanted me to move a mile. She struggled against me on the floor, trying to stand until her body gave out, her mind shut down, and her memory surrendered. All together in a pile of penance in between us. She sucked in air and took me in again as if she just remembered it was me who was there with her. When she couldn't fight me any longer, she wrapped her arms around me.

Bawling like a newborn baby.

Crying an ocean of tears.

Sinking among her sobs.

I held onto her the entire time. Never letting go. Until she believed that she wasn't alone. Giving her hope in a moment of nothing, but despair.

Weeping, "Keith said it was normal for me to feel like I'd been raped because it was my first time. And every girl's first time is never what it is in the movies. Up until that point, some directors had only touched me, made me touch them… nothing even close to what they did to me. *Nothing.*"

"Where the fuck is he? He can't be here wit' you. Cuz he ain't up your ass."

"He's doing damage control with another one of his clients back in L.A. I just don't understand… why would he lie to me?"

"Cuz he's a very sick fuckin' man. Who preys on innocent little girls who just don't know any better. Wit' your mom gone and your dad—"

"Noah, it was happening way before my mom died."

I jerked back, once again fucking stunned. "What?"

"It's always happened. I mean, not with every executive. They're not all like that, thank God, but some of them are."

"And your mom didn't know?"

"No. I told you, she pretty much let Keith take control over my career. She said it was in my best interest, that I was safe with him. I could trust him, that he loved me like I was his own. Always telling me I was lucky to have him as my manager/agent, and in my life."

"Jesus Christ, he had you both fuckin' fooled. I still don't understand how you haven't seen right through him, after all this time. To me, it was so fuckin' obvious that the motherfucker was manipulatin' you. I shoulda put him to ground years ago, and saved you from this life of never sayin' no."

"Noah, you can't—"

"What, Skyler? What can't I fuckin' do?"

"He's Keith Keyes, everyone knows who he is."

"I don't give a flying fuck if he were God. I'm gonna send him straight to Hell."

"Noah—"

"Times up, Romeo!" Vlad announced through the door with a curt knock. Snapping our attention over to him. "Stop fucking and come fight."

Skyler's body immediately tensed in my arms, now understanding why I was there in the first place.

"Skyler! Your PA and security detail are waiting for you downstairs. She looked stressed, but don't worry, I kept her occupied."

"Give me ten minutes, yeah?" I called out, only staring at the upset woman sitting in front of me.

"Alright, just hurry. Everyone is already waiting on you."

"Yeah, Noah. Your audience awaits for you to go kill another person." She went to stand up, but I grabbed her wrist. Pulling her back down.

"Cutie—"

"That's Vlad isn't it?"

I brushed a piece of stray hair away from her face. "Yes."

"What the hell? So he knows about us?"

"Apparently."

"So is that why I'm here?"

"Evidently, you're my birthday present."

"Well, then I'm your two-million-dollar gift."

"So you gave him a deal, yeah?"

"You're not sweet talking your way out of this one. You're still doing this, Noah? Fighting to feel? You can't keep living this life. It's not—"

"I know."

"Noah, I'm serious."

"Cutie, I know. This is my last fight, alright? I fuckin' promise. I mean after I snap Keith's fuckin' nec—"

"Skyler, I gotta go. Text me the address to your hotel. I'll be there as soon as I can, and we'll figure shit out, together. No more leavin'," I spoke with conviction, "You're mine."

She deeply sighed, and reluctantly nodded. Hating that I was going to fight.

"I love you, Skyler *Morgan*."

That made her smile, and with that I kissed her one last time.

Hard.

And deep.

And long.

Before I stood up and left.

Never imagining where the night would lead me. From killing one man, my opponent…

To trying to save, another.

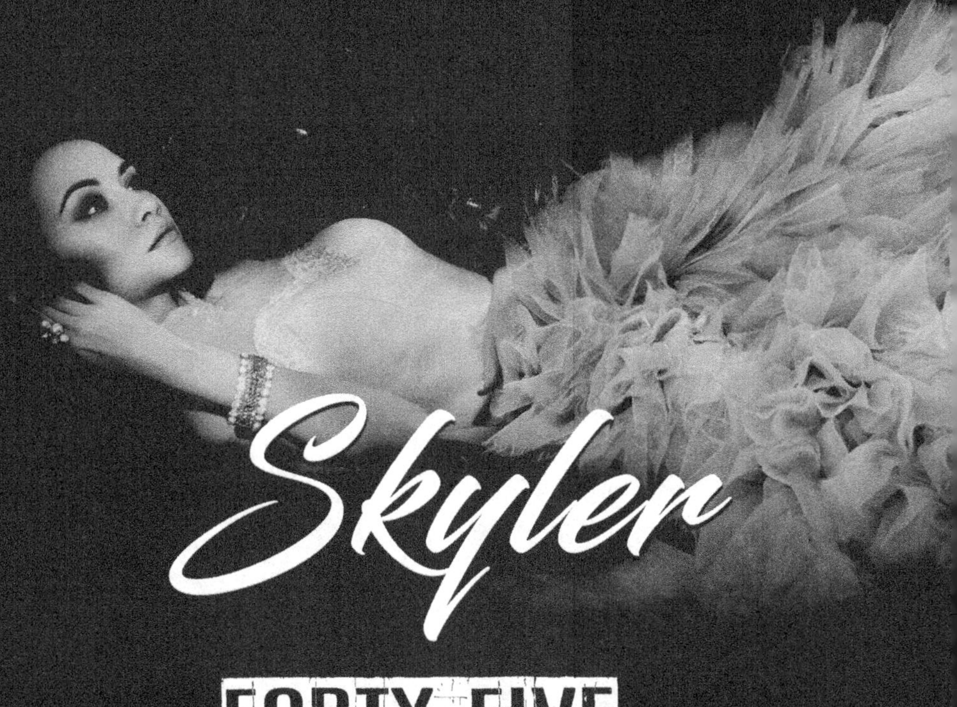

FORTY-FIVE

After watching Noah leave to go fight, I picked myself up off the ground, contemplating what the fuck just happened. It was a whirlwind of emotions, from one thing to another. Feeling like a fucking fool for having blind faith in a man who did nothing, but whore me out. Making me think the entire time it was normal, when in reality, it was the furthest thing from that.

How could he do this to me?

My mind couldn't process all these revelations fast enough, and I found myself lost in thought for I don't know how long. Minutes felt like hours. Until I was walking on autopilot toward the bathroom, fixing my makeup while I tried gathering whatever was left of my bearings. Before I made my way back downstairs.

As soon as I walked past a man I instantly recognized from the news and press, my mind and eyes quickly shifted, wondering what the hell District Attorney Damien Montero was doing here of all places.

Was he a blood thirsty voyeur too?

What the fuck?

I didn't have time to give it much thought when Pepper and my guards, ushered me to the exit. Though my eyes still lingered on the DA as we left the estate, watching him follow a woman to where I assumed the fight was.

Only adding to my afflicting thoughts of Noah tearing into someone again, shedding more unnecessary blood and violence.

Risking his life for what?

Fueling the emotions all over again.

Once we were sitting in the limo, I settled into the leather seat, closing my eyes.

"How'd it go with Jack—"

"Not now, Pepper." Not wanting to have any conversation with her or anyone else for that matter.

My head was fuckin pounding, spinning with every sentiment known to man, mixing in with all my unraveling thoughts and questions.

How do I handle Keith?

How do I even fire him?

Should I go to the press?

Tell them what's been going on behind closed doors in the fantasy land of Hollywood?

Should I call my dad?

Tell him first?

How do I stop Noah from killing Keith? Or…

Do I let him?

"Skyler," Pepper pronounced, standing by the open door of the limo. "We're here."

"Oh." I stepped out, grabbing the hem of my dress. "I must have dozed off."

How do I get away from Keith?

Would he even let me go?

Should I confront him?

Do I confront them all?

"You have an early morning tomorrow," Pepper briefed, making me realize we were now in the elevator. "I'm going to head to my room, but I'll wake you—"

"Actually, I want you to cancel my entire week."

She jerked back. "What?"

"You heard me. I'm exhausted. I need a break. I want the week off."

"You never take time off."

"No shit, it's why I'm telling you cancel my week."

"Skyler, you have a full schedule like always. I can't just—"

"You can, and you will."

"But what about your obligations? You're going to be letting people down."

"Shit happens."

"Since when? You go to work with a fever."

"Pepper, I don't answer to you. Last time I checked, I pay your salary. Now cancel my week or—" the elevator doors dinged open "—I'll have to replace you and find someone else who will."

Without giving her a chance to reply, I stepped off the elevator with my guards in toe. Letting them know Noah was going to be arriving at any time and they were to grant him access right away. Nodding to them, before I walked into my secluded, penthouse suite and shut the door behind me. Briefly taking a moment to myself, I leaned against the frame. Just remembering to breathe.

In and out.

There wasn't a damn thing I could do about any of this right now, and if I stopped moving, I would more than likely break the fuck down all over again. And for the first time in I don't know how long, I didn't want to do it alone. Not when I had Noah back in my life, helping me carry my burdens. Taking a deep breath, I had to try and remain calm.

"You know what you need… a nice, hot bath," I suggested to myself, walking into the master bathroom. "I'll relax, loosen up some tension, and by the time I'm done, maybe Noah will be back."

Turning the nozzle on the huge circular hot tub, I tossed in the bath salts and bubbles that the hotel provided on the counter, and undressed. Welcoming the warm water as soon as I stepped into the bath. Sitting on a comfortable spot against one of the jets.

I closed my eyes, hearing every manipulating word Keith ever said to me through the years.

"You don't want to disappoint anyone, especially your mom, do you?"

"I'm sorry, sweetheart, I didn't make the rules. It's just how it is in Hollywood. You want to be a shining star, right? It's what your mom always wanted."

"It's okay to like it, Sky. You're consenting to it. You're not doing anything wrong. Let your body enjoy it."

"You want that role, don't you? Nothing in life comes free."

And the worst one being…

"I love you, Skyler. You're like a daughter to me."

When I heard what sounded like the door to the penthouse shutting, I called out, "Noah?" but I didn't hear him reply.

Grabbing the cotton robe the hotel provided, I got out of the tub and quickly threw it on. Not wasting another second before I walked toward the living room. Needing to feel his presence and arms around me for the rest of the night.

As soon as I rounded the corner into the kitchen, I came face-to-face with the last man I expected to see.

A pissed off…

Motherfucking Keith.

He didn't waver. Coming right at me, spewing, "What's this bullshit I hear that Jackson Ellis hauled ass out of the room he was in with you?"

I instantly stepped back, grabbing onto the lapels of my robe. Suddenly feeling beyond vulnerable and exposed.

"Who told you?"

"Who do you think? Pepper!"

"So what? You just have her watching me now?" I wrapped the fabric tighter around my body, tying it as tight as it would go.

"What the fuck?" he scoffed out. "Of course I do. I need to make sure you're safe at all times. It's what any father would do."

Unable to control my emotions any longer, I roared, "You're not my father!"

He jolted back, stunned and blown away.

I instantly felt as if this was going to end up badly, so I didn't falter. Stepping past him, going straight toward the door where my guards were protecting me on the other side.

"Don't you walk away from me!" Keith seethed, gripping onto my wrist. Forcefully yanking me to face him again.

"Stop it!" I struggled against him to get away, screaming for my head of security, "Tony! Tony! I need you!"

"Sky, what the fuck is wrong with you?" Keith snarled, fighting me to stay in place.

"Tony! Please!"

"Jesus Christ, Skyler! He's not here! I sent them away!"

I froze, every part of my body locked up. Screeching, "What? Why?"

"Because I wanted some goddamn privacy to figure out what the fuck is going on!"

"Let go of me! I mean it, Keith! Let go of me, now!"

"What the fuck has gotten into you? Huh? Why are you acting this way? You're being fucking crazy!"

"Because of what you've been doing to me!"

So many bad memories came rushing back. My heart racing, my blood boiling, my mind playing tricks on me. Taking over all my senses.

"Did to you?! What the fuck are you talking about?!"

"I know, Keith! I know the truth! So you can stop fucking lying to me!"

"Lying to you? For fuck's sake! You're not making any sense? Are you high right now?"

I used his moment of confusion to rip my wrists out of his firm hold. Stumbling back, I caught myself on the kitchen counter. Not hesitating for one fucking second, grabbing a knife from the block with trembling hands. Holding it out in front of me.

Warning him off.

With wide eyes, he cocked his head to the side. "Sky, what the fuck do you think you're going to do with that?"

From the second Noah made me realize Keith's true colors, I contemplated this moment.

The expression on his face…

What he would say…

How he would react…

When I exposed him, yelling, "Protecting myself from you! Seeing as all you've ever done is sell me off to the highest bidder!"

Nothing could've prepared me for what happened next.

Keith sprang into action, knocking the knife out of my hand. Smashing my body face first into the wall as hard as he could, causing me to instantly see fucking stars. He knocked the wind right out of my lungs from the impact and his strength alone.

With a death grip on the back of my neck, he pinned the side of my face and body down, not allowing me to properly breathe or catch my bearings. My chest heaved and my eyes watered, gasping for air that wasn't available for the taking. All the blood draining from my face, down to my lips that trembled with the instinctual desire to fall apart.

"You fucking bitch," he raged into my ear from behind. "After everything I've done for you. I turned you into a fucking star! You'd be nothing without me! Nothing!"

My heart stopped.

As soon as he started singing, *"The sun'll come out tomorrow, bet all those dollars that tomorrow."* Swaying his hips, making me feel his erection digging into my back.

"Keith, what are you—"

"Shhh… shhh…" he whispered, my body seizing. "No more talking. I'm done hearing your fucking mouth. You think you can what? Leave me now? Is that what you think is going to happen?"

"How do you expe—"

"Shut the fuck up!" he sneered too close to my face, making me jump. Feeling his hands go to my thighs, slowly working their way up my sides. "You're just like your fucking mother."

My heart stopped.

I swear it just stopped.

"The day she fucking drove your dad's SUV into the river and died… I swear… when she found me in the studio room alone after your one-on-one interview with the director… I tried explaining to her that I'd never let anything happen to you. She just happened to walk in on the director with his hand on your thigh and she was reading into things."

"Oh my God…"

It all made sense now.

Why she was acting that way.

"I can't do this anymore, Daniel. I just can't keep doing this. I can't believe I let this happen. How did I let this happen? How did I do this to our family?"

Why she couldn't drive.

"I don't know what to say, I don't even know what to think. I'm so confused, Daniel. I just can't believe I let this happen to us."

Why she didn't try to fight for her life.

"I'm sorry, Skyler baby, I'm so sorry. I should have never—"

She thought she deserved it.

"I don't know, Skyler… to be honest, I think I just got lucky that she lost her shit in the SUV and ended her own life in the process."

Uncontrollable tears streamed down the sides of my face for what felt like the hundredth time that night. Everything that followed happened so fucking fast, but slow at the same time.

"All this time… all this fucking time… you made me believe you about everything you were putting me through… you made me think you loved me… were there for me… using everything with my mom to hold power over me… saying all she wanted was for me to be a shining star… all of it was lies… you made me think of you as my fucking father! How could you do this to me… how could you make me feel like I was your daughter when all you ever wanted was to whore me out?! I fucking loved you! Do you hear me?! You were my only family! You made me think you were my only fucking family, you fucking bastard!"

He didn't answer any of my questions, and part of me thought he would…

Instead, he leaned closer into my ear and whispered, "I will say this… I was very fucking surprised that your mom didn't say anything to your dad, but I guess… shock and shame make you do some crazy ass shit. What was your loss, was just simply another one of my fucking gains. And now…" he coaxed in an eerie tone, thrusting his cock in my ass again. "It's about time that I fuck your pussy the way I've wanted to fuck you since you were little girl."

Before I could scream bloody murder, he threw me onto the floor so fast I never saw it coming. Slapping me across the face and tearing open my robe. Holding me down by my mouth in the process.

"You're mine! You're fucking mine! Do you hear me, you little whore? I fucking own you!"

Pure panic coursed through my body as he moved his hand and placed it over my throat. Squeezing the fuck out of it, enough to where I could barely breathe.

I closed my eyes. Reliving every single time a director put his hands, his mouth, his dick all over me, making me feel like a whore.

"Open your eyes. Open your goddamn eyes."

I did, my teeth chattering and my body shaking.

He deliberately roamed his hands from my neck down to my stomach.

"You don't have to do this," I pleaded in a tone I didn't recognize.

It was like I was there, but I wasn't. I watched everything unfold in front of me as if I was having an out-of-body experience. He leaned over, his entire body hovering above me. I heard him lower his zipper, and that's when I mentally checked out.

My mind protecting me from what he was about to do.

My face fell to the side as more tears started flowing.

My eyes shifted to the knife within reach.

And I moved in autopilot.

Grabbing ahold of it for dear life, I didn't think twice about it. Brutally stabbing him over and over again…

Until his body jerked forward, making me realize he was dead.

I. Killed. Him.

Finally taking control of my life.

THE DAILY NEWS

News hit yesterday that well-known agent/producer Keith Keyes committed suicide at legendary Hollywood Roosevelt Hotel in Los Angeles, California. More on this story as it develops.

NY Times

It's been one month since Keith Keyes took his own life in such a tragic way. Celebrities from all over the world have been mourning the loss of this agent/producer ever since learning of his untimely death. Reports have surfaced that Mr. Keyes led a double life, and did indeed have demons he hid well. Several sources have confirmed that he struggled with Bipolar Disorder and manic episodes which leads us to believe why he would end his life so brutally.

USA TODAY

It's been six months since Oscar-winning actress, Skyler Bell, has last been seen. She was reported to have attended the funeral of her former agent/manager and longtime friend and confidant, Keith Keyes. Where she appeared to be struggling with the loss of the man she has described as a father figure in several interviews. We assume the three-time platinum winning singer and songwriter is taking time for herself to grieve the loss of such an important man in her life.

CNN

It's been over a year since renowned actress, Skyler Bell, has been seen. Several news stations have started to report the actress as MISSING in action. She is not only missed by her fans, but the industry as well. Police have had several reports from people who have claimed to have seen her, but they were all dead ends.

Skyler Bell, if you read this, we all miss you.

HUFFINGTON POST

Not only did news hit the media today about Skyler Bell's return, a year and a half since she was last seen at her long-time agent/manager Keith Keyes funeral. But the legendary actress has entered the spotlight with a vengeance. Claiming to have written a tell-all book about growing up in Hollywood and the secrets that will be revealed.

LA Times

Skyler Bell is back in the news, hitting the number one spot on the New York Times bestselling list with her debut memoir, titled, Lost Girl. Where she has shed light and removed skeletons from Hollywood's elite doors. Exposing several film directors and executives on using their power and authority to molest and rape her as long as she's been in the industry. Causing a media uproar with the help of District Attorney Damien Montero, justice was finally served to these so-called powerhouses and landed them in prison. Giving many other actresses the courage to come forward and share their story as well.

Skyler Bell became the voice for women all over the world.

Washington Post

With Skyler Bell's New York Times Bestselling Memoir, Lost Girl, hitting the list at the number one spot for the last ten weeks in a row, it has shed a possible new understanding on why Keith Keyes could have taken his own life so brutally. Perhaps knowing that the young actress was going to expose the decades of manipulation and abuse brought on by his hands. Deciding to end his own life, rather than her ending it for him.

The irony is not lost on us.

NBC News

Finally, we have some happy and exciting news to report! After two and a half years of Skyler Bell's journey since her brainwashing, manipulating agent/manager took his own life. The voice of women all over the world has reported getting married over six months ago on a private island in the Dominican Republican, with long time soulmate, as she described, Noah Jameson in her memoir. They were last seen cruising the Caribbean on their yacht named Lost Boy. Some media sources say she is pregnant with their first child. Although, neither information has been confirmed from her team, us here at NBC News believe it's true and couldn't be happier for the girl who has endured decades of hurt. Skyler has changed several things in the industry for the better, because she had the courage to show her demons. She has taken a step back from the constant limelight and is extremely private about her life. Which is completely understandable for how far she's come. We respect her privacy and wish her all the best.

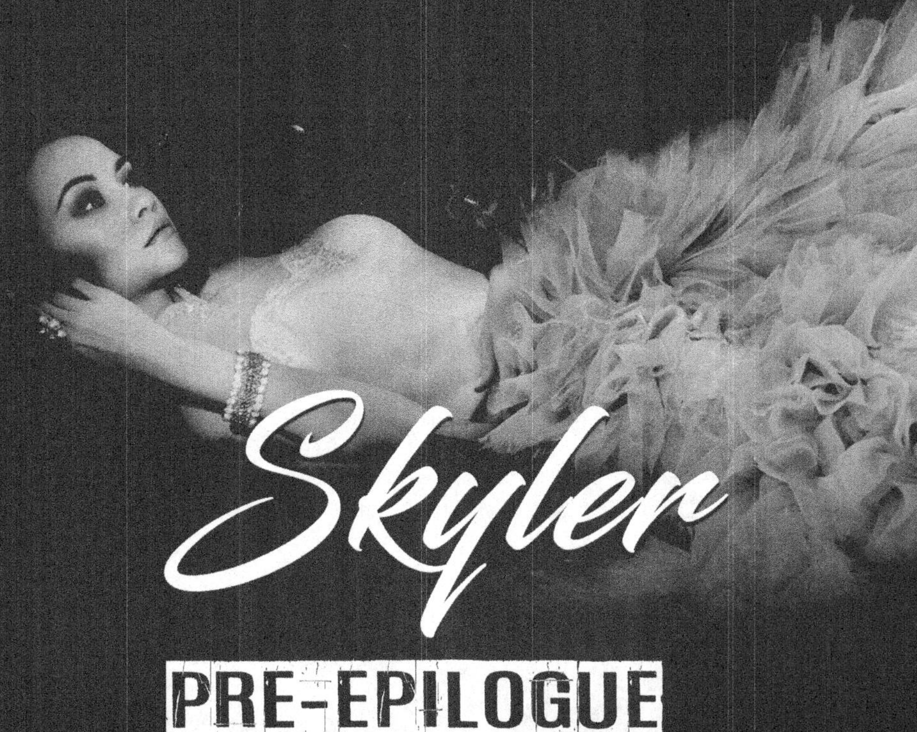

Skyler

PRE-EPILOGUE

Confessions of a Found Girl

So much had happened in our lives in the last two and a half years. Years that I sometimes thought I wouldn't survive. Till this day I still remember the expression on Noah's face when he rushed into the penthouse suite and threw Keith's lifeless body off me.

"Oh fuck," he breathed out, making me shudder out of my skin as I backed into the wall. Scooting as close as possible, seeing so much red. Blood everywhere…

On my hands, my body, my soul.

Wanting to cover my ears and close my eyes, find my happy place in tomorrow.

"Baby, baby, baby," Noah coaxed with nothing but agony and distress in his tone, pulling me into his arms. "You're okay, Skyler, you're okay… I'm here now. I gotcha, Cutie, and I ain't ever letting you go."

"Noah… what did I do? What the fuck did I do?"

"You did the right fuckin' thing. You hear me?" He pulled away, gripping onto the sides of my face. Looking me dead in the eyes, speaking with conviction, "And now I'm gonna take it over from here."

"Okay…"

He started touching my neck, my arms, feeling around my limbs. His eyes shifting with the movement of his hands. "You alright? Did that motherfucker touch you?"

"I'm okay... please... just hold me. I just need you to hold me."

He didn't have to be told twice, he held me until I thought I was alright, although, it couldn't have been further from the truth.

Even though Noah hadn't shown up until mere minutes after I took Keith's life that night, in a way it had been a blessing in disguise. Unexpected circumstances caused him to be late, but he made connections and a lifelong gratitude with a certain District Attorney who ended up saving *my* life.

Noah's corrupt lifestyle also ended up becoming a blessing in disguise. Vlad "handled," Keith Keyes. Washing my bloody hands of it all. He contacted a man who went by the name, Bossman.

I didn't ask any questions, all I knew was my slate was wiped clean when I woke up the next morning to media chaos of Keith brutally committing suicide at the Hollywood Roosevelt Hotel.

And the rest was history…

I spent my entire life being *Skyler Bell*, always working under some sort of life-changing pressure, so to fall back into the role and pretend to be the grieving client for his funeral, was definitely one of the hardest roles I had ever played, but I performed it nonetheless.

After the funeral, Noah and I spent months and months in hiding, mainly to escape the public eye. Completely going off the grid. Abandoning my dad, my career, my life, only leaving me with the man I loved most in this cruel world. Thankful that I finally had him by my side.

In every sense of the word.

The first months were the hardest, at least for my mental state of mind. I woke up in a fit of nightmares, remembering my mom's death, Keith's, all those producer's hands on me.

The list was endless of all the shit I was reliving.

Noah would just hold me, whisper how much he loved me, how everything was going to be okay…

The prior months were a whirlwind. Cutting ourselves off from society to travel around the world on Noah's yacht.

The one he finally made us a home.

Other than a few brief phone calls to my dad now and again, to tell him I was alright. And the same with Noah, keeping in touch with his mom and brother. We were technology free.

And after the first year, things did start settling down.

The nightmares were less and less.

The memories fell somewhere in the back of my mind.

And even though I was content and happy, living somewhat of a stress-free life, I couldn't get away from the guilt, the remorse, the shame I felt for something that was never my fault to begin with. I hated that more than anything…

Until one morning I awoke and decided to truly take control of my life. You see, killing Keith didn't do anything but permanently remove his existence, from actually seeing him day to day. It didn't exorcise him from my mind, he was still there…

Lurking.

Waiting.

Fucking smiling.

So I simply grabbed a piece of paper and pencil, and began purging all my demons onto a manuscript. Spending an unhealthy amount of time, day and night, writing everything that had happen to me. While Noah worked on restoring boats in the Caribbean.

Coming to the realization I couldn't hide anymore. Knowing I wouldn't be able to live with myself, if I knew young girls were getting molested every day in the industry. Someone's daughter, granddaughter, niece.

Someone…

Just…

Like…

Me.

Was being used only to gain fame for someone else. It was never about me becoming a shining star, it was always about Keith becoming one as well.

If there were more girls, women, in this business being brainwashed by men like Keith, thinking it was a normal thing that came with wanting to be in the spotlight. By pedophiles whispering in their ears that the bigger they wanted to get, the more sexual acts they had to perform.

Then it was duty to myself and these girls to have our voices fucking heard.

Once and for all.

No matter the consequences.

It couldn't be worse than what we'd already gone through.

After a year and a half, my entire story was written on paper. Through blood, sweat, and tears. Ready to be shown. Exposing what really happens behind closed doors in the city of dreams.

Hollywood.

The seedy bullshit that young girls and women endured all for the price of fame. All for price of selling their souls without even knowing it. Making me sick to my fucking stomach every time I even thought about it.

With the support and love of a lost boy named Noah Jameson, we returned to Miami with my manuscript in hand, meeting Bossman at the docks. Going to see the only man who could get my story out and raise awareness for these young girls all over the world. While convicting the sons of a bitches that preyed on the innocent.

No one other than…

District Attorney Damien Montero.

He restored me back to life.

Finally, truly allowing me to be free.

By the time we went to see him, the press was eating me alive with headline reports of Skyler Bell missing. Making my disappearance sound like I was kidnapped, and not just stepping away from the Hollywood spotlight. So I wasn't surprised in the least when pictures of me filled the TV screen with more headlines that read, MISSING. When I went to explain to Mr. Montero, at his newborn son's party, all that had happened to me.

When in reality, I was just lost.

Damien, as he insisted I call him, was more than eager to take my case. Vowing that we were going to take the motherfuckers down…

Suspect after suspect were exposed, stripped of their careers and thrown to a life behind bars. Names like Jackson Ellis and Christopher Anderson, just to name a few.

My book was then published six months later, hitting the *New York Times* number one bestselling list several months in a row. Pushing me back into the spotlight, but this time it was for the greater good.

I gave up acting and singing to raise awareness full-time. Traveling city to city for lectures, book tours, and retreats. Starting my own charity that focused on providing young girls therapy. Where I sat in a few times, needing treatment as well.

For the first in my life, everything was right in my world.

Because *Skyler Bell* died the night Keith did.

But…

Skyler Morgan, me, she would live on…

Forever.

NOAH

Epilogue

EVERAFTER OF A FOUND BOY

"Beep, beep, beep… Very hungry pregnant woman comin' through, clear the hell outta the way people," I laughed, walking in front of Skyler, signaling my hands like the airport workers do, bringing in a jumbo jet.

Making everyone laugh, including Skyler.

"You won't like her when she's fuckin' hangry."

Earning me a slap on the back of the head for that one. "You hush your mouth, there are children everywhere," she reprimanded, grabbing herself a plate and silverware at the MC barbeque.

We had just gotten back to Southport a few nights ago, after spending six months down in the Dominican Republic. Where Skyler and I got married in a private ceremony on the beach. Away from prying fucking eyes and the occasional paparazzi that still lingered after Skyler's Hollywood scandal came to light.

I technically asked her to marry me…

I'd just finished once again eating her for breakfast, she'd always been my favorite goddamn meal.

Murmuring against her lips. "Now, I need ya to go slip on a pretty white dress for me. I'm takin' my girl somewhere."

"We're not going to finish?" she giggled in between kissing me

"You did." I grinned. "On my fuckin' face." Kissing her one last time to prove my point before I made my way off the bed.

As soon as we walked down to the secluded beach, holding hands, there was a minister, and an older couple as our witnesses, we met down there at the marina we kept the yacht at. Ysabelle owned a bar, and her husband, Sebastian owned his own charter business. Both giving us VIP treatment, showing us all the best spots to fish, eat, and party. The best of the fucking best that only the locals knew about.

"Hey!" She jerked me back. "You didn't even ask me! That's quite cocky... even for you!"

"Didn't have to. You yellin' 'Yes, yes, yes' while my face was in between your legs this mornin' answered. Not my fault you missed the question."

"You asked me while I was in mid-orgasm? How does that even count?"

"Cuz your squirtin' pussy answered for you."

She laughed the rest of the way toward the minister, fucking beaming.

"Do you, Skyler Morgan, take Noah Jameson to be your husband? To have and to hold, for better or for worse, for richer, for poorer, in sickness and in health, to love and to cherish. From this day forward until death do us part," the minister declared, and I could already see from the expression on Skyler's face, the response from her pouty little mouth was going to be sassy.

"Hmm..." She cocked her head to the side, testing my patience. "Let's see..."

"Skyler," I warned in a familiar tone. Ready to say it for her if I had to.

"What was the question again?"

"Cutie..."

"I mean I don't really remember it? So I'm just kind of confused on what the Minister is even talking about?"

Grinning from ear to ear, I got down on one knee with the ring in my hand. Saying, "Marry me?"

She smiled, big and wide, lighting up her entire face. "We do."

Literally knocking me on my fucking ass.

I didn't waste any fucking time, trying to get her pregnant once her book hit the shelves six months ago. Wanting to end that chapter of our lives and start a new one with her. Adamant that I was putting a baby in her, making love to her over and over again.

The day we exchanged our vows, was the same day we finally gave one another what we always wanted.

A family.

Together.

Living our best life on our boat Lost Boy became our priority. Doing nothing but finally breathing and enjoying one another's company without any goddamn drama or bullshit between us.

Ma wasn't too happy with me when we called to tell her we'd gotten hitched. Spewing some shit about, "Robbing her of seeing her baby boy and new daughter-in-law getting married and we at least better have a few photos for her to cry over." Although, she did say she couldn't have been happier for us, finally finding our way back to one another.

Skyler's old man was more laid back and less fucking dramatic about it than my ma. He was just happy and grateful that I called him up one night to ask for his blessing. Knowing it would mean the world to him and Skyler. Things were good between them, better than they had been in a while. Her father was sober, working his steps, attending meetings. Him and Ma were even friends. Supporting each other when needed.

Two and a half years flew by since she laid one of her biggest demons to rest. By putting him to ground her damn self. I'd be lying if I said I didn't wish I would've done it for her, but it worked itself out. It gave Skyler the strength to finally take control of life for the first time and I couldn't have been more fucking proud of her.

My girl turned into my hero.

Creating a huge difference in the world with not only her singing, but the voice of women to be heard.

Making every damn person in our families beyond fucking proud.

Now, she was six months pregnant and glowing, so goddamn beautiful. Constantly taking my breath away. Her pregnancy was good to her and in turn Skyler was good to me, her hormones made my already horny girl incessantly crave my cock.

My mouth.

My tongue.

My fingers,

Everything about my touch, begging me to make her come.

And who was I to deny her the pleasure of sitting on my fucking face. Squirting all over the damn place. To the point where we needed several sets of back up bed sheets.

The sacrifices I made for happy wife, happy life, were endless.

Including, feeding her at all hours of the night. I don't know where the fuck the food was going other than in her round bump. Because you couldn't tell she was pregnant, unless she turned to the side. She was still petite, except you wouldn't think that with how much she hogged the bed. Saying something about our son being cold and needing my heated skin to warm him up through her belly. Pretty much sleeping on top of me, worse than she did before.

"Can you serve me seconds?" she asked with that pouty little lip that always made my cock twitch.

"Cutie—"

"Please… the baby is still hungry." She grabbed my hand and placed it over her stomach. "Feel. See, he's kicking because he's still hungry. Feed me, so I can feed him."

I laughed, kissing her lips. "Ya know I can't resist anythin', when you're beggin' me like that." Already thinking about how much more of an appetite she would have for food and my cock, when I finally knocked her up with triplets.

"I know, that's why I do it."

"What do ya want? Besides my cock in your mouth."

"Noah! Oh my God, they're kids everywhere."

She wasn't exaggerating, there were shitlins everywhere. We were at the End of The Road Clubhouse for the weekly Sunday family barbecue.

Everyone was there, from ma, to Skyler's dad. Creed and my sister-in-law Mia, and their kids. The good ol' boys as everyone called them. Who happened to be Mia's family that ended up joining our MC. Which was really fucking funny because none of them used to ride. I think they were going through a mid-life crisis together or some shit.

Their kids' kids were here as well. I swear, every person here was connected in some shape, way or form.

We were all just one big happy fucked up family, each having their own story to tell.

"No shit, baby." I grinned. "So everyone must love to fuck as much as we do."

Her mouth dropped open, only provoking me to lean forward to get close to her ear. "Close your mouth, Cutie… unless you want me to stick my di—"

"Oh my God! I'm getting my own food. Because now you're just making me wet, but I'm still hungry."

I grabbed her hand, sitting her back down. Smiling, "I fuckin' love you."

"Yeah? Then prove it… feed me."

I laughed again, I couldn't help it. Not when she was fucking adorable like that.

"If you don't soon, then this baby boy is going to kick his way out soon. I'm surprised I don't have broken ribs from the mini-linebacker I'm carrying." She pulled her white, flowy sundress taunt on her belly, and as if on cue, my boy started to kick again. "It's your fault, I swear you get him all riled up as soon as he hears his daddy's voice."

"Is that right?" Squatting down to the grass, I held both of my world's in my hands. Placing my mouth up to her belly to have a little one-on-one chat with my son. "Listen here, son."

Causing Skyler to giggle.

"You be good to your momma, she has enough on her plate. Wit' just bein' married to me. So stop fussin' in there, yeah?"

"Aiden," Skyler voiced, bringing my attention to her.

"What, baby?"

"Aiden's here."

I stood, turning around. Watching as Aiden stumbled through the backyard, clutching onto a bottle of Jack.

"What the fuck?"

He'd been here a few times over the years, usually with Bailey and their kids, but never alone or drunk as shit.

I quickly made my way over to him, grabbing onto his arm. "Aiden, what's going on? Did you drive here like this?"

"Bailey…" he slurred, staggering all over the place. Barely able to stand.

"Jesus Christ, man. What the fuck?"

Taking another swig from his bottle, he tried shoving me away. "Bailey… Bailey… Bailey..."

"For fuck's sake, Aiden." I'd never seen him like this before, rendering me speechless as soon as the words,

"She's gone… My Bailey… Left me. Forever," flew out of his mouth.

THE END.

For Noah and Skyler.

LOST BOY

Made in the USA
Las Vegas, NV
19 May 2024